## About the Authors

In a testosterone filled home (a husband, five boys between ages fourteen & eighteen, and one squeaky boy guinea pig), it's hard to imagine not going insane. The trick is to escape. So, in her charming Southern world filled with politics, football, and after school snacks, **Carolyn Hector** utilises her knack for spinning every plausible situation into a romance story. Find out what she is up to on Twitter @WriteOnCarolyn or find her on Facebook.

*USA Today* and *Wall Street Journal* best-selling author **Janice Lynn** has a master's in nursing from Vanderbilt University and works as a nurse practitioner in a family practice. She lives in the southern United States with her Prince Charming, their children, their Maltese named Halo; and a lot of unnamed dust bunnies that have moved in after she started her writing career. Readers can visit Janice via her website at: www.janicelynn.net

With the publication of *Temptation's Song* in July 2010, **Janice Sims** celebrates fourteen years as a romance writer. In fourteen years, she's published seventeen novels and had nine stories included in anthologies. When asked why she writes romances, she smiles and says it's the only genre in which happily ever after is a foregone conclusion. Plus, where else are you going to find a perfect male?

# Mistletoe Kisses

**CAROLYN HECTOR**

**JANICE LYNN**

**JANICE SIMS**

**MILLS & BOON**

First Published in Great Britain 2021
By Mills & Boon, an imprint of HarperCollins*Publishers* Ltd
1 London Bridge Street, London, SE1 9GF
www.harpercollins.co.uk

HarperCollins*Publishers*
1st Floor, Watermarque Building,
Ringsend Road, Dublin 4, Ireland

MISTLETOE KISSES © 2021 Harlequin Books S.A.

*The Magic of Mistletoe* © 2015 Carolyn Hall
*Winter Wedding in Vegas* © 2015 Janice Lynn
*This Winter Night* © 2013 Janice Sims

ISBN: 978-0-263-3026-46

MIX
Paper from
responsible sources
FSC™ C007454

This book is produced from independently certified FSC™ paper
to ensure responsible forest management.

For more information visit: www.harpercollins.co.uk/green

Printed and bound in Spain
by CPI, Barcelona

# THE MAGIC OF MISTLETOE

**CAROLYN HECTOR**

I would like to dedicate this book first and foremost to my husband and two kids. Thank you for allowing me the time to write. And to the Hotties of The Colour of Love Book Club.

I have to acknowledge Scott Kopel, Janet Atwater-Manuel, David Dickerson, Rhea Lathan and Aron Myers, who stormed into my office and demanded I strum up the courage to hit the submit button.

# Chapter 1

"Hold still, I've almost got it." Macy Cuomo parted her thirteen-year-old daughter's hair down the center. As Gia sat at on a stool in front of the vanity in the downstairs bathroom of their two-story home, Macy stood behind her, working the comb through her hair. The door remained open to get rid of the heat from the curling irons, flat irons and hot combs all plugged into the wall.

"Jeez, Mom, why can't you just send me to the hair-dresser's to get a blowout like Talia's mom does for her?"

Talia's mom, Jaime Jones, had an ex-husband who made child support payments on time. She also spent more time with a bottle of wine than she did with her own children. Those were some of the reasons why

Macy wasn't going to follow anything that Jaime did for her daughter. "Oh, but think of all the bonding time we get." Macy offered a wide, sweet smile as she slid the flat iron down to the end of Gia's long dark hair.

Finally Gia sat still. With her oldest quiet, Macy concentrated on fixing her hair. The music for the local Tallahassee morning news show filtered through the air. Macy's eight-year-old son, MJ, had sprawled his little body out on the living room floor and was tossing his baseball up in the air.

"Oh, MJ, turn that up!" Gia yelled, craning her neck to peer into the living room.

"Hold still!" Macy said again.

"Mama, it's Duke Rodriguez!"

*Duke!*

She needn't be reminded who the man was. Every weekday morning for the past two weeks, the flat-screen television mounted on the wall had remained on the news station. The guest host of the local morning show, Duke Rodriguez, united the three of them for various reasons. MJ made up his part of the fan club because of Duke's history as a professional baseball player. Gia, the budding media queen, followed the sports-figure-turned-news-anchor for his ability to merge politics with social events of the world in his broadcasts. As for Macy, she adored him for the main reasons every red-blooded woman did—the man was hot. Macy's stomach fluttered with butterflies every time his deep voice entered the room. Not that she'd ever act on it. He was a celebrity, for God's sake. Not to mention she had no time for a man in her life.

Duke's baritone laugh emanated from the television in the living room and drifted down the hall. Macy leaned out of the doorway to get a better look at the dreamy man.

"Mario Junior, do not stand so close to the TV," Macy yelled as she pulled the comb through the roots of Gia's hair.

"Aw, Mom!" whined MJ as he stepped backward to the oversize brown leather couch, nearly tripping over his white tennis shoes on the way.

"Just do it. And put your shoes on!" Macy glanced at the cell phone in Gia's hand. The minute Gia realized her mother was looking, she held the phone against her chest. Macy rolled her eyes toward the ceiling, not understanding how Gia could get so offended over her privacy when she posted every emotion, feeling and thought on Twitter.

"But Mama!" MJ petitioned loudly.

A lot of mothers could only envision what their children were going to be when they got older. Macy was positive MJ was going to be a lawyer. He loved to argue, and by the early age of four had always come up with good cases. But today he was going to lose. Macy was in no mood. She was already running behind schedule and should have been walking out of the house right about now. She had several errands to run before she had to get to the storage center and start pulling out her equipment.

"They're just about to get to the Santa story. Remember, we saw him last week!"

"I want to see!" Gia said, scrambling from the chair

the minute Macy set the flat iron on the edge of the sink. She clicked the button off and turned off all the other salon-style hair equipment, then followed Gia into the cluttered living room. Yet another thing Macy knew she was going to have to do at some point today before Mario came over to pick up the kids. Her ex-husband would surely tease her if he saw the mess, especially considering that had been one of her complaints about him during their divorce.

Macy leaned against the arm of the couch and pushed the long sleeves of her thin blue shirt up to her elbows. She crossed one leg over the other and realized she needed to put on her shoes, too. Quickly running upstairs to her bedroom, she grabbed a pair of braided flip-flops. Typically she didn't wear flip-flops with jeans, but today she had so much to do that they were convenient. Besides, the late November weather was still warm and balmy. She made it back to the living room in time to hear her daughter sighing. What a way to start a chaotic Monday morning. One more half day of school, and the kids would be out for Thanksgiving break.

"Duke!" Gia gasped, all lovesick. Macy could have sworn her moody teenager even batted her eyelashes at the television screen.

"And I bet the local high school baseball coach is going to ask for his old job back." Duke chuckled. As the family all gathered in the living room, the high definition of the television captured the cheeks of Duke's cohost turning a bright shade of pink, as they had every day since he came to WKSS.

"Speaking of Santa, we're expecting a sighting."

Juliette Walker twirled her hair around her finger and blinked flirtatiously at Duke. Obviously the young co-host was as smitten with Duke Rodriguez as Macy.

This morning, he wore a well-tailored black suit, crisp white Oxford shirt and a red tie. Without acknowledging Juliette's attempt to flirt, Duke shuffled the papers together in front of him in his large hands; a megawatt smile tugged at his square jawline, involuntarily exposing his dimples. Even after being away from sports for ten years, Duke still maintained a fit frame—broad shoulders and a tapered waist. He kept his straight black hair short and close-cropped. Unlike the typical news anchor, Duke wore a well-trimmed goatee to frame his luscious, full lips. Macy cleared her throat to keep from swaying when Duke blinked his thick lashes.

"Already?" Duke asked.

"Yes, I hear he'll be at the mall this Black Friday morning. Oh, I can recall the days of going to the mall and sitting on Santa's lap. What about you, Duke?"

Duke shuffled his paperwork and nodded his head. "I tried to milk Santa for all that I could."

"No way." Juliette gawked.

"It's true," Duke said with a nod. "But it had to be the right Santa, you know what I mean?" he asked, but didn't give Juliette a chance to reply. "I mean, that Santa I saw setting up down at the mall looks like a total fake. Did you see his beard?"

A sinking feeling washed over Macy at that very moment. She pushed herself off the wall. "Okay, kids, let's finish getting ready…"

"Wait!" Gia exclaimed.

"...to this day, I'm almost tempted to sit on a Santa's lap if he's got a real beard."

"You wouldn't dare!" Juliette said.

"Well, maybe not now. I mean, I tried to let every Santa I saw know what I wanted for Christmas until I was about thirteen. And at that point my mom had to smack me on the head and tell me that Santa isn't..."

The scene before Macy felt as if it moved in slow motion. Macy and Gia both tried to get to the television to turn it off before that damn Duke ruined everything. Gia was singing "Fa la la la la" loudly and running toward MJ to distract him. Macy ran in front of the television, tripping over MJ's shoes in the process before she could turn it off. But it was too late.

"...real."

MJ stood there as his large round brown eyes glistened with the threat of tears. "Did he just say Santa wasn't real?"

*When you out Santa as a fraud on public television, there are bound to be some repercussions.*

Duke Rodriguez found this out the hard way, especially when the woman whose attention he'd been trying to get wouldn't reciprocate any smile he offered each time their eyes met. The caramel beauty in the cream-colored dress stood under the mistletoe, refusing to return his notorious dimpled grin. Fortunately, his invitation to his boss's annual Thanksgiving dinner had not been rescinded. And he owed that to his mother, Janet Rodriguez, for teaching him to own up to his mistakes and hold his head high.

By coming to the party, he hoped to show the rest of the news team at WKSS, who were present at the studio to drop their children off at the daycare, how sorry he was for outing Santa. He brushed off being subjected to juvenile hostility from his colleagues. He hadn't been pushed out of a food line since kindergarten, yet today one person purposely cut in front of him. Another person had swiped the last fork before he could reach it, and then just as he'd reached for a ladle of eggnog, the woman before him let it slip into the creamy punch bowl, slopping the beverage all over the front of his shirt and suit jacket. He handled it with ease and a tight-lipped smile. The story of him revealing Santa Claus as a fraud would blow over soon enough.

"I feel responsible for not fully explaining how family-oriented our staffers are at *Tune In, Tallahassee*. The station likes to go all out for the children at our day care and some of the children we've had on our spotlight segments. We host a party, trim a tree and I even dress up like Santa. Send me the bill for your dry cleaning."

Duke glanced up from his poor attempt to clean the stain off his white button-down shirt. The autumn-colored napkin he used had begun to shred, leaving orange, yellow, and red paper streaks. "I'm going to hold you to it, Pablo."

Chuckling, Pablo nodded his head. With each bob, Duke caught a glimpse of the beginning signs of the horseshoe-patterned baldness of his thinning hair but decided not to tease him right now. Pablo kept his hair curly and low. Duke usually kept his hair as short as Caesar himself. A lot of people often thought he and Pablo were brothers. They were close to the same height, but Pablo had him by maybe a half an inch. Had Pablo not spent the summer back in the Dominican Republic, they both would have been the same hazelnut shade of brown. While Duke liked to dress in finer clothes, Pablo had always been comfortable in a pair of jeans and a polo shirt. Today he wore a red pullover. Duke guessed it was to announce the upcoming Christmas holiday.

"Whatever," Pablo said. "This is the least I can do for inviting you into the lion's den. I never would have guessed—" Pablo handed Duke another napkin, a white one "—considering what a rock star you were two weeks ago, that you'd go down in flames."

"Thanks," Duke grumbled, taking the napkin from his overdramatic friend. As one of the highest-rated news anchors for Multi-Ethnic Television, someone who never took time away from work, Duke knew his career in journalism was far from endangered. Duke enjoyed working for the Orlando, Florida–based company. Multi-Ethnic Television, with affiliate stations all over the nation, prided themselves on diversity, not only in the news anchors but in their shows, as well. Every sitcom, cooking show, or drama or reality series showcased different nationalities from the Caribbean, Africa, India and everywhere else that made up America's cultural melting pot.

With his contract renewal set to be signed at the beginning of the year, MET checked in with him every other week to verify his happiness. He also figured they wanted to know if their *DC Nightly News* anchor planned on returning to the news desk after he finished covering the morning anchorwoman's period of maternity leave.

But they might be getting their journalist back sooner rather than later. His time in Tallahassee might be limited, thanks to the hordes of soccer moms threatening to change morning shows and local business owners flooding Pablo's email inbox, warning they might remove their holiday ads as long as Duke was on the air. Duke's arrival in Tallahassee earlier this month seemed so long ago.

Just because his best friend was his current station manager didn't mean Duke had gotten off any easier. After shouting at him all morning long, Pablo suggested Duke do some serious investing in PR work if he wanted to help save the ratings. Despite his limited time in town, Duke prided himself on maintaining a positive image.

The anchorwoman he was subbing in for was Pablo's wife and the mother of Duke's three—now four—godchildren, so he was really here more so as a favor. He'd leaped from being a baseball star to being in front of the camera in DC, filling people's homes with current events for the past fifteen years, without missing a beat. Being down here with Pablo and his family, however, made him wonder what things he had missed out on in life. After the New Year, Duke had some serious decisions to make.

*Somewhat*, a little voice nagged him.

"Oh, and her name is Macy Cuomo," Pablo leaned in and whispered, "in case you were wondering. She's single and a very good friend to Monique and me."

He was wondering. He'd been staring at the petite beauty since she walked in the front doors of the Baez family's home two hours ago. There were no obvious signs of her flirting with anyone else, either. Once she'd laid her manicured hand on a man's chest as she tossed her head back and laughed at something that was said, but that was it. At that moment, Duke would have given anything to be that man.

"What?" Duke tried to shake off his gaze, realizing Pablo was speaking to him.

"Yeah, you look like you need to cool off," Pablo said, pushing something into Duke's hand. "You're sweating from staring at her. Take this."

He looked down to his left and spied the green bottle of beer in Pablo's hands. Frost billowed off the beverage.

"You guys have the heat on as if it were freezing."

"It's sixty-eight degrees outside," Pablo countered with a shake of his head. "You forget our moms bundled us up at seventy degrees in the DR."

"And yet you're wearing *chancletas* with jeans?" Duke chuckled. "I heard Thanksgiving is going to be in the seventies."

"Leave my flip-flops alone." Pablo laughed, lifting his foot. "Anyway, you know that's not what I meant. I'm just glad to see you're back on your feet and looking at a quality woman."

"So I've been staring?" Duke looked back at the angel in cream. Pablo was right; he had been away from the Dominican Republic for a while now. He forgot how much he missed a shapely woman with all the right curves in all the right places. This woman named Macy now stood with Monique, cooing over two-week-old baby Lucia. There was a maternal vibe coming from her that worried him. Most of the women he dated never lasted long if they started cooing over children. Duke could offer a woman jewels, trips, cars and other luxury gifts, but not a baby. A childhood illness had scarred him, prohibiting him from being able to give her a biological child. So why bother leading her on any further?

"Let's just say that you've been staring so much you've got Monique wanting to play matchmaker. If I didn't come over here to get you, I am sure she would have been printing out your wedding invitations."

*Matchmaking time,* Duke thought with a wicked grin. "That doesn't sound too bad. I think my best-friend-in-law has great taste."

Pablo choked on his beer and looked at him as though he'd grown a second head. "What?"

"I'm serious."

"You didn't say that when she tried setting you up with her college roommate."

The college roommate in question had had a unibrow and a questionable Adam's apple. She was one of the five girls Monique shared a room with. Duke had agreed to go on that date sight unseen. Pablo spent the entire double date apologizing for the misfortune.

The two friends looked at each other, both realizing they had the same image in their minds. "At least this time I can see what I'm getting up front."

"And at least this time I can tell you that she's not like the women you've gone out with, Duke. This one is a nice family girl."

Feigning hurt, Duke clutched his chest. "You wound me."

"Mo will wound you if you hurt her." Pablo slapped his best friend on the back playfully and led him across the room to where the woman in question was.

A few people glared at Duke. And then it dawned on him that the reason why this Macy wouldn't look at him must be because she'd already heard the story of his outing Santa. Through a frozen smile, Duke leaned over to his friend. "So you don't think that this lady heard about my Santa mistake on the morning news, do you?"

"Hell, who do you think was the first person to call me?"

"Ugh," Duke groaned and stopped walking.

Pablo pressed the bottle of beer against Duke's shoulder to push him forward. "Face the music. At least when Macy sees Lucia with her *padrino*, she won't think you're a complete ass."

As godfather to Pablo's first three children, Wellinson, Angel and Maylen, Duke knew that women held a soft spot for men who liked kids. Women blatantly hit on him whenever he took the children out to the park or to a game, slipping him their business cards or hotel key cards.

Growing up in Mao, a city in the Dominican Republic, Duke never realized he was poor. His father, Ramon, would say they were blessed. Christmas traditions were more like a big celebration with fireworks and lots of eating. When he got older and came to the States at eighteen, he realized that other people around the world celebrated completely differently from him. It was all about the commercialization of the season. And when it came to his godchildren, Duke was in sync with everyone else.

Duke fell back into step with Pablo. They crossed the hardwood floors of the living room, ignoring some of the eye-rolling that took place when Duke walked through. In the dining area, they found Monique beaming at the sight of them approaching. She opened her arms for him to hug. Duke reached for her and twirled her around. The tie of her black wrap dress flowed through the air as the curls of her blond hair bounced up and down.

"You look way too good to have just given birth two weeks ago," Duke said. "The both of you look great." He smiled down at baby Lucia. "*Dios lo bendiga.*"

"Oh, Duke, you always know what to say." Monique giggled and batted her blue eyes at him.

Their playful banter always warranted a growl from Pablo. "Don't listen to her," Pablo grumbled miserably. "She passed over my head the minute she found out she was pregnant."

Macy looked up from the baby for a moment. Duke noticed her light brown eyes and felt his breath get caught in his throat. She was breathtakingly beautiful.

"What's that?" she asked.

Duke took the opportunity to explain; hopefully his translation of a Dominican superstition might impress her. "Oh, you see, in the Dominican, if a woman passes over the top of her husband's head, he will get all her morning sickness."

Her perfectly manicured eyebrows came together in confusion. "I still don't understand."

"Most women carry the brunt of the morning sickness. Her body has to pass over his head. I mean, usually this happens when the man is sitting on a step and the woman will swing her leg over his head, like a high kick." Duke winked and held his hand over the top of his head. Did he really wink? He wished he could take it back. She seemed so sophisticated. Did she smell like sweet coconut? Suddenly, his train of thought was lost, and he just stood there staring at her, willing the next words to come out of his mouth.

Saving him, Pablo used his beer hand to nudge Duke once again and pointed toward the front stairs. Duke knew Pablo had had the house built for his wife. The stairs were a grand ordeal, coming right out of the pages of *Gone with the Wind*. "See that sixth step right there?" He looked back at Duke and Macy to make sure they were watching. "I was walking by these steps, minding my own business, when my wife nearly flew from that step onto the floor over the banister right over my head. It was like watching one of those bad seventies movies."

"Hey," Monique laughed, "I was barely eight weeks pregnant and still jogging every morning. but there was no way I could pass up a chance to test out the superstition."

The image made everyone laugh. Duke noticed how Macy was even prettier up close and smiling. The lighting framed her heart-shaped face, highlighting her café-au-lait skin, haloing the top of her light brown curly hair. Because of her flawless skin, he could not determine her age. The news anchors he'd worked with would kill for the illegal lengths of Macy's lashes. Her brown eyes crinkled in the corners as she stared at the three of them, her lips parted. Duke still stared, trying not to be a pervert, but the dangerous curves on her reminded him of the beautiful women back home—thick in the thighs, breasts and behind. His breath caught in his throat again. Asking if she was a model would have been something she'd already heard. She could have been on television. He wondered if she was in the business. He prayed not, because the last thing he wanted was to get involved with another woman in the industry. His last relationship had played out in the gossip tabloids from beginning to end, leaving a bitter taste in his mouth.

A lull fell across the foursome. Seemingly nervously, Monique cleared her throat. "So Duke, are you enjoying yourself? Pablo wanted to make sure you got some of the old Dominican traditions."

"Everything is great. Who made *pasteles en hojas*?"

"Pablo." Monique beamed. It didn't surprise Duke to learn that. The *masa*, or dough, was made up of plantains and other root vegetables. Getting it to the right consistency took a lot of time.

"That's good. It will go great with the bottle of Anis del Mono I had shipped in."

For most people, the anise in the liqueur had a strong flavor like licorice, thus making it an acquired taste. Ready for the strong Spanish liqueur, Duke looked around the room at the traditionally festive holiday atmosphere. Christmas was less than six weeks away, and they'd already had their home decorated in bright red, green and white. The Christmas tree in the family room had to be about seven feet tall and was decorated with matching red and green ornaments.

"The food, the decorations, everything looks great, Mo."

"Well, I can't take all the credit," Monique said.

"No?" Duke could see Macy out of the corner of his eye. She held baby Lucia close to her and with expertise. Despite Duke's status as godfather to all the Baez kids, he still always felt awkward holding one.

Monique hit herself lightly in the head. "Oh my God! Where are my manners? Macy, this is Duke Rodriguez, practically one of the family. Duke, this is our dear friend Macy. She's the one who did all of this." She waved her hand around the room.

"It's a pleasure to meet you," Duke said, extending his hand. Since she was holding the baby with both arms, she couldn't shake. Duke felt a little foolish. Quickly, he shoved his hand in his pocket.

"Nice to meet you." Her words sounded polite, but there was a clip in her voice that told Duke she was just being nice.

Not counting the echoing chuckle as Pablo took a sip from his beer, there was another awkward silence between them. Kenny G's melodic holiday saxophone notes were easily heard as the sound system dispersed the music through the rooms. Forks scraping against plates and champagne glasses being clinked in toast filtered through the air, as well. Monique raised her eyebrow in Duke's direction. He could read it. She'd done her part, and now it was time for him to make an impression. After years of dating, years of having women throw themselves at him, Duke felt something strange; he was at a loss for words.

Macy didn't seem the slightest bit awestruck looking at him. She'd barely glanced up when Monique made the introductions. With one hand in his pocket and one still holding his now-room-temperature beer, Duke stood there, rocking back and forth.

He towered over her by a good half a foot. Up close, he could see that her chocolate-brown hair was highlighted with little streaks of gold. She still wouldn't give him eye contact, but he could see that she had the longest lashes and barely any makeup on her top lids. When she smiled down at baby Lulu, he could see her regal cheekbones rise slightly.

Monique reached over and popped her husband on the arm. "Oh my gosh, I told you not to let me forget the thing."

"Ouch. The what?" Pablo asked, rubbing his arm.

A person had to be blind not to notice how Monique tilted her head toward the kitchen. She was obviously trying to give the two strangers a moment. Macy wasn't blind, but she was clearly devoting all her attention to the baby in her arms. "Macy, will you be a dear and watch Lucia for me for a second?"

"Not a problem," Macy replied sweetly, looking up for a moment.

Even when they were alone, Macy avoided Duke's

eye contact. He wasn't going to leave until she smiled at him. "So you're a caterer?" he guessed.

"I cater to people, but not like you may think."

Her voice was thick, melodic. Maybe she was an aspiring singer. "Well, that's interesting. You know, I just may be in need of your services."

Finally she looked up, but when she did, he truly felt the icy glare of the *mal ojo* she gave him. He shivered. The evil eye told him she wanted nothing at all to do with him. "I'm booked."

"But I didn't say when." He tilted his head down so she could see him give her an award-winning smile. He also didn't give up that easily. If she saw it, it didn't have any effect on her, though.

Macy squared her shoulders and finally gave him a direct stare. Duke could see that her eyes were a golden brown. Her lips made a cute bow, even if they were frowning at him. "I don't need to know, Mr. Rodriguez. I'm pretty booked until the time you're gone."

Duke pressed his lips together to keep from grinning too hard. She knew how long he was going to be in town? That gave him a glimmer of hope she'd been following his time in Tallahassee. "I would pay you double what your normal fee is."

"It doesn't matter what you want to pay," Macy stated again. "I'm extremely busy, and I don't think you understand what exactly it is that I do."

"Okay, okay, maybe we can talk about it over dinner?" Taking a long sip of his beer to figure out what he was going to say next, Duke nodded his head. "Oh wait, I guess you don't like to cook since you do it all the time, right? You, um, did the cooking for tonight, right?" he asked when she gave him a funny look. Her left eye squinted a bit, and her smile was crooked, devilish almost.

"I did the decorating," she clarified.

Duke looked around him, the furniture, the caramel-colored walls with the white trimming, and the fixtures. "Oh, you're an interior decorator."

She smiled, finally. He thought he could leave now, but he was too captivated. Her smile lit up the room. It ignited something within him. Something he hadn't felt in a long time. His mother used to say he was going to fall in love at first sight, but he wasn't quite sure if this was it. All Duke knew was that he did not want to leave this woman's side, even if she was making it obvious that she didn't want to be around him.

"I'm more of an exterior decorator, especially for the holidays."

"This is interesting," Duke replied with a raised eyebrow. Women always fell for that move. Dwayne "The Rock" Johnson had nothing on him. "You mean you painted the house?" She was so dainty and feminine, it wasn't something he expected.

"No." Macy shook her head and huffed. She was obviously growing irritated with him. He'd never had that happen with a woman. Brown curls bounced from side to side, framing her face. "I did the holiday decorations outside."

Duke recalled the Santa, the snowmen and the elves playing outside. It was quite the picturesque scene. There were a few homes in his neighborhood that were putting up their decorations, also. In fact, he'd gotten a letter in the mail about keeping up with the neighborhood traditions. "The decorations are great. Maybe you can do the same at my place."

She half smiled this time, then adjusted Lucia so that she was resting over her shoulder. Duke noticed that her ring finger was naked. "As I've said, I'm busy, Mr. Rodriguez." She tried to move away, but Duke stepped in her way.

"Hey, maybe I can do a story on you. This sounds like a fascinating one."

"Sorry," Macy said. Her snarky half smile told him she could go toe-to-toe with him and with anything he had to offer. "You're obviously new here. A story has been done." She moved to the right, and Duke moved to the left, blocking her once again. She sighed impatiently as she looked at him. The light from the skylight hit across her eyes, turning her eyes a seductive shade of golden brown.

"I feel like you're upset with me."

"Now why would I be upset with you, Mr. Rodriguez?" This time she offered a forced toothy smile, showing her dimple on her right cheek. "We've just met."

*She was being sarcastic.* He liked that. Women weren't sarcastic enough with him. They pretty much caved to whatever he said.

And then a bomb went off in the pit of his stomach at the ultimate possibility. *Maybe she genuinely just was not attracted to him.* His years of speaking in front of the camera, eloquently, went out the window. He found himself beginning to stutter, "Well, I…"

And then she ambushed him with her reasoning. "Could it be because yesterday morning while I was getting my kids ready and listening to the morning news, you exposed Santa as a fraud in front of my eight-year-old? Do you realize how many mothers had to explain to their children that you're just a pompous ass whom Santa stopped visiting a long time ago and that you're just so bitter that you wanted to ruin Christmas for everyone?"

He winced and snapped his teeth together as she gave him a thorough tongue-lashing. When she quieted down, Duke felt guiltier than ever. Pablo had said she'd been the first to call and complain. How soon he'd forgotten, after being lost in her beauty.

"Oh…" He scratched at the back of his head, still at a loss for words.

A few people within earshot overheard and were snickering, championing Macy.

"I'm real sorry about that. Maybe I can talk to her…"

"Him." She corrected him quickly.

Duke nodded. "I'm very sorry. Can I do anything to fix this situation?"

Once again Macy shook her head from side to side. "I highly doubt it."

"Can I at least take you to dinner sometime? Maybe take your son out for a tour of the studio?"

Macy sighed irritably. He could see that she wasn't a person to make angry. If her eyes could literally shoot daggers, he'd be dead right now. "There is nothing you can say or do. What's done is done, Mr. Rodriguez."

"Duke," he corrected her.

"What?" Macy pulled her neck back in confusion.

"My first name, it's Duke. My friends call me Duke."

"You are such an athle-tante."

"A what?" Duke laughed.

"It means you're like one of those celebrity athletes who think you can say and do whatever you like you're some society debutante." Rolling her eyes, she choked out a haughty laugh, then shook her head no. "I'm not interested. So you have a nice evening, Mr. Rodriguez."

Dumbfounded, Duke stood there and watched her disappear around the corner into the kitchen. If she went through the swinging doors without looking back, then he knew he didn't have a shot at her. His heart slammed against his ribs, a strange reaction he'd never felt before from just meeting a woman for the first time, because when she reached the door, she pushed one side open, stopped and cast a glance over her shoulder, directly at him.

# Chapter 2

The day after the party, Macy found herself sitting in her office, thumbing through various sketches she'd worked on all morning. The swivel chair squeaked as she leaned back in a half stretch, half yawn, her eyes surveying the room. In times like these, she still did not believe how blessed she was to have such a successful career. The two-story Victorian office she owned in historic Frenchtown had doubled as the home where she'd raised her children until she earned enough money. Now she traveled in to work from her ranch-style home just outside the city limits.

For ten years, Macy had worked her fingers to the bone, using her skills as an interior decorator for a corporation and moonlighting during the holidays as an exterior decorator to help pad her little nest egg. Oh, how hard the first two years of starting her own business were—she'd been in the middle of a divorce from her best friend at the time, Mario Polizzi, and taking care of an infant and a precocious child.

Macy owed a lot to Mario, and it was easy to maintain their friendship now simply because they both realized they never should have gotten married. Mario and his family had played a big part in Macy's life ever since her parents had passed away. Since they dated exclusively throughout high school, they both figured marriage was their next step. Getting pregnant right after prom sped up their plans. While trying to rebuild her life, Macy took on clients who needed help with their outside decorating ideas for the holidays. That business became a niche in town and led her to become extremely successful.

In a few weeks, all the homes in Tallahassee would be judged for their holiday spirit. Each neighborhood nominated a winner and posted their favorite home on Pinterest. From there, the home with the most votes collected a win. The award, courtesy of the mayor's office, came with a cash prize, but more important, clout in the community for having the most spirit. In the past ten years, one of Macy's homes had always won. Her biggest competitor was herself. But she never took all the credit. Each customer would sit down with her and give their ideas of what they wanted. Macy just put it into motion.

Now here she sat, a successful decorator, and she couldn't focus on one single thing. The Christmas clock down the hall ticked away. The bells on the front door indicating a visitor were silent. In a way, Macy hoped the feeling of excitement when she heard her bells chime over her front door would never go away. It kept her on her toes. There was always a challenge lurking around the corner, but right now she desperately needed some motivation. The Wainwrights' ideas weren't sparking anything with her.

The Wainwrights were her latest clients. They were a middle-aged couple, married for twenty years, and wanted to finally get involved in the Christmas tradition. None of Macy's suggestions had worked for them, and none of theirs were things Macy could pull off. She couldn't make real snow appear and stick for the duration of the holiday season. They had a hard time understanding that if they did not sign their contract, Macy would not to be able to help them. They were going to have to stop just showing up every other day with their latest outrageous ideas.

Tucking her pencil behind her ear, Macy adjusted the cowl-necked sweater and strained her ear for her latest Christmas gadget, a buff, half-naked Santa with one hand on his hip and the other behind his head while he gave off a hearty "ho, ho, ho."

Any distraction was welcome right about now. The lead from her pencil barely made any marks. For the first time in a long time, her mind was elsewhere. Her wrists flicked a few times, sketching the outline of a face that had haunted her all night long. From the curve of his lips to his chiseled jawline, Duke Rodriguez's face was burned into her brain. Two cups of coffee couldn't get her to concentrate. Duke's cocky smile, his eyes and the way he flirted with her yesterday flashed through her mind.

Matters didn't get better when the office timer went off and the television screen popped on, directly to WKSS channel seven. Duke's deep baritone voice filtered through the office. She'd turned her back on the television, but she could still hear him as if he were right behind her. She would never admit it out loud, but his deep voice with the slight island accent made her stomach flip with butterflies. The fact that he had this kind of effect on her bothered her to no end. She was supposed to dislike him. And yet she couldn't stop thinking about him.

There had been a whisper running through the Baez home last night when he'd dared to show his face. Everyone with children who watched *Tune In, Tallahassee*, the morning show, fumed with anger. Macy expected her friends to break out the pitchforks, but all Duke had to do was walk in the room with that nice suit on, smile his dazzling smile and flash those big brown eyes of his, and everyone reconsidered their boycott. Macy found it best to hold her grudge against him. To have a crush on him from afar was one thing; it was a different story when he was in the flesh, flirting with her. And it was obvious yesterday evening that he had been hitting on her.

Macy had caught Duke staring at her quite a bit at the party but refused to give him eye contact. A man like him probably had a hundred women throwing themselves at him. And then there was the horrible way he got himself introduced. He should have been ashamed of himself for putting Pablo and Monique in a position like that. But that didn't stop him. He actually had the nerve to try to hire her. She was glad she had a busy schedule. She had five homes to decorate tomorrow, and then every day until a week before Christmas she was busy.

The heavy bells on top of the door chimed. Macy perked up. Despite her dislike for Duke's personality, Macy felt her heart sink a tad when she spied her assistant Serena Berks coming in the door. She had no idea why she would even think a man like Duke Rodriguez would come to her place of business. She didn't know what she would have done with him if he had shown up, but then a devilish little voice nagged at the back of her mind, reminding her that it hadn't been *that* long since she knew what to do with a man.

Down the hall, there came a grunting, a cursing and a sniffling. Poor Serena was dragging in a huge plastic mouse statue with all her might. At five foot two, Serena was just two inches shorter than Macy. The giant mouse, decked out in a red-and-green stitched scarf, had to have been about five seven. Serena's bobbed red hair was disheveled around her freckled face.

Macy had hoped to find one or both of the male assistants she'd hired to help lift and cart around some of the heavier decorations. It was the peak season for exterior holiday decorating and the musclemen, Spencer and Andy, hadn't shown up. Usually, they broke the frat boy stereotype by being reliable. But late last night Spencer had left an apologetic message about not being here this week. She prayed it was a horrible prank.

Getting up from her desk, Macy peered down the hall to where she had a view of the front door. She shook her head and hid her smile as she twisted her hair into a bun and secured it with her pencil.

"Hey," Macy pouted. "Santa didn't announce your presence."

"That's because I threatened him within an inch of his life if he called me a *ho* one more time." Serena projected her voice a little louder so that it could be heard upstairs and in the backyard. "A lil' help here!"

"We're the only ones here," Macy shouted as she walked back to her desk and closed her sketchbook.

The outline of the Wainwrights' lawn was just about done. She hoped they would be happy with it. They'd better be happy. This would be the third time changing things around, and Macy's time was precious, not to mention that her staff seemed to be dwindling for the Thanksgiving holiday.

"Here," Macy offered, picking up the pace down the steps and into the foyer, "let me help."

"No, you don't have to," Serena argued as she stood the mouse in his upright position. The unplugged giant mouse stood with a black nose, which, when plugged in, turned red. The plastic book of Christmas carols in his hand was open. From a distance no one could read the words, but up close someone had written, "Who let the dogs out?" as a silly joke.

"Where are the boys?"

Biting her bottom lip, Macy hesitated to tell Serena the truth. From the looks of her dust-covered garnet-and-gold T-shirt and jean shorts, the bookkeeper's morning had started off rough. She must have climbed over everything in the shed just to find the mouse. Going into the storage space went above and beyond the call of duty.

At thirty, Serena had been her assistant for the last four years while she worked on her BS and now her MBA at Florida State University. She was a pencil pusher who kept up with Macy's schedules and appointments, yet here she was doing all the grunt work. She wondered if Serena would believe that the boys had been toppled over by a giant snowball. It was highly unlikely. The weather for Thanksgiving was scheduled to be a balmy seventy-eight degrees.

"They left an apologetic message on my answering machine saying they left early for Thanksgiving. I kind of hoped they were joking."

"No way! I thought they agreed to be here over the break."

Macy rested her hands on her hips as she studied the mouse. "I know. But according to the message, they somehow—" she rested her finger on her chin to recall the exact way the boys had phrased it "—scored some serious tickets." She mocked Spencer's surfer-boy accent with air quotes.

Serena's laugh turned into a hacking cough. She shook her strawberry-tinted head. "That's pretty lame of them. They worked last year. They understand how this is the busiest weekend for you."

Shrugging, Macy tried to smile, already figuring how to handle things. In a way, she looked forward to working alone tomorrow and Friday. She was prepared.

Key organizational skills helped keep Macy sane. What took most grown men all day to do, she could complete in an hour. She had a few homes in the morning with light decorations. Extra hands stringing up the lights might have been nice, but Macy could handle the work; after all, she'd started this business ten years ago with no help.

The only stickler in her plans was the Wainwrights' home, simply because they kept changing their ideas. Typically the slots for holiday decorations got booked up by the Fourth of July. Every weekend until just before Christmas, she was busy. Most trusted Macy's ideas. A lot of homeowners' associations even required their neighborhoods to decorate unless religion prohibited it. Doing the work on her own wasn't a problem, especially since the kids were at her former in-laws' house. Perhaps it would be a bit of a hassle trying to unload her truck, but she could get it done.

*"Achoo."* Serena sneezed.

Panic ripped through Macy's body. With the boys gone, she was going to have to lean on Serena more. "Are you okay?" she asked slowly.

"Just a sneeze," Serena said, swatting the mouse on the ear. "He did this to me, stupid dusty thing...*achoo!*"

Macy raised her left eyebrow in question. "Maybe you ought to drink some orange juice just in case. C'mon, I believe I spotted some when I put up some leftovers last night."

"Maybe," Serena answered as she followed Macy. "Oh, and I forgot to tell you who I ran into yesterday while you went to the party. Remember the party I wasn't invited to?"

"Who?" Macy asked with a sigh, anticipating Serena's guilt trip.

The sound of their footsteps on the hardwood floors blocked out Serena's exasperated sigh as they crossed the former living room, now a sitting room. Macy straightened a Christmas ornament on a seven-foot Fraser fir tree and kicked one of the shiny green display presents with red polka dots out of the walkway. On the other side of the stairs, across from the living room, was once Macy's dining room, now two downstairs offices. In the back of the house was the kitchen; access was gained from the thin hallway from the offices or directly straight back from the front door and living room. Macy opened the white double-door refrigerator. Pictures of previous jobs she'd had over the years mingled with Gia's and MJ's old drawings.

"I saw Mr. Officer and a Gentleman."

"Who?"

"Ugh, Lawrence, the pilot you dated."

Macy hardly called going out with Lawrence Hobbs dating. The whole reason Macy had gutted her Victorian home was to meet clients here in the spacious waiting room or in one of the back offices, or even better, at their homes to better survey the landscape. Lawrence, on the other hand, had one reason or another to meet her at a coffee shop, café and even the park to pick her brain about decorating. Eventually, the two of them figured out that Serena should do all the scheduling. Lawrence, a sweet man, had retired from the air force and settled down in Tallahassee. At the party yester-day, someone mentioned he'd started his own private airline, albeit a small one.

"You mean the pilot you kept leaving me alone with when he came over here?"

"Yes. I think he seemed really interested in how you were doing. I think you ought to give him another chance."

"Really?" Macy said very quizzically with a raised eyebrow. "Because when I saw him yesterday as well, at said party you weren't invited to, Lawrence mentioned his new girlfriend, one of the judges from last year's holiday decoration contest."

Serena opened her mouth, but closed it quickly. Her matchmaking skills were lost on this case, no matter how hard she tried. This time of year, dating was out of the question for Macy. Macy smiled and thought of her children and how they would react if she started dat-ing. Their father, Mario, dated. Hell, he'd been dating before they divorced.

Macy shook her head as she bent over to look for something nutritious for Serena. These days, Macy kept the refrigerator stocked with various juices from or-ange to grape and apple. Today, she seemed to have only orange left. Next to the drinks were containers of leftover turkey and all the fixings. She'd made extra plates last night for herself and the boys to eat after work. Now realizing they weren't coming in, she had extra extra leftovers. Grabbing a glass from the dish-washer, Macy poured Serena some juice and patted the bar stool. "Drink up."

"Orange?" She frowned, being ornery. "But I don't like orange."

"Beggars can't be choosers, Serena."

"But I'm not begging." Serena tried to argue, but Macy just stared at her. Playfully pouting, Serena climbed onto the high-backed bar stool. "Fine, I'll drink even though I'm not sick. So what do you think about Lawrence?"

"I don't think much about him," Macy answered honestly. Lawrence was a nice-looking man. He was about five eleven with cocoa-brown skin and a trimmed beard; his was one of many faces Macy had seen yesterday. He had come over and given her a hug and thanked her again for the work she'd done on his house, but told her this year there were so many changes in his life that he wouldn't be around to enjoy the decorations.

Serena rolled her eyes and gave a huff. "He was looking mighty hot when I saw him. He was on his way to the party I wasn't invited to."

*But was he as hot as Duke Rodriguez?* a little voice nagged in the back of Macy's brain.

"Hmph." Serena's eyebrows rose. "That was a pretty funny look you just gave. Did you meet someone? Oh, wait, tell me—how was meeting Mr. Dimples?"

With a droll eye roll, Macy shook her head at the nickname her thirteen-year-old daughter had given the obnoxious anchorman. Serena didn't help matters whenever Gia came to the office after school. They had been fans of the anchorman before he came to Tallahassee, and now they were bursting at the seams at him being here. Gia had actually wanted to miss going to her grandparents' house for the week just so she could go to the Baezes' holiday party and see Duke.

"Exactly as I expected."

That had been the understatement of the year. He was also a bit more than what she'd expected. Monique warned her ahead of time that Pablo had invited Duke home for some old-fashioned Dominican cuisine. He'd arrived in a bright red Ferrari, and parked front and center of the driveway for everyone to see as they entered the house. She'd spied him the minute he walked in. Duke was good-looking, but of course he knew that. He was the only one in the room wearing a two-thousand-dollar suit. The average household in Tallahassee brought that in during one month.

"Oh my God, did you speak to him?"

"He spoke." Macy shrugged.

"Were you nice to him?"

"I spoke," Macy said with a coy smile.

The last thing Macy had said to Serena about Duke before the party was that she was going to give him a piece of her mind when she saw him. She'd come into the office seething on the morning of the incident, demanding to know where he got off telling the world that there was no Santa Claus. Andy and Spencer had sworn they'd never seen Macy so worked up before. Velda Thompson, her grandmother, had taught her to always act rationally. It was a long and hard lesson for Macy to learn, but she thought this situation deserved a few foul words. Grandma V must have been rolling around in her grave.

"Did you give him a piece of your mind?"

"I told that athle-tante…"

"Oh-em-gee!" Serena stopped her with squealing. She sounded just like Gia. "Please tell me you did not call him that."

Macy shrugged. "I may have."

"I'm going to die of embarrassment. He probably thinks you're some sort of freak."

She couldn't have been that much of a freak if the man still tried to come on to her. Macy decided to omit the part about Duke's nerve to hit on her at the party. Serena was always trying to push single men in her direction, despite Macy's lack of time for one. Her business was booming, and when she wasn't working, her kids kept her busy. But that never stopped her assistant from trying. Serena would always bail her out of meetings after she did a background check on the single men. She claimed that seven years of not dating, let alone no sex, was not good for a woman.

But Macy had brushed off Duke's flirting as she did with most of the men she'd come across. A lot of men tried to use the excuse of hiring her for a job. Duke Rodriguez was no different than the rest. Well, he might have been hotter than any man she'd ever laid eyes on, but what did it matter? She had no time for someone like him. And he had no time for her. Duke wasn't going to be in town long, and Macy saw no reason to start something that couldn't be finished. Monique was only on maternity leave until after the Christmas holidays. She would return with the coverage of ringing in the New Year. Her stance on dating, even if it was Duke Rodriguez, wasn't going to change. So what if he had those deep dimples or those luscious lips that made even eating food look sexy?

"Answer my question." Serena took a long sip of juice, but kept her eyes on her boss. "What happened?"

"Nothing happened, per se. He did ask if I could work for him."

The news made Serena choke. Macy didn't believe her for one minute. She was the mother of two kids who always tried faking sick. Finally Serena settled down and asked, "And you turned him down?"

"As it is, we're already short-staffed, and you're getting sick. How am I going to take on another client?"

"I'm not sick," Serena said, fighting back a sneeze. Macy watched Serena's eyes redden as she tried to hold it in. If she wasn't getting sick, then she was having a major allergic reaction to something. Her nose was a faint pink.

Macy folded her arms across her chest and leaned against the counter. "Want to bet?"

"I am working through this. I need to hear good things. Tell me more about him, Macy," she whined.

"What is there to tell?" Macy's upper lip curled. "He is a typical man."

"Ugh! You are so lucky you met him," Serena moaned. "I wish I could have."

The doors over the glass front door opened with a jingle. The Santa monitor went off with a deep *ho ho ho*. Serena made a funny face the minute Macy got up to walk over to the door. Serena had closed her eyes, crossed her fingers and begun chanting.

"*I wish I could win a million dollars. I wish I could win a million dollars.*"

The wonders of that girl never ceased to entertain Macy. Serena was always doing something superstitious like that. She thought if she spoke a person's name out loud and the person appeared, the same thing might happen if she spoke out loud her next wish, usually concerning money. Every time she drove by a graveyard she held her breath and crossed herself; she picked up pennies on their tails off the ground and turned them over so the next person could have good luck. Macy headed out the kitchen doorway to catch a glimpse of her customer. Instantly, her throat went dry and she felt that whiplash appeal in her neck at the sight.

There, standing by her sexy Santa, stood the one and only Duke Rodriguez, dressed down compared to yesterday. Gone was the custom-made suit, but what he had on was still just as bad: jeans made to fit his long, powerful legs, a blue T-shirt that fit across his broad chest just a little too tight and a black leather coat that probably cost the same as her fee for one Christmas-decorated house. His dark hair was cropped against his head, framing his olive-skinned face. And as he smiled, knowing she was ogling him, his deep dimples popping out as he had the nerve to modestly blush. He could have easily stepped out of the pages of *GQ* magazine.

She knew she'd been clear yesterday when she said she was too busy. "Can I help you?"

"I certainly hope so," Duke said with a dangerous, juicy, bad-boy grin. He caught Serena's attention and nodded his dark head in her direction. "Hey, how are you? I'm Duke…"

"Rodriguez," Serena answered for him as she moved with lightning-like speed, nearly bowling Macy over just to shake his hand. "I know. Second-string shortstop for the Yankees for two seasons before you started work as a sports correspondent, prime-time anchor on ESPN for a few years, and then working from New York and DC. I've followed your career. We're so glad to have you in our little small town."

"Well, who knew a high school kid like yourself would be so into the news? I'm flattered."

The person most flattered was Serena. She gave an unrecognizable high-pitched giggle and swayed back and forth. Her face was the same color as the red in her shirt. Macy refrained from rolling her eyes as Serena beamed at his flattery. "Oh, no, I'm not in high school."

"This is my assistant, Serena." Macy made the quick introduction to keep Serena from making a bigger fool of herself. "What do you want, Mr. Rodriguez?"

"Now, didn't I tell you that my friends call me Duke?"

Macy raised an eyebrow and folded her arms across the front of her short-sleeved red sweater. "Mr. Rodriguez."

Serena gently reached over to wrap her arm around Macy's shoulder. She squeezed her just a little too hard. "Excuse my boss. She's a bit delusional."

Duke nodded and smiled. "I see. Well, I was hoping that was the case yesterday when I asked for Macy's services."

"I told you yesterday, Mr. Rodriguez."

"Duke," he corrected.

It was useless. She could spend the rest of the afternoon playing this Abbott and Costello bit over whether or not to call him Duke or Mr. Rodriguez. Macy huffed and caved in. The sooner he left, the sooner she could get back to work. "Fine. I told you the situation yesterday, *Duke*. I simply don't have time to decorate your house."

"I'll pay double."

"No."

"Please hear me out." Duke held his large hands out, pleading. Macy spied how smooth they were, compared to hers. Subconsciously she wrung her calloused hands together. A celebrity athlete like him was used to snapping his fingers and having people, specifically women, jump to his aid. Well, Macy knew she wasn't one of those women. If he wanted her help, he should have booked her six months to a year in advance, like the rest of her clients. "I'm begging. I came home yesterday and someone had egged my front porch."

"Damn kids." Serena *tsk*ed and shook her head.

"The sad thing is that I don't think it's the kids. It's the mothers in my neighborhood. The day before that, someone hung Santa in a tree and toilet-papered my house. I spent all night trying to get 'Santa Killer' off my front door."

An image of Duke standing in his doorway in nothing but a pair of red basketball shorts while scrubbing the door with a sponge and a foamy white bucket of soap entered her mind. She could picture the muscles on his back flexing as he held on to the door for balance while he reached down and soaked his sponge. A warm glow spread up Macy's chest as she blinked the image out of her mind and focused her gaze on her guest. "I'm really sorry for what you're going through, but I'm sure things will blow over."

"You know, I could always come over and stake out your place for you," Serena chimed in.

A tint of red touched Duke's cheeks. "Thanks, but I think what I really need to do is throw a good old-fashioned Christmas party just to show everyone that I'm not the ogre that they seem to think. Outing Santa was an accident."

"Sure, just like telling that athlete he needed a vasectomy, or telling a teen actress that she might want to consider dropping her parents as managers," Macy ticked off. "Or what about you telling that singer that he ought to come out of the closet?"

"So you've followed my work?" He wiggled his eyebrows at her. His mouth opened wide into a smile. She hated that she thought about how kissable his lips looked right now.

Perhaps wiggling his eyebrows was a dealmaker when getting a woman to come home with him, but Macy reminded herself that she wasn't interested. To prove it, Macy rolled her eyes and feigned disinterest with a slight yawn. "My thirteen-year-old daughter follows you. I just happen to be the type of parent that monitors what she watches."

"And so she and your eight-year-old son were watching?" He cocked his head to the side and grinned. "And you were watching me, too?"

Shifting her weight from one heel to the other, Macy shrugged her shoulders. "For your information, I happen to watch the show every morning. I was doing that before Monique went on maternity leave." The slow, lopsided smile Duke gave her was admittedly sexy. His attempt at what he must have considered his A-game was sad. "But I may start watching the other channel."

"See, that's exactly what I'm trying to avoid."

"Perhaps we need to sit down for this," Serena said.

Looking over at her, Macy noticed that her assistant was breaking out in a sweat. The last thing she wanted was for Serena to get sick. She had finals coming up soon and she needed all the studying she could get. This was exactly why she wanted the boys here this weekend: because she wanted to give Serena a break.

"Yes, please come in and have a seat." She stepped aside and waved her hand to the left, toward the parlor area. The hardwood floors echoed with the heavy footsteps of his rather large feet. Duke sat down in the Queen Anne chair and crossed one leg over the other. He filled the chair like royalty. Serena sat beside him on the adjacent matching couch, still batting her eyes at him. Macy stepped into the kitchen first to grab Serena's glass of juice.

Once everyone was situated, Macy sat down and sighed. "So what is it you're trying to avoid?"

"Well." Duke placed both feet on the ground, rested his elbows on his thighs and leaned forward. "You seem to care about Monique, and you are aware Pablo is practically my brother. I just want to do a good job for them.

I would hate for Monique lose her viewers due to my stupidity."

"Aw, you are so sweet," Serena cooed, leaning forward in her seat. She folded her hands underneath her chin and cocked her head to the side. It looked uncomfortable as she sipped on her juice.

If the girl flirted any more, she'd be sitting in his lap. Macy shook her head at her. Was she really going to believe this? It was a ploy, Macy thought. Somehow, Serena was doing one of her matchmaking schemes. Macy leaned back in the chair opposite him and studied his face.

"I told you, I don't have time. On top of everything else, two of my employees took off this weekend, which is going to push any time that I have to the limit."

"What if I paid triple?"

With that, Serena choked on her juice again.

Macy ignored her. "It doesn't work like that, Duke. I have limited time."

"Well, technically, you just have the homes tomorrow to do for the ones that are out of town." Serena offered up the schedule. "Too bad we're missing our handymen to help out." She gave Duke a wink. Reaching out, Serena touched Duke's biceps. "Oh my, what big muscles you have."

He at least had the sense to blush. "Thank you."

"Serena." Macy sent a warning glance at her friend. "Control yourself."

"What? I'm just pointing out that our usual muscle guys are going to the big game this weekend and I guess they drove down early."

"So I can help," Duke said excitedly. "I'm off until Monday, but even still, after that I am done with the morning news by seven. I can help you during the day with your work, and that will free up your time to help me throw my party, right?"

Serena sat back in the couch and grinned, ignoring the evil glare Macy shot her. "Beggars can't be choosers, Macy. Besides, don't forget that the boys are going to have exams coming up soon, so they're not going to be able to help out as much over the next few weeks."

"No." Macy shook her head.

"Why not?" Duke asked.

Serena leaned forward and faced Macy, putting her hand over the side of her face so that Duke couldn't see what she was saying, even though her whisper didn't do what it was supposed to. "He's paying triple, Macy. With your new house, the additional sheds you've ordered and the two trucks, the money will come in handy. Remember, I do the books…it'd be nice to see a chunk in there."

"No," Macy hissed.

"Why not?" Duke and Serena chorused.

"For starters, we typically meet up at four in the morning."

"Um." Duke cleared his throat. "I'm doing the morning news. I'm always up at four."

There was nothing more Macy wanted to do than to protest, but if she did she would only look silly. Monique and Pablo were her dear friends. They were the first people to help her get her business started, by offering free advertising. Every year, she decorated their home for free, just because she felt she owed them. What Duke had done was stupid, but Macy also knew he could be the cause of viewers leaving Monique's show. She couldn't let that happen.

She could handle working with Duke. She could handle his cockiness. Lord knew she'd been through worse with Mario. Macy gave Duke a once-over. She still doubted, regardless of his solid six-foot-four frame, that he had ever done manual labor. Had he been on a ladder? Could he string lights? Would he know how to test if one bulb was broken and what to do if it was?

Macy's mental argument raged on in her head. He'd be more in the way than anything else. And more likely Duke would ask to work inside. If that were the case, she figured he'd sit inside half the time while she stayed outdoors. That would work out perfectly, because then she wouldn't have to spend too much time with him.

Folding her arms across her chest, she looked at him and reluctantly said, "Fine."

"Well, that settles that," Duke beamed. "I'm all yours."

# Chapter 3

The pot of coffee finished percolating at the same time someone knocked softly on the door. Macy stopped briefly on the bottom step in the waiting room and glanced at the grandfather clock chiming away at four in the morning. Since the kids were spending Thanksgiving with their father and his family this holiday season, she'd stayed at work last night. She slept in her old bedroom, curled up with anticipation for her day with Duke Rodriguez. Fortunately, Serena was going to act as a buffer.

Macy had awoken thirty minutes ago. *And what a wasted thirty minutes it was.* Not only had the Wainwrights rejected her latest designs she had bike-messengered over last night, she'd spent the first minutes trying to figure out if each pair of jeans she had in the closet of her bedroom made her look too bulky. When did she ever worry about her clothes? First thing in the morning and Duke already flustered her. Ten minutes ago, she'd settled on a pair of dark-washed jeans, comfy gray furry boots and an over-size long-sleeve gray shirt.

Cutting into the silence of the early-morning hours of the house was another knock. Macy literally stood still until the third knock, still debating whether or not she would greet Duke at the door before or after her first sip of coffee, or even let him in. She decided on the latter and opened the door. Sexy Santa greeted her with his usual *ho-ho-ho* greeting, which made her grin as she did so.

"Good morning," she said sweetly. Her fingers twisted the scrunchie wrapped around the doorknob and maneuvered the band to her wrist.

Duke Rodriguez filled the doorway with the essence of a man. Macy braced herself against the door's frame to stabilize herself from her weakening knees. He wore another pair of well-fitting jeans that hung low enough on his hips, a black V-neck T-shirt and a pair of classic wheat Timberland boots. The front part of his shirt was tucked into his jeans, showing off the obvious silhouette of his washboard abs. His face had a slight morning stubble, which made him look even more rugged. His mouth opened wide as he smiled at her. "And good morning to you!" he said cheerfully.

"I didn't think you'd really come." Macy held the door wider. "Come on in, the coffee just finished brewing." She braced her back against the door, watching him stroll inside, and then pressed the door closed with the weight of her body. "You drink coffee, don't you?" she asked, walking past him. While she twisted and secured her hair into a high ponytail with the tie around her wrist, she listened for his heavy footsteps following her into the kitchen.

"I'm Dominican," Duke said with a heavily accented, matter-of-fact yet pompous tone.

*He was Dominican?* As if that was an answer! Of course she knew of his Dominican heritage. Duke put the "Spang" in Spanglish, flipping from English to Spanish at the drop of a hat depending on the person he was interviewing, typically making grown women swoon. Macy groaned inwardly when she realized that it seemed as if she knew everything about him.

He was Pablo's best friend.

He was Gia's major crush.

Macy knew just about everything there was to know about the man, whether she wanted to or not. She knew he was born and raised in Mao, a city in the province of Valverde, played baseball well enough to earn him a scholarship to the States, played with the Yankees for a while and then used his major in broadcast journalism to become a sportscaster, landing him his major break as a serious journalist during the 9/11 attacks. Duke's voice had brought her out of a dark time in her life.

The 2001 attacks had sent Macy into a depression. Having lost her journalist parents, who died in a car accident heading to cover the aftermath of the World Trade Center bombing, Macy stayed up night and day watching the coverage. Had her parents been alive, they'd no doubt have injected themselves into the report as well, the thought of which, crazy as it was, infuriated Macy once again. Their desire to cover the news had always overshadowed staying at home and raising their little girl. But there was something about the way Duke reported the news, the way he let his genuine emotions out, that struck a chord with her. Without having old video of her parents reporting, Macy had never felt the bond. Duke stood in front of the rubble and as he helped the people surrounding him, he helped her see the human side of a reporter and somehow forgive her parents. Sometimes she felt she owed Duke everything.

The infatuation had died when he outed Santa.

"We can grab a cup before we go out. Maybe Serena will call by then."

Instead of sitting at the kitchen bar, waiting to be served, Duke stepped into the kitchen and lifted the carafe. The black liquid brew steamed from the top. Through the short sleeve of his T-shirt, the bulge of muscle of his biceps caught Macy's eye. Obviously the man worked out. She never noticed how small the eight-cup maker looked until it was in his hands.

"Where do you keep your cups?" Duke asked.

"Up there." Macy nodded toward the closed cabinet above the sink and headed to the refrigerator. "So because you're Dominican, it's automatic that you like coffee? My dad was half Italian. Should I automatically like pasta?"

"Well, of course, and if you're making *baccalà* for the Feast of the Seven Fishes on Christmas Eve, count me in!" Duke half smiled over his shoulder.

She was shocked he knew of those traditions. When

most families had a nice turkey or ham or even a pizza on Christmas Eve, Macy grew up eating various seafood dishes, from *baccalà*, or salted cod, all the way to lobster ravioli. Christmas Eve was a day when most Italians fasted until Midnight Mass. "It has yet to be determined if you are invited or not."

"Well, I have a few weeks to win you over."

She turned so he could see her roll her eyes. He just grinned even wider. "Anyway, you like coffee?"

"I just simply meant that I grew up in the Dominican Republic, where generations and generations of my family worked on coffee plantations. Besides milk, it was probably the one thing I drank all the time."

"Well, there goes that myth," Macy mumbled, casting a glance up and down his frame.

"What myth?"

She hadn't realized he'd heard her. "I'm always telling my son that drinking coffee will stunt his growth."

The left eyebrow on his handsome face lifted in a question. "Your son, the eight-year-old, drinks coffee?"

"He wants to do what his mom and dad do," Macy explained, shaking the two cream bottles from the fridge as she chose her words wisely. Typically most men toned down the flirting mode when she mentioned a father in the picture.

"Oh?"

Did she hear a fleck of disappointment in his voice as he set the cups down on the counter? Glancing over to see if he was looking at her, which he wasn't, she noticed his biceps again as he reached for the cups in front of him.

The infatuation she swore had died out now reignited. Her knees weakened, and she reached for the counter behind her. *Muscles shouldn't make me weak.* Mario had muscles for days and she never got so gaga over them. *Focus*, she told herself. She watched his long fingers wrap around a mug. She liked that he chose a Santa cup and a snowman cup. There were plain old-fashioned ones up there, but given that her place of business centered around Christmas, she liked to keep the theme going for clients.

"So, where's your husband when you're out working?" Duke asked with his back turned. His voice had changed from disappointed to nonchalant. Perhaps he was trying to cover for hitting on a married woman. A slight tinge of guilt hit her. She turned, ready to face him, when he turned around. He had such broad shoulders that fell down into a tapered waist. It was a shame he was sculptured so beautifully.

"He's home with his parents and the kids." She shut the door with her hip and brought the creamers toward him. "I have Christmas Ginger and Holiday Hazelnut. And I don't have a husband."

"But you said…" Duke came back to the other side of the kitchen; he leaned a hip against the counter and placed his elbow on top of it to lower himself to her height. She noticed that all morning long, while she'd been sketching hard jawlines, she hadn't realized that Duke's cheeks slightly resembled a chipmunk's, which made him look very boyish. He nodded his head. "You said 'mom and dad.'"

Macy raised her eyebrow and matched his smile. "Well, in your defense, I did. So what do you want?"

He blinked during the long pause while their eyes locked. Macy's breathing became shallow, and she prayed he did not notice. Finally he shook his head. "Oh, you mean the cream?"

What else could she have meant? When his left eyebrow rose devilishly, Macy quickly got the point of her open question. A once-forgotten pitter-patter fluttered in the pit of her stomach. "Yes, the cream."

"I'll take mine black."

Macy shrugged and poured some of the hazelnut in her Santa cup. "I have this sinking feeling that Serena isn't coming today," she confessed out of nowhere. Maybe she just wanted to let him know up front that it was going to be a long day with just the two of them. She wasn't sure if she could trust herself to be around him all day long. "You're more than welcome to back out if you want."

Without even blowing, Duke lifted the snowman to his mouth and drank. "I'm staying."

"It's Thanksgiving, you know."

"And happy Thanksgiving to you." Duke grinned, tilting his cup in cheer. "Stop trying to come up with excuses. You can't do all this yourself." He waved one hand in the air at the decorations.

"You don't even know what *this*—" she mocked his movement with her free hand over her head "—is."

"Technically, you *can* hang up Christmas decorations all by yourself." Duke set his drink down. "You did do it all yourself before, didn't you? Climb trees and string lights, haul all your own stuff that you have stored in a warehouse not far from here. But just because you can doesn't mean I'm going to let you. Speaking of which, there wasn't a car in sight on my way over here, so we should make good time to get back here at nine so you can watch the parade."

Truly flattered, Macy beamed and bit back a smile. "I see you did your research and watched the video on me?"

When Macy first got up and running, Monique had done a piece on Winter Paradise, Macy's decorating business. She and her cameraman followed Macy around when she didn't have any help. It was just the promotion she needed. The video was now ten years old. The segment had ended with Macy climbing onto her couch in her red-and-white-striped footy pajamas, cuddling next to a then-three-year-old Gia. Although Macy wished that part could have been on the editing floor. She'd decorated Monique's house for free as long as Mo promised never to show the clip again. Duke had to have gone to great lengths to find it in the old tapes at the studio.

"I like to know what and who I'm working with." He nodded and slowly smiled. "So I went home last night, studied you. You're very impressive."

Heat from her blush toasted her cheeks. Duke Rodriguez stood in her kitchen, giving her compliments. Slowly Macy tried to relax, resting her hip against the counter. "Not everyone enjoys Christmas as much as I do. I might be the only person who gets goose bumps when stores start putting out holiday decorations before Halloween."

"I don't know about Halloween." Duke winked. "Someday I'll have to tell you how we celebrate Christmas in my hometown."

"It doesn't even snow there," Macy teased easily.

"And seventy degrees is ideal Christmas weather?"

Macy raised her eyebrow. Touché. "Well, the weather will be colder come Christmas."

He nodded his head in honorable acceptance of her comment. "I have to say, I watched your video over and over." He glanced around the kitchen, letting out a long sigh. "So this is where you raised your kids?"

"Yep, up until this year."

"I bet you have a big tree."

She nodded, admitting the truth. "What about you? Are you going to put up a tree?"

"Sure, if you think I need one."

For a moment, she forgot that she was going to decorate his place. "Oh yeah, right."

"Did you forget about me just that fast?" he teased.

*As if,* taunted a voice in the back of her mind.

"I bet with your reputation around town, you're able to get the best tree."

"The first tree," Macy boasted, "although this year, I don't have time to get the first one."

He smiled back at her. "I bet you're like royalty around here."

"Nah, I just like to make sure that everyone is happy through the holidays."

Nodding, Duke leaned against the counter, mirroring her. Through half-closed lids, his eyes focused on her lips. Self-consciously, Macy licked them, wondering freakishly what it would be like if he kissed her right now. Her throat went dry, and she couldn't think of a thing to say. The silence growing between them only provided more time for her to stare at him with her naughty thoughts. She prayed for a break in the awkward quietness. She prayed for anything to stop the wanton thoughts she was having about this man she barely knew. *C'mon, Serena, show up!*

Finally he spoke. "So how did you get the name Macy?"

"Well." Macy took a sip of coffee first, glad for the distraction from watching him staring at her mouth. She had thought for a moment that he was going to kiss her. And if he had, she might not have moved. "I was born during the Macy's Thanksgiving Day parade."

If he hadn't choked on his coffee, the surprised news would certainly have shown on his face. Duke's eyes opened wide; his mouth hung agape. "What?"

She gave him a slow smile. "It's true. My mother was a local weather girl who insisted on covering the parade. My father was also an anchorman. They lived in Jersey and commuted to New York City. Since my mom wasn't due until New Year's Eve, she thought everything would be okay. Then, just as Snoopy was coming down Thirty-Fourth Street, her water broke, contractions came and they hid her in a float."

"You're joking."

"Nope." She took another sip and hid her smile behind her mug. "Somewhere in this universe is a recording of my public entrance into the world."

"Interesting." Duke's melodic hum sent a wave of chills down her spine. "How did you end up in Tallahassee?"

With a shrug, Macy sighed. "Well, with my parents busy covering the world news, my grandparents took me in."

Duke straightened to his six-foot-plus frame and raked his hand over his cropped black hair. "That's pretty cool. My family believes in closeness. Hey, wait a minute, today must be your birthday, right?"

"No, this year my birthday falls on a Sunday."

He pressed his lips together as if to make a mental note about it. *He didn't have to*, she thought to herself. They just met two days ago.

*Technically.*

Surely, with all the chatter between the two of them, she felt they knew each other already. She knew all about Duke's career choices, and she knew all about his relationships with the starlets he'd interviewed over the years. She also knew about the serious relationship he had been in. If Gia hadn't mentioned it, Serena would have, or Macy could have easily caught wind of it in the grocery store line, looking at the tabloids.

Up until recently, Duke Rodriguez had been with a tall, raven-haired beauty named Kristina Barclay. They'd been together for about a year, which at least told Macy that the man was able to commit to a relationship. And then over the summer, they'd split, and neither would comment as to why.

Soon after their separation, Duke had been photographed at every nightclub from DC to New York City with one gorgeous leggy woman or another. Macy just assumed it was because Duke probably didn't want to settle down. He was close to forty and set in his own ways. Why else would a grown man leave a perfectly good job at a national news station in DC and travel down south just to help out a friend?

"Big plans? It's your what? Twenty-eighth?"

"Nice try." She smirked. "But if you didn't figure out from the interview, then I'm not going to tell."

She watched him stretch. She'd never paid attention to a man stretch before. It never seemed erotic, yet he managed to make it so. Heat crept around her neck, down her chest. Duke's chest seemed to double in size as he inhaled. His stretch came with a groan, a low, grunted sound that rose from the pit of his belly to his Adam's apple. When he finished with his yawn and stretch, he leaned against the counter, both elbows on the countertop. He seemed closer to her. And with him bent over like that, he was eye level with her.

"I am sure I can figure it out." He was confident in what he said and the way he smiled at her. She wished he'd stop doing that, because every time he did, she felt like a schoolgirl with a crazy crush. "So let me get this straight. Both your parents were in broadcasting and you're giving me grief about my slipup? Are you saying every broadcast was perfect?"

"Of course they did slip up every now and then. But it's just different when it's your own kids."

"I guess I would understand more if I had kids of my own."

"None?"

He shook his head no and reached for his coffee again. "No."

"Too busy planning your own career?" Macy said with a snarky smirk.

"Actually, I found out when I entered college at Miami."

Macy recalled her grandfather boasting about Duke's reputation as a third baseman phenom. The major leagues were interested in recruiting him. Even at eighteen, tall and lanky, his dark Caribbean looks had caused a buzz. Now here he stood in the flesh, filled out in all the right places, and still causing quite the buzz. Macy swallowed hard and pushed down the memory of all the fantasies she had of him.

"I came to the States for a summer workshop and got pretty sick. The docs worried it was meningitis, but turned out I had mumps again."

"Mumps?" Macy repeated, cocking her head to the side. She tried to imagine Duke's square jawline swollen.

"Turns out I am one of the few people who can contract it a second time," he continued, "especially since I was never vaccinated as a child."

"Second?" Macy shook her head. "I don't understand."

"I told you my folks worked on a coffee plantation. They really couldn't afford to take the day off to take me to the doctor."

It was her turn for her mouth to drop wide open. "Seriously? What kind of damages can that cause?"

"You mean, besides not being able to have kids?"

Macy's mouth opened with shock. For every interview Duke did on television, someone had always turned the question around on him and asked about his desire to settle down with a wife and children. Now perhaps she understood about not having any children. "I'm so sorry," she breathed.

Duke chuckled nervously. "I don't know why I just told you about that." He pressed his lips together, flattening them against his teeth. "Yep, but don't feel bad for me. I have the Baez kids that love me, and I love them as if they were my own. I get to spoil them without having to do any of the potty training."

"Ha! I'd love to see you changing diapers."

"Hey, I've changed my share. I just never want to go through getting a kid up every single night to go to the bathroom." He let out a visible shiver as if the reminder brought back bad memories. Macy had to laugh. She had had her share of sleepless nights with MJ and Gia.

"You're sweet to help them out." Maybe he wasn't such a prima donna.

"They're the sweet ones for sharing their kids with me, considering my situation." Duke blinked; his long lashes only made her envious. "So far, the kids still look at me as their hero when Mami and Papi won't buy them what they want."

With a combination of a groan and a laugh, Macy shook her head. "You and Serena would make a perfect couple, ya know." She cleared her throat and rubbed the back of her neck at how uncomfortable the words sounded out loud. Duke was not hers to even claim for herself or anyone else, but the thought of seeing him intimate with someone didn't sit well with her. He was still inches away from her face.

Duke glanced at the counter where she nervously fiddled with her cup of coffee. He reached down with his forefinger and stroked the side of her finger. As expected, his hands were soft and warm. An unexpected result was the flight of the butterflies in her belly. He leaned closer. Macy watched him tilt his head as he approached. Her breath was caught in her throat.

"Thanks for the offer, but—" he brushed his lips gently across hers "—I feel it's important you know that I am extremely interested in you."

"Extremely?" Macy squeaked out. Her heart thudded against her rib cage so loudly that she just knew he could hear it.

"Extremely and only."

To confirm his words, Duke pressed his lips against her. He tasted like coffee, strong and sweet. His mouth moved with an expertise that she'd never experienced before. Their connection was magnetic. His bottom lip curved perfectly against hers. Regardless of their height difference, their bodies fit together like a glove, molding against each other. His large hands supported her lower back, pulling her close to him. She could feel the hardness of his body, and swayed. Macy closed her eyes and allowed the feeling to take over her body. It was as though she was floating on a cloud and she never wanted to come down. She could be kissed like this forever. But forever wasn't an option for them.

Every fiber of her was on fire. How long had it been since she'd been properly kissed like that? Her insides liquefied, from the tip of her tongue down, sending searing heat to the valley of her nether areas. With just one swoop, he could easily lift her onto the counter. And she knew if she didn't stop this, she would allow him.

Thinking logically, Macy pressed her hand against his broad chest. She couldn't do this, not now. She cleared her throat. "Um, speaking of Serena, I wonder if she's okay."

Just as Duke raised an eyebrow, the phone next to the utility desk rang to the tune of "Jingle Bells." Macy took just a few steps to catch it on the second ring. "Hello." She leaned against the desk and watched Duke's amused face.

"You jinxed me!" Serena croaked on the other end of the line.

Macy balanced the phone on her shoulder, closed her eyes and crossed her fingers. "*I wish I'd win the lottery. I wish I'd win the lottery,*" she chanted, and then picked the phone up again, ignoring Duke's quizzical expression. His eyebrows went up in surprise and his lips threatened to emit a laugh, turning up at the corners.

"Oh my God. I knew my ears were burning. I'm dying here and you're talking about me?" wailed Serena, sounding congested, stuffy and sneezy. Macy didn't have to guess to add "feverish." Perhaps this wasn't one of Serena's tricks of trying to set her up with a single client.

Covering the phone, Macy mouthed to Duke that she was speaking with her assistant. The break was obviously needed for him, as well. He moved over to the sink, turning his back on her, and braced himself with his hands on either side of the sink. "No, we were just wondering how you were doing."

"Mr. Dimples showed up?"

"Of course." Macy hid her smile and turned around. "Everything will be fine here. You take care of yourself, and I'll be over later with some soup for you."

"Please don't kill him, Macy. I love him."

Chuckling, Macy nodded. Her body was still vibrating from the electrifying kiss. "I won't."

"And when I get better, you can thank me."

"For?" Macy glanced at the speaker part of her phone.

"For letting you spend time with your celebrity crush." Serena disconnected from the line before Macy got the chance to respond. She turned back to face Duke with Serena's words lingering in her mind. Her celebrity crush had kissed her. She touched the pad of her thumb to her bottom lip and almost let out a schoolgirl giggle. A *clink* from the sink brought her to reality. Duke had managed quietly to wash out their mugs and set them in the adjoining sink.

"You didn't have to do that," she said.

"I didn't mind." He turned around and leaned against the sink, mocking her pose. Their feet almost met in the center of the kitchen but didn't touch. "It was the closest way of giving you privacy, so that your assistant can tell you to be nice to me." He wiggled his eyebrows up and down, teasing her. "I'd say you're off to a nice start."

Macy could feel herself blush before she could open her mouth. Her cheeks tingled. "Look, that type of thing can't happen again."

"What thing?"

"The kissing." She cleared her throat in an attempt to sound professional. "I don't make it a habit of kissing my employees."

Duke nodded and looked down at her feet. He tapped her toe with the tip of his boot. "You do realize that I'm not really an employee of yours."

"I know. But we have to work together over the next few days…"

"I haven't figured out when I'm going to throw the party, so it might take weeks."

"Well then, weeks. Either way, getting involved is not a good idea," she said, squaring her shoulders and standing up straight. Weeks? She was going to have to spend more time with him than expected. Being around a man who could kiss like that and had professed his desire for her… Macy shook her head, not knowing how she was going to be able to resist him.

Slowly, he stood up and nodded. "Are you involved with someone?"

"No!" she exclaimed, appalled that he would think she would just kiss someone if she were involved. "I'm single."

"Are you not attracted to me?"

She closed her mouth as quickly as she opened it and searched for a logical answer. "Well, I'm not going to say that you're not attractive."

"I think there was a compliment in there." As he

smiled and licked his lips, she couldn't help but watch, recalling how that same exact tongue had just grazed hers. Her heart raced when he pushed himself away from the counter and moved closer to her. She craned her neck, promising herself not to budge. He was a good six inches taller than her. He placed his hands on either side of the desk, trapping her. The dimple in his cheek deepened when he grinned. *Mr. Dimples.*

"Maybe there was. Do I think you're good-looking? Sure. But so does half the world." Macy kept her breath steady, despite her fast-beating heart, and prayed she sounded as nonchalant as she tried to make herself sound. "I just know you're not going to be here long, and I think that starting something that can't be finished is a ridiculous thing to do. I have responsibilities, children, work…" She ticked off more things that she had to do while he stroked the side of her face with the back of his fingers.

"I think that all depends on what your definition of finishing is. Are you looking to get married?"

"God, no!" she blurted out.

"Are you looking for a live-in boyfriend or something?"

She shook her head no.

"Then it just depends on two people's definition of spending time together."

"We barely know each other," Macy heard herself say. Did she say it, or was it more of a plea? Either way, it was a ridiculous thing to come out of her mouth, especially when her heart was speeding up, knowing he was going to kiss her again. And she was going to let him. She closed her eyes as he lowered his lips to hers and kissed her softly.

"I can't help but feel like I know you. I like talking to you." He moved his mouth by her earlobe. She knew she should protest, but it just felt so damn nice to be touched this way.

"Why do you want to get to know me?"

"I'm infatuated with you, Macy Cuomo." He rested his forehead against hers and looked into her eyes. "I haven't stopped thinking about you since I saw you in the foyer of the Baez home. Would I like nothing more than to forget about this day and place you on this counter and make love to you all day? Yes. But I know you're a woman who takes her work seriously."

Had he known that same thought ran wickedly through her mind just a few minutes ago? His bold honesty scared her. She shivered. "Infatuations come and go."

"But isn't it fun discovering each other along the way? What harm could come from going out to eat?"

Macy inhaled deeply. "I have a Thanksgiving meal we can eat together when we're done working."

"So then dinner is a good start."

"Just dinner?"

"I'm a forty-year-old man, Macy. Just having a quick roll in the hay is over and done with for me. Can't we get to know each other? If you find you're not attracted to me, just think, my contract with WKSS is up in a few weeks, and you won't have to deal with me."

"Oh, how romantic," Macy said with a droll eye roll.

However, how often did a woman have an opportunity to kiss her celebrity crush?

"I just want to be around you." He kissed her again; this time, he trailed his lips along her chin and down her throat to the crook of her neck. The backs of her knees began to sweat.

"Yet you keep kissing me."

He pulled away with a tight smile and pointed his finger upward. "Then you might want to stop standing underneath the mistletoe."

# Chapter 4

For once, outing Santa had worked in Duke's favor. After coming home from Pablo's party, Duke had found college kids toilet-papering his front lawn. The two guys sang like canaries, confessing they sought revenge for their boss, Macy Cuomo, who'd come into work pissed off about him exposing Santa as a fraud on television. Instead of calling the cops, Duke had used the situation to work in his favor and bought the frat boys off, sending them down to Miami on an all-expenses-paid football vacation. And he wasn't the slightest bit sorry.

Duke rapped his knuckles against the bright red door of the Winter Paradise office and leaned in close to try to hear Macy coming down the stairs. How was it possible his knuckles ached? Who knew manning a staple gun required such a steady hand? A day hanging up

Christmas lights beat a two-week training session at a top-notch gym. His thighs burned from climbing up and down Macy's narrow red twenty-four-foot ladder.

"Good morning," Macy sang, yanking the door open and closing it quickly behind her. The naughty Santa behind her called out his usual *ho-ho-ho* greeting.

Because she closed the door so quickly, Duke did not get the chance to step backward, so Macy stood pressed between him and the door. He contemplated pinning her against the door and showing her what a good morning it already was.

"Good morning," he finally breathed, taking a moment to appreciate her exposed legs in a pair of tiny shorts. Her smooth stems spilled into a pair of low-top pink canvas shoes, and her hair was pulled high in a ponytail on top of her head. The white shirt she wore reminded Duke of one of his old baseball tees, with pink for the sleeves and rim of the collar. His heart slammed against his rib cage and his palms began to sweat. *Maybe it's the heat*, he thought. Yesterday the weather started off cool, and by midmorning, the skies had turned very summery. Getting used to the Thanksgiving holiday being so warm was going to take some time, but the sight of Macy in a pair of shorts, tennis shoes and thin top was something to help ease his mind.

Macy hiked her purse onto her shoulder and worked her way around him and down the steps. Turning her face up toward his, she smiled and blinked, fluttering her long lashes. "Are you ready?"

The porch light highlighted her face. Duke enjoyed a woman who didn't cake makeup on with a shovel. High-definition television drove a lot of women to all sorts of crazy facial antics. When his television-personality ex, Kristina Barclay, traveled, she carried her own luggage filled with makeup. As a television personality, Duke occasionally endured a powder puff here and there, usually after fighting the artists tooth and nail. Macy just wore some mascara and lip gloss. Her long lashes framed her light brown eyes. Her lips were tempting enough to kiss again as he had yesterday, but the last thing he wanted to do was scare her off. After his blatant confession about his infertility hadn't scared her off, he thought he might actually have a chance.

Duke did not like the idea of comparing Kristina and Macy. He and Kristina meshed because they both wanted the same thing out of life—success. While his father was the most influential man in his life, Duke never wanted to travel the same farmer's path. He knew his family had sacrificed quite a few luxury items such as braces, dresses—even getting the family car fixed— in order to send him to baseball camp, which was what kept Duke striving harder to succeed. He owed it to his family.

Making good on his debt hadn't been hard for Duke. He'd been enamored by the rich lifestyle of the scouts who came over to watch him play ball. He wanted the fancy car and a passport stamped from countries around the world. Being able to come and go without any romantic responsibility in life dazzled him. He'd seen his college teammates settle down with a family before graduation, limiting their dreams, and Duke did not want the same. He liked his fast cars and to come and go whenever he wanted. Kristina had never expected anything more from Duke. She found his inability to have children a blessing. Before Kristina, the women Duke dated hinted that they wanted a family. Some even tried to trap him by claiming to be pregnant. Knowing he would not have children of his own had never bothered him until now.

Being around Macy gave him a glimpse of what life would be like if he slowed down. He felt nothing but good vibes looking at the family photos and school projects hanging on the walls and refrigerator of Macy's business kitchen. Growing up in Mao, his mother had decorated her refrigerator with his accolades. Meanwhile, the subzero fridge in his condo in DC remained bare. In fact, the factory seal might still be on it, which reminded Duke something was missing in his life. But until he figured it out, slowing down had never felt good.

Last night probably had to have been the highlight of his time in Tallahassee—maybe the highlight all year. There was no need for a fancy restaurant; Macy's meal in Tupperware dishes she'd set aside for her two workers was superb. When they'd finished with the last house, Macy invited Duke in to share a small meal and watch some television. She said it was somewhat of a tradition with her employees.

He looked down at the woman in front of him and had to grin. He thought of all the women he'd known in his life, and by far none of them had impressed him like Macy Cuomo.

"Not that I'm complaining about looking at your gorgeous legs, but aren't you a bit underdressed for climbing rooftops?" His head turned in typical male fashion and smiled appreciatively at her backside as she waltzed down her brick walkway. Her shorts hugged the curves of her hips. Duke followed her to the side of the house where she kept her Jeep.

"We're not doing any decorating just yet," she called over her shoulder, opening a door. "We're doing a little shopping."

She cast an innocent smile. Her doe eyes fluttered at him. Duke had done enough Black Friday segments that he knew there was nothing "little" about shopping today. He stood his ground and waited for the engine of the automatic garage door to quiet down after opening up. "You know, studies have shown that the best day to get deals is actually Christmas Eve."

"What?"

"I'm just saying, you're not going to find the best deals today. Don't you want to relax?"

With her hand on the door of her red pickup Jeep, Macy shook her head and laughed at him. "If you can't hang, you are more than welcome to go back inside. I have a hideaway key underneath the Christmas deer's hoof by the front door. I'll let you know when I'm pulling up and you can help me with my bags." Before she got in the truck, Duke swore he saw her smiling. He liked it.

Duke cast a glance back at the Christmas-decorated lawn. Unlike the other lawns they'd worked on, hers was subtle. A few lighted deer casually grazed on the grass. Simple white lights trimmed the roof of the house, as well as the picket fence. He shook his head and grinned as she backed her vehicle into the driveway and rolled down the window. Duke came over and leaned against the driver's-side window. "So you just want to use me for my muscle, eh?" To add to the joke, he flexed his biceps.

Macy shook her head and laughed. "Let's see if we can get those twigs built up before the holiday season is over."

For the most part, Macy presented herself as all work and no play. All day yesterday, he thought the kiss between them must have been a mere fluke, but just now when she bit the corner of her bottom lip and batted her lashes, he knew better.

Duke opened the door on his side and hopped in. "Let's hit the roads. Today *is* one of the busiest shopping days of the year."

"Don't worry," she said with a wink, "I've earned myself a place at the front of all the lines."

He half laughed. "That's funny, because with my puny arms I seem to get to the front of all the lines, too."

Macy walked through the aisles of major stores like a celebrity; salesmen followed her aimlessly with large flats, grabbing and reaching for everything she pointed at and said she wanted. Shopping with Macy was interesting, to say the least. Duke was completely unprepared for it.

At noon, they stopped and had lunch. Duke insisted they sit down and take a break from the hustle and bustle. Macy chose a small bistro called Nicole's. The restaurant was pleasantly placed just outside Lake Ella, which was near the downtown area. Together, they dined, seated across from each other at a wrought-iron table with a green umbrella shading them from the afternoon sun. Ducks quacked on the water, while children ran toward the edge to throw whole pieces of bread into the lake. Duke took a long drink of his sweet tea.

"Tired yet?" Macy taunted him.

He had yet to see her break a sweat. Meanwhile, his feet were hurting. "No."

It was a lie. He knew it. She knew it.

Slowly she smiled, held her red straw between her fingers and guided it toward her glossy lips. "It's okay if you are. I'm surprised you haven't crashed by now."

"I don't see how you do it." Duke sighed in relief and relaxed against his chair.

Macy shrugged her shoulders. "It's a lot easier when my kids are with their father. Otherwise, I'm dragging them around with me and putting them to work." She held her hand in the air before he could even think to say anything. "And before you say anything, yes, Gia is old enough to watch MJ, but if I left them alone, then my cell phone would ring off the hook over the two of them fighting."

"I had a hard time getting my brothers and sisters to listen to me when we were growing up."

"How many do you have?"

"I have three brothers who are older than me—Bobby, Sandino and Erik. They live in the States. And then my two younger sisters, Ana and Theresa, both live back home near my folks."

"So your folks are still alive?"

"Yeah." Duke stretched, not sure how comfortable Macy was talking about parents, considering she'd lost hers in the bombing attacks when she was a teenager. "My parents still get around. One of these days I'm going to get them to come to the States for the holidays. Tell me more about your kids. MJ's eight, so that's what? Second grade?"

He liked that she beamed when she spoke of her kids. Her face lit up like a Christmas tree. Her dark eyes softened, and any trace of tiredness was gone. Her cheeks gave a slight hint of pink as she blushed.

"Third. And Gia is in ninth grade."

Duke winced. "Oh, sorry. I remember when my sisters went through high school."

He still recalled their tears due to rejection from boyfriends; the mood swings were just teenage angst. There was also the embarrassment Ana and Theresa had dealt with, not only from their parents, but their brothers, as well.

"Should I assume they were sweet little girls until they hit high school?"

"Exactly. But it's all about knowing how to talk to kids." Duke relaxed in his seat.

Their waitress arrived with their lunches. Macy had ordered the grouper sandwich with seasoned fries, which sounded so wonderful Duke got the same. They ate quietly for a few minutes, just enough time to satisfy their hunger, and then Macy cleared her throat. He was glad for that, because he liked a woman who could carry on a conversation.

"So with your vast experience with kids, teenagers in particular, you think you know how to handle them?" She was playing coy. A dimple popped out in her cheek when she tried not to grin at him.

"Of course. I think kids just appreciate honesty."

"Like outing Santa?" she interjected with a lopsided smirk and a raised eyebrow.

He bowed his head for a moment and then lifted his eyes toward hers. She'd bitten the corner of her lip again. "I'm sorry that slipped out. You know I wouldn't do something that cruel on purpose."

"Mmm-hmm." He eyed her suspiciously. The more she sat grinning at him with her Cheshire Cat smile, the more he wanted to lean over and kiss her.

Kissing her yesterday had kept him fueled during the day and night. His body had been so wired from spending time with her that he barely slept. He'd actually tossed and turned in his bed last night until he just lay on his back with his hands behind his head and thought about her lips against his.

"Seriously, if I have to re-create the North Pole myself, I will do so if it means helping you prove to MJ that Santa still exists." He reached across the table and touched the back of her hand. Her skin was soft, like the petal of a rose.

Macy scoffed and rolled her eyes, but didn't move her hand. "No need to go all extreme. As a matter of fact, you don't have to keep working with me if you don't want."

Every time she got nervous, she came up with one excuse or another to let him out of his obligation. Yesterday, he'd foolishly hit his hand with a hammer while tacking up lights, and she tried to let him off the hook. The truth was, he'd been so preoccupied with their last kiss that he hadn't been paying attention.

As the traffic around them grew louder with the afternoon shoppers, Duke squeezed Macy's hand slightly. "Will you stop trying to offer me a way out of this arrangement? I said I am helping."

"Yes, but that was so I could do your house. I'm just saying, I'll still do your house."

"You don't seem to get it."

"Get what?"

"You don't seem to have time any other way, so this is my selfish method of getting to spend time with you." He thought she would eventually figure that one out.

After a minute of his hand resting on hers, Macy conceded and nodded her head. "I supposed I should be grateful for your help. I can't believe Andy and Spencer would bail on me. I know that Serena is sick…so I guess I *should* stop."

Duke hid his smile at her reluctant "should." Either way, Duke didn't mind. He let go of her hand and sat back, smiling like the cat that ate the canary. He knew he should have felt guilty for buying off Andy and Spencer, but he didn't. He had Macy all to himself.

"Have you thought about when you want to have your party and who you want to invite?"

"What about Christmas Eve?" Duke picked up his drink, pushed the straw out of the way and sipped from the cup. Macy did the same. He liked that she didn't look at him with such hate, like she had the first time they'd spoken. He wanted all the folks at the WKSS studio, as well as the viewers he'd pissed off, to accept his apology. In Mao, having a village party took little effort, so why not do the same here? "And I want to invite everyone."

She half choked on her drink. "Everyone?"

"Yes, I'm going to announce it on the morning news this week. I wanted to discuss it with you."

"Duke, your party is going to cost a fortune."

"Money is no object, and I want the house to be really festive, so whatever you want to charge me, have at it."

"That's three weeks away."

"Do you need more time?"

He liked the way she pressed her lips together when she was in thought. "No, we can do it."

Duke gave her a devilish smile and grin. Macy rolled her eyes, but her cheeks flushed. When was the last time someone had openly flirted with her? A gorgeous woman like her...men surely threw themselves at her feet left and right.

"I mean the party," Macy quickly clarified. "What kinds of food do you want?"

"Whatever you think would be good." He shrugged, not caring about the food or the cost of things. The only thing that mattered to Duke was that he was spending more time with Macy, and he had three weeks to secure her presence at his party, not as his caterer and decorator, but as something more. Something much, much more. What? Duke didn't know. It dawned on him that he had no game plan here.

Macy was reluctant to get involved with him because he would be leaving after the New Year. But what kind of life would he return to? He hated the fact that his personal life was displayed in the tabloids. Prior to Kristina, he never thought of marriage. Though his parents had been happily married for what seemed like an eternity, there was more to life than marriage—or so Duke thought.

Kristina had proposed to him in more of a businesslike manner. Like Duke, she'd attended college in South Florida. They both wanted to conquer the media world. He never imagined they'd be what the viewers called a power couple. Late last spring, after celebrating at a successful music award show, Kristina laid out her proposal, including all the endorsements they'd receive for product placements as a married couple, and she already had a date set for when they'd adopt a child and introduce it on a special report. At the time, he had no idea how to answer her.

Truthfully, the whole idea sickened him. His parents married for love, not business. His father made a grand scheme of a proposal to Duke's mother. Without being able to provide the potential for a child, Duke felt a proposal should at least be his decision. He hated not having control of his life, from the trainers who kept him fit to the ladies at the studios who chose his wardrobe. Feeling powerless scared him. And he'd taken a leave of absence from the DC news desk and headed down to Mao for some soul searching and got caught up with the baseball training camps back in the DR. The temporary break from the news desk and the permanent break from Kristina would change his world if he went back.

If? Funny how his "when" turned into an "if" now, he thought. A few weeks ago, he couldn't wait for the day when he got a late-night phone call with a story breaking. Now his mindset was a bit more relaxed. If he decided to renew his contract, he wasn't sure it would be with the DC affiliate. At work, there was always someone picking out his clothes. Thanks to a trainer who kept him fit, he remained in the magazines as a sex symbol. He always had someone to keep him on track.

There was something about Macy, Duke thought as he shifted in his seat. What he liked about her was the refreshing way she dealt with him. She gave him a task and allowed him to complete it without handling him with kid gloves. She gave him what he'd sought after for a while. She treated him like a man.

He got simple joy from just being around her. She was refreshing. She was entertaining. He enjoyed being around a woman who didn't count every calorie before it entered her mouth. He liked that when they were shopping, she didn't dictate orders to everyone around her. People seemed to follow her every whim because they genuinely liked her, not because they were scared of her. Kristina demanded fear from everyone. She may have not wanted Duke for his money or for a family, like other women he'd dated, but she did crave attention. The more, the better.

"Is everything okay with your food?" the waitress asked, rushing over to the table. She'd already come by for a picture and an autograph, and had him speak with her grandmother on the phone, who seemed to be in love with him.

Kristina would have called the manager over and had the woman fired by now. Macy sat back and grinned the entire time; she'd even made a sarcastic joke here and there each time the waitress came over with something new, but it was never anything malicious, just a joke on him. Duke realized he must have been frowning. The thought of Kristina did that to him. He pushed his plate away, folded his hands across his lap and smiled. "Yes, thank you. Everything is just perfect."

After she left, Macy was still looking at him. "You *were* frowning," she confirmed with a raised eyebrow.

"Sorry, I didn't mean to."

Macy sat back in her seat and folded her hands in her lap just as he had. The sun hit her face, lighting her chocolate-brown eyes. Her skin blended with the sun, making it golden. *Damn, she is beautiful*, Duke thought to himself.

"You know, I recognize that frown. You were thinking of an ex, weren't you?"

Duke knew better than to answer. But he wasn't going to lie to her. She didn't even seem bothered by it; she just asked the question the way a friend would. "I'd rather not say."

"That's probably wise," Macy mumbled, and then grinned. "But for whatever it is worth, you can work things out if you truly want."

He wanted Macy. Her attempt to sympathize with him was even more endearing. She was trying to give him hope that things could work out with Kristina. Perhaps his kisses didn't mean that much to her or just weren't sinking in. He leaned in closer. "If we're referring to what I think, trust me, I truly don't want things like that to work out."

"I can understand."

"You and your ex?" He knew she was married once before. He knew she had children with this man, and Duke didn't think of himself as the jealous type, but a part of him was glad that Macy's relationship hadn't worked out. Otherwise, this luncheon would have gone a completely different way. "How long have you been divorced?"

"Seven years divorced now, but we were the best of friends for the longest time before marriage," Macy shared with him.

"How did you two meet?" Duke thought the man had to be the world's biggest fool for letting her go.

"Both sets of my grandparents were friends with his parents, and they thought it would be cute to put us together because of our backgrounds. We each have a grandparent who migrated from Italy, so they insisted we attend the Sons and Daughters of Italy Club."

Duke didn't give a damn about Macy's background. A beautiful woman was a beautiful woman. In the DR, women came in every shade of color.

"We just knew we were destined to be friends."

As much as he hated to admit it, the thought of Macy still friends with an ex made him uncomfortable, unsure. He'd never felt that way before. Jealousy was not something he had in him. He used to think there were too many women in the world to get jealous, but then he met Macy. She was the only person he was concerned with right now.

When Duke took his initial break from the news desk, he'd done so with the blessing of the station production manager, Oscar Orsini. Oscar also produced Kristina's *Spotlight on Socialites* show. Without caring whether or not Duke accepted Kristina's business proposal of marriage, the two of them conspired together and planned out the Rodriguez/Barclay wedding; the list of sponsors and endorsements had taken over three pages in an email. Still with no idea how to say no to Kristina, Duke returned to DC and found out exactly why Oscar and Kristina were spending so much time together. Duke had guessed that, with his absence and lack of response, an affair between the two must have been foreseeable. This time, when Duke left DC, Oscar accepted his open-ended leave of absence.

How Macy's ex could just be friends with her was beyond him. He couldn't imagine watching her go out with a different man. And that was after only one kiss. He couldn't imagine how he would feel after making love to her.

"I doubt I can be friends with…"

"Kristina?"

He wanted to tell Macy he wasn't sure he could be just friends with *her*, not Kristina. But instead of telling her what he was thinking, he just cleared his throat. It didn't surprise him that Macy had heard of Kristina. He'd tried as much as he could to keep private life private; stories got out.

Since he'd been away from the limelight in DC, he

hadn't had that problem as much, and it was refreshing. When he played baseball, he was used to reporters asking him questions after a game, but when he became an anchorman himself, it almost seemed as if he was stalked every time he went out with Kristina. The more he thought about it, the more he realized Kristina could have easily phoned in their whereabouts.

"I really can't see Kristina and me being friends, just because we have nothing in common."

"Is that why you two broke up?" Macy asked and then quickly shook her head. "I'm sorry. I shouldn't have asked such a personal question."

Relaxing in his chair, Duke chuckled. Macy could ask him anything in the world. Considering he'd already told Macy about his infertility, why not go ahead and blab about Kristina's infidelity? But he did not want to come off as wounded. The tabloids already speculated a breakup, along with a graph of how many events Kristina attended alone. It was only a matter of time before the truth came out. He just didn't want to bring that drama here. "It's okay. I haven't spoken about the situation. Without divulging too much, let's just say that we had a difference of opinion." He held back a grin when she started to nod her head in understanding and reached for her tea. She was on the edge of her seat, clearly waiting to hear the whole story. The whole world had been on the edge of its seat.

"She wanted to get married, didn't she?"

Duke had left DC first and as a result, the media pegged him as the bad guy. Typically, he didn't care what people thought about him. As long as he knew the truth, he was okay with what others thought. But today it was different. It affected Macy's view of him.

"Yes, she wanted to get married, but not for the reasons you may think. In her eyes, we were this power couple in the news."

"You guys did rival Jay-Z and Beyoncé or Brad and Angelina for a while in the media," Macy chimed in with a cocky smile. "Not like I paid attention or anything."

"You're good for my ego." Duke clutched his heart and wobbled to the side a bit in jest. "The whole media thing was not my idea. I wanted something low-key. Believe it or not, I like the idea of an intimate relationship, one that's not plastered over the gossip tabloids."

Slowly Macy nodded her head as if she understood. He doubted she did. No one did. "Yet you continued the relationship with her?"

"I just went with the flow of things. But we had different ways of getting ahead in life. I thought journalism meant getting the story by any means necessary. I just never thought sleeping with someone to get a story was the way to go."

Obviously he'd surprised her with the revelation. Her mouth opened to a perfect O. "I thought…" She let her words trail.

"You guessed I strayed?" Duke asked with a raised eyebrow.

"Well, uh," she stammered, her light eyes averted toward the condensation sweating from the glass of tea. "You do have that bad-boy quality about you. And when the news of the two of you breaking up hit, you were seen with a bunch of different women."

He'd been told that before. He knew. His history as a baseball player allowed him to behave in what would be considered a bad-boy way. But he was in his twenties then. He'd grown. Just because there was a woman in every zip code waiting to give herself to him didn't mean he had to act upon it.

"I can admit that the way I handled myself wasn't the right way, but I quickly was reminded that my bad-boy streak in life was over."

"May I ask who reminded you?"

"My sister Ana." Duke cleared his throat, not proud of himself, but he had this feeling that Macy wasn't going to judge him. "I was in a hotel when she called me on my cell phone and asked if I knew the name of the woman lying next to me. And when I didn't, she asked how I would feel if some guy didn't remember her name."

Macy covered her mouth and sat back. Her eyes narrowed on him. He winced inwardly, praying that she wasn't judging him. "So then you left?"

"More or less. Pablo called me soon after I talked to my sister. He reminded me also about how I said I wanted a relationship. I actually always saw myself settling down with just one woman, kind of like my folks. And I envy Pablo's married life with Mo."

Macy nodded her head in agreement. "They are a great couple."

"I think so. I mean, I knew them both in college, and I can't say I've ever seen two people so perfectly suited for each other." He shrugged at his own honesty. "I always wanted a good woman on my arm, someone who made me realize my priorities but still loved me for my imperfections. You know, the kind of woman you would do anything for."

"That sounds very romantic, Duke."

"I'm a very romantic guy. Just give me a chance," he countered.

Picking up her glass, she visibly hid her smile. "After you just told me you went through a slew of women after you got your heart broken?"

"That's cold, Macy." Duke blew out a low whistle and shook his head. "She didn't break my heart."

"But you guys were engaged."

"Yeah, but…"

"Didn't you want to marry her?"

Maybe she should have been the reporter with her rapid, on-point questions. He liked that Macy didn't candy-coat things. She challenged him. "No, I didn't. But it didn't mean I appreciated being deceived, either."

Her eyes diverted to the ground and then moved back at up to him. "Sorry."

"It's okay." He shrugged. "In a way, it was a blessing in disguise."

"How do you figure?"

"Because it led me here."

He liked it when she blushed again. She tucked a strand of hair behind her ear with her fingers.

"So, are you going to give me a chance?"

Blushing, she rolled her eyes skyward. "What is it you want from me?"

"It depends on your definition of *want*," he began as

she raised her eyebrows in question. So he followed up with a reply. "In DC, I didn't really have time to date around."

"Sounds like you got around enough," she interjected quickly before clamping her hand over her mouth. "Sorry!" she added with a playful giggle.

"Anyway, being a journalist, I never had time to do the typical dating thing. I would have to cover one event or another. Kristina, I guess, was convenient to date and understanding, since she was a reporter, as well. Our schedules matched."

Macy nodded and took another sip of her drink. Just seeing her lips move over her glass made his body stir. He readjusted the way he sat so that he wouldn't make it so visibly obvious how much he wanted her. "Makes sense," Macy was saying. "My schedule for dating has been a bit off-kilter."

"So you're saying you haven't been on a date in a while?"

"Ah, let's see." She tilted her head back, giving him a glance of her beautiful neck, sculpted just for his lips. He cleared his throat, hoping it would settle the stirring in his pants, but it didn't. "I went out a few times with this one man for lunch. Does that count?"

"It depends. What does he do for a living?"

"He's a pilot."

"A pilot?" he asked. Macy didn't strike him as the type of woman who went for flyboys. Of course, she also didn't strike him as the type to go for former athletes, either, especially because of the special word she called him. There had to have been another reason. "Were you talking about work?"

Duke wanted to know if she'd kissed the pilot, but refrained from asking. He didn't want to know. He didn't want to think of some other man making her squirm as he did yesterday.

"His house won first place last year in his neighborhood."

"Then you didn't date him. He was a client. If he was a smart pilot, he would have flown you to another city for lunch."

"So what do you have in mind? I bet you can't think of much, now that you're in slowpoke Tallahassee."

"Tallahassee's not so bad," he said honestly. The weather was different, especially for this time of year, but prior to his outing Santa, the people had been friendly. And then of course, there was Macy.

"How do you like it?"

Duke leaned back in his chair and smiled appreciatively at her beautiful face. Just looking at her made him grin. Her smile challenged him. He couldn't use any line as he could on another woman, and he wouldn't want to on her. "I have to admit, I've absolutely fallen in love with this town."

The same reddening flush from earlier reappeared at Macy's cheeks. "I see."

The fact that she clearly tried as hard as she could to resist him affected him. Duke had to shift in his seat and remind himself that he was a grown man, not a boy easily aroused by a smile, but there was just something about Macy. "Do you? Do you really?"

In an apparent attempt to change the subject, Macy cleared her throat, but Duke leaned in closer and took her hand again. "I know you may think it's soon, Macy, but I can tell by the way you react every time I touch you, you're just as curious about where things can go between us."

"I—I..." She fumbled for words and stuttered.

"I am just asking for you give me a chance." He leaned closer and pressed his lips against hers. She tasted sweet like tea, but he knew she had her own sweetness. He had tasted it yesterday and had to abstain from taking more. Macy was the type of person who needed to take things slow. He respected the fact she had two children. As a matter of fact, he couldn't wait to meet them. But in the meantime, images of making love to her flooded his mind. The feel of her mouth made his body pulsate. It was all he could do to keep from taking her on the table right now. But he knew he couldn't.

People from nearby tables oohed and ahhed at the two of them, and a few of them even clapped. Macy pulled away for a split second, and then her body melted into his, just as it had done yesterday. Her hands clasped the sides of his face as she pulled him closer to her. She was an expert kisser. If they weren't in public, Duke would have pushed everything and acted on impulse. His heart slammed against his rib cage. A car horn sounded behind them, and though he was sure he wasn't the cause of it, he heard tires screech against the street.

Pictures formed in his head: Macy and his mother standing in the kitchen talking and laughing. Picturing his mother while he was kissing Macy wasn't ideal. But he thought it meant something. That kind of domesticity, something he'd never pictured before, especially not while kissing a woman. Reluctantly he pulled away.

He liked the way her long eyelashes fluttered as she tried to come back into focus. When she did, she blinked and smiled shyly. "Mmm-kay."

# Chapter 5

Birthdays in his childhood had always been a big event, Duke reminisced, pulling his Ferrari into the circular driveway of Macy's ranch-style home off Mistletoe Court for her birthday celebration. The family didn't have a lot of money growing up, but they always had a good time. Family and friends would come from miles away to eat and then head out to swim on the beach. Many would spend the night, which was already cramped with three brothers and two sisters having to share two rooms. The girls, of course, had their own room, but the male cousins slept in his room, thus making it impossible to walk across the floor in the middle of the night to go to the bathroom.

Duke pressed his lips together, impressed with Macy's style of home. From what he'd learned, she used to live in the office of Winter Paradise. It was easy to see how that Victorian-style house had been a home and how it turned into her place of business. Her new house was quite impressive itself. He'd prefer a spread like hers for himself one day. Once Duke had graduated from high school and didn't have to live with his siblings, he thought he would always want his own spread. Living in New York and DC hadn't helped him see his dream come true, but being down south certainly had opened his eyes for him.

The ranch-style home sat on a large piece of property far from the curb. At one end, the garage connected to the outside porch, which was lined with three rocking chairs on one side and a hanging swing on the other. On the side where the garage door was, there were four large windows decorated with a trim of white lights. Near the end where the swing was stood a bay window with a dressed Christmas tree.

When Macy reminded Duke this morning on the phone about her small party, she failed to clarify how many people were coming. What Macy defined as an intimate gathering turned out to be at least a dozen cars or so parked in her driveway, street and lawn. When she had originally asked him over, Duke was under the impression she'd invited her family, maybe Pablo and Monique. Judging from the cars parked outside, he doubted he'd be able to get any alone time with Macy. As disappointing as that was, he was still eager just to be under the same roof as her. Before getting out of the car, he reached into the backseat for the rectangular box, perfectly wrapped in a light pink. He'd discovered over the past few days that her favorite color was, surprisingly, pink. With her job, he would have half expected Macy to like red and green. The contents of the small box rattled. A smile tugged at his lips. He couldn't wait to see her face when she opened it.

As his foot hit the first step, he heard a group of girls screaming from upstairs. He reached for the doorbell, but before he could pull his finger away the door jerked open. Duke straightened to his full height and flashed his award-winning, camera-ready smile.

"Duke Rodriguez, well damn, ain't this something. I've been a fan of yours for quite a while," exclaimed a stocky man with arms big enough to bench press his Ferrari. He was close to six feet tall, but not by much. What he might have lacked in height, he made up in muscle. The man must have been a professional bodybuilder. "I'm Mario Polizzi."

Duke extended his hand, swearing privately this man was trying to break his hand for no reason…then he quickly made the connection. "Oh, Macy's…" He couldn't bring himself to say "ex-husband." This man was obviously more of a meathead than someone who was smart enough to hang on to a woman like Macy. Mario's loss was his gain. Duke smiled and gave his hand a firmer shake. "It's a pleasure to meet you."

Releasing the viselike grip, Mario smiled broadly and his dark hooded eyes lightened up as he grinned. "I'm really glad you came over today. I've heard so much about you…*ow-ow-ow*."

Mario's face suddenly twisted in a cringe; his eyes squinted and his mouth tightened as if to keep from cursing. Duke couldn't imagine anything would cause the man pain. Didn't he work out every single day? Duke checked out his muscles popping out from his blue tank top. Not only did he have one of those barbed-wire tattoos across his biceps, but there was also a much smaller hand pulling the hairs on his arm. Duke couldn't see who the hand belonged to, but he had an idea.

Mario shook his head. "I'm sorry," he said in a robotic tone, "I've never heard anything about you before in my life." His eyes widened and stretched while his head nodded to whoever it was behind the door. Duke caught the hint.

"Well, it's a pleasure to meet you either way. Polizzi. Related to any of the Polizzis in DC?"

"So because I'm Italian, I gotta know everyone whose last name begins with a consonant?"

Duke opened his mouth to apologize, but when he did he saw the hand on Mario's arm pull the hair again. "Ow, ow, ow." Mario winced, his eyes visibly watering, but then he playfully punched the air just a fraction before Duke's ribs. "I'm just messin' with you!"

"So I heard there's someone here who knows a little bit about journalism. Someone named Gia?"

"Oh my God, he knows your name!" squealed a squeaky, girlie voice from behind the door.

The door pulled open wider and Duke came face-to-face with a mini replica of Macy. He now knew exactly what Macy looked like as a young girl—all legs, hair and big brown eyes.

"Gia, honey, this is Duke Rodriguez. Duke, this is my daughter, Gia, the aspiring reporter."

Frozen like a deer caught in the headlights, Gia stared at Duke. There was a slight sound of "hi" or "hello" that came out of her mouth, and then her two friends flanking her grabbed her hands and pulled her up the stairs. Behind the closed doors, he could hear their screams.

"Did I do something wrong?" Duke asked Mario.

Mario reached into his back pocket and extracted a black cell phone. "I'll tell ya in a second. C'mon in. Can I get you a beer?"

"A beer sounds good."

"So you're an alcoholic?"

Duke did a double take. "What?"

Mario's face spread out in a smile. Duke recalled the photographs of young MJ on the office refrigerator. He definitely saw the connection. Mario made the same punching gesture toward Duke's ribs and laughed. "Aw, I'm just messin' with you."

"Mario, get away from him," Macy said, coming from down the hallway. She was dressed in a beige strapless sundress that reached down to the floor. Her thick curly hair framed her face; images of running his fingers through it entered his mind. Duke noticed her shoulders were bare, but for a gold crucifix that hung around her neck. His mother would love her already, just knowing she was Catholic.

"Why are you answering my door? You're supposed to be gone." Playfully, Macy punched at Mario's beefy arm before she turned and smiled up at Duke. She stood on her tiptoes, and instinctively Duke leaned down. She kissed him delicately on his cheek. Her lips were soft.

The kiss was gentle, but he'd been thinking about her all morning long, so that was enough to send a stirring under his belt. "I'm sorry if he's trying to get to your head."

"I wouldn't try anything like that," Mario said, voice cracking. The phone in his hand chirped. "Hey, dude, you're totally on fleek."

"Mario!" Macy exclaimed.

In his defense Mario held up his phone in one hand and pointed at it with the other. "Hey, that's not me. Your daughter posted this on Twitter."

Macy took hold of Duke's arm and led him down the hallway toward the living room, to the left of the stairs where Gia and her friends disappeared. "You'll have to excuse Mario, and take him with a grain of salt," she said.

"You two seem to get along well," Duke replied.

"Please don't be fooled by our banter." Macy shrugged her shoulders. "His family and mine go way back."

"I think I recall you mentioning it." Duke hoped he came off nonchalant. "But now you two are friends, for the kids' sake."

"It's easier being friends." Macy laughed nervously. "We watched a lot of friends go through divorces, and their fighting tore their families apart. We're the happiest divorced couple you'll ever meet."

Where Macy's office downstairs was full of Christmas memorabilia, her new home was quite different. On one side, family portraits lined the hallway in black frames against the beige walls. The other side resembled a bar that overlooked the sunken living room, with no sign of Christmas coming.

He spied the Baezes and nodded their way, knowing he'd talk to them in a minute. Duke wanted to soak in Macy's family pictures. He noticed an old picture of Macy when she graduated from high school, the standard photograph of casting a glance over her bare shoulder. Her hair had been pulled up; she was as gorgeous then as she was now. There was a wedding picture of an Italian-looking man with bronze skin and a woman with a café-au-lait complexion; he immediately recognized them as Macy's parents. Macy had inherited her mother's thick curly hair and her father's almond-shaped eyes.

The hallway ended with the kitchen to the right and the living room to the left. The pictures on the wall ended as well, but from what Duke could gather from them, Macy still appeared to have had a normal upbringing with both sets of her grandparents. She at least did all the things typical American girls did, from amusement parks to horseback-riding lessons and camping trips. He liked the various captured moments of her kids growing up. "When Gia is good, she's his, but when she's bad, she belongs to me. Go figure," Macy was saying.

Slightly uncomfortable with the closeness between the two of them, Duke tried to laugh off their friendly banter. She did say that she and Mario were destined to be just friends. "She got a phone for her birthday over the summer," Macy was explaining as she led Duke into the spacious kitchen, "and half the time the only way we can know what's going on in her life is through her Tweets."

Being in the media, Duke was familiar with Twitter. He refused to let everyone know where he was and what he was doing 24/7. As far as he was concerned, there was only one person he'd share that information with. He glanced down at the birthday girl beside him and grinned. "I almost forgot—this is for you."

Macy took the pink package slowly and shook her head. She bit her bottom lip as she looked down at the bow on the top. Her slim fingers toyed with the edges. "You didn't have to get me anything."

"Sure I did. It's your birthday."

He knew she was going to protest. So he took it from her and set it on the round oak table in the corner of the kitchen. The island in the center of the kitchen was filled with several trays with meat ready for the grill—chicken, steak, hamburgers and hot dogs.

Macy and Duke faced each other. She still held his hand. He could see her chest rising up and down from nervousness—something he adored. She couldn't fake innocence. "You can open it later," he whispered into her ear. He deserved an award for not nibbling on her lobes right now. Every inch of his body told him to kiss her, but unfortunately someone interrupted them.

"Duke!"

In the living room, Duke saw Pablo seated next to his wife on an overstuffed beige couch. Pablo got up to shake his hand. Monique held on to baby Lucia and beamed at the sight of Macy's hand possessively wrapped around Duke's forearm as she led him into the sunken living room.

With his free arm, Duke extended his hand toward his friend. "*Hola, hermano*, how's everything?"

"Great. Great," Pablo said, shaking his hand. "Are you ready to get back to work in the morning? Or have you been loafing around and you won't be able to get up?"

"Oh, he's been up," Macy spoke up for him. Still holding on to the handshake, Pablo eyeballed Duke, who tried not to laugh. He knew at some point during this party he and Pablo were going to have to talk. He leaned over to kiss Monique properly on both cheeks, and then planted a kiss on Lucia's head. The baby was fast asleep.

Music played in the background. He thought he recognized a bit of *bachata*. No doubt Pablo had been a part of the music selection. When his generation was growing up, the elders dismissed the heavy guitar and bass music as a fad they prayed would go away, even going as far as banning it in some places. But like most things, the more the adults tried to stop something, the more kids flocked to it. Now it was widely accepted within their crowd of music lovers.

Through the sliding glass door, Duke spotted a few couples out on the sprawling back porch swaying to the beat of the music. Duke had the sudden urge to sweep Macy into his arms and dance with her. He would love to feel her hips against his as they danced. But maybe now was not the right time.

Monique leaned forward in her seat, careful not to

squish the baby. "So Duke, how do you like the morning show?"

"It's good. Refreshing," he answered honestly.

"I loved getting up and spreading the news. I know it hasn't been long since I've been on maternity leave, but I miss going out and getting the story," Monique said.

Duke looked over at Macy and explained what he knew. "When we were in college, Mo uncovered every news story possible."

"She did it to get close to me," Pablo boasted. "She covered all the sports, too. Mo may have endured a lot of baseball games, but it was really so she could get an interview with me."

Playfully, Monique pinched Pablo's arm. "He's half right," she said to Macy.

"Here you go, man." Mario came over to the group with a cold bottle of beer already opened.

Duke thanked Mario and took a sip. "Actually, to be honest with you, I haven't missed the investigative side of reporting."

"It'd probably be hard to be an undercover reporter," Mario piped in, "with you being a famous baseball player and then being on ESPN for so long."

Duke nodded and took another sip of his beer. But he couldn't lie. He couldn't go anywhere without someone bringing up his time with the Yankees or as a sports reporter. No one remembered his interviews with politicians or his reports on Middle Eastern leaders. His job in DC had covered everything from politics to the local limelight. He reached his goal, breaking the mold of a dumb jock. Duke wanted to be the face viewers watched on television and trusted to bring them the news. People related to him and remembered his sports career. Sometimes, it took extra time to keep his guests focused on the story at hand, rather than reminiscing over past games. "My previous careers have had their drawbacks."

"Sit down, Duke," Macy said, fanning her hand toward the couch opposite Pablo and Monique. They fell into the cushions at the same time. Their hips touched, causing Macy to giggle slightly and adjust herself so she could look at him. As he looked into her eyes, it seemed like the rest of the world had been shut out. Duke leaned in closer and pressed his forehead against hers.

"Thank you for coming," she said quietly as she leaned over.

"You know I wouldn't have missed it for the world." Out of the corner of his eye, Duke didn't miss Monique elbowing Pablo in the ribs when he sat down.

"So Macy," Monique began, "how's your new helper coming along?"

Macy glanced up at Duke and beamed. "He's turning out to be not as pampered as I assumed."

"Pampered?" Pablo choked. "You thought *he* was pampered?"

"You know the celebrity type." Macy rolled her eyes when Duke looked over at her. "Always having someone doing things for them."

He touched his heart and sank bank into the cushions of the couch. "*Athle-tante* is what you called it, right?"

Macy shrugged and hid her smile.

"So what happened to your usual helpers?" Mario

asked, perching himself on an arm of the couch just above Monique.

"They got tickets and a hotel for the Miami game."

"*The* Miami game?" Pablo leaned closer, scratching at his chin. He cut his best friend a glare. "You don't say?"

Duke shot his friend a glowering smile. Pablo knew about the tickets, as well as the hotel. Before seeing Macy, Duke had planned on taking Pablo down for the game. Of course everything else fell into place for him with Andy and Spencer. Now was not the time for a confession, but eventually he'd tell Macy the truth. It was best to change the subject. He looked up at Mario and guessed that would be a great way to start. "So what line of work are you in, Mario?"

"Landscaping." Mario whipped out a business card from the small square pocket of his tank top. "Let me know if you need any help."

"God, Mario," Monique groaned, "only you would try to make connections at a birthday party."

Mario blew a kiss at Monique. Duke took the card and looked at it briefly before slipping it into the back pocket of his jeans. "Are you ready for work, Mo?"

"A little bit. I'm enjoying the time I have with Lucia."

The longer he was covering her position, the more time he got to spend with Macy. The room filled with the rest of their guests. Francisco Cuomo, Macy's paternal grandfather, came over for a little while, just long enough to share a few stories of Macy's childhood and her bad temper. As soon as he left, Macy begged Duke to forget everything her grandfather said and just remember that she'd learned to overcome her anger through her mother's side of the family.

Duke got a chance to meet the younger Mario, MJ, when he and Wellinson, Pablo's son, came inside to see how much longer the food was going to take. When the kids opened the door, Duke's stomach growled at the delicious smell of the grill going. After a while the men, Duke included, went outside to check on the grill. Apparently Mario was manning it and seemed to be doing a good job.

Typically when Duke was gathered in the center of a male conversation, everyone wanted to know about his history with the Yankees. Since Duke's passion was baseball, he didn't mind it too much. Growing up, he'd always felt he was best at the sport. Before he hit eighteen, the pros were already calling. Instead of jumping into the major leagues, Duke opted to get an education first. He missed the days of living in the DR and being able to play all the time, all year long. When he became a sports reporter, he was still connected to the game, even though he covered all sports from baseball to golf to football. Most of his friends who weren't in the business were always curious about his ability to get tickets for games, whether for the Super Bowl, the World Series, or even big-time college football, like the one last night in Miami.

Pablo was staring at his best friend when Mario brought up the game this weekend. "You aren't fooling anyone," Pablo said once Mario left to bring in some cooked meat. "I know you got rid of Spencer and Andy."

Coyly, Duke smiled and took a long gulp of his beer.

The sun was shining brightly. He was glad he'd worn a T-shirt and jeans, but wished slightly to have worn some shorts as Pablo had.

Macy had a huge backyard. Pablo's kids and other children were playing a game of tag, screaming and running around like crazy. He remembered those days when he and Pablo used to run around like that. There wasn't much he and Pablo didn't share. "I'm pleading the fifth."

"Because you're guilty."

"Of being infatuated," Duke admitted.

"So what is the deal?" his friend asked. "You've obviously found your way in with her. Now what do you plan on doing with it?"

Duke leaned against the brick wall near the grill. "I'm not sure. She strikes me as hesitant about going any further with me, other than a few kisses here and there."

Pablo choked on his beer. "You kissed her?"

"I'm not going to kiss and tell."

"But you will with me." Pablo grinned and took another sip to clear his throat. "I told you Macy is special. Don't pull any stunts with her."

He didn't have to be told that Macy was special. "I know that. And I'm fine with the way things are right now. I really enjoy just being able to spend time with her. She's unlike anyone I've ever met."

"And speaking of people you've met, Kristina called the station looking for you. She's been getting a bit testy with my secretary, too."

Duke guessed Kristina had given up on contacting him by phone after he let her daily calls go straight to voice mail. Daily turned into weekly. After a few weeks of this, Duke just blocked her number and sent her emails straight to the trash. He half expected Kristina to give up on contacting him, but being the reporter that she was, she wasn't going to let go until they spoke. But he had no desire to speak to her and he had no desire to think of her right now, now that he was finally enjoying himself. He made a mental note to eventually call her back. Pablo's secretary, Desiree, didn't deserve harsh treatment from Kristina. But he didn't want to think about that today, either.

Blatantly changing the subject, Duke sighed. "So the kids are doing great with the new baby?"

"Just fine. As a matter of fact, Lucia will be christened the week after New Year's. I know your deal with Orsini says you have to return New Year's Day to renegotiate with MET. Do you think you can make it back?"

That just put things into perspective for Duke. He knew he was going to have to leave. The main reason Macy didn't want to get too involved with him was because she thought he was going to have to leave. His date to renew his contract with the MET Network was looming. If he chose not to return to the news desk in DC, his agent might find a station in Florida for him. After being away for so long Duke had a hard time strumming up the desire to return after that lifestyle. He had plenty of money to stay in Tallahassee for a while, whether it was at WKSS or not. He had no reason to get back. "I might just not leave."

Judging from the surprised look on Pablo's face, the news was unexpected. "Are you serious?"

Casually, Duke tossed his head back to laugh, with full intent to spy on Macy through the sliding glass door. She was facing him, but seated on the coffee table, playing with the baby and talking to Monique. Occasionally she would look up, tuck her hair behind her ear and smile in his direction. Every fiber of his being was on fire. He doubted he'd have a moment alone with her right now, but all he wanted to do was hold her in his arms and kiss her again. He appreciated how she made sure at her own birthday party that everyone was welcomed into her home, how she treated them like family. It was something his mother used to do—very warm and inviting.

"I'm serious as a heart attack."

"This is great for the station! I can rearrange things. Mo, of course, wants to come back, but I can figure out where to put you in the station. With your work in DC, you could handle the politics in Tallahassee with ease."

Before Duke could tell Pablo to hold off on etching his name onto an office door, Wellinson came over with MJ. Wellie gave Duke a high five. The boy was getting tall for eight years old. Wellie was his partner in crime. Back when he was a baby, Duke used to take him to the park, and the boy had become a babe magnet, not that Duke needed it.

Now he stood there right beside Duke, both of them waiting for Pablo to look the other way. They had their chance when Pablo lifted the grill to flip a few burgers. Duke slipped Wellie a ten-dollar bill. It had been his tradition to slip the kids some money on the side.

"Wellie says you played baseball," MJ said, tugging

at the hem of Duke's shirt. "He said you were a short-stop like me."

"That's right, I was," Duke answered with a grin. Now was his chance to win over the boy for whom he'd spoiled Christmas. "Do you want to play a bit?"

Enthusiastically MJ nodded his dark head. "Can we?"

"Can we what?" the boy's father asked, opening the screen door with a tray full of raw meat.

"Play baseball," Wellie and MJ chorused.

"Sure, why not? We have a few minutes before the food is all done," Mario said. "I call Duke's team!"

The sun had begun to set by the time the game was over. The food had been ready for a while, and tables covered in red-and-white checkered cloths were set up out back to accommodate all the guests who had arrived. Hamburgers, ribs, fish, potato salad—everything imaginable at a summer picnic was available for this late-November birthday feast. The pièce de résistance was the three-foot-tall birthday cake with candles on top. He stood next to Macy as she pulled her hair back and blew out the candles. Her face was bright red with embarrassment as everyone sang "Happy Birthday" to her. He liked that about her.

After several pieces of the chocolate cake, Duke found himself full. He collapsed in a cushiony lounge chair in the corner of the porch. Monique and Pablo had to leave to get the kids home and in bed for school in the morning. A few other neighbors and friends left, as well. MJ sat at Duke's side, still going on about the things he'd learned. Macy had gone up front to say goodbye to the rest of her guests.

"Thanks for teaching me all that stuff today," MJ said.

"Oh, no problem—anything for you." And it was the truth. Duke easily took a shining to the boy.

"Are you being extra nice because you outed Santa?"

"W-what?" The question obviously caught him off guard. Duke jumped to his feet.

No one told him that MJ was precocious. He sat there, grinning devilishly. "It's okay. My mom freaked out about it, but I already knew Santa wasn't real. I've known since I was a kid."

"You did?" Unfamiliar with this territory, Duke scratched the back of his head. "But your mom…"

"She loves Santa. I've just been pretending to believe in him, but I already know she's the one who puts the presents under the tree."

Duke cleared his throat. *Where is Macy?* Or where was Mario, for that matter? "Well, you see…"

"It's okay—" MJ stood up and patted Duke on the arm "—I'm going to tell my mom next year I know." Then he held out his little hand. "Let's just keep that our little secret."

Not knowing what else to say or do to that, Duke extended his hand and shook MJ's. He wouldn't say anything to Macy yet about him knowing about Christmas. Who knew? MJ might get a big surprise this year.

"Now that looks like a nice picture," Mario said, coming out the back sliding glass door. "MJ, I'm about to go. Walk me out?"

"Sure." MJ turned his head up at Duke and winked. "Thanks again."

Mario stepped forward and also extended his hand, just as his son had a few minutes ago. "Duke, it was a pleasure to meet you and play a game of baseball."

There was still the strong pressure in Mario's hand—dominance. Duke squeezed back hard, as well. "No problem. You should have been in the pros. You certainly have the arm for it."

Letting go of his hand, Mario flexed his throwing arm. "Sure, I had the arm for it, not the discipline. But thanks for the compliment. And I'll see you at the Ugly Sweater Party, right?"

"The what?" Duke leaned in closer, just in case he hadn't heard correctly.

Mario chuckled. "Ask Macy about it."

"Ask Macy what?" Macy asked, appearing in the doorway. Their eyes met and Duke felt his heart flutter and sink to the pit of his stomach with excitement. It had been a while since he felt this kind of exhilaration from eye contact with a woman. He liked the way she lowered her lashes and blushed. She tucked a strand of hair behind her ear as if to help distract herself. "The Ugly Christmas Sweater Party," MJ answered for everyone. "You have to wear the ugliest sweater you own, and if yours is the ugliest, then you win."

"Duke, you don't seriously want to go to that, do you?" It was the first time all evening Gia had said a complete sentence in front of him. She still had her phone in her hands, but her friends were gone. She'd changed into a pair of baggy sweats and her face was devoid of any makeup, reminding him even more of her mother. "Mom!" Gia shrieked with widened eyes. "You can't let Duke embarrass himself like that! It's one thing if Dad does it, but one bad picture could ruin his career!"

"Hey, I'm just finding out about this." Macy leaned against the door frame, her arms folded delicately across her chest. "Mario, would you go home and quit causing trouble around here?"

"Okay, okay. Kids, walk me out."

And finally, they were alone.

Duke breathed a sigh of relief. He had enjoyed spending time with everyone, but it was the first time in three straight days that he hadn't spent the whole day with her alone. The percussion-filled beat of a Milly Quezada song filtered through the speakers.

"Ah, the Queen of Merengue," he said with a smile. "What do you know about this?"

Macy shrugged. "I know a little somethin'."

"I've wanted to do this with you all day." He walked to her and extended his hand.

She took his hand and allowed him to pull her against his body. To the beat of the music, he moved their bodies as one in a slow dance. "You know how to merengue?"

"I'm Dominican," Duke responded simply.

Macy grinned and rolled her eyes. "I'm not even going to question that."

They danced for a few minutes. He could feel her heart beating and was sure she could hear his heart as she laid her head on his chest. Each step she took, right to left or back and forth, just sent images in his mind of how good things really could be between them. He meant what he said when he told Pablo that he wouldn't mind staying here. Something about Macy made him feel at home. The music stopped, but they stood together in the growing moonlight.

Macy looked up at him, batting her lashes. "My kids loved you. You even got Gia to speak with her mouth and not her Twitter."

"I loved your kids. They're great, and you've done a wonderful job with them."

"Thanks."

"Have you opened your present?"

When she shook her head no, her hair released the intoxicating scent of coconut. "I was waiting until everyone went home."

"You should open it now."

"I can't with you watching."

"I'll wait out here and you let me know if it's okay."

In protest, Macy wrapped her arms around his shoulders and molded her body against his. It killed him to peel her off, but he did and turned her around by her bare shoulders. "I'll be out here waiting."

Grudgingly, she turned and disappeared inside. Duke went back to the lounge chair and stretched his long legs. He thought about how he really could get used to these warm Tallahassee nights during the holidays. This time last year, he was wearing a wool coat, gloves and a scarf just to keep warm. He'd spent the holidays reporting. And last year he'd made a promise that he was going to get back home to Mao for the holidays. If he wasn't working.

Sure, he was working somewhat this season, but it was different. He was with Macy. His thoughts got lost in all the things he wanted to do with her. Time passed into minutes. After a while he realized Macy hadn't come back out. He wondered if she'd fallen asleep. Was he supposed to have let himself out? Curious, he got up from his lounge chair with a moan and went to the door; it was slightly open. He found Macy curled up on the end of the couch staring at the television, crying.

Panic surged through his veins. Her eyes were bloodshot red, and her nose matched. "Did I do something wrong? What is it?"

Sniffling, Macy untucked her legs from her position in the couch. She clicked off the remote control and slowly walked toward him. "I can't believe..."

"Was it wrong?" Duke smacked himself upside the head. "That was so stupid of me. I'm so sorry I didn't..."

She cut him off, throwing herself at him, wrapping her arms tightly around his neck, bringing him down to her level. Her tongue swooped into his mouth, capturing his tongue, claiming his mouth. Her hands clasped the sides of his face. His libido went into overdrive as she allowed him to bring her back down to the couch.

He still didn't have a clear idea why she was crying, but his body could only react to her soft lips against his. Her long dress was gathered around her thighs. Duke kissed her neck and then her shoulders. He peeled back the top of her dress for just a peek at one perfectly pink pert nipple. He ducked his head down for one quick taste. She gasped beneath his touch, and her fingers dug into his shoulders.

The front door slammed shut, and like two naughty teenagers, Duke and Macy scrambled to sit up. He helped her pull the top of her dress up and adjust her hair back over her shoulder. Her eyes were still glassy as she giggled and pulled his shirt down. He hadn't even realized she'd managed to pull it up so much.

"Hey, Mom!" Gia said, coming down the hall. She leaned over the ledge and looked at them.

"Are you crying?" MJ asked.

With a choked sob, Macy began to cry again. Duke cursed inwardly. Now the kids were going to think he was some sort of creep.

"They're happy tears," she reassured them.

"I think I upset your mom with her birthday present," Duke tried to explain. The kids came down the hall and into the living room. Gia sat on the couch and pulled MJ into her lap.

"What happened?" she asked.

"He just gave me a wonderful present that I never thought I'd ever get the chance to see."

"What did he give you?" MJ asked.

"My parents…" Macy sniffed. "It was a video of the Macy's Thanksgiving Day parade, the day I was born."

Duke eased back into the cushions of the couch with satisfaction. Finding the tape and getting it shipped here had been totally worth the effort, just to see the look of surprise and appreciation on Macy's face. His gesture to bring her a piece of her past opened up the doors for a brighter future for the two of them.

# Chapter 6

With the Thanksgiving holiday behind them, the Christmas spirit began to spread to everyone in town. Thanks to Duke's help, Macy completed one of her most successful weekends yet. He'd turned out to be more reliable than expected. What she did not expect was her overflow of emotion for him. This celebrity crush was manifesting into something else, and Macy had no idea what to do with it. Since laying eyes on him in person, he'd had such a profound effect on every aspect of her life, and it was hard accepting he would be gone after the New Year.

Every day after he did the morning show, Duke would show up at Winter Paradise, just as promised. He worked diligently, helping her get all her homes done ahead of schedule. At the office, he bonded with Andy and Spencer while loading and unloading the shed. For Serena, he would call up his single friends and talk her up. If she ever made it to New York City or DC, she was going to have a busy time.

And then there were the evenings when Duke would insist on driving her home, and of course Gia and MJ would beg him to stay for dinner. When he talked about going out and finding a Christmas tree to chop down, the kids invited themselves to tag along, which led to an impromptu road trip after school. Of course, upon returning home, they had to show him the proper way to decorate a tree. Macy and the children always decorated their trees alone. But having Duke in the house with them seemed natural.

In just a short amount of time, Duke had become an intricate part of her life. And now Macy had plenty of time to work on his home. The Wainwrights ended up deciding not to go with Macy's company, which was fine with her. The positive side of not working with the Wainwrights meant it now gave her more time to work on Duke's place. After receiving written permission from the owners of the house Duke rented, Macy set forth a plan to work on the decorations.

Taking her eyes off her work for a second, Macy briefly looked up and spied Duke straddling the other end of the black shingles on the roof with the hammer in one hand, a nail in the other and an extra nail in his mouth. His triceps glistened in the sunlight. Sweat trickled from his brow, and he'd never looked sexier. The man concentrated on his task at hand, and maybe more so because they were finally able to work on his house, albeit in the evening. Of course he would have to have a two-story colonial-style home. It was pretty; Macy had seen the prestigious neighborhood when she searched for a home for her family. No matter how successful her business was, this neighborhood was still nowhere near her price range.

They'd spent the earlier part of their afternoon wrapping lights around the four pillars on his front porch. With the shutters being black, Macy thought it would be best just to light candles and hang wreaths on the four large windows on the bottom floor and hang more from the ones on the second floor. They were working on framing the top of the house with white lights, and more or less eye-flirting with a few stolen glances, her batting her lashes at him, and sending a few smiles back and forth after getting caught checking out one another.

And she had to give the man credit where credit was due; he certainly did know how to fill out a pair of jeans. The dark blue Yankees shirt he wore wasn't too bad, either. It fit across his broad chest like a second skin. She could almost feel those strong arms around her now. But Duke had been nothing but a gentleman. And as much as she hated to admit it, she was waiting for him to kiss her again. The thought of making out with him on her couch caused such a fire in her belly that she barely needed a jacket for the cooling weather.

"Are you watching me?" Duke asked with the nail still between his lips.

"I'm just making sure you're hitting the nail on the head." Macy recovered her composure. "I would hate for you to knock a hole in your roof. It might not rain right now, but the summers are notorious for afternoon showers."

"Lucky for me I won't have this house in the summer." Duke chuckled. He swung his hammer once and then extracted the other nail. Carefully he scooted closer toward Macy with the other string of lights following him.

The comment left a sour note in Macy's ears, reminding her once again he would be leaving. Was there really a point in getting involved with him? Monique had highly encouraged it after their talk last Sunday at her birthday. She'd known Duke since college and said she hadn't ever seen the glow he'd been sporting since getting involved with her. Serena had confirmed the same thing about Macy when they were alone at work together. Both women felt an affair was exactly what was needed. But Macy wasn't sure she was that kind of girl.

Duke was a heartthrob in the outside world. He was used to fast living, fast cars and fast women. And he was going back to that world. Macy's everyday life as a working soccer mom didn't fit in with that. Right now, he was miles away from it. Though a lot of people were mad at Duke for outing Santa just before Thanksgiving, he still had a huge following. A few people in town had stopped them when they were out together. There were the occasional homeowners who conveniently stayed home once they heard Duke Rodriguez was helping her out for the chance to meet him. She'd seen the photos in the tabloids of Duke spotted at celebrity and political events and had no idea how she would handle seeing him in person at a red carpet event with women throwing themselves at him.

She didn't think she could have a brief affair. No matter how good it physically would have felt, she didn't think she could survive the heartache once it ended. She knew she would get too attached to him, and recovering from a broken heart was not on her list of things to do.

Inhaling deeply, Macy tried to think about how she was going to handle things. She didn't want to fall in love with a man like Duke Rodriguez. A Mariah Carey tune about what she wanted for Christmas blasted from her truck's radio.

*BAM!*

Torn from her thoughts, Macy watched Duke hammer. "Are you following the pencil pattern I drew?"

"Yes, Miss Macy," he mocked.

Macy shrugged her shoulders, hit her nail on the head and scooted closer as well, making sure her next nail hung exactly where it was supposed to. "Did being a smart-ass get you were you are today?"

The hammer in his hand stopped in midair. He looked up and gave her a devil-may-care grin. Macy told herself she wasn't the devil and she didn't care. So what if his mouth looked so inviting? So what if he had dimples so deep, you could swim in them? Those chocolate-brown eyes weren't going to work on her. "Do you mean did my smart ass get me on top of the roof with a beautiful woman who knows how to work a hammer?"

Tugging a stray hair behind her ear to keep from blushing, Macy shook her head. "I stand corrected. It must have been flattery."

*Bam.* One hit on the head again and the nail sank into his roof. He moved closer to the center.

*Not bad,* she mused at his work. Macy tapped her nail twice and then hit it all the way in. She moved closer.

Another amused laugh filled the air as Duke reached for another nail out of his back pocket. He slipped one out and a second one behind his ear. "I didn't get here on just flattery and sarcasm," Duke said. "I worked very hard to get where I am, you know."

"Yes, from New York to DC." Macy hummed and hammered.

"Well, there were a lot of small towns along the road."

"Which is better?"

"Small towns or big?" Duke held his hammer in mid-air again and pondered that thought. His eyes glanced skyward for a moment before settling on hers. "There's good in both, I guess."

"Where has your favorite been?" She hammered and moved closer.

Duke looked down and hit the nail, scooted closer and took out two more nails. "Here."

"Here?" Macy half laughed. "I find that hard to believe."

Repeating his task, Duke moved closer. "Why? You're here."

"I was raised here," Macy said, as if that made a difference.

"But you didn't leave." He hammered and slid again. Her heart slammed against her rib cage with each inch he came toward her. "Did you think about leaving?"

Had she thought about leaving? She wanted to laugh, but it was too tragic that she couldn't. For as long as Macy could remember, her grandparents had raised her. But Tallahassee was also her parents' home, and the idea of leaving made her feel as if she was betraying their memory. "I've thought about it. But it was never the right time."

"Kids?" Duke nodded with understanding. The closer he got, the more Macy found herself studying his face. His cheekbones were high and his jawline squarely chiseled. There was a bit of a five-o'clock shadow on his face, which only made him look dangerous. She guessed a man who was into sports and a reporter wouldn't have seen the reason to stay in one place.

"Sure, kids kept me here. I mean—" she half shrugged "—there was school, and then Mario was here, and my grandparents. There were lots of reasons to stay here. I like the peace and quiet. I saw what living in the limelight did to my parents as famous reporters, and when they died, I even experienced it." Macy exhaled a sad sigh at Duke's quizzically raised brows. "A couple of reporters bombarded my grandparents' door when they died, shoving cameras in our faces asking how we felt about their deaths. I barely had time to process anything, and there they were. I don't see how you deal with it."

"I don't miss it," Duke admitted. "I've gotten so used to the little amount of fans I have here."

Macy offered a half smile before fiddling with a bulb on the string of lights. If Duke hadn't been in the limelight, she never would have developed a celebrity crush.

Of course, now she realized his TV and real lives were totally different. She much preferred the man before her.

"Do you at least travel, as in a vacation?" he asked, breaking her train of thought. In the distance, a train's horn blew and bells rang, indicating its arrival.

Macy shook her head no. For no reason at all, she did not travel. Thanks to the income she earned over the holidays, she had nothing to do during the spring and summer but plan for the next holiday.

"You ought to. I like Tallahassee, but I can admit that I miss seeing the seasons change. You know, right about now it would be snowing in New York City."

"I've never seen snow," Macy replied. She was used to the look on everyone's faces when she disclosed that information.

Duke's eyes bugged out. "Really? Your re-creations of snowy scenes are impeccable."

"It's a snowman." She gave a shrug and looked down at the ground.

"How could you not have seen snow?"

"Well, with my folks working, they came down here when they could for the holidays. I'd go up there for the summers."

"You've done such a fantastic job with your imagination, then." Duke nodded his head down toward his front lawn.

His yard was filled with a snowy Christmas scene that came straight out of a Norman Rockwell painting. Fake snow was sprinkled on the ground of Duke's spacious front yard. He didn't have many trees, which made some decorating easy. It was only hard because she had to use what leftover statues she had in storage. Coming up from the driveway, she created a real bridge that looked wooden from afar but was made of a simple hard plastic. Snow covered the railings.

On one side of the bridge, Macy had carefully put statues of fawns playing. Underneath the bridge, she created a small pond. She hid the extension cord underneath the snow and plugged it in around back. On the other side of the bridge was a snowman equipped with a fake carrot that looked real enough to eat. For good measure, she stuck coal from her grill down the front of the middle ball to represent a shirt.

"It's a great snowman. It looks like one I built my first time seeing snow." Duke hammered again and then moved closer. He chuckled to himself and shook his head. "My first snow, I sent my sisters a bag of it."

"Didn't it melt?"

"Yeah, even with express mail."

Macy leaned back and laughed, imagining what it might have been like to get that in the mail. Duke was really turning into someone she couldn't have imagined. He liked his family, he was kind and he was, in his own way, humble. He wasn't afraid of hard work or taking orders.

"Have you brought them here to see snow?"

Smiling, Duke slowly nodded his head. "I've brought my sisters here. My parents haven't been."

"Ever?"

"No. You see, where I'm from, the Christmas countdown starts in October, and my folks are really busy."

"I told you I'm the type of person who gets excited

about the Christmas displays before Halloween," Macy said, leaning in, listening.

Duke nodded. "I noticed that. There's something about being home and smelling your mother's and aunts' cooking. Bosses hand out double *sueldo*…"

"Bonuses?"

With a wink, Duke smiled. "Not just any bonus. It's pretty much what you make in a month. It helps spread cheer for families that might not have enough to spend on their kids. On Noche Buena—Christmas Eve—we go to a special mass called La Misa del Gallo."

As he filled her with stories of back home, there was a certain sadness in Duke's voice that Macy couldn't miss. "You miss them, don't you?"

"I do, I miss my city. This sunset reminds me of it."

"Oh yeah? *Mao*. Did I say that right?"

"You did. But it was also called Ciudad de los Bellos Atardeceres."

She looked at him with one eyebrow raised for translation.

"The City of the Beautiful Sunsets. But right now, I'm beginning think it's the company you keep that makes someplace spectacularly beautiful."

Her heart lurched in her rib cage. She cleared her throat and tucked a nonexistent strand of hair behind her hear. "Maybe you should go back soon."

"I will one day. Maybe next year I'll go."

Again, Macy was reminded that Duke's being here was just temporary. She was going to miss him when he was gone.

"You didn't ask me why I like it here the best."

"Okay," Macy said slowly, uncomfortably. A part of her wanted to move away, but if she moved too quickly she would fall. She looked to her left, but the late-afternoon sun was setting earlier, leaving a beautiful orange glow that blinded her. Trees hugged Duke's backyard, and from this angle there was nothing but dense darkness.

Duke placed a hand on the roof, on either side of her hips. His eyes wide, he touched his forehead to hers. "Because if I hadn't come here, I wouldn't have met you."

"If you hadn't outed Santa..." she started to remind him, but then forgot all that she was going to say when his lips reached out and brushed hers. He pulled his head back to see if she was okay with it. Macy felt such a shock of pleasure that she smiled. She actually smiled at him.

He leaned in closer, turned his head to the right and closed his eyes. His upper body held his weight as he deepened the kiss. Their tongues touched with a zap of electricity. He must have felt it, too, because he pulled away for a second, just a second, and she felt him smile against her mouth. Macy wanted to lean closer, but that was too bold, and besides, she could fall.

Duke's hands touched her thighs, his thumbs on her inner thigh while his fingers spread across the thick-ness of her legs. Slowly they moved to the curve of her waist. As their tongues danced, his hands were on her back, and he pulled her closer to his chest. For a quick moment, Macy felt herself panic. This wasn't safe. This was dangerous. She couldn't breathe at first, and then she could feel his arms crossing over, and his fingertips held on to her shoulders.

Finally, she breathed.

She recalled one time when her *nonna* came home from the hospital with a small oxygen tank. Macy had wanted to see what it was like. Maybe now was not the time to recall that memory, but the thrill of the risk felt somewhat the same. Macy was so scared that she would get caught, but at the same time she could breathe with such clarity. Her lungs were clear; her mind was clear. She felt as if she were walking on a cloud.

"If I hadn't outed Santa," Duke finished for her, "I probably wouldn't have been able to kiss you."

Just then the phone in her back pocket rang. Macy looked at the number, frowned and answered it. She watched Duke's face as he watched hers, trying to read what was wrong. She hung up the phone after a few *okay*s and *uh-huh*s.

"Is everything okay?"

She half smiled. "It was just a reminder of why this—" she wiggled her hands back and forth between them "—is an impossible situation. My life is too complicated right now for a relationship."

Disappointed at her own admission, Macy pushed away, but Duke held on to her hand.

"What is it?"

"It's just one of those days. Gia's at school, and she had to stay late because her media teacher needed help while he was doing something else. Mario was supposed to pick her up, but he got caught up with MJ…"

She growled with frustration. "I'm sorry, but this is just typical of Mario. He's so irresponsible!"

Duke cupped her face and gently made her look at him. "So, okay, she needs a ride? Let's go get her."

"It's not just that, Duke." Macy felt herself melting looking into those eyes of his. "It's a ride today, a dozen cookies tomorrow. Someone is sick and puking in the future... My life is unpredictable, Duke, and your time here is short."

He dipped his head down, capturing her lips with his. Gently, his mouth coaxed hers open and his tongue slid across her lips, breathing life into her once again. "So let's go get Gia. I can help with cookies tomorrow, but hopefully no one will be puking later."

"You really didn't have to come with me," Macy was saying with her hand on the passenger's side of her truck. They were pulled up in front of the local high school. Duke had seen Macy angry before and was glad this time that he wasn't on the receiving end of it. If he'd had any questions about her relationship with Mario, it was all answered by the way she went off on him on the ride over. Apparently, Mario was supposed to pick up Gia after school, but got caught up at MJ's karate class. And that had been one of the basic complaints Macy had about him. Duke liked the guy, but even without being a parent himself, he knew you had to learn how to multitask. Apparently, things like today happened more often than not.

Duke released his seat belt and rushed out his door

to help Macy out, even though she had one leg on the ground. "You know I didn't mind. It's quite domestic."

He wiggled his eyebrows at her and ignored the fact that she rolled her eyes at him.

"If you like being domestic, I'll give you my grocery list." She slightly laughed. "I'll be right back here," Macy called over her shoulder as she entered the building. "Try to stay out of trouble."

Trouble. Duke snorted outwardly and leaned against the passenger-side door. He looked all around him. There were a few cars left in the pickup parking lot of the high school. When he was younger, there had been no one to pick him up, so he and his siblings had to walk. There were no buses, but their mother made sure each and every single one of them knew the importance of going to school. Duke had had coaches to keep him steady. If he didn't go to school, he wouldn't play.

In the distance, Duke thought he heard the familiar sound of a bat cracking against a ball. He'd know that sound anywhere. As if on autopilot, he headed toward the direction the sound came from. Off to the left of the building, he spied a baseball diamond. His pulse quickened, as it did every time he saw a field. His hands itched to throw a ball or swing a bat. A group of kids dressed in what Duke assumed were the school colors of blue and white were tossing around the ball. There was someone on the sidelines with a clipboard. The man didn't look tall enough, or nearly muscular enough, to have ever played ball before. Duke hadn't realized he was chuckling until the man looked up, waved and started walking over toward him.

"You're Duke Rodriguez!" the man stated.

"I am," Duke confirmed slowly as he extended his hand. "I didn't mean to interrupt your practice."

"Bah!" the man grunted with a flick of his wrist. Behind him the other members of the team were coming up the hill. "You weren't interrupting much. We're down a coach, as you may have heard. Oh my God, of course you heard. You commented on it on the news the other week when, you know..." The smaller man elbowed Duke in the ribs and with his other hand, covered his mouth and whispered, "When you outed Santa."

*Here we go again*, Duke sighed inwardly. "Yeah." He scratched at the back of his head. "I'm sorry about that, Coach."

"Don't be. I thought it was a hoot. Oh, where are my manners? I'm not the coach here. I'm the media teacher, Bob Nogowski. I'm just filling in until we can find a more suitable coach. Uh-oh, here they come." Bob nodded toward the boys coming up the hill.

The boys, all fifteen of them, all seemed to be over six feet fall, and each and every one of them spoke at once, introducing themselves and shoving their hands in front of Duke to shake. He did his best to keep up with the names. Out the corner of his eye, he spied Macy with Gia walking toward the car. He hoped he didn't embarrass Gia.

His attention was diverted momentarily as the kids asked questions like lightning. It amazed Duke that these kids could recall his batting average back in the day. They had to have been in elementary school when he had that old life. It also amazed him that he'd already been reporting the news for a few years now, and it dawned on him that everyone, besides Macy, always referred to his days as an athlete.

Within the crowd of questions, Duke heard someone clear her throat. He looked up and saw Macy standing behind him. Her arms were folded, but she had an amused crooked smile and one eyebrow raised. "You are such an athle-tante!" she teased.

One person who wasn't smiling was Gia. She looked more mortified than when he'd first met her. The last thing he wanted to do was upset her. Perhaps these were her friends and he was invading her privacy or something.

"Sorry, hon, I heard the swing of the bat and the rest was history. Hey, Gia, sorry if I kept you waiting."

"Gia, your mom's dating Duke Rodriguez?" one of the kids said to her.

"Uh, well…" Gia fumbled to find the words. She looked down and around, then toward her mother for help.

"We're very good friends," Macy supplied.

"Cool."

Duke wanted to say they were more than just friends, but he was a bit preoccupied watching Gia and another boy. Obviously, the two awkward teenagers wanted to talk to each other. The boy shuffled his feet in the dirt and twisted his body left and right in his letterman's jacket. Since he'd begun spending more time at the Cuomo household, Duke hadn't heard Gia mention anything about a boy. She talked about school, her media teacher and some of her girlfriends. But not a boy, not a boy in particular.

A sudden surge of protectiveness crept over him.

Duke remembered the boy's name was Jimmy and he was the only freshman on the varsity team. He was tall and lanky, but that was typical for a fourteen-year-old. He seemed like a good kid at first, but now that he was blushing the same shade of red as Gia, Duke wasn't too sure. Her eyes widened and her mouth dropped wide open.

Duke wrapped his arms around Macy's and Gia's shoulders. "Well, I've kept my two favorite ladies waiting. Guys, have a great season."

There was a bit of protest from the guys, including the temporary coach. Duke promised he'd try to come to one of their practice games before he left. Jimmy stepped over and tugged Gia's arm. She went with him to the side so they could speak privately. Duke kept a watchful eye out for them, just in case.

"Any time you want to come by," Bob said, shaking Duke's hand, "it would be perfectly fine with me. We could really use some pointers out here."

The team backed the coach up on his open offer. Duke started to shake his head no. He already had a job to do, and when he was done at the station he was rushing to spend time with Macy. "Well…"

"I'll be honest with you, I could use some help here," Bob said. "I'm the media pro. Ask Gia."

"You should," Macy encouraged him with a smile.

"I'll have to see what my schedule is like and I'll

have Gia let you know. She might not like me being around."

Jimmy and Gia rejoined them, some of the boys already pleading with Gia. Duke tucked Macy closer to his side as he said goodbye to everyone and walked off. When they got closer to the car and, more importantly, out of sight and earshot of the team, Gia did some odd skip move toward the car. She spun around at the locked door and faced them. Duke still had the keys and unlocked the door with them in his hand.

"Oh my God!" Gia squealed. "Jimmy actually knew my name! He's the first freshman to be on the varsity team! The *varsity team*! I am so excited! He wants to take me to the Christmas dance this next week! Can I, Mom? Can I? Oh my God! Thank you, thank you, thank you, Duke, for coming to pick me up!" With that, Gia pulled out her cell phone and began Tweeting as she entered the backseat.

Duke hadn't realized that Macy slipped her fingers into his as they walked toward the car until she squeezed his hand. "I think she's an even bigger fan of yours now."

"Oh yeah?" Duke beamed, aware of the crush Gia had had prior to meeting him. "How do you know?"

"She actually told you the news before you heard it on Twitter." Macy looked up and smiled. Seconds later, her phone was chirping, indicating a Tweet.

They stopped walking once they reached the back of the car. Duke turned her toward him and took both hands in his and smiled down at her. "That's progress, right?"

Her lashes batted against her cheeks as she looked down at his chest to contemplate his question. He liked the way her eyes turned a golden brown when the sun hit them just right. She was smiling, but the smile hadn't gone to her eyes. It reminded him of the first time he'd laid eyes on her and she wouldn't really look at him. Something was wrong.

"It's progress," she agreed.

"I hear a 'but' in there somewhere."

"The kids and I have really enjoyed spending time with you with this week. I just fear that they're going to get too close."

"What's wrong with that?"

"You still have a contract in DC." Macy looked down. "That means you're leaving once the New Year rolls around."

"Yes and no." Duke gave a long sigh. He hadn't shared his thoughts of staying on with the DC station with Macy. How crazy did it sound that he didn't want to leave Tallahassee? He enjoyed being able to sleep through the night and not have to get up at all kinds of hours to get a story. Macy and her children had helped him get ready for his upcoming party, and since last week, he absolutely looked forward to getting off work and finding out what they'd been up to all day. Family. He missed being a part of a family.

But what did he have to offer them? Macy wasn't interested in his fame. The children were over being starstruck. Without all that, was he still enough for them? When he returned to Mao last summer, his father thought Duke was crazy for taking a break from the career he'd worked so hard to build. His mother had stood up for Duke in her own way and reminded him that even with all the accolades he received and parties he attended, they did not mean as much without his own family. Duke half agreed. He did want a family, and one was waiting for him in DC with Kristina, but it wasn't the one he wanted. More and more, each day he saw himself with someone like Macy. He just didn't want to scare her off too soon. "Does that mean that we have to stop seeing each other when I leave?"

Her eyes lit up just as Gia's had a few moments ago. The idea obviously hadn't crossed her mind. "That can get expensive."

"Let me worry about that, okay?"

"Okay, Mr. Athle-tante."

He had plenty of money to travel back and forth if he wanted. He hadn't been a careless athlete. He'd helped out his folks as much as they would let him and then kept the rest of his signing money away in savings. Then of course there had been the money from his job at ESPN and now. "I've got that covered. I just want you to stop bringing up New Year's Eve being the end of things, because it doesn't have to be."

Macy stood up on her tiptoes, bringing her lips to his. "I like the sound of that. And I'll try not to bring up New Year's Eve."

Duke responded at first with a kiss, slow, sensual and meaningful. He pulled away and wrapped his arms tighter around her waist. "Well, that's the best Christmas present ever!"

# Chapter 7

Mario's annual Ugly Christmas Sweater Party was in full swing by the time Macy and Duke arrived with the kids. His two-story house was filled with friends from work and friends from way back in the day. The kids made a plate from the buffet table and disappeared. Last year, Macy recalled, Mario recruited her for last-minute details. This year things went off without a hitch, which only made Macy happy because now she had plenty of time to spend with Duke. Macy shared a few pastries with Duke before he was pulled away by a group of guys for sports talk.

To keep up with the theme tonight, Macy wore a minidress decorated to look like a Christmas tree, garnished with tiny red, green and gold balls. She clinked every time she walked, and she hung out by the fireplace, occasionally stealing glances across the room and enjoying every butterfly flittering around her stomach. She twisted a strand of her flat-ironed hair around her forefinger. Gia had spent all evening on her hair and would have had a fit if she saw her twisting it. Letting it go, Macy inhaled deeply, agreeing with everything Serena yammered on about. Macy nodded in the direction where Duke was standing and talking to Mario and Pablo.

Serena had encouraged Macy to give in to her libido where Duke was concerned, but she had no idea how complicated her life was with Duke in the picture. In the afternoons when it was slow, Duke offered to pick up Gia from school after he helped the baseball team with drills. Some days, he would bring MJ with him to help chase balls. After practice and work, he would come by Macy's office, pick her up and take them all out to eat. In the evenings when homework was due, he would help out, whether it was Gia with her media class or MJ with his math, while Macy worked on dinner. When the kids went to bed, she and Duke would sit on the couch, kissing away like two teenagers until it became too uncomfortable for either one of them. Both had agreed not to do anything silly, like getting caught on the couch by Gia or MJ. And Duke's spending the night would seem to send the wrong message for the kids. So Duke and Macy were forced to handle their relationship like grown, mature adults. A lot of cold showers were taken on Macy's part.

Last night, Gia asked Duke to take her to the upcoming dance with Jimmy. Having a Ferrari could have had something to do with it. And it had been Gia who picked out the green cardigan Duke wore tonight, with a snowman family down at the bottom; what looked like snow falling on the family was actually cotton balls sewn onto the garment. It fit. It fit well, Macy thought, looking at Duke's broad shoulders stretching the green twill.

In her eyes, Duke was the epitome of the perfect man. Besides having a sculpted body of a god, he knew how to make her feel like the only woman in the room—in the world, even, whenever he looked at her. Sure, he had a megawatt smile that dazzled her each time she looked at him and his kisses brought every fiber in her body to life. But it was beyond the hard body, seductive dark eyes, or his chivalry. It was that and more that made Duke so desirable.

When they were together, he hung on to every word she said, listened to idle chatter from Gia and MJ. He was creative with the children, even when they bickered with each other, overdramatizing the issue they were fighting about, though the conflict usually ended with the kids defending each other. With MJ, Duke figured out how to distract him from being sad over Mario forgetting to take him to get a haircut. Duke talked MJ into going with him to the barber and they both came home with fresh cuts. According to MJ, the barber gave the boy a hot towel facial while he trimmed Duke's dark goatee. He was good with the children. He was good with her.

When she had mocked his hands weeks ago, she had no idea of the tenderness behind his fingers. The way he stroked her face when he kissed her goodbye, or the control he maintained when reaching over to massage her shoulders and feet after a long day. Every time he glanced at her with his deep brown eyes, he bored through another wall inside her. When he touched her with his large hands, every inch of her body wanted to melt. The past few nights, they had a few intimate moments on her couch. Macy could not believe how out of control she could get with him. Just the other night, she'd ripped off his shirt and almost begged him to make love to her on the couch downstairs, but he remained levelheaded. It wasn't as if he hadn't taken his shirt off when they worked during the day, but when the man stood hovered over her body on the couch at night, with candles set all around them, it was hard not to shake the feeling of his hard abs against her fingertips. But because she knew what he looked like without that sweater, it made the whole thing ridiculously funny at the same time. Macy inhaled deeply and focused on the man at hand.

It was a good thing Duke was so confident. He was good-natured through it all, teasing her and calling her a *celebutante* when someone would pull her to the side just to let her know they were voting for her homes in the decorating contest. He didn't seem to mind at all when her former client, Lawrence Hobbs, came over to wish her good luck on the drawing tonight when she was standing off to the side while Duke had gone to get them something to drink. When Duke arrived, Macy made the introductions and Lawrence was on his way. He wasn't bothered at all by the pilot. *It's nice to be in a mature relationship*, she mused to herself.

"Ugly sweater be damned," Serena said, holding her cup of eggnog in front of her mouth. No amount of slurping on the beverage could mask her grunted moan. "That man looks good."

"I will have to agree to that," Macy said, toasting her cup of apple cider in Duke's direction.

"Isn't it weird that Mario has a man crush on your boyfriend?" Monique asked, coming over to the two ladies. She wore a black sweaterdress with Santa on it that buttoned down the front. On the left side of the dress, Santa looked as if he was tiptoeing away, dragging his sack of toys behind him, but instead of toys spilling out of the open bag, it looked more like cotton padding, as if Monique stuffed her bra.

"I have two things to say." Macy looked at the outfit and laughed. "First, let me say that I hate you for getting your body back so quickly after having Lucia!"

Looking down at herself, Monique blushed. "Sorry, but I have been working double time to get things back in place before I show my face on high-definition television again."

"That's why I'm never having kids," Serena chimed in. "All that extra work to lose the weight? No thanks." She shook her head. Macy and Monique shared a look, knowing they had once both said the same thing before in their lifetimes.

"So what was the second thing you wanted to say?" Monique asked, ever the reporter. She hadn't forgotten how Macy had phrased her statement.

"Oh." Macy shrugged and took another look at Duke across the room. He looked at her at that exact moment and gave her a wink. The status of their relationship hadn't been publicly announced. She knew what they were when they were alone, but Macy wasn't sure if she wanted the world to know. What would happen when he went back to his celebrity lifestyle in DC and she had to watch his life pass her by in the tabloids from Tallahassee? "He's not my *boy*friend."

"Whatever! Man-friend, gentleman caller." Monique playfully pushed Macy's shoulder. "I hear down at the station that he's so eager to wrap up in the morning just so he can get over here to help you out."

"So?"

"So?" Monique stood there and gaped. "So as a reporter, you're only as good as your next story, and he hands off every bit of good news that comes across his desk."

That was something Macy wasn't aware of. She just assumed that because of Duke's high profile, there wasn't much investigative reporting he could do. "Oh, I didn't realize that."

"Did you also realize that Gia's dropped her crush on Duke?" Monique pressed on. "I haven't gotten a single Tweet about him and what he wore. Now it's all about some guy named Jimmy."

Macy had noticed she hadn't heard much else about Gia's love for Duke. Gia wasn't the first one anymore to turn on the television in the morning to catch Duke's broadcast while she got ready. Macy had figured that as a typical thirteen-year-old, she'd found someone else to crush on. "What do you think that means?"

"I think it means she's giving her mom permission to

steal her man," Serena interjected. "And I have stepped down from being the future Mrs. Rodriguez, as well."

"Oh, that's so generous of you," Monique said drolly.

Poking out her tongue, Serena leaned in closer to Macy. "And he'd be your boyfriend if you gave him some."

"Serena!" Macy blushed. "No."

"Why the hell not?" both girls blurted out. A group of Mario's guests looked at them as they walked by. The ladies regained their composure.

Monique leaned in closer and whispered, "Y'all haven't?"

Macy shook her head. "No, sorry to disappoint you guys."

"Again, I have to ask, why the hell not?" Monique laughed. "He might be my husband's best friend, but the man is gorgeous and totally into you!"

Leaning in, Serena whispered to Monique, not quietly enough though, "And you heard about the birthday present he got her, right?"

"No, what?"

"He gave her a copy of the tape of the Macy's Thanksgiving Day parade her parents were covering when her mother went into labor with her."

"Aw!" Monique covered her mouth, but not before Macy spotted her poking her bottom lip out. "He's your *angelito*!"

"My what?"

Shrugging, Monique dropped her hands to her side. "It's a Dominican tradition I've learned from Pablo. Each week, you receive a gift."

"Like a secret Santa."

"Something along those lines."

"So what are you going to give him in return?" Serena leered, wiggling her eyebrows up and down.

"When do you guys think I would have time for something like that? The kids do live with me."

"Do you want me to have them spend the night tonight with me?" Monique asked. "Maylen has been begging me to let her hang out with Gia since Gia gave her that makeover the last time she babysat them."

"We'll see." Macy shrugged. "We're in no rush."

"No rush? Don't you want to see what he's like in bed before he leaves?" Serena inquired.

As much as she wanted to find out, Macy still had standards to uphold. She rolled her eyes. "Not every relationship has to end up in sex, Serena."

"Well, all of mine have."

There hadn't been a serious or healthy relationship in Serena's life. She was young, though, no kids and in school. Macy shook her head and grinned. "And what kind of meaningful relationship are you in right now?"

Wincing, Serena pouted. "Ouch."

"Sorry." Macy tilted her head to the side and looked thoughtfully at her friends. "But we're in no rush because Duke said things didn't have to end after the New Year."

"Get out!" Monique's jaw dropped. "I didn't realize he was so serious about you."

"Apparently so." Macy beamed.

"And are you that serious about him?"

"I think I am."

"Well, if you sleep with him now, that can help you decide if you definitely are or aren't," Serena added. Macy made a mental note to not let Serena have another glass of eggnog.

Monique stood there, smiling. "I can't believe our two close friends are hitting it off so well. I think I'm going to cry!"

"Please don't," Macy quickly said as she reached out and stroked Mo's shoulder. "Let's see where things go before the waterworks come out."

Nodding, Monique sniffed back her tears. "Okay, I'll try not to."

"Or at least wait until they do the nasty," Serena mumbled.

What Macy didn't tell her friends was that tonight the kids were spending the night with Mario. When Duke took her home this evening, it would be the first time they were going to have a chance to be home alone. They'd been alone together before, but something about tonight was different. Duke had been a patient man. Despite each passionate kiss he gave her, she never felt pressured by him. It was nice to go out with a man who didn't expect more right away.

From across the room, Duke made eye contact with her. He stood as tall as Mario's Christmas tree, but he seemed broader than it. Her heart swelled at the sight of such a man. Duke broke the contact with a wink. He whispered something to Pablo and handed him his drink, then made his way across the room toward her. Macy felt her heart skip a beat as he approached.

Eartha Kitt's seductive croons of "Santa Baby" filtered through the air. Macy could think of one thing in particular she wanted. And by the end of the first verse, he was standing right in front of her.

"Care to dance?"

"Dance?" Macy managed to get out. Mario had moved all his furniture out, so that there was room for everyone. No one else was dancing. Before she could point out that fact, Duke pulled her by her wrists into the center of the room and held her against his hard body. Once again, his touch made her feel as if she was melting. Her knees went weak, but it didn't matter, Duke had her. His arms were wrapped around her waist, fingers resting at her backside. Against the fabric of his green sweater, his heart thumped through his chest. His square jawline twitched and his full lips broke into a smile.

Even with their height difference, Duke managed to crane his neck down to bring his lips close to hers. Macy's heart raced in anticipation of a kiss. For once, she was aware they weren't the only ones in the room. All eyes were on them and she claimed him, stretching her arms upward around his neck. Duke's thighs pressed against hers and they moved together as one. Everything was perfect. "Well, I guess that's a yes, then."

"Have I told you how beautiful you look this evening?"

She fit against his body comfortably, familiarly. "I think you may have said something about it when you picked me up."

"The statement still stands. I don't think I'm the only one who seems to think so, either." Duke nodded his head in the direction of Lawrence, who stood in the corner sipping his eggnog.

Macy cut her eyes back at Duke. "Well, thank you. Were you taking a poll?"

"No need. I'm Dominican. I can sense these things."

"Whatever," she said. "May I say how handsome you are?"

Duke grinned and nodded his head. "Thank you. You may."

"Well, all the ladies are discussing it, also."

"All of them?" he inquired with a raised eyebrow. "What about one in particular?"

"Which one were you concerned with?"

Chuckling, he grinned, exposing that devil-may-care dimple with his crooked smile. "I thought I was pretty sure I made myself clear as to which woman I was interested in on that first morning I came to work with you. But in case you need a reminder…"

Duke dipped his head and captured her lips in a sensual kiss. He tipped her chin up to meet his face. They swayed to the music, or so she thought. Macy felt as though she were floating on air. Somehow they danced like that until Nat King Cole's deep voice entered the room with "The Christmas Song."

"How are you enjoying your evening?" Duke asked.

Was it normal for a woman's body to be so turned on from a kiss? Macy's heart fluttered. "I think I'm enjoying it just fine. But then again, the night is still young."

"Oh yeah?" He pulled his head back to get a look at her. "What does that mean?"

She offered him a sly smile and shrugged in his

arms. "It means that the kids are spending the night with Mario."

"I think I heard him mention that. I know it sounds weird, but it was like he was giving me the go-ahead head nod."

Hiding her laugh, Macy pressed her head against Duke's broad chest. "That sounds about right."

"I have to admit that I was a bit jealous when I first met him."

"Really?" She craned her neck to look up at him. "Why?"

"Well, he is your ex-husband. You guys seemed very chummy."

She shook her head before he could say another word. "We're chummy now because we were friends before we got a divorce." Macy tried to pretend she did not hear sarcasm in his voice. "We have two kids together. I thought you would understand that in order to co-parent, we have to get along."

"Can I ask why you two split?"

She really didn't want to talk about Mario, especially when her body just wanted to be completely satisfied by Duke, but she felt she owed him that much of an explanation. "Let's just say that there were times that Mario just looked at me like we were buddies. And then one day this woman left a message at the house for him, letting him know that she wasn't pregnant after all."

"Ouch."

"It's okay." Macy shrugged. "At that point in our relationship, it was much more of a relief. I wasn't in love with him. I loved him and always will because he's one of my best friends, but I'm not in love with him."

"And you haven't dated anyone since because of him?"

"No, I haven't dated anyone because I was too busy running my own company."

"And now?"

"And now, I'm listening to my inner Grandma V's voice and taking time to stop and smell the roses."

"Who?"

"My Grandma Virginia," Macy explained. "My mother's mother."

She wanted to let Duke know at that moment that she was falling in love with him, but decided to save it for a more intimate setting. He looked down at her with half-closed lids. He was staring at her lips. And every time he did that, it made her blood pulsate.

"So, back to what I was saying," she brazenly said. "We'll have the house to ourselves."

Duke returned the sly smile. "Are you asking me to a sleepover?"

The image of them having a pillow fight on her bed filtered through her mind, though she highly doubted that kind of rolling around in the bed would happen. But the thought of what could happen made her stomach flip. She was ready. She was beyond ready. These cold showers she was taking every night were about to end.

"Maybe not the kind I used to have when I was a kid."

Duke cleared his throat and put a little distance between them. She'd gotten to know his body very well in the past few weeks. She knew he was as turned on and excited as she was, but his body reacted more physically when he was turned on. She thought it was cute how he would try to pull away. The first time she could recall him doing that was on Thanksgiving when they'd been interrupted by the phone call. She smiled, appreciated his being aroused by their kisses. At least she wasn't the only one.

"Be careful, Ms. Macy. I just might take you home right now."

A chill crept down her spine. Her cheeks heated in a blush. She wrapped her arms tighter around his shoulders and realized she could feel his heart beating. "And is there a problem with that?"

Dropping his hands from her waist, he took hold of her hand. "Let's get out of here."

Following his cue, Macy grinned and allowed Duke to maneuver her through the now-crowded floor full of dancers. The weather wasn't cold enough for a long coat, and even if it were, there was so much heat pumping through Macy's veins, she would have been fine outside. Duke stopped at the door. Macy looked up at him, feeling a slight disappointment. Had he changed his mind?

"Look." Duke pointed up toward the doorway. "Mistletoe. I think it's only proper that we practice the custom."

Before she could say anything, his lips had recaptured hers with the same kind of passion he'd shown a few minutes ago. Macy felt her blood pulsating. Knowing that the kids weren't going to be home all weekend long made her feel like a horny teenager. She giggled before deepening her kiss. "We should go. Now."

Duke reached for the door, but it was already opening. Macy was too busy grinning from ear to ear to pay attention. From across the room she could hear Serena whistle crassly at them sneaking off.

"Well, damn, Duke Rodriguez, if you aren't the hardest man to get a hold of."

Macy was still smiling and blushing when she turned to face who was at the door. The first thing she'd noticed was that Duke had dropped her hand, causing her to look at who was speaking.

"Kristina." Duke's warm voice had turned icy cold.

Kristina Barclay was as glamorous in person as she was on television. She was close to six feet tall with legs that went on for days. Obviously she didn't know it was an ugly sweater party; otherwise she wouldn't have poured herself into the black cashmere dress that stopped barely below her thighs and worn thigh-high black leather boots. She wore a black-and-white houndstooth coat to shield her from the dropping temperature. Macy bit the inside of her lip and studied the woman whom Duke had been so popularly linked to.

"Oh, you don't know how glad I am to find you here!" Kristina cooed. "I thought for a second that you might have actually flown home to that little village of yours. You always were talking about spending the holidays with your parents."

Macy had never been to Mao, but she took great offense at the way Kristina spoke of Duke's hometown. Knowing how much Duke cared about his family, she also didn't appreciate her dismissing Duke's love for them, either. How long had they known each other?

"Well, aren't you going to invite me in?"

"It's not my party, Kristina."

Unfortunately, Mario didn't catch the tension. "Kristina Barclay." He practically drooled as he pushed his way to the door. "Come in, come in!"

"Thank you," Kristina said, sauntering into the room. The music was still playing, but no one was dancing. Pablo had made his way across the room with Mario. "Pablo, haven't you been giving Duke my messages?"

"Now is not the time," Pablo said under his breath. Monique appeared at her husband's side.

"You knew she was coming?" Monique's question was more like a sentencing from a judge. Macy felt sorry for him because she knew Pablo was going to get an earful later.

"Now is exactly the perfect time." Her upper lip curled in a sneer as she looked at Pablo. "That senator from Tallahassee is stepping down. I would have thought you—" she turned and looked over her shoulder at Duke "—would have been all over it, seeing how you're in his hometown."

Pablo looked down at his phone. Macy looked around and noticed that everyone working for the station was checking their cell phone for the text messages. But not Duke.

Macy felt Duke tense again. "Not now, Kristina. Go away."

"I can't go away. The station has sent me down here

to this godforsaken town to cover the story. And Oscar wanted me to remind you that you're on loan here. Didn't you read the fine print?"

Duke spoke through clenched teeth. "I was rather preoccupied when I left."

"Well, your contract here is null and void with the station if there is a story. And—" she slipped off her coat, which Mario eagerly caught "—obviously there's quite the scandalous story here."

There was a gasp in the room. The front door, which was still open, began flashing with lights from the ground to the top of the door. Macy knew that a senator stepping down would certainly cause a stir, but she couldn't understand why it would call for the paparazzi to come out like hounds. She looked up at Duke. His eyes were now slits of anger. She cast a glance at Kristina and her mouth gaped in shock. There she was, dressed in her pearls that hung down between her breasts and rested peacefully on her perfectly round pregnant belly.

The last thing Duke wanted to do was subject Macy to his former lifestyle. The bulbs were going off. His heart ached at the sight of her face, her eyes wide and glued on Kristina's shape. He cursed under his breath. Macy left his side and stepped away. He reached for her, but she pulled back.

Behind her, Kristina cackled in her menacing way. "Oh dear, Duke, did you find yourself someone to keep you occupied for your time here?" She narrowed her eyes on Macy, her upper lip curled in a jealous rage.

"Sweetie, did he tell you that when he's done here, he's leaving and coming back to me?"

"Get out of here, Kristina," Duke lashed out at the woman standing in the doorway in the center of this mayhem.

"Duke, maybe you and Kristina can talk in the other room," Pablo suggested. Duke didn't miss Monique pinching his arm.

"Or she can just leave," Monique snapped.

"Gee, Monique, I thought we were friends." Kristina's voice lacked conviction.

Monique shrugged her shoulders. "*Duke* is my friend. And that right there—" she pointed toward Kristina's belly "—is some straight-up bullsh—"

"Mo," Pablo hushed her. He wrapped his arm around his wife's shoulder.

"Sorry," Monique mumbled. "But you know you're wrong for coming up here like this."

In desperation to speak with Macy, Duke shook his head no. He looked back around for her, but she was gone. Thinking he spied her being escorted through the kitchen doors by that Lawrence guy, Duke turned an angry stare at Kristina, who was still giggling there, enjoying the spotlight. Choking her right now would not be the right thing to do. The paparazzi were shouting out questions left and right.

"Duke, is that why you left her?"

"Duke, who's the new lady in your life?"

"Duke, are you going to finally marry Kristina now?"

Growling, Duke grabbed Kristina by the elbow and just started walking with her until he found a quiet room. "Gosh, Duke!" Kristina breathed when she looked around. "So quick to get me into bed again?"

They were in a bedroom. There were two twin beds against either side of the wall, and a desk separated them. Posters of Anderson Cooper, Don Lemon, Tavis Smiley and Rachel Maddow covered the walls on one side. Pictures of various baseball teams covered the other. It must have been Gia and MJ's room when they came to stay with their father. Thank God the kids were out on a hayride and weren't being subjected to this drama.

Kristina was sitting on the edge of the bed with its pink comforter, stroking her hand along the material. "It's kind of small, but I'm sure we can make do with it."

"What are you doing here, Kristina?" Duke folded his arms across his chest.

"I came to uncover a story."

"The senator's story or yours?"

She laughed and rolled her eyes. "Don't be silly. Do you think that I wanted things to happen like they did tonight?"

"Of course."

"Well, you're wrong. I'm just doing my job."

"And your job is to come into someone else's home and cause a scene?"

Trying to smile innocently didn't work on Kristina. She was always working an angle somehow. "Now, how could I cause a scene?"

"The paparazzi."

"I can't help it if they follow me everywhere I go."

He snorted. "You could if you didn't tip them off.

I've been here over a month now and I haven't had any trouble from them, and I've been on the news."

"This Podunk town isn't considered news."

Tallahassee had grown on him. Insulting the town was insulting him. His anger grew at her smugness. "If it wasn't news, then you wouldn't be here."

"Well, Oscar thinks…"

He stopped her before she could say anything else about their boss, with whom she'd had an affair. "Does Oscar think that's my child?"

"Of course he does!"

He cursed again, this time not under his breath. "You know this is not possible." He waved his hand at her physical state. The evidence of her affair not only angered him again, but reminded him of what he could not do as a man. The bedroom he stood in reminded him of what another man could do that he couldn't.

Throughout his entire life, he'd competed. He competed in baseball, journalism, and to stay on top of his game at all times. Another man providing a woman with a child was something he could not compete with. It was the one spot in life where he failed. And if he could not create his own family, what did he have to offer Macy?

Kristina pressed her bejeweled hand against her chest. "I know. And you know. And Oscar questions that. But more importantly Oscar's wife doesn't know that."

It had been rumored that Oscar's wife Allegra's family was in the Mafia. Nothing had ever been proven, but the rumors apparently had Kristina scared. "Tell him the truth, Kristina," Duke warned her.

"I can't."

"It's not my problem."

"It kind of is."

He pushed off the wall. "That's not funny."

Kristina picked a fleck of dust off her kneecap as she crossed her legs. Her belly was full. She looked as if she was ready to give birth at any moment. Oscar was crazy for sending her out on a story so close to her due date.

"It is. You know you wouldn't be where you are if it weren't for me."

That wasn't going to help her case. He looked around the room. "You mean in the bedroom of a friend's home in Tallahassee? Don't forget why I am here."

"You're here because you went on a booty bender." She sighed as if she were the bored one. "Some men go through a drinking bender, but you went through women quicker than I go through a pair of shoes."

He snorted at how wrong Kristina was. There was no booty bender or partying. His days were filled with responsibility. He enjoyed being reliable for Gia and MJ. There were no other women for him, only Macy. Duke's heart ached to see her again and talk to her. His mind raced back to Macy. He had to go find her. What could she be thinking right now? He was thankful someone had come earlier to take the kids on a hayride so that they weren't subjected to the circus outside. "I don't have time for this." He reached for the door.

"Are you going to find your girlfriend?"

"Don't bring her into this."

That got her reporting radar going. She straightened

her spine and raised her eyebrows. "So the little sweater girl is your latest thing, eh?"

"Good night, Kristina. I'm sure you can find your way out."

"I guess Sweater Girl knows all about how you got your job in DC."

It sounded like a threat as he was walking out of the room, so Duke stepped back in. "What did you say?"

"Oh." Kristina sighed and shrugged her shoulders. "I just was curious if she knew the truth about how I was the one who discovered you. You were just covering the sports in New York when I met you."

"I was actually doing just fine, Kristina."

"Yeah, but look how you left things in DC. The world will see you as a typical jock running from your responsibilities, leaving his pregnant girlfriend who's done everything possible for him when she's with child."

"Don't try to threaten me, Kristina." Duke shook his head, "because I could easily take this to the public and have you do a DNA test."

"You'd ruin me!" Kristina exclaimed in a panic-stricken voice. "You of all people should know how important our careers are."

"I really do feel sorry for you."

"C'mon, Duke. This can be our last news story together. The ratings have dropped tremendously since your leave of absence. With you resurfacing by my side, you can get a bigger raise for yourself from MET. Don't forget, I know your contract renegotiation is coming up soon."

"It doesn't matter," Duke said.

"Please, Duke. Your absence has only made social media go crazy, waiting for your return to national news. I know with me being pregnant and on camera with you, my return will be just as welcome after I have the baby."

"No."

Kristina sighed while trying to pitch her ideas. "I just need you to go along with this with me for a little while. This is going to be my last news break until I deliver, then I'm going to lie low."

"Not a chance."

"Think about your future, Duke!" Kristina wailed.

For the first time since she showed up, Duke gave her a genuine smile. "That's just it, Kristina. I am."

That wasn't a good enough answer for Kristina. Nothing was good enough until she had her way. She slunk off the edge of the bed. Doing her best seductive cat walk, as seductive as one could be with a huge belly protruding from her body, she came toward him. He straightened his spine. The smell of her overly chemically processed hair wafted to his nose.

She ignored his rigid body language and snaked her arms around his neck, drawing him down for a kiss. The minute their lips touched, Duke felt guilty and disgusted at the same time. He didn't want to push her away due to the baby, so he reached around his neck and pried her snakelike arms from around him.

"Cut it out, Kristina, it's not going to work."

With a high-pitched giggle, Kristina squared her

shoulders and wiped her bottom lip. "Oh, I think it worked out just the way I wanted." She nodded her head to the right of her where the window curtains were drawn open. In the distance, he could see Macy swiftly walking away.

# Chapter 8

Walking through the kitchen into the living room, Macy inhaled the sweet smell of her bakery cookie-scented candles. She checked the clock over the mantel. It was after midnight and she'd been home for the past three hours by herself. Lawrence had been kind enough to bring her home after the ruckus, since Duke was obviously so preoccupied.

As she tied the sash around her soft pink robe, common sense told her to blow the candles out. Common sense told her to get into a pair of real pajamas and just go to bed. But there was a nagging voice coming from somewhere inside that told her to give him a few more minutes.

Macy hadn't meant to leave Duke's side, but she'd caught a glimpse out the front door of the hayride coming back. As a child, Macy could never understand how her parents could just dump her off with her grandparents, but after seeing how the paparazzi flocked to the door... She would never want to subject her children to that.

Her mind kept replaying the incident at Mario's. Her heart ached for the pain that woman must have put him through. Duke had looked like death washed over him when he saw her. From what he'd told her, Macy knew things didn't end well with her. Kristina Barclay was certainly a piece of work. There was no doubting that she had seen her walk by the window outside Mario's house. They'd made direct eye contact and upon doing so, Macy had seen the devilish smirk across her face.

Trying to take her mind off seeing the two of them kissing, Macy turned on the television with the remote control. The midnight broadcast of an entertainment news program was already showing a recap from the paparazzi's point of view of Kristina and Duke. From their angle, Macy had a better view of Duke's face. She had felt his tension when she was standing beside him, but from the camera angle she could see it. His face was taut with anger, his lips pressed firmly together, and his eyes had turned a shade of black, soulless black. Macy shivered, reminding her never to get on his bad side...ever.

The idea of Duke being bonded for life to a woman like Kristina Barclay made her blood boil with jealousy. She wanted to scream and punch something. She wanted to fight for her man and she didn't know how to handle her feelings. When Mario's infidelity had been exposed, Macy was ready to move on with her life, without him.

She wanted Duke. But did she have him anymore? Kristina had a part of Duke inside her and Macy had no control of where this would leave her and Duke. She'd seen him with small children. He loved them. He doted on the Baez kids. Hell, he'd even carved a place for himself in Macy's family. But the dose of reality tonight threatened her future with Duke. Things had been so perfect between her and him. Why did Kristina even come down here? Of course, it was to reclaim Duke. Who wouldn't him as part of their family? Was it even possible for Duke to be the father? He'd told her he couldn't have children. In fact, he'd blurted it out during one of their first real conversations.

The clock struck one and woke Macy out of her slight doze. Her heart sank with the realization of the time. Duke still hadn't shown. Had Kristina's kiss meant more to him than she would have thought? Were they now wrapped up in the sheets on his bed? Jealousy was not an emotion Macy was used to having, but she had to decide if that was what she was feeling as she felt the frame of the remote control squeaking in her hand as she crushed it as she thought.

Macy tried to push the thought of him…the two of them…out of her mind. On TV, a nightly talk show host was going on about the season's shopping and preparation for Christmas, which was in just another week. It reminded Macy that Duke's party was on Christmas Eve. She'd had everything ready to go. His guest list was, well, everyone who could come. With the recent explosion of Kristina, she wondered if she would be on the open-invitation list. She clicked off the television, wishing it was just that easy to turn her thoughts of Kristina and Duke out of her mind.

Well, she thought to herself, no matter what…she still had a job to do, and she would still do the best job possible. Deciding to showing the two of them how a true professional should act, Macy sighed and stood up. She blew out the candle wicks, now drenched in the melted wax. Puffs of burning smoke followed her through the living room and the kitchen as she snuffed all the candles. As she walked down the hallway to head upstairs, there was a faint knock at the front door.

Her heart lurched into her rib cage. Instinctively Macy pulled her fingers through her hair. Without having to ask, she knew it was him. Macy opened the door and leaned against the side of it, staring at Duke with all the nonchalance she could muster.

"What are you doing here, Duke?"

"Macy!" he breathed, stepping closer. Obviously he wasn't thinking, either, because he reached for the sides of her face with his large hands and pulled her into a kiss. A deep kiss. She could taste the whiskey on his cool tongue. "You're okay!"

"Of course I'm okay." Macy pulled away but didn't move her hand or hip from the door.

"Are the kids okay?"

She reached her wrist out and pretended to look at a watch that wasn't there. "It's like five hours later, and you're just now asking me this?"

"I'm sorry. Things just got…" Duke straightened.

"Out of hand? Chaotic?" Macy offered for him. He was still in his ugly sweater. She wasn't sure if that was a good thing or not.

"But the kids are okay?"

She sighed. "The kids are fine. We were able to get them to Mario's neighbor before you and your girlfriend made a scene."

"Whoa." Duke dipped his head to look at her. She wouldn't look at him. Instead, she focused on the tip of the tree on his sweater. "Where is this coming from?"

"I saw you two."

He shrugged. "You saw us what?"

"I saw you two kissing." To see if he would deny it or not, Macy finally looked up at him. His mouth twitched with a smile. "You can leave now."

Duke shook his head. "I'm not going anywhere, Macy. We need to talk."

"Really?" She half chuckled with sarcasm. "You left the party with your girlfriend. Your very pregnant girlfriend."

"Ex," he quickly corrected. "And stop trying to get rid of me, Macy."

"Why should I?" Here it came. Her voice cracked. Macy cleared her throat. "Who are we fooling, Duke? I don't belong in your world, and after a night like tonight, you don't belong in mine."

"The hell I don't!" Duke pushed the door open. His large body filled the frame. She watched his large shoulders rise and fall with each controlled breath he took.

Macy found herself walking backward. She knew Duke would never hurt her, but he'd pushed himself into her foyer with such brute force. Her heart skipped a beat. A fire in her belly grew as he stood there looking over her. Since when had she become a sadist? She wasn't sure, but the thought of Duke throwing her over his shoulder right now and taking her to the couch gave her body such a rush that she could feel her lower extremities vibrate with sensation.

"I used to think it was cute the way you would try to push me aside every time you got scared, Macy, but it's really beginning to piss me off." He ranted a few words in Spanish. She was sure he was cursing as he paced back and forth in front of her, raking his hands over his head. "You know what I think?" he finally asked, in English.

"What?"

"I think you're just afraid to lose."

Macy tried not to laugh at that. "Get out of here, Duke. We can talk some other time."

"I'm not leaving until you hear me out," Duke said. "Kristina is not a part of my life, and that baby she's carrying is not mine."

"Why would she say it's yours? Why come down here and make the announcement like that?"

"Because Kristina lives for the drama," he explained. "But I did not get her pregnant."

"But you guys were involved."

"We were. And if she had it her way, we'd be engaged by now with a wedding sponsored by every corporation. If can recall, I left the news desk when all the rumors started about a possible engagement."

She did recall the tabloids speculating about his untimely leave from the news desk and counting all the sightings of Kristina out alone at public events. Macy nodded.

"Don't nod, tell me you believe me," Duke ordered. "You need to hear me when I say that I, in no way, shape or form, am involved with any of Kristina's scheming. The only person I care about is you. Do I make myself clear?"

A flash of excitement coursed through her veins. Was he choosing her? "Yes."

"Yes, what?" he asked.

Macy rolled her eyes. "Yes, I understand there is nothing between you and Kristina."

"And?"

"Duke, it's late."

"That's fine with me." Duke stopped pacing and glared at her. Her breath got caught in the back of her throat as she noticed the look in his eyes.

She shook her head in disbelief at the audacity of his intentions. "You can't be serious," she said as his mouth paused a millimeter before her lips.

"Very."

Without having a chance to react, Macy fell into Duke's embrace. He had one hand at the back of her neck while the other snaked around her waist, his thumb massaging the tie of her robe open. She'd been ready for this. She'd been waiting for this. The apex of her thighs began to melt with fire. Duke bent her backward. Inches from the ground, she gazed at the ceiling as his mouth began to open her robe. She could feel his grin when he discovered her naked underneath.

As one of his large hands still held her back in his arms, his other pulled open the robe completely, which pooled around his hand where he supported her back. There she was, bare, vulnerable for him to see. Duke took a caressing finger from her bottom lip down, over her chin, down her chest and between her breasts. She felt her body quiver as his fingers reached the curls down below.

"You are so beautiful," he whispered into her ear just before nibbling on her earlobe.

Macy struggled to stand up.

He shook his head. "Let me just feast on you right now."

She thought she'd said yes. The words couldn't form, but at least a sound of approval escaped her throat. She sucked in a breath of cold air when he took a nipple into his mouth; first one, then the other, then both at the same time, balancing her breasts in his large hands. Aimlessly, she reached for the sweater encasing him. She tugged at the material. Duke grinned and maneuvered her to the steps. He pulled the sweater over his head. The gold cross hanging from his chest blended in with his golden-brown skin and twinkled against the last of the candles Macy hadn't blown out yet.

Duke moved his bare torso between her naked legs and brought his mouth down on hers. He revived her with his kisses. He was so warm against her. So full of life against her. Her hands wrapped around his shoulders. Her fingertips splayed across the muscles of his back, down toward the waistline of his jeans. Moving her fingers around, she fumbled with the buckle. She couldn't quite pull the button from the hole and had to lean back to get a view of what she was doing. She cast a glance up at Duke, who was looming over her with his arms on either side of her. He inhaled deeply.

"I'm not going to let our first time together be right here on the steps."

Disappointment ripped through her. She was sure, as she slid his pants over his tailbone, that she could change his mind. "Really?"

"Really," he said, lifting her by her bottom and placed her up two steps. "You're going to lead me to your bedroom."

"I am?" She mocked him with as much bravado as she could. "How do you expect me to…" Her words once again were lost in her throat as he dipped his head between her legs, his tongue like a heat-seeker, and found her center.

"Oh. My…" Macy moaned at the feel of his vibrating tongue. She tried to think of baseball cards or cooking recipes—anything to keep her from coming so soon. His tongue slipped into her center, stretching her almost. She quivered and took deep breaths. The only way she could stop from exploding right now was to go up one more step. But with each step she inched up, Duke was right there, his lips pressing against her lower ones until she made it to the top step.

"Which room?"

"Th-there," Macy moaned breathlessly.

Duke swept her up into his arms and took her quickly to her bedroom. He placed her squarely on the bed and kicked out of his pants.

A few hours ago, Macy had been ready for this. She had candles going in her room. The chiffon mosquito netting was drawn on three sides of the bed already. Duke took a knee slowly onto the bed. Macy lay on her back and propped herself up by her elbows. She stretched her toe against his chest. Duke turned and pressed the high arch of her inner foot to his mouth and kissed it.

He was built like a Latin god. He had the world's most beautiful broad shoulders, tapered waist, six-pack abs and powerful thighs, not to mention the world's most beautiful erection staring right at her. He was playing with something in his hands. Macy glanced down briefly and noticed the foil wrapper. The realization of what they were about to do hit her. It excited her. She wasn't ready to stop looking at him. Her mouth watered at the sight of him. She sat up farther until she was on her knees and knelt in front of him.

She could feel him shiver as she pressed her lips against his. His hands stroked through her hair down to the small of her back and around her belly. He reached between her legs and felt her ripeness. She was going to die if she didn't have him right now. Macy reached down for his erection and took it in her hands. He was hard as steel and smooth as velvet at the same time. The tip of his head leaked slightly with evidence he was just as ready for her.

She pulled away from her kiss and raised one eyebrow at him, daring him to make the next move. "You've got me in my room. Now what…" Macy wasn't sure if she got the enunciation of the *t* out of her mouth before

Duke had grabbed her by her knees and flipped her on her backside again. She lifted her head to laugh and was greeted by his soft mouth nibbling on her bottom lip as he swiftly entered her body.

Her bones in her ankles crackled as she wrapped them around his waist as he drove into her. His body kept such a steady, fast pace she was sure they had run the Kentucky Derby at least four times by now. Duke extended one leg over his shoulder and drove home into her. Her breasts bounced rapidly and wildly. He took a nipple into his mouth as he took the other leg and threw it over his other shoulder. Macy braced one hand down on the mattress under her contorted body. The other hand pulled against the back of his neck.

Duke broke off kissing her breasts and growled. It was primal. It was erotic. Apparently, he felt all the sexual frustrations she'd been experiencing with him, and they both were finally able to let it out. And she did. Her body stumbled with a twitch and Duke moved, if possible, even faster, all the way out and powerfully back in again.

"Let it out," he whispered in her ear.

She released her scream with the first orgasm. Duke was right behind her, groaning louder and louder, until they both hit the peak of their climaxes at the same time. Chills spread all the way down Macy's body. She'd never experienced such a thing. It was the most beautiful thing ever.

It wasn't until they heard the sound of a sanitation truck coming down the street that they got out of the bed. Macy hadn't realized how tired she was. She also didn't realize that she had literally spent all night long making love to this beautiful man. They lay in her bed, their hands entwined.

"Please let me explain what happened this evening."

"I don't want to talk about it."

Duke turned on his side. Even though the candles had burned themselves out hours ago, Macy still knew Duke was looking at her. "You don't want to talk about what we just did?"

"Oh...that's what you wanted to talk about?"

"I used a condom with you, Macy."

"I know." She felt herself blush. "I think I remember putting it on you." She'd never been the one to do it before, but she'd seen enough episodes of *Real Sex* to know how to do it.

"It wasn't because I was worried about getting you pregnant."

"I know, Duke." Macy lay on her side and stroked his biceps, remembering Serena had said what big muscles he had. Her hand barely made it around one side of his arm.

"But you saw Kristina…"

Macy sighed into the darkness. "When you first came to the office, you told me that you had a serious illness as a child, resulting in you not being able to have kids."

"You remembered that?"

"Of course. I also remember you saying how Kristina betrayed you. It didn't take a genius to figure the rest out."

"No, I guess not."

"But I appreciate you trying to protect me tonight anyway." She scooted closer. "But don't think I appreciated seeing you two kiss."

"You were spying?"

"I would hardly call it spying when I was trying to get all the kids returning from the hayride to go to Mario's neighbors' and there you two were."

She felt the bed shift with his weight as he raised himself on his elbows. "I would hardly call that kissing her."

"And don't get me started on the circus at the door." She mimicked his movements and struggled to sit up. She started to turn on the light by her bedside, but realized that for the past few hours she'd been sweating up a storm. She must look a mess. The cameras tonight reminded Macy of Duke's glamorous world. She imagined everyone in it woke up flawless. "I can't imagine living under that kind of scrutiny."

"I never liked it."

"Then why did you put up with that?"

"It was just part of…" His voice trailed off into the darkness.

"It was what Kristina wanted," Macy summed up. She felt him nod. "It seems like you did a lot of things that she wanted." She thought about his situation with Kristina. From what she'd learned over the past few weeks, Duke owed a lot to Kristina. She wanted him to do the news; he did the news. She wanted to move to DC; he moved to DC. He made plans to visit his parents in the DR, and she didn't want to, so he didn't go.

Obviously, she wanted to put her pregnancy on him. What was he going to do?

"So…" Macy slowly drawled out. "What did she want?"

"Well, she wants me to go along with this pregnancy."

"What the hell?" She sounded jealous. But she couldn't stop herself. "You're going to let this lie continue?"

"I told her no."

"Why did she even feel she could ask that of you?"

"Macy," Duke sighed. "The baby isn't mine."

"And I clearly understand it's not yours," Macy clipped icily. "Why does Kristina think she can come to you and ask you to cover for her if you two have been over for a while now?"

"It's because of who the father of the baby is," Duke confessed. "Look, a part of me had gone along with Kristina's path. There was a time we both wanted the same thing. We both wanted to report the news. We both achieved that. I owe my success to a handful of people."

In the darkness, he reached for her, turning her body to its side, and pressed his against hers. "You know I'm under contract MET right now in DC, and it's my outstanding reputation as a news anchor that gives me leverage with the contract there and keeps me here in Tallahassee. I like having the upper hand when I come to a table to negotiate. Shaming or exposing Kristina won't help."

"And what about the giant elephant in the room?"

"Huh?"

"Her pregnancy, Duke."

"Well, you already know that it's not mine."

"True." She didn't like the sound of his voice.

"So to me, that's all that matters."

She sighed against the pillow. Her heart sank at his explanation. She would have much rather preferred he told Kristina to go to hell rather than let the world believe that it was his child she was carrying. She wondered what it was she had over him to make him think he had to protect her. That urge of jealousy struck her again. She wondered what that feeling would be like if Duke had been so protective over her.

A flash of panic wrenched at her heart. Tears pooled in the corners of her eyes. She realized right then and there that she loved Duke Rodriguez. And the heartbreaking thing was that he obviously did not feel the same way about her. Not once in his speech about his career and his negotiations had he mentioned her or the direction of their relationship. Kristina was a part of building Duke's career. What did Macy offer him for his future?

Macy controlled her breathing so that Duke couldn't feel her sob. Fortunately the garbage trucks down the street grew closer, drowning out any sound she might have made. She pulled the covers away.

"Where are you going?" he asked, holding her close.

"The garbage trucks are coming. If I don't get the trash out now, it will be doubled next week, and they're not picking up the day before Christmas, as usual."

Duke raised himself up on his elbow. "Well, hang on. I'll do that."

Macy pushed him back with her shoulder. "It's okay. I know where everything is. I'll be right back. You rest."

"We can sleep in, you know."

How well did she know that? Duke didn't have to do the news in the morning. She knew his schedule by heart. Weekends were his free time, which he spent helping her. But then Monday would roll around and of course, this Monday would be different. This Monday, he'd be working with Kristina. "I know. But I'll be right back. You get some rest."

The coolness of the sheets as he reached for Macy's soft and tender frame woke Duke from his slumber. The realization of what they'd done up until the wee hours of the morning began to register in his brain. He was more in love with Macy now than ever before. She was everything he'd imagined. And he couldn't wait to tell her.

Duke sat up in bed and looked around for any sign of her. He found her discarded robe neatly hung up against the back of the bedroom door. His jeans were folded on the edge of the bed. Reaching for them, Duke slipped them on and looked around for his shoes. The sun was already spilling into the room from the open curtains. The clock on her nightstand said it was eight. He'd slept in. But that was okay; he didn't have to go in to the station today.

He sniffed the air, expecting the faint hint of coffee or bacon or eggs, something. Not that he expected Macy to make breakfast or anything, but after a night like last night, he was sure if she wasn't in the bed with him when they woke up, she would be down in the kitchen.

She always had food ready to serve whenever he got off work and came directly over.

"Macy?" Duke called out, opening the bedroom door. He looked around the room before leaving. His sweater from last night had fallen on the floor by the bed. It was too warm to put it back on, so he buttoned up the top button on his pants and trotted down the stairs, anxious to see Macy again.

Walking down the steps, his heart raced as he remembered the details of what had happened there. He was smiling to himself when he reached the bottom step and walked down the hallway. He heard shuffling in the kitchen and decided he would surprise her. The surprise was on him.

"Am I interrupting?" Duke asked. His smile faded at the sight of Macy and her friend Lawrence huddled together against her counter. Macy was dressed casually in a pair of pink velour jogging pants and a plain white T-shirt. Her hair was pulled up into a ponytail at the top of her head. She smiled, but it wasn't a full smile. Something was wrong, he realized as she tucked a stray hair behind her ear. Her cheeks were flushed. Duke's eyes darted back to Lawrence, who shared the same embarrassed look. The hairs on the back of his neck rose.

Moving from Macy's side, Lawrence crossed the kitchen and extended his hand toward Duke. "Hey, man, I was just leaving."

"Don't leave on my account," Duke said casually as he firmly shook the man's hand.

"Oh, it's not that. I've just got, um…some errands

to run." Lawrence stepped backward, reached for some papers on the counter and then fumbled with them, rolling and putting them in the back pocket of his jeans. Duke thought the man's skintight white T-shirt was a bit much for eight in the morning, but chose to ignore it. He had to remind himself that even though the two of them worked closely together once, Macy was with him. Last night had confirmed that. "Congratulations on winning."

"Winning?"

"The—uh." Lawrence shifted his glance to Macy. It was a guilty look. Macy said they'd gone out a few times, but that there were no sparks. There certainly seemed to be sparks right now. Both their faces were flushed. "The ugly sweater contest."

Duke looked down at himself, knowing his chest was bare. The child in him flexed his pec muscles. "Oh. Yeah. Thanks."

"Well. Macy, I'll see you later?"

"Yeah, sure," Macy said, folding her arms across her chest. Duke could see the swelling of her breasts, and now that he'd had a taste of them, he didn't want to share with anyone, ever. "I'll walk you out."

"Oh, don't worry," Lawrence said nervously. "I can show myself out."

In his years as a reporter, Duke had come across some shady people. Grown men stuttering and stumbling over themselves was a telltale sign that something wasn't right. Lawrence was in too much of a rush to get out of there. It was just like the time he'd walked into Oscar's office and Oscar and Kristina had flown to opposite sides of the room like the Red Sea parting. He knew it was wrong to compare the two situations. Macy was nothing like Kristina. But there was still that nagging feeling in the back of his head. If Kristina could fool him, especially with the paparazzi always following her around, surely Macy could…

"Are you hungry?" Macy asked, breaking him from his morbid thoughts.

In an instant, Duke's thoughts went from morbid to desirous. He wanted nothing more than to place Macy on top of that counter. Every inch of his body went hard. His hand went to his growling stomach, but he wasn't hungry for food.

Macy's eyes followed his hand and then went back up to his face. Her dark eyes sparkled as they crinkled when she smiled. "You can't be serious."

"Oh, I'm very serious." Duke moved across the kitchen floor, enjoying the way Macy's throat moved up and down as she gulped. She braced herself against the counter, which was fine with him. He gently picked her up and sat her on the countertop. Their hips met. He stiffened instantly.

Wedging her hand against his chest, Macy created some space between them. "Wait, as much as I'd love to do this…"

Duke listened as he planted a trail of kisses against her neck.

"We can't. I've got some things to take care of."

"Like what?" Duke placed another kiss against the side of her mouth, purposely not brushing her succulent lips. If she wanted a kiss, she was going to have to turn her face for it.

"You're not making this easy."

"It's not supposed to be easy." Duke took hold of her hands and pulled them down to his waistband. "It's hard."

She blushed. He wasn't looking, but he could feel the heat from her cheeks as he nibbled on her ear.

"No, seriously. I have work to do."

"No, you don't. The judging went on last night." He continued kissing her earlobe. Little goose bumps appeared on her shoulder blade and arm.

Macy sucked in her breath. "I'm serious, Duke."

The sound in her voice was serious. Duke straightened up, but didn't move from between her legs. "Is it the Lawrence guy?"

"Wh-what?"

*She stuttered.* Duke's heart sank. It was the same stutter he'd heard once before. He looked into Macy's dark eyes for as long as he let her, which wasn't long before she looked and pushed him away. "That Lawrence guy. He was here pretty early in the morning."

"He's a friend of mine."

"Really?" Duke regretted folding his arms across his chest the minute he said the words. But it was too late. His tone and Macy's response had put them both in combative mode. He had to fix this. "I'm sorry, it's just…"

"It's just nothing," Macy snapped.

*Too late*, he thought. She was already squaring her

shoulders for battle. Duke raked his hands over his head. "Let's start this morning over."

Macy shook her head from side to side. Her lips were already flattened in anger. "No, that's quite all right. We might as well go and finish this."

"What is *this*?" Duke threw his hands up, still trying to surrender. His heart slammed against his rib cage in panic. Quickly he softened his voice. "I don't want to fight with you, Macy, especially after last night."

"Ohhh," cooed a voice behind them.

Duke cursed inwardly and turned around to see Serena leaning against the door frame. Her bright face was lit up with a quizzical grin. "Good morning, Duke, Macy. I didn't mean to interrupt, but the door was unlocked and I thought you'd want to see the results from the contest for the best decorated home."

Glancing back and forth at him and then her boss, Serena extracted a paper from the oversize bag on her shoulder. "You're upset." She noticed. "Maybe you've already seen it."

Now next to him, Macy shook her head. "No, not yet."

"Macy," Duke breathed. "We need to talk."

"I can come back," Serena offered.

"No." "Yes, please." Duke and Macy spoke at the same time. His eyes pleaded with Serena. "Will you at least give us a few minutes?"

"Don't tell her what to do," Macy interjected. "Serena, stay."

Confused, Serena looked between them again. She bit her bottom lip. "Well, since Duke is topless…"

"Serena," Macy warned.

"Fine, fine." Serena handed Macy the paper. "How about I just go sit out on the deck for a few minutes while you two talk?"

Macy took the paper, but shook her head as she scanned over the front page.

"Can you put that down, Macy? We need to talk."

"Why do we need to talk, Duke? I said I was busy."

"Busy doing what?"

Her eyes narrowed on his.

She cocked her head to the side in order to reexamine him. "Oh, you think because of last night that I am supposed to bend to your will?"

"That's not what I'm saying." Duke paused with his brows furrowing. "What is going on here?"

"Obviously, *this* is going on," Macy held up the paper for him.

There on the front page of the *Tallahassee Daily* was Duke's picture at the precise moment he was ushering Kristina off into the bedroom. Considering he'd done basically the same thing to her this morning, it wasn't a good look.

"Macy, I explained that…"

"Kids talk, Duke. How do I explain this to Gia? What do I say to MJ when his friends ask him about you being in a relationship with me, while this woman is claiming you're the father of her child on national TV?"

He scratched his head. "But I already told you I'm not."

Macy shook the paper at him. "Which means nothing

when this is plastered in the news. Jesus, Duke! What am I supposed to do now?"

"Nothing," Duke said, trying to control his irritation at Kristina. Damn her for coming back. "It will blow over."

"It will blow over with the two of you reporting the news together?"

"Now wait a minute…"

"No," Macy cut him off. "I'm not going to wait a minute while you figure everything out."

"Hold on now, Macy… I dropped the whole issue with Lawrence being in here so early in the morning."

"What?" She gasped with laughter. "You can't be serious about throwing that in my face when you have a pregnant girlfriend who you have to work with…"

"*Ex!*" he interjected. She shook the paper again at him as if that made a difference. He couldn't help what the paper wrote. He couldn't control it. "Okay, I think I see what's going on here, Macy."

The room grew quiet while Macy stood there, waiting for him to explain.

"You don't like the idea of me and Kristina working together. I understand that. But I think what it is, is that you're just afraid."

"Afraid?" she choked out.

"Yes," Duke replied matter-of-factly. "This morning you saw how good things could be for us, and you're just trying to push me away."

"Why would I do that?"

"I don't know why, but you've been pushing me away since we met. And you know what I think?"

"What?" she asked drily, with a sigh.

"I think you're afraid of a challenge."

Scoffing at him, Macy tossed the paper on the table. "What?"

"You're afraid of a challenge. Just think about the homes you did, homes you've won awards for. You don't like dealing with difficult people. You didn't like dealing with the Wainwrights. You didn't like their new ways of doing things and figured you would lose the contest if you worked with them. You don't want to work with me because you're afraid you'll lose me. Think about it, Macy...you're a sore loser."

"Are you calling me a loser?"

He sighed with deeply felt frustration. Counting to ten backward in Spanish, he shook his head. "That's not what I'm saying."

"Well, you're wrong about the contest. It's not about winning. It's about what I won. And it doesn't really matter because I did not win this year." With that, Macy snatched the paper back up and held it in his face. Her fingers pointed toward the small article at the bottom of the page. Duke could clearly see that the winning house was not hers. Instead, there was a proud middle-aged couple standing in front of a uniquely decorated home. He could only assume they were the Wainwrights. Macy set the paper back down and brushed past him. She stopped at the doorway. "But you're right about one thing—I don't like dealing with difficult people. You can show yourself out."

"Macy." Duke pleaded, "Don't be like this. We still have work to do together."

"Don't worry about it. I'll still do your party on Christmas Eve. But I don't want to look at your face until then."

Duke stood in the kitchen. He cringed when he heard a door slam and cursed when he realized it was the front door. Had she really left? Baffled, Duke turned around. Serena was now back at the doorway, shaking her head.

"What just happened here?" he asked her. If anyone should know, it had to be Serena.

"It seems as though the two of you had a fight."

"That was more than just a fight," Duke said, trying to steady his voice. "Did you have to show her the morning paper?"

Serena shrugged. "I really didn't come over here to show her the article about you and that Kristina woman. I came over here to see how she was doing since she lost the Christmas decoration contest."

"Is she really that much of a sore loser?"

"Duke, it never about her winning."

Duke nodded his head. "She said that. So what's it about?"

"It's about the money she would have won," Serena said, then she shook her head. "Or more about where it goes when she wins."

"So where does it go?"

"To the Child Victim Fund for kids who have lost both their parents."

Duke's mouth dropped open. He felt like a world-class ass.

# Chapter 9

"Well, you're absolutely miserable without him," Serena commented, standing in the doorway of the department store changing room.

Looking in the three-way mirror, Macy shook her head at Serena's reflection. The morning of Duke's holiday party was girl time at the mall. Monique brought Maylen along with Lucia because the baby hadn't been feeling well lately, and Mo wanted to keep an eye on her. Macy brought Gia, who insisted that Serena come. Serena had to come along to give her two cents whenever necessary. After brunch, Gia took Maylen to get their nails done while the older women tried on clothes. Lucia was so tired just from the ride over to the mall that she'd fallen asleep in her stroller, giving Monique a chance to try on a few dresses, as well.

In a skintight black velvet dress that showed off a figure that would rival any pinup girl, Mo stood next to Serena and was nodding at her comment. "She's right, you know."

Macy was trying on a dress. The bench in the changing room was filled with different dresses in different styles and different colors. Nothing seemed right. She only needed to look at her friends' frowning faces each time she opened the door to know that each dress wasn't the right one. If it didn't hug her body too tight, it made her look too matronly. It had been a week since she had that horrible falling-out with Duke. He had the nerve to question her friendship with Lawrence when he was going to allow the world to think that he was the father of Kristina's unborn child. She knew that the whole thing with Lawrence could easily have been cleared up with a logical explanation, but with the way he reacted toward her, he didn't deserve one. But it still didn't help how she was feeling now. What her friends were telling her was the truth.

She not only looked miserable, but she felt miserable, as well. Every morning she woke up with her heart feeling heavy. It ached. Duke had spent only one night in her bed and already her sheets felt empty and cold without him.

"Thanks a lot," she said drily into the mirror.

"It's Christmas Eve," Monique said cheerfully. "And tonight you get to see Duke after your ban…"

"I didn't *ban* him exactly," Macy quickly said.

Serena snickered. "It sure sounded like it to me."

"Either way," Monique said, laughing, "I know he can't wait to see you."

Duke had honored Macy's wishes by not trying to see her for a week. It gave her time to think. Perhaps working closely together since Thanksgiving had blurred her thoughts. She needed space, and this time apart allowed her to prepare for Duke's party. But she couldn't secretly help but wish he would have disregarded her banishment. If he was so eager to see her, he would have just come over, no matter what she said. And being the stubborn person she knew she was, she wasn't about to see him before tonight.

Since she knew his hours at the station, Macy was able to get in and out of his house when he wasn't there. Everything was set for his big party this evening. She hadn't kept track of who was coming, since it was an open invitation to the whole town. Macy banked on a lot of families not trying to come, thinking it was already going to be full. She also banked on the fact that it was Christmas Eve and most families already had plans. Macy had every caterer in town on call. She figured a few hundred orders of everyone's best dishes on the hour would keep the steady flow of guests satisfied.

Macy smiled at Monique and nodded toward her gown. "I like that dress for you. If you're not careful, you and Pablo are going to have another baby before the year is up."

"Are you ignoring what I'm saying?"

"Of course not," Macy said in a sarcastic tone. "Look, this time apart for Duke and me is good."

"Good how?" Monique and Serena chorused.

"Good because this is the way things are going to be when he leaves," Macy said with a shrug. She ran her fingers along the bustline of the red dress as she looked in the mirror at herself. She missed Duke desperately. She missed seeing his dimples when he grinned at her. She missed hearing his deep voice with its heavy accent when he was trying to be charming. She missed hearing about Mao.

But Macy also thought about the brighter side of Duke not being around her.

This week, she was able to get in and out of stores without someone stopping the two of them for Duke's autograph. Of course, while the hounding in public ceased, the hounding from her children increased when she came home from work. MJ and Gia wanted to know where Duke was and when he was coming back. *It is better this way*, she told herself.

"But he said he was going to come back and see you," Serena griped. Trying as hard as she might, Serena's efforts to get Macy to talk to Duke weren't working out. If there was a problem or a concern dealing with Duke's party, Macy made Serena handle it. Serena had tried to flake out on a meeting with Duke, but Macy had been one step ahead of her. She had to be one step ahead. If she wasn't, she would have easily fallen back in with Duke and not been able to resist his charm. She needed to stay strong.

"Sure, he would come back to visit, but I'm not sure I'm the stop-by-and-visit type of girl." Macy sighed. "Seeing how the paparazzi went crazy with him at Mario's party gave me an insight on what it really would be like to get involved with Duke."

Monique sighed impatiently. "You're already involved with him."

"And it's not better," Serena said. "You're slamming things around the house. You're moody. Andy and Spencer said they feel like they need to walk on eggshells around you."

"It really is," Macy argued with her friends. "Duke and I are in two different worlds. He was just taking a break from his celebrity life and I just happened to be a part of it."

Monique shook her head and *tsk*ed at her. "The paparazzi were here because Kristina called them. Duke had been here for almost six weeks and he hadn't been hounded like that. So it's not really a true experience of what life with him would be like."

"It is true," Macy countered. "Duke was here because he was getting into some pretty bad stuff, partying, drinking and whatever, and Pablo brought him down here to clear out his head. He was just here taking a break."

"That doesn't mean he hasn't fallen in love with you, Macy," Monique said.

"It doesn't mean that he *has*, either. He hasn't really said it, you know." Macy wasn't sure if that's what hurt the most—that she was supposed to stand by his side while he allowed this farce with Kristina to continue, or that she didn't know how he really felt about her?

"So if he said he loved you, would you reconsider things?" Serena asked.

"Well, if he said it right now, it would just be staged and not real." Macy shook her head back and forth as her friends groaned in frustration. She chewed her bottom lip for a brief second before she confessed her problem. "Do you guys realize that she wants him to go along with the charade, saying that the baby she's carrying is his?"

"That bitch!" Serena exclaimed, balling her fists against her hips. "Girl, just let me have one minute alone with her. I'll get her straight."

Macy shook her head. "As much as I wouldn't mind that, it still wouldn't help the situation. Duke's kindness to Kristina affects my family."

"But you have to realize, Kristina knows her career is washed up. She was nothing without Duke," Monique was saying. Macy had learned through Monique that since the Tallahassee station, WKSS, was an affiliate of her DC station, Kristina was allowed to be the guest anchorwoman. While Macy couldn't bring herself to watch Duke on television last week, she was glad to hear that Kristina was reporting the news from the field instead of right next to Duke. "But you know, I can understand that you have Gia and MJ to protect." Monique nodded her blond head, beginning to understand.

"Gia knows what's going on. She has already had enough people at school Tweeting her to find out what's happening, because everyone at school was getting to know Duke as the coach's helper, and that Gia was responsible for bringing him there. And now all that's going to change. He's going to leave." Macy inhaled deeply. If she thought about it anymore, she would start crying again. Sadly, she shook her head and reached for the doors. "Let me get out of this dress and find the right one. This one is too long."

As she closed the doors, Serena called out over the top of the door, "So if you're so sure things are going to end between you and Duke, why are you in search of the perfect dress?"

"Because even though he's leaving, I want him to see what he's going to miss."

On the other side of the door, she heard Monique and Serena agree with her reasons. She slipped out of the dress she was trying on and back into her jeans and black sweater. She flipped her hair out from her collar when she heard Gia and Maylen panting as they ran into the dressing room. There was a slight panic when she opened the door and saw both girls faces' were bright red. They were both speaking at once. Monique was trying to calm Maylen down.

"What is going on?"

"We found the perfect dress for you, Mom!" Gia cried.

"Okay, fine, let's go find it. Hang on, let me find my…"

Gia pulled on her arm. "We don't have time. It's Christmas Eve and there's one dress left and we got to get it before someone else buys it for tonight."

"Fine. Fine." Macy shook her head and laughed as Gia and Maylen guided her down the corridor of the top floor of the mall. They'd gotten there first thing in the morning, and it wasn't that busy. Now it seemed like people were everywhere. She started to understand the urgency and picked up her pace.

Behind her, Serena was laughing. Monique was running as she pushed Lucia in the stroller. They had to look like a sight. They stopped short in front of a little boutique, Desideri. From what Macy knew of the store, its wares rivaled Victoria's Secret lingerie. It catered to women of all sizes. Macy stood at the entrance, glancing up at the fancy black letters, then back down at her teenage daughter. She cocked her eyebrow. "What do *you* know about this place?"

"I Tweeted that I was at the mall with my mom who was looking for a dress. My friend Michaela's sister works here and says she has the perfect dress for you."

"How does she even know what my size is?"

"She saw you on the news at Daddy's stupid Ugly Sweater Party and knew exactly what you needed to shut Kristina Barclay up."

Great, the whole world's first impression of her was in that ugly sweater. *Damn Mario!* "I can't go in there. They sell lingerie." Macy clutched her heart and feigned outrage. "I am a mother."

"And clothes," Serena said, catching up to them. "I've been in here once or twice. C'mon…I'm sure we'll find something."

The curvy mannequins in the window were all wearing seductive satin or lace. Macy would have thought that pushing the clothing up front would have been a better idea. But she took going in there with a grain of salt. She needed a dress.

"Serena!" A tall, curvaceous woman beamed coming from behind the counter. "It's been a while."

"The saleslady knows your name?" Monique mumbled, amused.

Ignoring her, Serena stretched out her arms and gave the woman a hug and an air kiss on both cheeks. "I know, but I haven't had a good date in a while. Claire, these are my friends Macy and Monique, and their girls, Gia, Maylen and Lucia."

"I'm Michaela's friend," Gia said, extending her hand to the saleslady.

"The Tweet," said Claire. "I do have the perfect dress."

"Thank God," Gia breathed. Without hesitation, Claire grabbed Macy by the wrist and led her to the small dark pink dressing rooms in the back of the store. "It's already hanging up in the back. I know it's the perfect one."

"Well…thanks." Macy stumbled into the dressing room and found what looked like the perfect black dress. Judging from the length of the material hanging from the hanger, she expected it to stop short enough on her legs without making her look like too much of a schoolmarm or too much like an extra from one of those trashy reality shows. She worried about the spaghetti straps and the sweetheart top, but once she tried the dress on, she fell in love.

Outside of the dressing room, a commotion began to take place. Macy poked her head out to see that Kristina Barclay and her entourage of paparazzi had waltzed into Desideri unceremoniously. The photographers were capturing Kristina picking up various garments and splaying them across her belly to see if they would fit.

"You all can't be in here," Claire explained to them. "No cameras. The owners are very serious about that."

"Don't be silly. I'm Kristina Barclay," Kristina cooed.

"I know, but..." Claire tried to get a word in.

"And I'm here to get a dress for an important event this evening. I'm sure the owner, Gabrielle Owens, wouldn't mind. We've met several times, you know."

Not ready to step out of the dressing room yet, Macy watched her daughter's reaction. The material of the dress, firm as it was to keep anything from jiggling, hung around her waist. With her little fists balled up, Gia started to go into action, but Monique protectively stood in front of her. "Kristina, perhaps you can find someplace else to shop. I happen to know Gabrielle Owens Brutti *personally*, and I know she wouldn't appreciate your cameras in here."

As if on cue, Lucia stirred in her stroller with a gurgling sound. Kristina's face faltered for a moment for the camera, trying not to let Monique's words of truth hit her. She spied Lucia in her stroller. "Oh, is this the little one? I can't wait to have mine." She touched her belly. "Any day now, you know. And *we're* so excited."

There was no need for an explanation of who she meant by *we're*. But one of the paparazzi asked about Duke's whereabouts for the day and if Kristina was there to pick out a dress to surprise him at tonight's party. Macy seethed with an anger and possessiveness she didn't think she had the right to have. Duke might have explained what the deal was to her, but not the whole world. And right now, anyone listening would fall for the lies of Kristina's tale. Kristina sidestepped the questions with vague comments about surprising everyone tonight. Then, without asking, she reached down and picked up Lucia. Lucia opened her light brown eyes, took one look at the woman who was holding her, then to her mother and then back at Kristina, and promptly threw up. As much fuss as Kristina made coming in, she made the same, if not more, going out. She screamed in disgust as she rushed down the corridor. *Lucia the hero*, Macy thought. She made a mental note to kiss the baby for giving Kristina what she deserved.

Finally fully dressed, Macy walked out of the dressing room, and the boutique erupted with laughter. Subconsciously, Macy wrapped her arms around her shoulders. In the mirror, she thought the dress had fit like a glove but still managed to hide her bulges. The black straps came close to her shoulder, exposing much of her breasts. When she was looking in the mirror, she thought she'd looked sexy and sophisticated at the same time. She thought it had been perfect.

"Does it look that bad?"

"Oh, Mommy!" Gia gasped, spinning around. Her dark eyes lit up with excitement. "It's perfect!"

"She's right," Monique said, shuffling Lucia in her arms. "You look beautiful."

"That's definitely the one," Serena agreed.

"Then what were you guys laughing at?" She tucked a stray hair behind her ear, pretending not to know what had happened.

Gia held her phone in the air. "Check your Tweets when you get a chance."

"Otherwise, stay tuned for the evening news!" Monique wrapped her free arm around Gia's shoulders. "Honey, that dress is the one. Get it and let's get ready for the party of the year."

"So let me get this straight," Mario said, setting his beer on the counter in Duke's kitchen. "You thought for a second that there was something still going on between me and Macy? And then you thought there was something going on between Macy and Lawrence?"

As much as Duke hated talking about his private life with the man who once shared a life with Macy, he did. He sighed and picked up his own beer. He had a living room filled with guests who'd arrived early. Fortunately, Macy had the hindsight to have the caterers begin an hour earlier. He had been dressed in just a towel when they set up the first dishes. He had to admit that he was extremely disappointed when it hadn't been Macy at the door.

He'd abided by her wishes, giving her a week to think about things. It gave him a chance to get things in order, as well. Every day that he came home from work, he knew she'd been there. Not only could he smell her coconut scent, but he could see the differences her preparation had made in his home. She cleared out all of the furniture in the downstairs rooms and had a huge Douglas fir in the corner of one room. The large twelve-seat table had been taken out of the dining room and in its place she put several dozen tall round tables around which people could stand and eat the food.

The woman of the hour still hadn't shown up. Duke sought solace in his kitchen. Mario had done the same.

But Duke figured it was better access to the food coming in from the back door delivery and better access to the female servers to gather the food without running into the guests.

"Well, when you say it like that, I know I came off insecure."

"Yeah, you did," Mario said. "And I ain't messin' with you this time. You got this other chick Kristina pregnant."

Duke shook his head. "It's not my baby. I know that, Kristina knows that and more importantly, Macy knows that."

"Now, see, that's where you're wrong. My kids are involved in this. How do you think it looks for Gia or MJ? Do you think they would understand something like this?"

In the past days, he had time to think; Duke screwed things up. He thought that, as long as Macy knew the truth, everything would be okay. But Kristina not correcting the public misconception on who the father of her baby was had damaged everything Duke had built with Macy, Gia and MJ. "I am going to fix this."

Mario said, "I kind of took care of it for you."

Not knowing what Mario would do, Duke felt dread wash over him. "What did you do?"

"Excuse me, Duke," Serena said, poking her head in the doorway. Duke's feeling of impending doom went away, because if Serena was around, that had to mean that Macy was nearby, as well. Macy had pawned Serena off on him all week long. Every time he called Winter Paradise to ask a question or verify a charge,

Serena tried giving the phone to Macy, but he could hear Macy turn the call down. It was sad that just hearing Macy's voice had cheered him up a bit.

"Santa will be flying in soon. Are you ready?"

"Santa?" Duke asked with a raised eyebrow. "Flying in?"

"Yes, didn't you look at your itinerary?" Serena grinned. He shook his head. "No."

"Oh dang, maybe I left it back at the office. Macy thought it would be good for the kids who are here to see you publicly apologize to Santa for your mistake in a press conference."

Beside him, Mario chuckled.

Duke had to laugh, too. He remembered that he promised Macy that he would re-create the North Pole for MJ if need be to prove to him that Santa was real. Now the scenery in his front yard made sense. It really had turned into a winter wonderland, and to make matters better, the weather had cooled down to a nice thirty degrees. The people in his front yard admiring Macy's handiwork were all dressed in sweaters and earmuffs. Macy had set up a carriage ride for those who had to park farther down the street, and even they were covered up in blankets and hand muffs.

When he got home yesterday evening, he'd found one side of his front lawn fenced in with snow and what looked like a landing strip in the center of the snow. He thought about Lawrence being a pilot and realized that he'd played a part in tonight's events. Damn, he was an ass for jumping to conclusions. Why didn't she just explain that to him? He had to find Macy.

"Serena, where is she?"

Looking innocent, Serena shrugged her shoulders. "Who?"

"Macy."

"Mom's at the office." Gia offered up the whereabouts of her mother's location as she waltzed into the room. MJ followed his sister. They paused briefly and glanced at each other before running into Duke's arms. God, he'd missed them.

"Why isn't she here?"

"I think she's still working. She wants to send that money she would have won in the Christmas decorating contest to her charity, so she's trying to figure out the books."

"But I already donated the money."

Serena snapped her fingers and pointed at him. "I knew you did it!"

He felt like such a jerk last Sunday that he'd gone down as soon as possible and written a check to the charity. Even though he'd done it anonymously, the newspaper had written up a comment in the paper yesterday and said the organization was still blessed. If Macy had seen it, she would have known that the charity still received its money, but she wouldn't have known he'd done it. "That was a secret."

"Like you bribing Andy and Spencer with football tickets?"

Duke's mouth made an O.

"Don't worry. Macy hasn't figured either out yet."

Thankful for that, Duke nodded. "So where is she?"

"Well, I don't think she's coming tonight, Duke."

"What?"

"I think she had second thoughts."

This night wasn't going to be a success without her by his side. Before taking off through the back door, Duke knelt down to Gia and MJ's level to discuss a different agenda for the night. Serena held her clipboard close and listened intently to the new plan.

He might not have had the career he had without Kristina, but he wouldn't be the man he was now without Macy. Summer, fall and now winter had passed without him investing too much time in his journalism career, but he could not stand the thought of a few days without Macy, Gia and MJ. His family. He needed her and had to have her.

It took him thirty minutes, but he finally made it to Winter Paradise. Macy's car was still in the driveway. All the lights downstairs were off, but the one in the bedroom upstairs spilled onto the steps. He pictured her in the bed under the covers, ready to shut tonight out of her mind. He wasn't about to let that happen. Tonight wouldn't have taken place if it weren't for her. She had to be a part of it.

Once he was in the foyer, he heard Macy coming down the steps. He stood still, not wanting to frighten her. "Macy," he said into the darkness.

It didn't work. She screamed the minute she saw his figure.

"It's okay. It's me, Duke," he assured her, waving his arms and crossing the room quickly so she could see his face in the light coming from upstairs. Stumbling on something on the floor, Duke met Macy on the steps. He pulled her into his arms and held her against his chest. He bet her heart was pounding from fright. His was from love.

Macy clutched her heart. "Jesus, are you trying to scare me to death?"

"I'm sorry. I just had to see you."

"How did you get in here?"

"You told me where the hideaway key is, remember?"

She glanced at the door. "And the sexy Santa? I didn't hear him go off."

Duke chuckled at her questioning and stroked her shoulders with his fingertips. He couldn't see exactly how, but he knew her hair was piled on top of her head. "Because Serena taught me how to walk by without making him talk." He pulled his head back so she could see him grin in the light.

Macy sat down on the step, still trying to catch her breath. He felt bad, he really did, but in the faint light he could see the gown Macy was wearing and felt himself harden with desire. The black material came just above her shapely thighs. Her shoulders were practically bare, and her breasts looked as if they were being served to him on a platter. The heels she wore had to be at least four inches, and her legs were encased in a dark pair of hose. As she sat down, he noticed the top of the hose and realized she was wearing garters. A week had been too long without her.

"Macy, I came over to tell you how sorry I am. I got caught up in some jealousy quicksand and couldn't get out of it."

"Jealous of what?" Macy's voice cracked.

"It doesn't matter, but what does matter is, I love you."

"You love me?" she breathed.

"Yes." He nodded. "And I'm begging you to give me one more chance." He knelt down on his knees in front of her. The last time they'd been on a set of steps, they made love for the first time. He glanced up into her dark eyes and wondered if she was remembering the same thing. "I can't take being away from you for a week. I couldn't take being away from you for a day. Hell, I already told MET I don't plan on renewing my contract."

Her mouth opened to protest. "What?"

"I turned down their offer to relocate me to a Florida station. I don't want to spend another day away from you, Macy Cuomo."

"Duke, I don't know what to say."

"Don't say anything. Just come with me to the party. You can't stay here."

She shook her head. "I didn't get this dress for nothing. What on earth made you think I wasn't?"

"Serena!" they both agreed.

Macy's cell phone rang. She reached into a little purse Duke hadn't noticed her carrying and answered it, then quickly she closed her eyes and chanted, "*I wish I'd win the lottery, I wish I'd win the lottery, I wish I'd win the lottery.*"

She'd done it before, and he had seen Serena do it, too. He watched her talk about what was going on at the house. While she was on the phone, Duke took the opportunity to caress her legs. Curiosity was getting the better of him. Her calves felt velvety beneath his hands. He couldn't believe how much he'd missed her.

It wasn't just the days that were a problem; it was just being around her. He needed her. Without her, he was nothing. He loved this woman with all his heart.

After hanging up the phone, Macy stood up and reached for the light switch just beyond Duke's head. Her breast swept across his mouth. He wondered if she'd done that on purpose. "Look, I appreciate you quitting your job, but there's more…"

Duke quieted her with a kiss. His fingers pulled her face down to his. The fog he felt that he'd been in was lifted the minutes their lips touched. His thumb caressed her cheeks. She gave him life with each kiss. When he reluctantly pulled away, he heard Macy's gasp mirror the same way he felt. Relief. They both needed that.

"Oh my God," Macy said.

Now he knew his kisses were good, but… Duke followed Macy's gaze upward. Hanging from the ceiling were dozens of sprigs of mistletoe, strategically placed where they would have no choice but to kiss all the way across the room. The walls twinkled, not with a full light, but with several hanging icicle lights, illuminating the ceiling like the night sky. The rug he thought he'd tripped on happened to be Serena's version of snow, pristine white snow.

"I love you, Macy." Duke felt the need to reiterate that under such a romantic setting. He wished to God she would say the same three words to him. But since she wasn't going to say anything just yet, he opted to kiss her again for fear of anything she had to say that he didn't want to hear. She might not have liked the idea of him sticking around more.

Her skin was like silk beneath his fingertips. The strap over her shoulder slid off with ease. A teasing moan escaped her throat as she cupped his face. His thumb touched the outer area of her nipple. Carefully, he stroked her just right. His tongued danced with hers against the beat of their hearts.

Shaking her head, Macy pulled away at the same time as she ran her hands over his chest. Her eyes were filled with tears. His heart stopped beating for a moment as she spoke.

"Duke." Macy tore her lips away from his. She shook her head. "I want to do this, I really do, but I can't be involved with you when this whole Kristina thing is still looming over us."

He mentally cursed Kristina. "Macy." He heard himself breathe her name.

"I can understand two exes being friends. Mario and I are still friends, but I would never try to pawn off another man's child on him. And I doubt he would accept anything like that."

Relieved that was the only thing wrong, Duke laughed. This was easily fixable. "I know. And I know you two are just friends. Kristina and I are not like you guys. I'll take care of her as soon as possible." Duke stood up and pulled her up with him. They moved to the bottom step and now, with her come-get-me heels on, she was a few inches shorter than him. "But I need you and the kids by my side tonight."

"At the party?"

"And after," he said with a boyish grin, then kissed

her forehead. "Let's go before I just take you upstairs and see what it is you're wearing underneath that dress."

Macy tucked her hand in his. His heart thumped faster. "Hey..." She pulled him back before they reached the door. She pointed her manicured fingertips toward the ceiling. "Are we forgetting tradition? I love you."

Duke stopped short and turned her in his arms and abided by the laws of the mistletoe. "That is the best Christmas present I've ever gotten." He dipped his head down and captured her lips.

"Just you wait until later."

Playfully, he reached for the hem of her skirt. "Does it have anything to do with what's... Ouch!" She'd popped his hand away just as his fingertips felt the promising flesh under her gown.

"Hey, I've been meaning to ask you what the deal is with you and Serena and this lottery thing."

"Oh, nothing, it's just that every time we're thinking of someone or something and then that person or thing appears, we just chant that, just in case we're granted wishes."

"So what if I say how great it would be if you kissed me?"

She rose up on her tiptoes and snaked her arms around his neck.

"Mmm, I wish I'd win the lottery..." he whispered as he pulled back and kissed her, "I wish I'd win the lottery..." he said more softly and kissed her again. "I wish I'd win the lottery. Are you ready to go?"

"Mmkay," she managed to moan.

When they reached Duke's home, the party seemed

to be in full swing. There were people from the station, people from the homes he'd helped decorate and people he'd seen in general when around town with Macy. There was nowhere to park near his house, so they parked at the end of the street and took one of Macy's carriage rides back to his front lawn. From what he could see, tons of delivery trucks were parked across his back lawn. His front yard, including the street leading up to his house, had been filled with guests' cars. The gated side with the landing strip was now filled with... As Duke looked closer, he shook his head in disbelief.

"Are those reindeer?" he asked Macy, wrapping his arms around her waist as he helped her down from the carriage. The erotic smell of her coconut shampoo made him forget he was standing in his private winter wonderland.

Macy bit her lip. "I kind of went overboard last week."

"Dare I ask how much this is going to cost me?" he teased.

Rolling her eyes, Macy slipped her hand into Duke's. There was a table on the porch with a candy-cane tablecloth. Two microphones were set up in the middle of the table with two chairs in front of them ready for the main event. They made their way over the front lawn, through the crowds and up to the bottom step of the porch. Santa came to the door, and after a lull everyone began to ooh and ahh at what was to come.

"You should probably make your apology speech." Macy nudged Duke with her elbow. She grinned when he looked down at her. "What?" She smiled innocently.

"You said you were willing to do something like this for MJ. I just figured, why not for the rest of the city?"

He didn't mind. He was on cloud nine tonight, and nothing was going to knock him off. In a mock press conference, Santa and Duke sat at a table with some of the other reporters from WKSS and discussed what a bad boy Duke had been all year long, including telling everyone Santa did not exist. Duke made his apologies for not believing in the magic of Christmas. The kids and the parents seemed to enjoy it. When the conference was over, Duke welcomed everyone to his home and thanked them for coming. He also thought this was the proper time to thank Macy, as well.

"If you all would take a moment, please welcome my better half to the floor." Duke nodded in the direction of the DJ booth at Serena. A spotlight fell across Macy's frame. She looked like a movie star. Duke held his breath and remembered the first time he'd seen her. "This whole evening wouldn't be possible if it weren't for Macy Cuomo."

The onlookers clapped and cheered Macy on to the stage. Duke opened his arm and Macy stood against him. "Macy, I just wanted to say thank you. And I can't wait to see what happens between us when the New Year rolls around." What more he wanted to say was pushed aside when he looked over and saw Kristina and their boss from DC, Oscar, climbing out of a carriage, followed by his wife, Allegra, who walked off in a different direction once her feet hit the ground.

No doubt MET had shared Duke's news with the DC station. Oscar didn't look too happy. He was middle-aged, balding and burned out from his job as a station manager. He looked even balder since the last time he'd seen him. "Thanks, everyone, for coming, and enjoy your evening," Duke said.

Everyone clapped for Duke and Santa. They all began to disperse either into the house or around the lawn. Some came up to the table and shook his hand, thanking Duke for making his apology. When they had a break, Duke took hold of Macy's hand and they walked down the steps.

"What's wrong?" Macy asked as they walked through the crowd.

"I'm about to clear the air right now," Duke replied. While more people eagerly stuck their hands out at Duke, he tried to make his way to the other side of the yard. He waited patiently and tried to greet as many people as possible, all the while keeping an eye on the folks in the back. As he approached, Mario came out of nowhere and began shaking Oscar's hand obnoxiously up and down.

Mario looked up and grinned at the sight of Duke and Macy. "Oh, great! You two made up!"

"Hi, Mario, where are the kids?" Macy said, leaning over and hugging him. Duke didn't miss the glare Macy and Kristina shot each other.

"In the house, eating." Mario pointed his beefy arm toward the home. "I have been talking a lot with my cousin, Allegra. I just came to have a word with my cousin-in-law, Oscar. Duke, you must know Oscar Orsini, right?"

"I do," Duke answered slowly. "Did you say cousin-in-law?"

"Yeah, remember when you asked if I had any Polizzi family in DC?"

"Yea?"

"Turns out in this case, I really do. My cousin Allegra."

Kristina choked on air.

"Yeah, she's married to Oscar."

Duke noticed Kristina's eyes widen. He had to laugh at the situation. Kristina, who devoured having the attention thrown on herself, cringed at the thought of Oscar's wife finding out about her. "Really?"

"Yeah, actually she's in the kitchen, so why don't you guys wait right here and I'll get her?"

"You know," Kristina said nervously, "I don't think I'm feeling very well. You guys wouldn't mind if I left early?"

"Oh, but your entourage hasn't even arrived," Macy spoke up.

Kristina offered Macy a nonapologetic smile. "Well, you know how pregnancy can be."

"Mmm, yes, I do."

"Excuse me." Gia interjected herself into the adult conversation with her phone aimed between Kristina and Duke. "This is Gia, reporting live on Snapchat from what seems like the North Pole." She focused the camera back on herself for a moment to take a selfie against the snow-covered ground before focusing back on Kristina.

Duke raised a brow at the teenager.

"Kristina," Gia continued, "congratulations on your

pregnancy. For the inquisitive kids out there watching, Duke, are you the father of Kristina's baby?"

"Absolutely not."

A few of the folks eavesdropping gasped, Macy included. She covered her mouth with one hand while trying to corral her daughter with the other. Gia stepped out of her mother's reach and followed Kristina as she tried to disappear into the crowd. "Kristina, wait, the viewers want to know who the father of your child is."

"Have you lost your mind down here?" Oscar asked, gritting his teeth. "Or has this been your plan all along, to punish me for what happened between me and Kristina?"

"Oscar, was there some reason you came tonight?" Duke asked his former boss once Kristina had left.

Clearing his throat, Oscar nodded. "There was. I wanted to talk to you about your contract. You know I can sue you."

"For what? My contract is with MET, who set me up at your station. Might I remind you that you were the one who signed off on my leave of absence? Go ahead, Oscar."

"I don't think he's going to sue you." Mario draped his arm over the shorter man's shoulder. "Are you, *cugino*? I think we ought to go into the kitchen. I know Allegra doesn't like to be kept waiting." As he walked by Duke and Macy, he winked at them.

"Wow. What an evening," Macy said, sinking against him.

"Do you think you'll miss all this excitement when I'm no longer in the limelight?" Duke whispered in her ear.

"Is that your little dig on Tallahassee news not being so big?"

There was just something about the way she looked at him. It made Duke's heart swell. Her hair was piled up on top of her head with a few curls hanging down framing her face. "No, I meant now that I'm not going to make as much money, seeing how the local high school coaches don't make much."

"High school coach?"

Duke took Macy in his arms. "Yeah, you see, a little birdie told me that there was a high school baseball coach position open, and I was offered the job and I took it."

When her face lit up, he smiled. "Seriously?"

"Very much so. And I have to say that this last week has made me realize that my life is nothing without you."

Macy pushed away and folded her arms across her chest. "Nothing?" she squeaked out.

"Nothing," Duke repeated, enjoying the look of disbelief on her face. Gia returned from the crowd with MJ in tow. They flanked Duke. "I am more than willing to give up the fame and fortune just to be with you." Taking a deep breath, he got down on one knee.

Macy covered her face. "What are you doing?"

"Well, I asked the kids earlier and they agreed to have me. And now I would like to ask you to marry me."

"Oh my God!"

"Macy Cuomo, a week without you was the most torturous ever. I don't ever want to spend any more time away from you. Will you please marry me?" He realized the crowd behind him had quieted down and had begun paying attention to them.

"Well?" shouted someone from the crowd. Duke was pretty sure it was Serena's voice.

"Yes!" Macy cried.

Duke stood up and spun Macy around in his arms. "You just don't know how happy you've made me. I only wish my parents were here to meet you!"

Macy buried her face against his neck. He could feel her warm breath against his collarbone. "Duke, listen, that thing I was working with Lawrence on."

"It doesn't matter…"

"It kind of does." She wiggled out of his arms and slid down to her feet. "There's what we were working on."

Duke followed her bare finger toward the street where a long stretch limousine had pulled up. A chauffeur ran around from the driver's side to the back door and opened it. He did a double take at the sight of what he thought he saw.

"Ma?" The word escaped him as the emotions caught in his throat. His mother had stepped out of the backseat, followed by his father, his two sisters, Ana and Theresa, and then his brothers, Erik, Bobby and Sandino. Duke looked back down at Macy by his side. She was tearfully looking up at him.

"I didn't want to tell you what Lawrence and I were working on last week because I wanted this to be a surprise."

"How did you—"

"Pablo and Monique helped coordinate. Lawrence flew his plane and picked them up earlier this evening."

"Macy, I don't know what to say…"

"How about you just introduce me to my new family?"

A stroke after midnight, Macy stood on the porch, waving away Duke's last guest. He had gone inside to say good-night to his family and met her in the foyer. Macy closed the door behind her and held on to the doorknob. Duke was standing at the bottom of his steps.

"We have to stop meeting like this," she teased, cocking her eyebrow toward the steps. He looked breathtakingly handsome with his button-down Oxford shirt rolled up to his elbows.

"I don't think I'm ever going to look at stairs the same way," Duke said, walking up on her. His hands pressed against the door on either side of her head. "You know, I fell in love with you in front of the Baezes' stairs. You were standing right under the same mistletoe." He nodded toward the ceiling, encouraging her eyes to follow where he hung the dried plant.

"You did not." She beamed inwardly, but held her composure. "This is the same one?"

"*Es verdad.*"

She smiled. "I already agreed to marry you. You don't have to woo me with your tricks."

"Okay, *mi future esposa.*"

Macy closed her eyes and moaned, "We are not going to do anything with your parents in the other room."

"I'll be quiet."

"Yes, but I might not be." Macy giggled. "Hey, speaking of your parents, you know you didn't close your eyes and wish to win the lottery when you saw them."

He dipped his head down and inhaled a kiss. "That's because I already have, Macy. I already have won. Thanks to you and the children, I have my own family."

\* \* \* \* \*

# WINTER WEDDING
# IN VEGAS

**JANICE LYNN**

To my favourite nurse, Joni Sain!

You rock!!!

# CHAPTER ONE

DR. TAYLOR ANDERSON woke from the craziest dream she'd ever had. Apparently sleeping in a glitzy Las Vegas hotel stretched one's inner imagination beyond all reason.

Married. Her. To Dr. Slade Sain.

As if.

The man was such a player, she wouldn't date him, much less consider a more serious relationship with the likes of him. Sure, he was gorgeous, invaded her deepest, darkest dreams from time to time, but the man's little black book had more phone numbers than the Yellow Pages.

If and when she married, no way would she make the same relationship mistakes she had made during medical school. Never again was she walking down that painful path of inevitable unfaithfulness from a man she should have known better than to trust.

Yet her mind warned that last night hadn't been a dream, that she had married Slade.

Last night she'd drowned her awkwardness around him. She rarely drank, but she'd felt so self-conscious surrounded by Slade and her colleagues in a social setting, that she had overimbibed. She didn't think she'd been out and out drunk, but she hadn't been herself.

These days, the real her was quiet and reserved, steady and stable. Responsible. Not the kind of woman to go to a tacky Sin City year-round Christmas-themed wedding chapel and marry a man she respected as a brilliant oncologist, had found unbelievably attractive from the moment she'd first laid eyes on him, but thought as cheesy as the Jolly Old Saint Nick who'd, apparently, also been an ordained minister. Who knew?

Mentally, she counted to ten, took a deep breath, and opened her eyes. She was in her hotel room queen-size bed and Sexy Slade Sain was nowhere in sight.

She glanced at the opposite side of the bed. The covers were so tangled, who knew if there had been anyone other than herself beneath the sheets? Just because she usually woke with the bedcovers almost as neat as when she'd crawled between them didn't mean a thing. Really.

She wasn't in denial. No way.

Neither did the fact she was in the middle of the bed, sort of diagonally, and sprawled out. Naked. What had she done with her clothes?

What had she done with her naked body?

A knock sounded on the door leading out of the room. Feeling like she was suffering a mini–heart attack, Taylor grabbed at the tangled sheets.

"Room service," a male voice called through the door.

Room service? She pulled the covers tightly around her body. She hadn't ordered room service.

The bathroom door opened and a damp, dark-haired pin-up calendar model wearing only a towel—dear sweet heaven, the man had a fine set of shoulders and six-pack!—undid the safety chain.

Slade was in her hotel room. Naked beneath the towel and he was buff. The towel riding low around his waist, covering his perfect butt, his perfect… She gulped back saliva pooling in her mouth.

Despite her desperate clinging to denial of the cold hard facts she'd been willfully repressing, she knew exactly what she'd done with her naked body. What she'd done with *his* naked body. Why her bedsheets were so tangled. The details of how she'd come to the conclusion that marrying Slade was a logical decision might be a little fuzzy, but she'd known exactly what she'd been doing when Slade's mouth had taken hers. Hot, sweaty, blow-your-mind sex, that's what she'd done. With Slade. As much as her brain was screaming *No!* her body shouted, *Encore!*

"That was quick," Mr. Multiple Orgasms praised the hotel employee pushing a cart into the room. He stopped the man just inside the doorway. "I'll take it from here."

The pressure in Taylor's head throbbed to where at any moment she was going to form and rupture an aneurysm. Slade's wife. This had to be a nightmare. Or a joke. Or a mistake they could rectify with an annulment.

Could a couple get an annulment if they'd spent the night in bed, performing exotic yoga moves with energetic bursts of pleasurable cardio?

She closed her eyes and let images from the night before wash over her, of Slade unlocking her hotel room door, sweeping her off her feet, and carrying her to the bed and stripping off her clothes. She'd giggled and kissed his neck when he'd carried her across the threshold. Then he'd kissed her. Really, deeply kissed her. Even now she could recall the feel of his lips against hers, the feel of his body against hers, his spicy male scent. Heat rose, flushing her face, ears and much more feminine parts.

They so wouldn't qualify for an annulment.

Wow at the moves the man had hidden inside that fabulous body. His hands were magic. Pure magic. His mouth? Magic. Just *wow*.

She cracked open an eyelid to steal a peek. He tipped the man from Room Service from his wallet on the dresser, closed the door, turned and caught her staring.

"Morning, Sleeping Beauty." He gave a lopsided, almost self-deriding grin. "Some night, eh?"

She groaned and pulled a pillow over her head to where she just peered out from behind it. "Tell me that wasn't real."

He shrugged his magnificent shoulders. "That wasn't real."

Dropping the pillow but hanging on tightly to the sheet, she let out a surprised sigh of relief.

"But if by 'that' you're referring to our wedding at the North Pole Christmas Bliss Wedding Chapel—" the words came out with a mixture of amusement and shock, as if he couldn't quite believe what they'd done either "—well, according to our marriage certificate, that was very real."

Keeping the covers tucked securely around her, Taylor sat up. A wave of nausea smacked her insides. He stood there looking sexy as sin and she was going to barf. Great. Just flipping great.

"One minute we were kissing in the limo surrounded by Christmas music and that crazy peppermint spray the driver kept showering us with, the next we're getting married so we could have sex. Great sex, by the way. You blew me away." His blue eyes sparkling with mischievous intent, he moved toward her and she shook her head in horrified denial.

"Get back," she warned, covers clutched to her chest with one hand and the other outstretched as if warding off an evil spirit. Sure, there was a part of her that was thrilled that he'd enjoyed their night as much as she had, but it was morning. The morning after. And they'd gotten married. "That's crazy. We didn't have to get married to have sex."

Pausing, he scratched his head as if confused. "Not that I don't agree with you, but that's not what you said last night in the limo."

The movement of his arm flexed muscles along his chest and abdomen and sent a wave of tingles through her body, but that wasn't why she gulped again. She was just…thirsty? Parched. Still fighting the urge to barf. Forcing her eyes to focus on his face and not the rest of him, she blinked. The flicker of awareness in his blue eyes warned he knew exactly what she had been looking at, what she'd been thinking, and he wasn't immune to her thoughts.

"You told me you wouldn't have sex with me unless we were married," he reminded her.

She had said that. In the midst of his hot, lust-provoking kisses she'd thrown down her gauntlet, expecting him to run or laugh in her face. "So you married me?"

He glanced down at the cheap band on his left hand and shrugged. "Obviously."

Not that he sounded any happier about it than she felt, but someone should shoot her now. She was wearing a ring, too. A simple golden band on the wedding finger of her left hand. Because she was married. To Slade.

Slade was not the man of her dreams, was not someone she'd carefully chosen to spend the rest of her life based upon well-thought-out criteria. He was exactly what she avoided even dating because men like Slade didn't jibe with her life plans. How could she have had such a huge lapse of judgement?

The metal hugging her finger tightened to painful proportions. At any moment her finger was going to turn blue and drop off from lack of blood flow. Seriously.

She went to remove the ring, but couldn't bring herself to do it. Why, she couldn't exactly say. Probably the same insanity that had had her saying "I do" to a man she should have been screaming "I don't" at. Besides, she'd probably have to buy a stick of butter before the thing would budge.

"We should talk about this." He glanced at his watch. "But we have our presentation in just over an hour. You should eat."

She glanced at the bedside table's digital clock. Crap. She'd slept much later than normal. Then again, she'd stayed up much later than normal.

Nothing had been normal about the night before. It had been as if she'd been watching someone else do all the things she'd done, as if it had all been a fantasy, not real.

"You have to go to your room," she told him, needing to be away from his watchful blue gaze.

"I'm in my room." He shifted his weight and her attention dropped to where the towel was tucked in at his waist. His amazing, narrow waist that sported abs no doctor should boast. Abs like those belonged on sport stars and models, not white-collar professionals who saw cancer patients all day. "Last night we arranged for the hotel staff to move my things into your room while we're in class today."

They had stopped by the front desk and requested that. Wincing, her gaze shot to his.

"No." She was going to throw up. Really she was. How was she going to explain this to Gracie? She grimaced. "I don't want you in my room."

"Understood." He looked as if he really didn't want to be there either. "But we're married."

"Married" had come out sounding much like a dirty word, like someone who'd just been given a deadly diagnosis.

Guilt hit Taylor. She had told him she wouldn't have sex with him unless they were married. But wasn't marriage a bit far for a man to go just to get laid? He had a busy revolving door to his bedroom so he couldn't have been that desperate for sex. He must have been as inebriated as she had.

"How did we end up married?" she asked, pulling the bedcovers up to her neck. The less he could see of her the better. She already felt exposed.

"You told me you wanted to have sex with me, but that you wouldn't unless we were married. Our elfish limo driver said he knew a place that could take care of a last-minute license and we happened to be right outside it. We got married and had sex. You know this. You were there."

If she'd been into one-night stands, last night would have been amazing. But she wasn't. She was a mature, professional doctor who had learned her life lessons the hard way and had a beautiful little girl she was raising by herself to prove it. She'd vowed she wouldn't have sex again without being married first. Had she foolishly believed marriage would protect her from future heartbreak?

She'd wanted Slade so much. Had possibly wanted him for months, although she'd never admitted as much to herself. When their pointy-eared three-and-a-half-foot-tall limo driver had taken them to the chapel, she'd looked at Slade, expecting him to laugh at her condition.

When she'd seen him actually seriously considering marrying her just to have sex with her, a big chunk of the protective ice she'd frozen around her heart had melted, leaving her vulnerable and wanting what she'd seen in his eyes. Whether it had been the alcohol, the Christmas magic everywhere, or just Vegas madness, she'd wanted to marry Slade the night before. It made no logical sense, but she'd wanted him to want her enough to walk down the aisle to have her.

"We were drunk," she offered as an out. "We can get an annulment because we were drunk."

His expression pained, he narrowed his gaze. "Maybe."

His hands went to his hips and, again, she had to force her eyes upward to keep them from wandering lower than his face. The man was beautiful, she'd give him that.

"I wasn't sober," she persisted, clinging to the fact that she hadn't been in her right mind. She wasn't in her right mind now either. Her head hurt and, crazy as it was, she wanted him, but she couldn't tell him that. "Regardless, I want a divorce."

Raking his fingers through his towel-dried hair, Slade eyed Taylor grasping the covers to her beautiful body as if she expected him to rip them off and demand she succumb to his marital rights whether she wanted him or not. Did she really think so poorly of him? Despite the fact he'd not been able to say "I do" fast enough the night before, he didn't want to be married any more than she apparently did.

Probably less.

Sure, he'd been attracted from the moment he'd met her.

But although he'd have sworn she felt a similar spark, she'd brushed off his attempts to further their relationship.

Until last night.

Last night she'd looked at him and he'd felt captivated, needy, as if under a spell he hadn't been able to snap out of.

He took a deep breath. "A divorce works for me. A wife is not something I planned to bring back from Vegas."

Or from anywhere. He had his future mapped out and a wife didn't fit anywhere into those plans. He'd dedicated his life to breast-cancer research and nothing more.

Marrying Taylor had been rash—the effects of alcohol and Las Vegas craziness—and wasn't at all like his normal self. Women were temporary in his life, not permanent figures. He preferred it that way.

A divorce sounded perfect. His marriage would be one of those "what happens in Vegas stays in Vegas" kind of things.

Thank goodness she didn't harbor any delusions of happily-ever-after or sappy romance. They'd chalk last night up to alcohol and a major lapse of judgment.

Maybe there really was something about Vegas that made people throw caution to the wind and act outside their norm. Or maybe it had been the smiley little elfish limo driver, who'd kept puffing peppermint spray into the car, telling them they were at the wedding chapel that had made the idea seem feasible. Had the spray been some type of drug?

"Good." Taylor's chin lifted a couple of notches. "Then we're agreed this was a mistake and we can get a divorce or an annulment or whatever one does in these circumstances."

"I'll call my lawyer first thing Monday morning." Relieved that she was being sensible about calling a spade a spade and correcting their mistake, he pushed the room-service cart over next to the bed and stared down at a woman who'd taken him to sexual heights he'd never experienced before. Maybe that peppermint stuff really had been some kind of aphrodisiac.

Even with her haughty expression, she was pretty with

her long blond hair tumbled over her milky shoulders and her lips swollen from his kisses. Until the night before he'd never seen her hair down. He liked it. A lot.

He liked her a lot. Always had. He'd wanted her from afar for way too long. Despite the whole marriage fiasco, he still wanted her. Even more than he had prior to having kissed her addictive mouth. She'd tasted of candy canes, joy and magic. Kissing her had made him feel like a kid on Christmas morning who'd gotten exactly what he'd always wanted.

Which was saying a lot for a man who hadn't celebrated Christmas since he was twelve years old.

"Now that that's settled, there's no reason we can't enjoy the rest of the weekend. Let's eat up before this gets cold."

The covers still clasped to her all the way up to her neck, she crossed her arms over her chest. Her eyes were narrow green slits of annoyance. "Don't act as if we're suddenly friends because we both want a divorce. We're not and we won't be enjoying the rest of the weekend. At least, not the way you mean."

"Fine. We won't enjoy the rest of the weekend." He wasn't going to argue with her. "But we're not strangers." Ignoring her I-can't-stand-you glare and his irritation at how she was treating him as if he had mange, he lifted the lid off one of the dishes he'd ordered and began buttering a slice of toast. "I've been working with you for around a year."

"You see me at work." She watched what he did with great interest. "That doesn't make us friends. Neither does last night."

She had to be starved. While satisfying one hunger, they'd worked up another. He'd ordered a little of everything because he hadn't known what she liked. Other than coffee. Often at the clinic, he saw her sipping on a mug of coffee as if the stuff were ambrosia. Funny how often he'd catch himself watching for her to take that first sip, how he'd smile at the pleasure on her face once she had. He'd put pleasure on her face the night before that had blown away anything he'd ever seen, anything he'd ever experienced.

"You make your point." He sat down on the bed and waved a piece of buttered toast in front of her, liking how her gaze followed the offering. "But as we're in agreement that we made a mistake, one we are rectifying, I don't see why we can't be friends and make the most out of a bad situation."

Scowling, she shot her gaze back to his. "You and I will never be friends."

She grabbed his toast and took a bite, closed her eyes and sighed a noise that made him want to push her back on the bed and, friends or not, taste her all over again.

Perhaps she'd prefer it if he told her how much he was enjoying how she'd just licked crumbs from her pretty pink lips? How much, now that he knew disentangling himself from their impromptu marriage wasn't going to be a problem, he was anticipating making love to her again, because for all her blustering he wasn't blind. She'd looked at him with more hunger than she had the toast. Whether she wanted to admit it or not, she was as affected by him as he was her. They had phenomenal chemistry.

She leaned toward the tray, got a knife and a packet of strawberry jam, then nodded while she spread the pink mixture on what was left of her toast. Not an easy task because she refused to let go of where she clutched the bed covers, which seemed a bit ridiculous to him since he'd seen every inch of her. Seen, touched, tasted.

Slade swallowed the lump forming in his throat and mentally ordered one not to form beneath his towel. "In case you need reminding, we had a good time last night."

"I didn't."

"Don't lie." He'd been there. She hadn't faked that, couldn't have faked her responses, and he wouldn't let her pretend she had. "Yes, you did."

"Okay," she conceded with a great deal of sarcasm.

"You're good in bed. Anyone can be good if they get lots of practice and we both know you've had lots of practice."

"Lots of practice?" He hadn't lived the life of a monk, but he didn't go around picking up random women every night either. Sure, he never committed, but the women he spent time with knew the score. He wasn't the marrying kind and avoided women who were. "You want to discuss my past sex life?"

"Not really." Her face squished, then paled. "Although I guess we should discuss diseases and such."

He arched his brow. "You have a disease?"

"No." She sounded horrified enough that he knew she was telling the truth. They should have discussed all this the night before. And birth control. Because for the first time in his life he hadn't used a condom. Because for the first time in his life he'd been making love to his *wife*.

Slade's throat tightened. He'd not only gotten married the night before but he'd had sex without a condom. How stupid could he have been?

Was that why the sex had been so good? Because they'd not had a rubber barrier between them? Because they'd been flesh to flesh? He didn't think so. There had been something more, something special about kissing Taylor.

Besides, they'd used a condom the first time. It had been their subsequent trips to heaven that had been without one. He'd only had the one condom in his wallet and they'd still been high under the Las Vegas night air—or whatever foolishness had lowered their inhibitions.

"Do you?" she asked, sounding somewhere between terrified and hopeful his answer would be the right one.

"I haven't specifically gone for testing recently." There hadn't been a need. He had never had sex without protection before her and didn't engage in any other high-risk behaviors. "It's been a year or so since my last checkup, but I do donate blood routinely and have always checked normal."

His answer didn't appease her and she eyed him suspiciously. "When was the last time you donated?"

"About two months ago."

Relief washed over her face. "No letter telling you about any abnormal findings?"

He shook his head. "No such letter. What about you?"

Her gaze didn't quite meet his. "I've only been with one man and that was years ago during medical school. I've been checked a couple of times since then. I'm clean."

As unreasonable as it was since he was no saint and they were going to end their marriage as soon as possible, the thought of Taylor being with anyone else irked him. A surge of jealousy had his fingers flexing and his brain going on hiatus.

"He didn't have to marry you to have sex with you?"

# CHAPTER TWO

SLADE INSTANTLY REGRETTED his sarcastic question, especially when, with a pale face and watery eyes, Taylor glanced down at the plain gold band he'd put on her hand the night before.

"No, Kyle didn't marry me, but I did believe he was going to spend the rest of his life loving me. Silly me."

The fact that she'd been heartbroken by the jerk rankled Slade. Good thing she didn't want this marriage any more than he did. He'd hate to think he'd hurt her like that fool had. Regardless of what the future held for them, he didn't want to cause Taylor any pain. That much he knew. "What happened?"

She shrugged and the sheet slipped off one shoulder to drape mid-upper-arm. "He didn't marry me or spend the rest of his life loving me. End of story."

Hardly, but he wouldn't push. Such sorrow laced her words that his chest squeezed tighter. "I'm sorry."

"I'm not." Masking her emotions behind an indifferent expression he suspected she'd perfected over the years since her breakup with the guy, Taylor picked up a spoon and scooped up a mouthful of eggs. "He was an arrogant jerk."

Her lips were wrapped around the spoon and another jolt of jealousy hit him as she slowly pulled the utensil from her mouth.

She picked up a strawberry and bit into the juicy fruit. "Mmm. That's good."

"Speaking of good..." He watched her pop the rest of the berry into her mouth and lick the juice from her fingers, and struggled with the desire to do some licking of his own. "Last night really was spectacular, apart from the whole getting-married thing."

She met his gaze, nodded, then deflated. "Oh, Slade, what have we done?"

Hearing her say his name caused flashbacks from the night before. Until then, he'd never heard her say his first name. He liked the sound. "We got married, but we can correct that. We will correct that. As soon as legally possible."

"It's crazy that we got married. Why did we do that? We aren't in love, barely know each other and I don't even like you."

He gave a wry grin. "All this time I just thought you were waiting on me to win you over to my way of thinking."

"Professionally maybe, but not romantically."

"Professionally, I'm a good oncologist."

"You are." She winced. "I didn't mean it like that."

"Then what did you mean?"

"Just that I always thought you were a flirt and didn't take life seriously."

"I take my job very seriously." His work was the most important thing in his life and always would be. "I care a great deal for my patients and like to think I provide them the best care possible."

"You do. It's just that..." Her voice trailed off.

"It's just what?"

"I guess I let your personal life influence how I viewed you professionally."

"What do you know of my personal life?"

Her face reddened. "Not much. Just gossip really."

"Not that you should believe gossip, but what do the gossips say?"

"That you date a lot of different women."

"You think I shouldn't?"

She sighed and looked somewhere between disgusted and desperate. "What I think about your personal life doesn't matter. We'll get a divorce and no one ever need know about any of this."

Thankful that she was so practical about the whole thing, Slade nodded. "Agreed. We'll figure the legalities out on Monday and end this as painlessly as possible."

She eyed him, then gave a hopeful half smile. "Maybe we'll get lucky and there's some kind of 'just kidding, I've changed my mind because I was stupid in Vegas clause.'"

Thank goodness Slade felt the same as she did. They'd made a horrible mistake, knew it and would make the best of a bad situation.

Not that she could believe he'd married her.

The man was gorgeous, amazing in bed, could have any woman he wanted and usually did, according to her female coworkers who loved to discuss the handsome oncologist's love life latest. Why would he have married her? Taylor was admittedly a stick-in-the-mud, boring homebody. Her idea of fun was a good book while soaking in a bubble bath or playing with Gracie. Her ideal life would bore him to tears. No confetti and blow horns anywhere in her reality or her ideal future.

From what she knew about Slade, they couldn't be more opposite.

*Opposites attract.*

She winced at the inner voice in her head playing devil's advocate. Okay, so she'd admit she wanted to rip Slade's towel off and have that encore performance. Not that she did anything more than wrap the sheet around her, grab the cup of coffee from the tray, and, head held high, strut into the bathroom to take her shower.

Of course, that only reminded her that his naked body

had been under this hot stream earlier and had she wakened in time she could have joined him. Her husband.

What a joke.

But right now she had to get her act together, because they were presenting to a group of oncologists, pharmacists, marketing representatives and others on the benefits of a new cancer-fighting drug they'd been researching.

At some point today she should probably tell Slade that not only had he become a husband the night before, he'd also become the stepfather of a precious six-year-old little girl.

She winced.

Yeah, that might shock Slade enough to have him scrambling around in hopes of finding a twenty-four-hour Vegas divorce court.

Although she had a photo of Gracie on her desk at work, she doubted Slade had ever been inside the room, that he'd ever had reason to be in her personal office. Yes, they worked in the same multifloor cancer clinic. But prior to their being chosen to go to this conference to discuss the research being done at their facility, they'd not really interacted except when he'd sent her running by asking her out.

Because she avoided men like Slade.

Had for years.

The last time she hadn't, she'd ended up pregnant and alone.

Nausea hit her. After their first time she and Slade hadn't used birth control. He'd only had the one condom, and they'd been too delirious to acknowledge the ramifications of unprotected sex.

How stupid was she? Was he?

The timing in her menstrual cycle wasn't right for pregnancy, but she wasn't so foolish as to think it wasn't possible.

Her hand went to her bare belly. Was she? Had she and Slade made a baby? Dampness covered her skin that had nothing to do with the shower water. She loved Gracie with all her heart, would do anything for her precious daughter, but she'd never planned to have more children. Not without finding a man who met all her criteria for Mr. Right, which included what kind of father he'd be to Gracie.

Then again, she'd never planned to get married to a man she barely knew either, and she'd done that.

Her parents would be so proud. Ha. Not. Her actions this weekend would just once again affirm their disappointment in her.

She finished rinsing her body, then stepped out of the shower and eyed the half-empty cup of coffee.

She picked up the cup and, with great sadness, poured the lukewarm liquid down the sink drain.

No more coffee or anything else that wasn't healthy for a pregnant woman until she knew for sure one way or the other that she and Slade hadn't created a new little life.

Slade leaned back in his chair and watched the impressive woman woo the crowd with her smiles and witty sense of humor.

Taylor went through the slide presentation she'd put together on the data their oncology clinic, Nashville Cancer Care, had collected on Interallon, a new experimental cancer-fighting drug they'd been successfully administering as part of a larger nationwide research trial. Remission rates of metastatic breast cancer had increased by 40 percent in patients who'd received the trial medication over current treatment modalities. They were hopeful FDA approval would be soon so the medication could be administered more widely.

Taylor pushed back a stray strand of pale blond hair behind her ear and pointed a laser at the current slide, referring to a particular set of data.

He'd slid his fingers through that soft, long hair last night. Not that you could tell just how long or lush her hair was with the way she had it harshly swept up. Neither could you tell how gorgeous her big green eyes were behind those ridiculous black-rimmed glasses she wore. Definitely you couldn't tell how hot and passionate her body was beneath her prim and proper gray pantsuit and blazer.

She epitomized a professional businesswoman presenting data to a crowd of health-care professionals who couldn't possibly appreciate how amazing she was.

Slade scanned the crowd, noticing several of the men watching her with a gleam in their eyes. Well, maybe some of them did see just how amazing she was, but he pitied them. She was his. His wife.

He couldn't believe he'd gone that far.

He usually had no problems with women, but Taylor had always been different. For months he'd not been able to convince her to give him the time of day and he had tried. Repeatedly, he'd struck up conversations only to have her end them and avoid him.

She made a comment, misspoke a word and poked fun at herself, getting a laugh from their audience. Slade skimmed the crowd, noticing several of the men seemed to be further enchanted by the woman on stage.

Green slushed through his veins, clogging the oxygen flow to his brain. Had to be since he sure wasn't thinking straight because his brain—or was it just his male ego?—was screaming, *Mine. Mine. Mine.*

"Now…" She flashed another smile at the crowd, pulling them further under her spell. "I'll turn the podium over to Dr. Slade Sain to present specific case studies and then we'll field any questions together."

They walked past each other as he took the podium and she returned to sit in the seat next to his at a table that had been set up at the front of the auditorium. He tried to meet her gaze, to smile at her and tell her what a great job she'd done, but she kept her gaze averted, purposely not looking at him.

Which annoyed Slade.

He stewed all the way to the podium and then did something almost as stupid as slipping a golden band around a woman's finger when he had nothing to offer her but more broken dreams.

"Ladies and gentlemen, give my wife a round of applause for the great job she just did."

Taylor's face paled.

Slade's face probably did, too. What had he just done?

Several of the people in the audience who knew them gasped in surprise. A few called out their congratulations.

When their gazes met, Taylor looked annoyed, but then she pasted on a smile for the crowd.

Their colleagues and class attendees settled down and, despite the horror bubbling in his stomach that he'd just made their mistake public, Slade got serious. He believed in the benefits of Interallon and wanted others to have the opportunity to significantly benefit from the still-experimental medication. Despite whatever was going on in their personal lives, it was his and Taylor's job to educate their colleagues, to get others involved in the medication trials, as the pharmaceutical company pushed to have the FDA expedite approval.

He went over their case studies, answered questions, then pointed to one of their colleagues whose hand was raised with a question. The doctor had started out with him and Taylor the night before, but they'd ditched him and a handful of others when they'd left in the limo.

"Sorry to change the subject off Interallon, but when did you and Dr. Anderson get married?"

"Last night." Slade glanced toward Taylor. Her green eyes flashed with anger beneath her glasses, but she kept a smile on her lovely face. No doubt he was going to get a tongue-lashing when the presentation finished. He deserved one. He wanted to scream and yell at himself for his stupid remark, too. "Next question."

The man raised his hand again and spoke before Slade could call on another person. "You and Dr. Anderson got married last night? When you left dinner, you got married?"

Taylor stood, walked over to the podium, and took the microphone. "Dr. Ryan, you'll understand if Dr. Sain and I request personal questions be saved for a later, more appropriate time. Right now, we prefer questions regarding Interallon and the success our clinic and the other clinics involved in the trials taking place are having with this phenomenal resource in our battle against a horrific disease."

Put in his place, the man nodded. Taylor immediately called on another person and fielded a question about the medication being used in conjunction with currently available treatments.

"At this time, the studies using Interallon in conjunction with other cancer-fighting modalities are just starting to take place. Nashville Cancer Care will be heading up one of those trials early next year."

Another flurry of questions filled the remaining time and no one brought up their nuptials again until after the class was over. Several of their colleagues shook their hands, patted their backs and gave them congratulations.

"I didn't see that one coming," Dr. Ryan commented, looking back and forth between them. "I didn't even know you two were seeing each other."

Slade narrowed his gaze at the other man. Cole Ryan had been one of the men eyeing Taylor on stage as if she was a piece of candy to be devoured. A growl gurgled in Slade's throat, but he managed to keep it low.

Taylor closed her laptop and picked up a file folder with her notes inside. "I prefer to keep my personal life private. Obviously, Dr. Sain and I disagree on that particular issue."

"Dr. Sain?" Ryan chuckled, then slapped Slade on the back again. "Your wife calls you Dr. Sain?"

Slade glanced at Taylor's scowl, the stiff set to her shoulders and the tight line of her mouth. He was an idiot. He deserved her anger. He didn't even know why he'd made the stupid announcement. Other than the fact that he'd been overcome with jealousy. "When she's upset."

"Trouble in paradise already. That's a Vegas wedding for you." The man laughed again, not realizing just how much he was getting on Slade's nerves. Odd, as he usually liked the doctor, who also practiced in Nashville.

"Well, congrats anyway." Cole gave them a wry look. "For however long it lasts."

Slade packed up his briefcase and followed Taylor from the conference room and down the long hallway that led out into the hotel's main lobby.

Ignoring the lush Christmas decorations and colorful slot machines scattered around the huge lobby, Taylor didn't say a word directly to him until they were alone in the elevator. Then she rounded on him, opened her mouth to speak, then stopped, closed her eyes in disgust and took a deep breath. When she opened her eyes again, anger still flickered there. "How dare you make that little announcement during our presentation?"

"I shouldn't have said anything."

"You made a joke of our presentation," she accused, practically snapping at him.

"No, I didn't." He would never intentionally do anything to take away from the importance of Interallon and the results they were getting with the medication.

"Yes, you did. Rather than paying attention to what you were saying, half the people in the room were busy Tweeting that we'd gotten married."

"You're exaggerating." He hoped she was exaggerating.

"Really?" She dug in her bag and held up her phone. "This thing has been buzzing like crazy since you made your little comment. Forget the fact that our marriage is a sham, but how dare you make a mockery of my work?"

"That's not what I was doing." Guilt hit him. She was right. They were getting a divorce as soon as it could be arranged. The fewer people who knew of their mistake the better. He'd been out of line to say anything.

"That's exactly what you were doing." She looked as if

she'd like to hit him, but instead just gritted her teeth and made a sound that was somewhere between a growl and a sigh.

"You're right," he agreed with sincerity and regret. "I shouldn't have said what I did. I'm sorry, Taylor."

That seemed to take the steam out of her argument, as if she hadn't expected him to apologize. Rather than say more she just rolled her eyes upward, her long lashes brushing the lenses of her heavy-framed glasses.

The elevator beeped and the door slid open. She practically ran out. Slade followed, his eyes never leaving her as she marched to her door, dug in her bag for her room key card, then slid the card into the slot. He got there just as she pushed open the door and went inside, not waiting for him.

Slade hesitated only a second, then caught the door before it closed, and went inside to try to repair the damage he'd done.

He wasn't very good at this husband thing.

Good thing he didn't plan to be one for long.

# CHAPTER THREE

TAYLOR GLANCED AROUND her hotel room and wanted to scream. Those weren't her things.

They were Slade's things.

Her blood boiled. How could he have been so stupid as to have announced that they'd married? She'd just wanted to have a quiet quickie divorce. She had not wanted anyone to know. Now everyone knew. Right before Christmas. Ugh.

She threw her bag down on her bed, wincing when she recalled her laptop was inside. She clicked on her phone to see who the latest text was from. Her parents? No doubt they'd hear of her latest "major life mistake" soon enough.

The text was from Nina. Great. Had her friend said anything to Gracie? She prayed not. No way did she want Gracie to know what an idiot she had for a mother.

Married in Vegas to a virtual stranger. Brilliant example she was setting for her impressionable young daughter. Shame on her. No doubt her parents would remind her of that over and over.

I just read that you married Slade Sain! Is that true? Hello, girlfriend, have you been holding out on me? I didn't know you two were an item and I'm your best friend!

"We need to talk."

Clutching her phone, Taylor spun at Slade's words. "You need to get out of my room."

"This is our room."

"Get out," she repeated.

"Taylor." He raked his fingers through his hair. "I'm sorry I messed up. You're right that I shouldn't have said anything. Unfortunately, I did and I can't take the words back."

"I didn't want anyone to know I married you!"

Something akin to hurt flickered across his face. "Not that I want to be married any more than you do, but am I such a loser that you're ashamed of me?"

Surprised that he sincerely looked offended, Taylor sank onto the foot of the bed and sighed. "This is crazy. I don't want to argue with you, Slade. I don't want to say hurtful things. I don't want you here. I don't want to be married to you. I don't want anyone to know. I don't want to face our colleagues at this dinner tonight, knowing that they're going to be watching us."

"That's a lot of 'I don't wants,'" he mused, his voice gentler than before. He knelt down on the floor in front of her. His eyes searched hers. "What is it you do want, Taylor?"

Although he wasn't touching her, his nearness made her insides tremble. Probably from disgust that she'd married him. "To forget this ever happened and to not be married to you of all people."

"Of all people? Ouch."

"I'm sorry if I'm wounding your ego, but don't pretend that it's anything more than that," she pointed out, wishing he'd move away from her. How was she supposed to not look at him when he was right there, kneeling in front of her? "Yes, we had sex together and it was good. But we aren't in love and we won't ever be. This was a mistake and what's worse is that it's now a public mistake." Oh, how she hated that anyone knew how big a mistake she'd made. "And above all else I don't want Gracie to find out."

Confusion furrowed his brows. "Who's Gracie?"

She might as well tell him. "My daughter."

Shock registered on his face and for a moment she thought his knees were going to give way. "You have a daughter?"

"Yes, I have a daughter." She snorted. Just as well Slade wasn't the man of her dreams, because his reaction to the news of Gracie would have killed any chance he had.

Face a little blanched, he shook his head. "You don't have a kid."

He sounded so confident in his immediate response that Taylor wanted to laugh. Only she wasn't feeling very amused at the moment. She was feeling crowded with him so close to her and annoyed at his reaction.

"Sure I do." She narrowed her gaze, hoping he'd take the hint at how much she disliked him. "Perhaps you noticed the stretch marks along my hips last night when we were…" Her cheeks heated. Crazy after the things they'd done the night before that she couldn't bring herself to say the word *sex*.

But whereas she was annoyed, his expression remained shocked. "You have a beautiful body, Taylor." His tone was as gentle as it had been before, but there was a dazed look to his eyes. "And no more stretch marks than other women have with fluctuations in weight of a few pounds."

He would know.

Ugh. She hated it that her mind went to him with other women. But, then, he did go through women just as fast as Kyle had, so why wouldn't her mind go there? He was a player. A player she had married and was going to divorce.

"Puh-lease." She didn't even attempt to hide her sarcasm. "I've given birth. I know my body changes. I don't know what game you're playing, but get real."

"You have a beautiful body, Taylor," he repeated, so matter-of-fact that something cracked deep inside even if his words only meant he hadn't really looked at her.

"The body of a woman who has had a baby. If you'd paid attention last night, you'd have realized that."

He ignored her snap, stood and paced across the room. When he turned to look at her, he didn't meet her eyes. "When?"

"Gracie is six."

The skin on his face pulled tight. His jaw worked back and forth in a slow grind. "The guy in medical school?"

She nodded and couldn't hold in her bitterness. How dared Slade look at her with accusation in his eyes? He had no right to judge her! "Give the man a prize. Of course he's Gracie's father. I told you he was the only man I'd ever been with."

"There are other ways women become mothers, Taylor," he pointed out, his voice level and patient, even though color stained his cheeks at her outburst. "A strong, successful woman like yourself may have decided to have a child and sought a fertility clinic, for all I know."

Strong, successful woman? Ha, what she really wanted to do at the moment was curl up into a ball and cry. How strong and successful was that?

"Because, like I've said, you don't know me. This just proves my point."

His jaw flexed again. "A point I tried to correct on numerous occasions, but you didn't want to let me know you."

"Of course I don't want to let you know me. You've ruined my life." She was crying now. She didn't want to cry, but from the moment he'd made his comment about his "wife" during their presentation and her phone had started vibrating in her bag, she'd wanted to cry. There was no more holding the tears back. Yep, strong and successful, that was so her. Just ask her parents.

"Please, don't cry, Taylor." He sounded almost as lost as she felt. "I want to make you smile, not cry."

The last thing she wanted was to cry in front of him, but she couldn't make the tears stop. She cried for her parents and how embarrassed they were going to be by her. Again. She cried for Gracie and how her mother's moment of stupidity would affect her. And she cried for herself, that she'd been so easily led astray after six years of living an exemplary life.

"Tell me what I can do to make things better."

"Go away," she immediately informed him.

He stared at her for long moments then gave a slight nod of his head. "I'm sorry I've upset you, Taylor. I'll go for now. I have a meeting at noon anyway, but I will be back later to change for dinner. I hope you'll be ready to talk, because whether we like it or not we are married, people do know and we need a game plan on how best to deal with this so that it has the least negative impact on both our lives."

"I heard a rumor today."

Slade winced. He should have known better than to answer the phone when he'd seen who was calling. "Hey, Dad."

"Is what I'm hearing true, son?"

"Depends on what you've been hearing."

"You married?"

How did he answer his father? The best man he'd ever known through and through. A man who cherished the bonds of marriage, a man who had lost his precious wife, Slade's mother, to cancer, and carried that bond still in his heart, despite the fact he'd remarried several years back to a good woman.

Slade couldn't lie to his father. "Guess some rumors are true."

Silence ticked over the phone line.

"Have to admit I'm surprised," his father said slowly. More silence. "She pregnant?"

Slade's face heated. Not that he could blame his father for asking. Everyone who really knew him knew he'd never planned to marry, that he had dedicated his life to medicine, to finding a cure for a disease he hated.

"Not that I know of. She does have a kid, though." Hadn't that one been a shocker? Not only had he married but he'd also become an instant father. Not that it really mattered. He wasn't likely to meet Taylor's daughter. They'd divorce, pretend as if none of this had ever happened, and that would be the end of their Vegas mistake.

Which was exactly what needed to happen, so why did the image of Taylor's tears flash through his mind and make him wish life was different? That he was different?

Then again, hadn't he learned at twelve years old that wishes didn't come true? If they did, his mother would still be alive because he'd wished more than any kid had ever wished. He was sure of it.

More silence.

"For a man who just got married, you don't sound very happy. You okay, son?"

Okay? Again, the image of Taylor's tear-streaked face popped into his mind. No, he wasn't okay. He'd married a woman he wanted physically, cared for as a person and whom he didn't want to damage emotionally. "I'm fine."

"You're not in some kind of trouble, are you?" Worry weighed heavily in his father's words. "This is just so un-expected."

Slade could almost laugh. "I'm not in trouble, Dad."

At least, not the kind his father meant.

"Well, then, congratulations."

Congratulations. Because he'd gotten married. And become a father. Why did his tie feel as if it was stran-gling him?

He couldn't even respond to his father's comment.

"She must be something special," his dad continued.

Images from the night before flashed through Slade's mind, images of sharing laughter with Taylor, of holding her hand as they'd climbed into the limo to leave the hotel, of kissing her in the back of the limo, of how his heart had pounded in his chest as he'd slid a ring onto her finger and promised to have and hold her forever...

Maybe he was in trouble, because as much as he didn't want to be married, didn't want to think about the fact she was a mother, he did want Taylor in his life.

If only she weren't so complicated. If only they hadn't gotten married.

"Taylor is special," he admitted, then realized just how much he'd revealed in his three softly spoken words.

"I'm glad to hear that. After your mother died you avoided getting close to anyone. I'm glad you've met someone worth the risk."

Slade's ribs threatened to crush the contents of his chest they constricted so tightly. He hadn't avoided getting close to anyone. He'd just made a conscious decision to dedicate his life to finding a cure for breast cancer. His father didn't understand that. Maybe no one could. But to Slade, doing all he could to prevent others from going through what his family had was his number-one life priority.

"Dad, I hate to cut you short." Not really a lie. He loved his father, enjoyed talking to him normally, just not today, not when he was reeling from the past twenty-four hours, from the fact he'd woken up with a wife and a kid. "But I'm on my way to my dream job interview with Grandview Pharmaceuticals." A dream job that would give him every opportunity of achieving his number-one life priority. "I'll give you a call next week when I'm back in Nashville."

"Hello, my darling, how was school today?" Taylor said into the phone to her daughter. The first rays of happiness were shining that day.

"Good," the most precious voice in the world answered. "Aunt Nina said I was very smart."

Although she was no blood relation, Gracie had called Taylor's best friend "Aunt" for as long as Taylor could remember.

"Aunt Nina is right. You are a smart girl. And a very pretty one."

Gracie giggled. "You always say that."

"Because it's true."

"I miss you, Mommy." Gracie's voice sounded somewhere between sad and pouty. Taylor could just picture her daughter's expression, see the sadness in the green eyes that were so similar to her own.

"I miss you, too." More than words could convey.

"When are you coming home?" Gracie demanded.

"I'll be flying home tomorrow evening. You and Aunt Nina are picking me up from the airport."

"Are you bringing me a prize? Aunt Nina said if I was good while you were gone that I'd get a present."

"Aunt Nina said that, did she? So close to Christmas? Well, I'm sure if she said that, then she's right."

Gracie talked to her a few minutes more, then handed the phone to Nina.

"She's something else, isn't she?" Nina immediately said into the phone.

"I hope she's not been too much trouble," Taylor told her best friend.

"Are you kidding me? I've loved having her here. She's helped me decorate my house and you know me, I'm one of those who never has things done the week after Thanksgiving. This year, I'm way ahead of the game, and she and I have had a blast getting everything done."

Taylor understood. Gracie was a blast and loved Christmas almost as much as her mother did. No doubt the little girl had garlands and lights strung all over Nina's apartment.

"Good. When they told me I would be going on this trip, my first thoughts were what I'd do about Gracie. I've never left her before."

"Are you sure your first thoughts weren't about getting an early Christmas package from a certain sexy oncologist?

Or perhaps the two of you just got carried away beneath some Vegas mistletoe?"

Taylor sighed. She had known Nina would ask about Slade. Especially since she hadn't answered a single text message from Nina or any of her other friends and colleagues. What was she supposed to say? *Yes, I messed up again. It's what I'm good at when it comes to the opposite sex.*

"You might as well tell me, because you know you're going to. Best friend, remember?"

"I remember."

"So what's up with you becoming Mrs. Dr. Sexy?"

Taylor winced. "Please tell me you didn't ask me that in front of Gracie."

"She's watching her favorite television program and is totally oblivious to what I'm saying."

"Don't count on it. She picks up on a lot more than people give her credit for."

"Fine, I'll walk into the kitchen." There was a short pause. "Now, tell me if what I read was true."

"It's true."

Nina squealed. "You and Dr. Sain got married? How romantic! Tell me everything."

"There wasn't anything romantic about it." Which wasn't exactly true. Drunk or not, he'd been sweet when he'd slid the wedding ring onto her finger, had lifted her hand and placed a kiss over the gold band. Just the memory goose-bumped her skin.

"You got married to the sexiest man we know and there wasn't anything romantic about it?"

She sank her teeth into her lower lip. "Not really."

"Which means there was at least something romantic going on," Nina concluded. "Hubba-hubba. This is huge. You got married. I can't believe it."

"That makes two of us."

"This is so unlike you. You're, like, never spontaneous. I

just…" Nina paused and Taylor could just imagine her friend shaking her head while she tried to make sense of what was being said. "So, tell me the details. How in the world did you and Dr. Sain get married?"

"A bunch of us had dinner, went to watch a Christmas show and then I ended up in a limo with Slade. We drove to a cheesy year-round Christmas wedding chapel and exchanged vows. Alcohol was involved."

Nina moaned. "Please tell me it wasn't a drive-through ceremony."

"It wasn't." Although if it had been, would it really have mattered? "Santa Claus married us."

"Santa?"

"An impersonator, but, yes, Santa. There were even elves snapping pictures and throwing fake snow at us." Ugh. Taylor rubbed her temple. "What am I going to do, Nina? I got married last night."

"Celebrate the fact that you married the hottest guy around and will be the envy of every female at the clinic?"

"I'm serious."

"Me, too. So, how was he?"

"Nina!"

"That good, huh?"

"That good," Taylor agreed, unable to lie. "Better than any man should be." Better than she'd thought any man could be. He'd set her body aflame and made her ache for more. "But I can't stay married to him."

"Why not?"

"We never should have gotten married in the first place. We were under the influence and made a huge mistake. Besides, he is about as opposite from what I want in a man as possible."

"You want ugly, not sexy and not good in bed?"

"You know what I mean." Would her temple please stop throbbing?

"Fine. I know what you mean, but you did get married.

Show a little more enthusiasm, please. Didn't you joke last year after Christmas that you should have asked Santa for a man? Well, girl, you must have been at the top of the nice list this year for Santa to have delivered Slade Sain."

She did recall joking with Nina that she should have asked Santa for a man. She didn't want to be alone, raising Gracie without a father. But she'd much rather that than to have let the wrong man into her life. She sighed.

"We're going to get a divorce just as soon as it can be arranged." She twisted the gold band on her left hand. Why hadn't she taken it off? Why did it feel seared to her very being?

"Too bad."

Taylor pulled back her phone to stare at it. "I can't believe you said that. I made a horrible mistake last night. Can you imagine what my parents are going to say?"

"Who cares what they say, Taylor? You can't keep trying to make up for disappointing them by getting pregnant out of wedlock. These are modern times. Women have kids without being married. You finished school and have made a great life for you and Gracie. If your parents can't see what a wonderful woman you are, then phooey on them."

In theory, Taylor knew her friend was right. In her heart, she hated to disappoint her parents again. They were devoutly religious, had the perfect marriage, couldn't understand how she'd let herself become pregnant out of wedlock and although they loved Gracie, they'd never let Taylor forget how disappointed they'd been.

"I know you, Taylor," Nina continued. "I'm not sure how you and Slade ended up married. There must have been some major Christmas magic in the air last night. But quit stressing and enjoy the rest of your honeymoon before planning your divorce. Reality will set in soon enough."

"I'm not on a honeymoon and reality set in first thing this morning."

"Technically, you are on your honeymoon," Nina pointed out. "You got married last night."

Taylor dropped backward onto the bed. "Crap. You're right. I'm so stupid."

"You're the least stupid person I know."

Taylor just groaned.

"Obviously, there was something between you two last night that triggered the 'I do's,'" Nina pointed out in her ever-optimistic way. "You married a superhot guy who you had really great sex with and now he's your husband. Why not quit worrying about the details and the pending legal 'I don't's and just enjoy your honeymoon?"

If only life were that easy. "You don't mean that."

"Why wouldn't I? You never do anything for yourself, Taylor. You're always working or doing things for Gracie. For the next twenty-four hours don't worry about anyone but yourself. The act is done. You're married and on your honeymoon with a hunk. Take advantage of that, of him and his skills. What's going to happen in the future is going to happen regardless of whether or not you grasp hold of what life's presented to you on a silver platter. Or, in this case, what Santa's wrapped up in a pretty bow. I say go for it, work off some long-overdue steam, and make some memories before going your separate ways."

Ugh. Her friend almost made sense. Almost. "You're not helping."

"Sure I am. I'm just not saying what your determined-to-be-a-prude ears want to hear."

"I hate it when you're right."

Nina squealed again. "So, you're going to do it? You're going to let your hair down and rock Dr. Sain's world?"

She wasn't so sure she could rock his world, but he had seemed to enjoy the night before. They had been hot.

"I'm not sure I know how to let loose anymore," she admitted, positive it was true. She enjoyed life, but all her free time did revolve around Gracie. "And I didn't say you were right that I should let my hair down. Just that what you were saying wasn't what I wanted to hear."

"You want me to tell you that you should hightail it back home and file for divorce without indulging in some fun with your husband first?"

File for divorce. Pressure squeezed her heart. People in her family didn't divorce. They didn't get pregnant out of wedlock and they didn't marry virtual strangers in Vegas and they didn't divorce. That was her family.

But she would be three for three because she would be filing for divorce. To pretend otherwise was ridiculous. She and Slade had suffered lapses of judgement, clouded by lust and alcohol. That much she could admit to. She'd wanted him last night. When he'd kissed her, she'd melted and forgotten everything but him.

"I'm waiting for an answer."

Taylor's grip on her cell phone tightened. "I'm a mother, Nina. Regardless of what I want, I can't just go around indulging in fun whenever I want to. It's not that I don't want to indulge in fun, because I do." Oh, how she wanted to imbibe more of Slade. "He was amazing. An affair with him would be amazing, but I need to end this without doing anything that might complicate things."

"Too late. Things are already complicated."

Taylor's gaze shot to the open hotel room door and the man who stood there. Crap. When had he opened the door and how much had he overheard?

"Sorry, Nina, but I've got to go." Her gaze latched on to Slade's and she refused to look away even when that's what she wanted to do. How was it he made her feel so on edge with just a look? "My husband just walked in."

# CHAPTER FOUR

FRUSTRATED, SLADE STARED at the woman lying on the bed. Clicking off her phone, Taylor slowly rose to a sitting position. Which was exactly where he'd left her.

She'd left the hotel room, though. He'd gone to a presentation, had sensed her sneaking into the meeting room and had turned to catch her sliding into a seat in the back of the auditorium. When the meeting had ended, he'd glanced her way. She'd been gone.

He'd forced himself to go to all the programs he'd marked on his agenda, even though he'd had a difficult time staying focused on what the presenters had been saying. At noon, he'd had an interview with Grandview Pharmaceuticals, the company that owned Interallon and that was renowned for their headway in the fight against cancer.

John Cordova, the older man who'd interviewed him, had commented on how they needed someone dependable, someone able to make long-term commitments, to see things through, to fill the position. The man had then congratulated him on his recent marriage.

Slade had withheld the fact that his marriage wasn't a long-term commitment but a mistake. He'd gotten the impression that a divorce so quickly following his marriage wouldn't have won him any brownie points in Cordova's eyes.

His phone call with his father played through his head.

His father was going to be so disappointed in him when he told him the truth.

His temple throbbed ever so slightly. He found himself wishing he could lie on the bed beside Taylor, talk to her about the interview, about his goals and dreams, about his mother and how much he missed her, about the concern in his father's voice and how he hadn't had the heart to tell him that his marriage was over before it even started either. He wanted to talk with her the way they had the night before because talking to her, being with her, had felt so right.

Too bad Taylor was staring at him as if he were a serial killer.

Last night had been different. When she'd looked at him, he'd seen something more. That something more had triggered some kind of insanity. She'd wanted to have sex with him, and that knowledge had shot madness into his veins. She'd challenged him with her condition about marriage and, gazing into her eyes, he'd lost his mind and the ability to walk away from the temptation she'd offered.

He had the feeling that before all was said and done, his insanity was going to cost him a lot more than he'd bargained for.

She cleared her throat, reminding him that he had been staring at her for way too long.

"I need to change for the dinner program."

A semiformal conference farewell that was more socializing than anything else.

"That's fine." She watched him from behind her big glasses, which he'd really like to lift off her face so he could better read her expression.

"Not really, but I guess for the next day we don't have a choice. The hotel is sold out and I don't plan to move to another hotel."

She nodded as if she'd already known. Perhaps she'd called the front desk and asked.

Slade had never been an awkward kind of person. Usually, he could come up with something funny to say, something to smooth over any situation. This wasn't any ordinary situation, though. This was him standing in a hotel room with his wife, whom he didn't want to be his wife and neither did she want to be his wife.

He raked his fingers through his hair then, shrugged.

"I'll just grab my suit and change." He opened the closet door and removed a garment bag. "I'll hurry in the bathroom so I won't interfere with you getting ready. If you're going, that is."

"I'm going."

He nodded and turned toward the bathroom.

"With you."

He paused, but didn't turn around. "Why?"

"As far as the world is concerned, we're happy newlyweds. If we go separately, we'll have to answer too many questions. I don't know about you, but I've dealt with enough questions about our marriage already today."

Slade looked up at the ceiling, counted to ten, then turned. "That's my fault. I'm sorry. You're right. I prefer not to raise questions, but even if we're together, people are going to be curious."

"You're right, but at least if we're together we can keep our story straight."

"I won't lie to anyone who asks about us."

"You're going to tell people that you married me so you could have sex with me?"

When she said it out loud, he agreed the reason sounded ridiculous. Still…

"Isn't that why most men get married?" he said, fighting to keep his tone light. "Because they want to have sex with the woman they are marrying? I definitely want to have sex with you, Taylor."

"I suppose so," she responded, ignoring his last comment. "Or we could just tell them that we were drunk and didn't realize what we were doing."

He certainly hadn't been thinking clearly, but he distinctly recalled exchanging vows with her, promising to care for her forever, to cherish her and yet they were planning to end things before they'd even got started.

He stared at her, wishing he could read whatever was running through that sharp mind of hers. "Shall we tell them we married because we were drunk or because we wanted to have sex?"

Her gaze darted about the room as if seeking the answer somewhere within the four walls. Finally, she shrugged. "Take your pick. Both are true."

Taylor pulled her dress out of the closet. Her gaze settled on Slade's clothes hanging next to hers.

Other than her father, she'd never lived with a man, so seeing the mix of Slade's belongings with hers had her pausing, had her eyes watering up again.

What an emotional roller coaster she rode.

Her safe, secure world felt as if it was crumbling around her.

She'd quit taking chances years ago. Had quit living in some ways. Oh, she lived through Gracie, but what about for herself? Nina was right. She didn't do anything for herself, just lived in a nice controlled environment where she planned for all contingencies.

Too bad she hadn't had a backup plan for an unexpected Vegas Christmas wedding.

While Slade was in the bathroom, she changed into her dress, took her hair down from its tight pin-back and pulled it up into a looser hold. She had her contacts in her purse, but wasn't sure what it would say if she put them in when she almost always wore her glasses.

How ridiculous was she being? What did it matter what she looked like?

Still, she dug in her purse and put in her contacts. She

was just blinking them into place when Slade stepped out of the bathroom.

Wearing only his suit pants.

Taylor's body responded to his bare chest like a Pavlov dog to its stimulus. The man was beautiful.

And hers.

Not for long, but at this moment Slade Sain was hers more than any other man had ever been.

Just as she was his more than any other woman had ever been his.

Maybe.

She frowned because she really didn't know that to be true. "Have you been married before?"

Her question obviously caught him off guard. "No. Why? Have you? Never mind, silly question with that one-guy thing. You haven't."

"No, I haven't," she agreed, averting her gaze from his intense blue one. "I just wondered if you had."

Despite the tension between them, he grinned with wry humor. "Wondering if I make marrying a habit?"

Exactly. "Something like that."

He slipped his crisp blue shirt on one arm at a time, then buttoned his cuffs. "I've never been married before." He paused, stared at her with a serious look. "I've never even contemplated marriage."

Her feet wanted to shuffle but she somehow kept them still. "Why not?"

Smoothing out his shirt, he shrugged. "I have other plans for my life besides a wife, two point five kids and a white picket fence."

Her chest spasmed at just how different they really were, because once upon a time she'd dreamed of being a wife with kids and that proverbial white picket fence. "I'm sorry."

"Don't be. We're human and made a mistake. People do it all the time."

He wasn't telling her anything she didn't know. So why

did his words shoot arrows into her chest? "Not me. Not like this." She winced. "I mean, obviously I have made mistakes before, but I thought I'd learned better than to make this kind."

"Marrying me makes you realize you haven't evolved as far as you'd hoped?"

"Something like that. We were practically strangers and got married." Sighing, she closed her eyes. "Before last night you probably didn't even know my eye color."

"I knew."

His answer was so quick, so confident, that she couldn't question the truth of his response.

Staring at him, she asked, "How?"

He shoved his hands in his pants pockets. "I know more about you than you seem to think."

"Like what?"

"Like how much you love coffee."

She rolled her eyes. "Lots of people love coffee, so that's just a generic assumption that could be said about a high percentage of the population."

He shook his head. "You like two teaspoons of cream and one packet of sweetener."

She frowned. That was how she took her coffee. For a moment he had her, but she hadn't made it through medical school by being easily duped. "You saw me make my coffee this morning."

"You're right," he agreed, walking back to the closet to pick up his sleek black dress shoes. "I did. But I already knew how you took your coffee because I make a point to be near the lounge when you go for your morning cup at eight forty-five every day."

That he knew what time she took a coffee break was a little uncanny. Maybe she was more easily duped than she'd realized.

"What else do you know?"

"That you smile a lot at work. That your patients love you. That Mr. Gonzales has a crush on you."

"Mr. Gonzales has a crush on every female who works at the clinic," she pointed out about one of her favorite patients. The older man came in weekly for his lung-cancer treatments and the staff adored him.

"You're his favorite."

"Maybe." She watched Slade sit on the bed and slip on his socks, then his shoes. "What else?"

He lowered his foot back to the carpet but remained seated on the bed. Good. She didn't want him towering over her. "Blue is your favorite color. Not a regular blue, a turquoise blue."

"How would you know that?"

"Because you wear that color more than any other."

He knew what she wore? Why would he have noticed her clothes? Especially since she usually had her lab coat on over whatever she wore?

"You're starting to creep me out a little."

"Surely you noticed that I'd been trying to get to know you for months. I start a conversation and you end it with a few words. I walk up to you and you walk off. I ask you out, you say no."

Of course she'd said no. He wasn't her type.

"You talk to all the women at the clinic," she pointed out.

"I talk to everyone at the clinic. Not just the women."

"True, but you're a horrible flirt."

He looked amused. "I've never made any bones about the fact that I enjoy women but that I have no intentions of settling down. I wanted to take you out, for us to enjoy our time together, and then us both move on to what we really want in life."

Taylor gulped. He sounded so much like Kyle…only Kyle had never been so honest with her, had never told her that he'd been seeing other women, that she hadn't been special. Quite the opposite. He'd made her believe she'd been his one and only.

"I date, Taylor, and I have flirted with women in the past. But for however long it takes for our lawyers to sort out this mess, I will be faithful to you. You have my word on that."

Something in his voice rang of truth, but she couldn't think straight for the heat flushing her face.

"I wasn't… I mean… I haven't slept with a man for over six years so it's a safe bet to say that for however long we're married I'll be faithful to you as well."

From his seat on the bed, he stared at her. "You're a young, beautiful woman, Taylor. Why is it that you've not had sex in six years?"

She gave him a classic "duh" look. "Because I have Gracie."

Obviously, he knew nothing about raising a six-year-old girl, about being a good mother, about trying to live up to her parents' expectations of her to be a responsible woman. Apparently.

"Being a mother doesn't make you less of a woman, Taylor. Or make you have fewer physical needs."

"Being a mother means I have to make responsible decisions because my choices don't just affect me, but her as well." With each word she said, bits of her carefully constructed facade crumbled. "She's not going to understand that I got married while in Vegas."

"Don't tell her."

Taylor bit the inside of her lower lip. He was right. She could just not tell Gracie. She and Slade would divorce and her daughter would never know the difference. Only her daughter really did have big ears. What if Gracie found out and *she* hadn't been the one to tell her?

She didn't begin to fool herself that her parents wouldn't find out. They'd be so disappointed. Again. Not that they didn't love Gracie, but that Taylor had once again not followed their norm would earn another tsk from her mother and another sigh from her father.

"What if Gracie overheard something or someone else told her? That wouldn't be fair to her."

His expression was pinched. "I'm sure you know best."

"Clearly not."

"Or you wouldn't have married me?" His tone held wry humor.

"I'm sure for other women and under different circumstances, a woman marrying you wouldn't be considered a bad thing. But not me."

Sliding his hands into his pants pockets, he frowned. "Why not?"

Seriously? He was asking her why not? The man was the office playboy and she was the quiet mouse.

"You have to admit you aren't exactly daddy material."

Daddy material. Not that Slade wanted to be daddy material, but Taylor's words stung. So, he had absolutely no experience being a father and had no desire to learn. That didn't mean he'd be a bad one. Every guy started somewhere.

For her to judge him so unfairly irked.

"Has it occurred to you that I could already have a child on the way?"

Her face paled to an icky green shade. "We made more than one mistake last night, didn't we?"

Slade's chest threatened to turn inside out. His heart pounded and his throat constricted at the ramifications of what they were discussing. "If you are pregnant, Taylor, I'll take care of you and our child."

Taylor surprised him by sinking onto the bed beside him. "Gracie is the best thing that ever happened to me, but I don't want another kid, Slade. Not like this."

Which meant she did want more kids someday. No doubt she was a wonderful mother. Too bad he didn't want a wife and kids because he couldn't imagine anyone better than Taylor.

He sighed at how different they were tonight with each other compared to the previous night. The night before they'd both been carefree, full of lust and passion for each other.

"I wish we could go back to last night."

"Why?" she whispered from beside him. Why she whispered he wasn't sure, but somehow her low voice seemed exactly right.

"Last night I wasn't your enemy."

Her head fell forward and she stared at her hands, no doubt at the shiny thin band on her left hand. With the way she felt, why was she still wearing the cheap strip of gold?

"You aren't my enemy, Slade."

Her words should have comforted him, but her tone wasn't complimentary.

"You're right," he conceded. "I'm your husband. That's worse."

"I'm sorry." She sounded as if she truly was.

"Tell me, Taylor, would things have been different this morning if we'd had sex without getting married?"

She shrugged. "I don't think I would have had sex without marriage. Not really. After I got pregnant with Gracie, and Kyle signed away his rights, I vowed I wouldn't give myself to another man unless he married me first." She toyed with the gold band on her finger, then stood and walked across the room, turning to look at where he sat. "Foolishly, I equated marriage as being loved truly and completely." She laughed a little, but there wasn't any real humor in the sound. She spread her arms and gave a smile that was more sad than anything else. "Look at me now, desperate for a divorce less than twenty-four hours after getting married. Guess that old saying about being careful what you wish for definitely applies in this case."

Slade couldn't bear the self-condemnation that shone in

her eyes. He crossed the room to stand in front of her. He knew better than to take her in his arms, although that's exactly what he wanted to do. Instead, he traced his finger along her hairline, then cupped her chin. Her eyes, unfettered by her glasses, glittered up at him like big and beautiful emeralds.

Guilt hit him. She wanted exactly the opposite from life. She wanted that white picket fence and two point five kids. Instead, she was married to him.

"I am looking, Taylor. I see a woman who fascinates me, a woman who is strong and good and beautiful. A woman who turns me on and makes my blood boil. We aren't enemies. We made a mistake in getting married, but we're in agreement on ending the marriage. Our mistake is a fixable one." Did he really believe his own words? He wasn't sure. He just didn't want their mistake ruining her life. "I want to spend the evening with you without what happened last night as a barrier between us. Even if just for tonight."

She considered him a few moments, emotions playing across her face. "Just for tonight? Pretend that everything is okay? Why?"

"Why not? What do we have to lose by putting forward a united front? We both want a divorce. We're on the same page. Why suffer through the evening alone when even despite our emotional turmoil the physical is still booming between us?"

She blinked up at him. "It's what Nina said I should do... I want to, Slade, but... Okay."

A flicker of emotion he couldn't label burned to life within him. Crazy because the last thing he needed was to get more entangled with Taylor. A voice in his head reminded him that he was married to her. How much more entangled could one get?

# CHAPTER FIVE

SLADE WAS THE perfect date. Maybe because he was trying so hard. Taylor knew he was trying and appreciated the effort he was exerting to make her evening as stress-free as possible, especially when she knew he wasn't any happier about their current circumstances than she was.

The meal had been the usual conference menu of a spinach salad, slightly rubbery chicken, green beans and potatoes. For dessert, they'd had a key lime pie that had been quite good.

The final speech of the conference had finished and now the attendees were mingling, with a few heading onto the dance floor and others to the main section of the hotel to gamble.

"You guys want to come with us to the blackjack table?" Dr. Ryan joined the conversation they'd been having with a couple of oncologists from Gainesville, Florida.

Slade's gaze connected with hers and she shook her head.

"Sorry, bud," Slade told his colleague. "But Taylor and I won't be doing any gambling tonight. I was just about to take her out onto the dance floor."

The dance floor? Taylor wanted to protest, but Cole Ryan was watching her reaction a bit too closely so she just smiled.

"Ha, marriage is a gamble every night," Dr. Ryan joked as Slade took Taylor's hand and led her from the group.

"I never knew he had such a sour disposition regarding marriage," Taylor mused, trying to focus on the other man and not on how good it felt for Slade to be holding her hand, on how her heart was racing at his nearness, at how her skin burned at his touch.

"Perhaps it's only your marriage to me that sours his disposition."

Taylor frowned. "You think he…? No, I mean he asked me out once, but that was a long time ago. We just didn't hit it off that way."

"That way?" Slade's face darkened and if Taylor didn't know better she'd think he was jealous. But that made no sense. They had no real ties to each other, only plans to divorce as soon as possible.

"You know, like…" She paused. She'd been going to say like she and Slade had because the biggest problem she'd had with Cole Ryan had been that there had been no sparks. Otherwise he'd been a decent guy who had met most of the criteria on her Mr. Right list.

Slade had the sparks covered and then some. Right now, with her hand in his as he led her onto the dance floor, she knew exactly how they'd ended up where they had the night before. When he touched her, fireworks went off inside her body. Last night he'd had the whole Fourth of July show exploding within her.

She swallowed, willed her body to not give in to its carnal reactions to Slade, to focus on anything but the fire between them.

Dinner had gone well. He'd had intelligent conversations with the other people at their table, had included her, asked her opinions, and sat back and let her give those opinions with admiration in his eyes. He'd been attentive, pulling out her chair, touching her frequently, smiling at her often. When an overly pompous member of their table had gone on and on about the latest article he'd written about the denucleation of a cloned T-cell, they'd shared a look that had spoken volumes without saying a word, because they'd known what the other had been thinking. His wink had reached inside her and touched something tender.

If she hadn't known he was Dr. Slade Sain, playboy extraordinaire, if she hadn't made the mistake of marrying him, she might think he was someone she would like to date. Which was kind of silly since she was already married to him. And he *was* Dr. Slade Sain, playboy extraordinaire.

He'd said he'd be faithful for however long they were married. An easy promise since they planned to talk to divorce attorneys as soon as they returned home. Still, tonight, at this moment, it was easy to pretend that their attraction was special, that the future was full of wonderful possibilities.

What was it Nina had said? To let loose and enjoy herself? That she was married to a hunk so why not enjoy it for the rest of their Vegas stay? To worry about tomorrow... tomorrow.

Slade pulled her into his arms and, her arms around him, she buried her face into the curve of his neck. He smelled so good. So perfectly male.

He was perfectly male. His body. His mind. His sense of humor.

She wanted to cry. She wanted to forget who she was and who she had to be. She wanted to be that woman Nina had told her to be, even if only until she had to fly home tomorrow evening.

Slade drew back and looked down at her. "You okay?"

She nodded and toyed with where his hair brushed the back of his collar. "This pretend stuff isn't so bad."

One corner of his mouth lifted. "Agreed. You are very beautiful, Taylor. No pretending."

Her breath caught because he looked at her as if she were the most beautiful woman he'd ever seen. How could he look at her that way? As if she was the only woman who existed?

"Thank you. You aren't bad yourself." She attempted to lighten the heavy longing clouding her good intentions.

"If you could read my mind, you'd think every thought in my head was bad."

"Oh?"

He shook his head.

"You can't say something like that and then not tell me what you were thinking."

"Says who?"

"Me."

His lips twitched. "I'm thinking that perhaps holding you in my arms in public wasn't such a good idea, because having you pressed against my body makes me respond in a very nonpublic way."

"I noticed that."

"Kinda hard to miss."

"Did you say hard?"

His mouth was close to hers. So very close. "Isn't this about the point in our conversation where we got into trouble last night?"

"The point where we started being suggestive?" she whispered against his lips. For twenty-four hours she could let go and just be a woman who was with a man who turned her on, a woman who was with a man who wanted her.

"The point where I wanted you so badly I couldn't think of anything else but having you."

"There's only one problem." She stared into his eyes, seeing passion and something so intense it stole her breath. For twenty-four hours he was hers. Twenty-four hours and what they did wouldn't change anything. Twenty-four hours and then they'd return to reality.

"What's that?"

"I won't sleep with anyone who isn't my husband."

"And your husband?" he breathed against her lips. "You'll sleep with him?"

"Sleep? If you think we will be sleeping anytime soon, then you aren't nearly as turned on as I am."

He kissed her. Right there on the dance floor his mouth covered hers for a gentle kiss that was so potent it demanded everything she had yet gave so much more.

When he pulled back, he leaned his forehead against hers. "If we do this, nothing changes between us. We'll still end this as soon as possible. You know that, right?"

Taylor was pretty sure all that could change between them already had. They couldn't ever go back to the way things had been. With the way he was looking at her, she didn't want to. Tomorrow night they'd be back in Tennessee, reality would take over and they'd never have this moment again.

Nothing would ever be the same and if she thought about it that would terrify her.

So, instead, she clasped her hands with his and told him with her eyes what she wanted.

The night before they'd been frantic for each other.

Now, back in their hotel room, Taylor felt just as frantic, but was enjoying Slade's slow stripping of her way too much to urge him to go faster.

She wavered between eyes closed in ecstasy and open to view the fantasy of his caresses. She watched him in the dresser mirror. He stood behind her, his hand on her dress, his other at her waist as he slowly slid her zipper down her back. His mouth trailed kisses in the wake of exposed skin, causing goose bumps along her spine that scattered outward in pleasured awareness of his gentle caress.

He reached the curve of her spine and slid his hands beneath the silky material. "You aren't wearing a bra."

"There was no need. The dress has built-in support."

"Lucky dress to be next to these." His hands were now on her bare breasts, covering them, cupping them as he straightened to kiss her shoulder. His gaze met hers in the mirror as his lips spread more kisses along her nape. "Very lucky dress, but it's got to go."

He maneuvered the material to where it fell to her waist, then slipped the dress over her hips to leave her standing in her black lace panties.

His body pressed against her from behind, he examined her reflection. "You are so beautiful, Taylor."

"Don't look too close or you'll see my many flaws," she half teased, self-conscious of the changes pregnancy had left on her body. She didn't have a lot of stretch marks, true, but she did have them.

Slade spun her, knelt in front of her and brushed his lips over the small silvery streaks that marred her abdomen near her right hip.

"You are beautiful. All of you," he praised, his lips moving to her left side and kissing the tiny silver lines there.

Taylor shuddered, her hands going to his shoulders as her knees threatened to buckle.

Weak as water. She'd heard the expression used in the past but had never really understood the term until this moment. Her legs were weak as water, threatening to let her spill to the floor in a gooey gush.

His tongue traced over her belly, darting into her belly button. His hands molded her to him, helping to support her.

He moved higher up her belly, causing her breath to suck in as his face brushed against her breasts.

She closed her eyes and just felt. She felt every touch, every caress, every move of his body against hers.

She felt every emotion, every ounce of passion, every demand for more.

When she could stand no more of his sweet, torturous foreplay, she tugged on his shoulders. "Please, Slade. Please!"

He stood, took her mouth with his, and kissed her so hard that she thought they might always stay that way, that their locked lips knew something far beyond what their minds did, that they belonged together.

Not breaking their kiss, he lifted her. She wrapped her legs around his waist, not liking that his pants were in the way, not liking that he was still so dressed when she was so naked.

When he lowered her onto their bed, breaking their kiss, she immediately tugged his shirt free from his waistband. "I want to touch you."

"Good." His breathing was heavy. "I want you to touch me."

"I mean now. Before. I want to touch you the way you touched me."

His hands stilled from where he'd been unbuttoning his shirt. "I'm all yours."

Taylor sneaked a peek at the man sitting in the airplane seat next to her. He'd offered the guy who had originally had the seat a hundred dollars to swap and the guy had traded without hesitation. Currently, Slade's nose was buried in the program he was reading on his computer tablet.

"Quit looking at me like that."

"Sorry." Heat flushed her face. "Like what?"

"Like you are trying to dissect me."

"Sorry. That wasn't my intention."

Slade clicked a button on the tablet, closing the program he'd been reading, then turned to her. "What was your intention?"

"Pardon?"

"Why were you looking at me just then?"

"I…I don't know."

"Yes, you do. Tell me."

"That's ridiculous."

"You were thinking about this weekend, about all the things that happened between us, and you were wondering about what's going to happen once this plane lands," he supplied for her.

"You're wrong."

His brow arched.

"At least, partially. I was thinking about this weekend and what happened between us, but I already know what's going to happen once this plane lands."

He waited.

"Nina and my daughter will be waiting to pick me up. I'll go home with them. You and I will get divorced and will forget this weekend ever happened."

He digested her words for a few minutes, seeming to accept her prediction. His lips thinned to a straight line. "Except for the whole getting-married thing, I don't regret this weekend, Taylor."

Her heart fluttered at his words, but she tried not to read too much into his comment. Did she regret the weekend? The past twenty-four hours had been amazing. Waking up in his arms and making love first thing this morning, then again in the shower before they'd checked out of the hotel had been amazing. Dealing with the ramifications of what they'd done at the North Pole Christmas Bliss Wedding Chapel was what wasn't so amazing.

She tried not to touch her ring. She failed.

"We were in Vegas. People do silly things in Vegas. We'll be home soon and the best thing we can do is forget any of this ever happened," she whispered, even though she seriously doubted any of the surrounding passengers could hear their conversation.

"I basically agree. A wife and kid aren't on my agenda, but I'll admit—" he gave her a sexy grin "—you're going to be hard to forget."

Not nearly as hard as it was going to be to forget him.

"Maybe we could still see each other occasionally," he suggested.

Oh, how he tempted her. But to delay the inevitable would only complicate an already bad situation even further.

"We had a fun little fling this weekend, but when this plane lands everything goes back to normal. I'm a single mother with a very busy schedule. I just don't have the time or inclination for an affair with you."

"We're not exactly having an affair," he pointed out. "We're married."

"A marriage we both want ended as soon as possible. Santa Claus married us in a building that looked like a life-sized gingerbread house. Elves sold us our rings, took our picture, witnessed the ceremony. Who knows if our certificate is even real? It's probably not since it was issued after normal business hours."

Guilt hit her. She sounded crude and uncaring. But, really, what did he expect? They didn't even know each other. Not beyond the physical. That she knew quite well. She'd saved every pore on his body to memory because she'd known she'd want to pull out the memories and relive them.

"It's something to have our lawyers look into. If it's not real that would certainly simplify things.

"I don't get that lucky," she mused, thinking how great it would be if their wedding turned out to not be a legally binding union.

He took her hand into his. "You're right. Our wedding ceremony being a sham would be in both of our best interests."

She'd just said the same thing. So why did hearing him say the words cut into her chest? Make her want to hold on to his hand all the tighter?

She might have only spent two nights in his arms, but part of her felt he was hers. No doubt her feelings were just associations to the phenomenal sex they'd had. Women had been associating great sex with emotions for centuries. He'd done great things to her body in bed and out of bed. Of course she'd feel possessive of him.

What was she thinking? She wasn't thinking, that was the problem. That had been the problem all weekend.

"Physically, I still want you, Taylor. I'd like to see you again."

Physically, she still wanted him, too, but she couldn't afford an affair with Slade. "I've more to think about than just myself."

"Your daughter?"

"Yes. Gracie is my whole world. I won't expose her to this mess I've created."

"I'm really not interested in meeting your daughter or becoming a part of your day-to-day life."

"Just in meeting up with me for sex?"

"I guess that makes me sound like a jerk," he admitted, and she wasn't going to argue with him. He sounded exactly as she'd known all along.

"It doesn't make you sound like someone I want to invest more time in."

"I guess I understand that, considering you do have a kid." The look on his face said he didn't really. Or maybe it was just the prospect of her being a mother that caused the look of disgust. "I'm being selfish in that I want you in my life still."

"Just without the entanglements of marriage and my daughter?"

His grin was self-deprecating. "There I go sounding like a jerk again."

"I'll contact a lawyer and we'll divorce quietly. We both know it was a mistake, that we can chalk this weekend up to a great sexual adventure, and we can go about undoing our mistake in a completely civil way."

He studied her a moment, then nodded. "I guess you're right. I just…"

"You just what?"

"I enjoyed our time together."

His words struck deep inside her.

"That makes two of us," she admitted. She'd had such high hopes that someday she would find the right man, would marry and have a happy little family. The house, white picket fence, children, happiness.

"Seems a little sad when we are so physically compatible," Slade interrupted her thoughts.

"Perhaps." A lot sad, really. "But better we be logical and end this now than risk things getting messier."

He took her hand into his, laced their fingers and traced over her skin with his thumb. "Things would only get messier if we let them. As long as we knew the score, that we weren't long term, we could give each other great pleasure."

Taylor sighed. If Gracie hadn't been involved, she might give in to the temptation deep within her. But her daughter was involved. Gracie needed stability. Not a mother who ran out and got married in Vegas to the office playboy, planned to divorce him but wanted to keep having sex with him until the divorce was final. Slade made her act out of character, made her behave rashly. She owed it to Gracie, to her daughter's future and well-being, to make responsible choices.

Having an affair with Slade wouldn't be responsible.

"Therein lies the problem. I don't want to continue this in hopes it wouldn't get messier." When he started to interrupt her, she rushed on. "Admittedly, it would be a pleasurable mistake but a mistake all the same. We were in Vegas and got caught up in the silliness. Let's end things now while we can still be civil to each other and this, hopefully, won't ruin our ability to work in the same clinic together. I really like my job and don't want to have to look for something else."

"Mommy!" Arms spread wide, a pint-size fairy princess ran toward Taylor. "I missed you."

The moment she was off the escalator that led down to the airport's baggage area Taylor knelt down to her daughter's level and scooped her into her arms. She kissed the top of Gracie's head, breathing in the fresh baby-shampoo scent of her blond curls. "I missed you, too!"

"You shouldn't go away for so long ever again," Gracie scolded.

"It was only three nights."

"That's too long."

Three nights in which a lifetime of changes had taken place because as much as she told herself she would put the weekend's events behind her, it wouldn't be that simple. If only.

She hugged Gracie tightly. "You're right. That was way too long to be away from my best girl."

"I'm your only girl," Gracie reminded her with a giggle. "Aunt Nina and I put up her Christmas tree and she let me hang the ornaments and a stocking with my name on it. Do you think Santa will leave my presents at Aunt Nina's house?"

"Maybe Santa will leave you a present at Aunt Nina's, too, but Santa knows where to leave your presents." Taylor squeezed her daughter and kissed the top of her head again. Emotion clogged her throat at how much this talkative little girl meant to her. "That's some outfit you have going there."

Taylor raised her gaze to Nina.

"What can I say?" Nina smiled and shrugged. "She wanted to be a fairy princess. Who am I to deny her inner princess?"

"I am a fairy princess," Gracie corrected Taylor's best friend and nurse, then redirected her attention to her mother. "Aunt Nina wouldn't wear her princess clothes because she thought she might get 'rested, but I think mine are beautiful." Gracie spun as if to prove her point, curtsied, then snuggled back to where her mother still crouched down.

"Oh?" Taylor arched a brow at her friend, smothering a laugh at the mental image of Nina wearing a fairy-princess outfit in the Nashville airport.

"I figured someone would call airport security if I came

in dressed like a cartoon princess," Nina admitted, gesturing to her jeans. "I tried to convince Gracie I was a princess in disguise, but she wasn't buying it."

"Princesses don't wear jeans when they're in disguise," Gracie reported matter-of-factly, her fingers going to Taylor's hair and twining beneath the pulled-back strands. Playing with Taylor's hair was something Gracie had started as a baby while nursing and something she reverted to almost always if she was in Taylor's lap or snuggled up next to her. Taylor treasured the bond with her daughter and dropped another kiss to her forehead.

"Did you bring me a present from Vegas?"

Taylor's stomach plummeted. Gracie's present. How could she have forgotten Gracie's present? She'd even mentioned to Slade this morning that she needed to stop by one of the hotel's many gift shops and pick out something special for her daughter. Instead, she'd gotten wet and wild with him in the shower and completely forgotten.

She stared into her daughter's wide expectant green eyes. Oh, yeah, she'd been irresponsible this weekend, had been a big disappointment to her child and would be mailing off her application for Worst Mom in the History of the World later this week. Yet another reason why ending things with Slade was the right decision. He made her forget things she'd never have forgotten otherwise. "I—"

"I think this is for you."

Taylor almost toppled over at the sound of Slade's voice. They'd purposely parted at the gate. He hadn't wanted to meet Gracie any more than she'd wanted him to. He'd leaned in, kissed her cheek and told her he'd had a great time, minus the whole wedding thing. She'd laughed, nodded and ducked into the bathroom to hide the moisture that had stung her eyes.

Still in a kneeling position, she glanced up at where he stood, his overnight bag draped across his shoulder, his clothes impeccable, not looking at all as if he'd been on a plane for several hours. He held a fuzzy stuffed bear wearing a pink tutu and a glitzy pink crown on her head.

Where had he gotten that? One of the Nashville airport gift shops? Had to be. He'd been at her side at the Vegas airport.

His face was pale and yet had pink splotches on his cheeks as he stared at her daughter. He eyed her as if she might morph into a monster and devour him any moment.

Gracie, never one to be too shy, spotted the bear and grinned with excitement. "I think you're right."

Her tone sounded so mature, so confident that had it not been Slade holding the bear, had he not been looking in such a shell-shocked and leery way at the little girl, Taylor would have laughed at her daughter's expression and words. Instead, all she could think was that she wanted to grab Gracie and run far away from him.

Which made no sense.

She didn't need to protect her daughter from Slade. Yet that's exactly the instinct that rose to the surface. Not that there was any need. He looked ready to bolt at any second. He should have stayed away.

"Hello, Dr. Sain," Nina greeted him, looking quite intrigued. "I hear congratulations are in order."

Taylor wanted to kick her friend, but had to settle for a warning look. Gracie's fingers left her hair and moved to hold Taylor's hand as she eagerly eyed the bear.

"Thanks," he answered, some color coming back to his face. Regaining his composure, he flashed a smile that would weaken many a female knee.

Good thing Taylor was already kneeling down because her knees wobbled.

Gracie felt her shift and frowned at her. "Mommy, are you okay?"

Not really, but she couldn't tell her daughter that because Gracie would want to know what was wrong. What could she say? That she'd spent the past two days having wild Vegas sex with this man, her husband, but now she just wanted to go back to her ordinary life and forget anything out of the ordinary had happened?

Was that what she wanted? What she really wanted? Or did she want something more? Something that made no logical sense whatsoever? Something he'd never give her and so she didn't dare even think it? If she'd had the slightest doubt, seeing his reaction to Gracie would have reconfirmed that he wasn't right for them.

"Mommy is fine, Princess Gracie." This came from Nina, who apparently took pity on Taylor's inability to talk. "She's just had a long flight home from Vegas and is a little tired."

When no one made a move, Gracie gestured toward the bear that an also silent Slade still held. "Did my mommy bring that for my present?"

Perhaps she wasn't the only one struck speechless because, despite the smile he'd flashed, Slade just stared at Gracie as if he'd never seen a kid before, then tentatively held out the bear to her.

First getting a nod from Taylor, Gracie took the bear and cuddled it. "Thank you. I love her. I'm going to call her Vegas, Princess Vegas, because she came all the way in an airplane to live with me."

Slade opened his mouth, probably to tell Gracie the truth, that he'd bought the bear in a Nashville gift shop, but Nina stopped him.

"Gracie, that's a really cool name for a really cool bear. Can I see her?"

Gracie hugged the bear, but then showed it to Nina, pointing out a tiny pink bejeweled necklace on the toy.

"Thank you." Taylor finally found words as she straightened.

His gaze shifted to Gracie.

Taylor cast a nervous glance toward her daughter, who was still busy checking out the bear with Nina. Her friend was trying to look as if she wasn't paying attention to Taylor and Slade, but was, no doubt, soaking up every word.

His expression was serious. His blue eyes dark and intense. "I felt responsible for you not having her gift."

Taylor swallowed. "It's my fault, not yours. I let myself get distracted."

"I'm sorry, Taylor." His gaze held hers, then shifted back to Gracie. "So sorry."

"Mommy, can we go home now?" Gracie interrupted, tugging on Taylor's hand. "I want to show you the picture Aunt Nina helped me paint and we need to find a Christmas tree. Aunt Nina's is so beautiful."

Nina shot her an apologetic look at not being able to keep Gracie distracted longer.

Taylor didn't care. She didn't want to be having this conversation with Slade.

"I'm sorry, too." Taylor spotted her suitcase rolling out on the nearby baggage carousel. "Now, if you'll excuse me, I'm going to grab my bag and go home to catch up with my daughter. Goodbye."

Just before it got too far for her to catch this time around, Taylor pulled her bag off the rolling contraption. She smiled at Nina and Gracie, and pretended everything was great. "Let's go. Not sure I'm up to going out to buy a Christmas tree tonight, but I can't wait to get home and see that picture."

First waving goodbye to a stiff Slade and thanking him again for her bear, Gracie slipped her hand into Taylor's and began talking a mile a minute, as she usually did.

Too bad Taylor wasn't able to keep from looking back when they reached the glass doors to take them out of the airport.

Slade still stood right where they'd left him.

# CHAPTER SIX

SLADE LOOKED OVER his patient's labs. Her white blood cell count was too low to administer her chemotherapy.

"We'll recheck your levels next week and administer then if you're strong enough to handle the treatment."

The pale woman nodded. Twenty-three years old and fighting leukemia with all she had, Brittany Tremaine hadn't lost her hair yet, but was experiencing other devastating side effects of her therapy. "Whatever you say, Doc."

The young man beside her, holding her hand, leaned forward. "What do we do in the meantime?"

"In the meantime, she needs to rest, eat healthily, build her strength back up." Slade stood, shook the man's hand, then gave Brittany a hug that he hoped conveyed encouragement and compassion. It was what he felt for the young woman, what he felt for so many of his patients.

Oncology wasn't a profession for the faint of heart.

When his mother had died of breast cancer when he'd been twelve, Slade had become obsessed with fighting cancer. He'd held fundraisers at his school, become an advocate at raising awareness of the deadly disease, had known that he'd go into a profession where he could continue that battle and make a difference to where other kids didn't have to face the same thing he had.

Although there was a great emotional burden that came along with his job, there was also a great deal of joy and satisfaction with each success story. He prayed Brittany would be one of those success stories.

"I'll see you around the same time next week. If anything changes negatively before then, come back in sooner," he advised, tearing off a piece of paper from a preprinted pad he kept in his pocket. A motivational quote was on the sticky note.

Slade gave a quote to each and every patient he saw each and every time he saw them. Perhaps a silly habit, but he'd had several patients comment on his messages, that they'd kept them posted on their mirrors. One survivor told him she'd kept the quotes in a scrapbook and now shared the book with others when the need arose.

Slade knew all too well about saving quotes. He had a stack of them himself. He'd not looked at them in several years, but last night, when he'd gotten home from Vegas and unpacked his suitcase, he'd pulled the shoebox he kept the notes in out from his closet. He'd flipped through the protective album he'd placed them in years ago as a young boy, and he read each and every one. Right up until the shaky handwriting had become almost illegible.

Then he'd called his dad.

When he'd gone to bed he'd been an emotional wreck in some ways, but in others he'd known exactly what he had to do. Although he couldn't stay married to Taylor, he didn't want to hurt his family, or hers. Most importantly, he didn't want to hurt Taylor.

The best way to achieve all of that was for them to pretend they were happily married, then, when he hopefully got the job with Grandview, he could leave as the bad guy, and she'd not suffer any negativity from their impromptu wedding. Should he tell her about his interview? Perhaps, but at this point, he suspected she'd use the fact that he might be leaving to be that much more on guard with him. Taylor already aced on guard so he'd just wait and tell her if the need arose.

"Dr. Sain?" Nina interrupted his thoughts. "Sorry to bother you, but Taylor is in a room with a patient and I need someone to check a patient now, please. I believe she's having a reaction to her infusion medication."

Slade shoved his nostalgia down and followed Taylor's nurse to where a woman who appeared to be in her early fifties sat in one of the special recliners in the infusion lounge.

"Hello, Mrs. Jamison. My name is Dr. Sain. Your nurse tells me you aren't feeling well?"

"I'm itching all over." The woman scratched her neck to prove her point.

Slade skimmed his fingers over her exposed skin. Large red welts were forming. He turned to Nina. "Go ahead and stop her infusion. As long as she isn't allergic to the medications, give her an antihistamine and a shot of steroid."

"Yes, Dr. Sain."

He turned back to the patient. "Any difficulty breathing?"

The woman shook her head. "No, I just itch like crazy and feel a little light-headed."

He examined the woman thoroughly, waited for Nina to administer the medications he'd ordered. "Recheck all her vitals in fifteen minutes and pull me out of a room if you need to."

Nina nodded. "I'll let Taylor know what's going on with her as soon as she's out of her patient room."

As if she'd known they were discussing her, Taylor walked over to them. "Hi, sweetie. Tell me what's happening."

Mrs. Jamison began telling her about how she'd started itching during her infusion.

"Hmm, this is the second time you've received this particular medication. I don't recall any problems with the last infusion. Were there any after you got home?"

Scratching, the woman shook her head. "I felt fine, but I don't now." She cleared her throat. "I feel like my skin is on fire."

Although Slade had just checked the woman, Taylor began examining her. "Heart rate is tachy."

"I gave her an antihistamine and a steroid," Slade informed Taylor. "Hopefully the symptoms will start resolving soon."

The woman hacked then cleared her throat again. "I hope so," she rasped.

"Me, too," Taylor agreed, eyeing the coughing patient with concern. "I think we're going to have to give you another shot of steroid."

"Or maybe just go to epinephrine?" Slade suggested as the woman hacked again. "I think her lips are swelling."

Mrs. Jamison's gaze lifted to them. Her lips were swelling before their eyes. Her eyes watered. Her skin became more and more blotchy. "I feel like I can't get enough air."

"Nina," Taylor said, knowing her nurse would know exactly what she wanted.

"On it," Nina replied, rushing away from them.

"Respiratory rate is over twenty," Taylor said, although Slade wasn't sure if she was speaking to him or was just thinking aloud.

"Take slow deep breaths," Slade advised, in hopes of refocusing the woman's increasing panic. He grasped her wrist and took her pulse. Running over one hundred and fifty, her heart rate was also too high.

"I...can't," the woman denied, shaking her head while coughing. She was now wheezing audibly.

Nina rushed back with an injectable pen that she handed to Taylor. Taylor popped the cap and jabbed the pen down on the woman's thigh, through her clothes, administering the medication in the process.

Slade pulled out his phone and dialed for emergency services.

"I can't...breathe."

"The reaction should be slowing very soon with the medication we just gave," Taylor informed her patient, watching as Slade checked her pulse again. No doubt the adrenaline they'd just administered would push the lady's heart rate up even higher. No matter. There hadn't been a choice. She was going into anaphylactic shock. "You're having an allergic reaction to the chemotherapy medication. It's rare for that to happen but, unfortunately, from time to time it does occur. I'm giving more steroids through your IV and I'm going to admit you to the hospital for observation tonight."

The woman just nodded between wheezes.

"Your heart probably feels as if it's racing like crazy. It is. Although the medicine I just gave can cause an increased heart rate, what I expect to happen is that once your allergic reaction is under control, your heart rate will drop back close to normal."

Taylor and Slade stayed with Mrs. Jamison, keeping her calm and stable while they waited for the ambulance to arrive. Slade soothed the lady in the chair closest to Mrs. Jamison, easing her concerns regarding her own infusion.

"As Taylor said, it's very rare that someone has a reaction to their chemotherapy, but it does happen," he assured the anxious woman, when she asked for her treatment to be stopped for fear she might also react. "You still need your medication infused. Other than prayers, the medication is the best weapon we have at our disposal to fight your cancer."

The nervous woman kept eyeing Mrs. Jamison, but did nod agreement. For a moment Slade had thought she was going to rip out her central line.

Having most of their patients' infusions occur in a common lounge area with recliners and televisions was a good thing overall. It provided support and socialization during the long infusion process. But when something went wrong it could start mayhem.

Fortunately, although the other patients had kept a curious eye on what was happening, only the lady next to Mrs. Jamison seemed spooked.

The paramedics arrived, wheeling in a stretcher.

Taylor gave them a quick report while they loaded a still wheezing and hacking Mrs. Jamison onto the stretcher.

"That scares me," the nervous woman told Slade. "What if I react to my chemo, too?"

"I don't think that's going to happen, Mrs. Smith," he reassured the woman, squeezing her hand gently. "I know putting medications into your body is scary, but there are times when not doing so would be much scarier."

"The medications make me feel so bad," the woman admitted, a little weepy. "Sometimes I feel as if I would be better off to just not take them."

"Your last scans showed a reduction in the size of your tumor. The medications are doing their job. You're doing fantastically on the medicines. To stop them halfway through would be a shame."

Taylor had stayed with her patient until they loaded her onto the ambulance. When she came back into the lounge, she came over to them.

She smiled at Mrs. Smith then glanced at Slade. "Thank you for taking care of Mrs. Jamison."

"You're welcome, but you did all the work."

"I'm not sure why Nina didn't come and get me to begin with. Mrs. Jamison was my patient."

"I had just finished with a patient and was in the hallway. It would have been silly to pull you from an examination room when I was available."

"I suppose you are right." She looked pensive, as if even though she couldn't argue with his logic she didn't really want to agree with him. "Still, I hate it that you had to take care of one of my patients."

Who did she think she was fooling? What she was really saying was that she hated that they'd had to interact. She'd avoided him all morning, including skipping her morning coffee. What was she trying to prove? It wasn't as if the entire office didn't know they'd married and was watching their every move with great curiosity. Such juicy gossip spread like wildfire and, no doubt, the entire clinic had known within an hour of Slade making his announcement during their presentation. If only he'd kept his mouth shut. If only they hadn't gotten married to begin with. If only his chest didn't feel a little like he couldn't breathe when he looked at her. Not that she was looking back. Her eyes were everywhere except meeting his gaze.

"It wasn't a big deal," he said finally, mixed emotions running rampant through him. He wanted her. But that wasn't part of the plan.

"All the same, thank you."

Taylor stared at Slade, feeling as if she should say something more, but what?

What could she possibly say to him? So much and yet, really, what was there to say?

"I had a no-show this morning—she's at home, sick. Can I help you get caught up again?" he offered, taking the pressure off her to come up with something to say.

She shook her head. "That isn't necessary, but thank you."

"I didn't think it was necessary. I just wanted to help you."

"I appreciate the offer, but I don't need your help."

Mrs. Smith was watching their interplay with curious eyes, all concern over her infusion apparently forgotten with the minidrama unfolding in front of her. No doubt the other staff members within viewing distance were also curious bystanders. She'd gotten several congratulations throughout the morning. No doubt Slade had as well.

She'd avoided him. Something she'd gotten good at long ago. Why had Nina gone to him? They'd all worked together for over a year. There were dozens of physicians at the clinic. Never before had Nina had any reason to seek out Slade. Go and marry the man, and suddenly her nurse was asking him to see her patients. Not okay.

Taylor didn't want him seeing her patients. Not when they were having allergic reactions. Not when he'd had a no-show and offered to help her catch up.

Not that she didn't trust him in that regard. He was an excellent doctor. She'd never heard any complaints or problems regarding the care he provided his patients. Quite the opposite. Everyone sang his praises. It was just that the less she had to do with him the better. He wasn't the man for her.

"I'll talk to Nina about not bothering you regarding my patients in the future."

His brow lifted. "Why? We all help each other when the need arises. That's always been the case in this clinic."

Out of respect for the curious ears listening to their conversation and because she didn't want their patients privy to their weekend activities, Taylor just smiled. "You're right. Thank you."

Not that she wouldn't be talking to Nina. She would definitely see to it that Nina went to anyone but Slade for assistance unless a patient's health would otherwise be compromised.

As if he could read her mind, Slade just stared at her. Disappointment showed in his blue eyes. Then he turned to Mrs. Smith. "I'm going to pop in and see whoever is next, but I want to be sure you're okay before I do so. You need anything?"

Taylor didn't wait to hear the woman's response. Slade had the situation under control and the nurses were providing good care for all the other infusion patients. She was going to catch up on her morning patients.

"Do you have a minute?"

Taylor glanced up at the man standing in her doorway. Her husband.

Ugh. Could she lie and say no?

She'd managed to avoid him for the rest of the day, but

had caught him watching her several times when she'd been talking to this patient or that in the infusion lounge.

The last thing she wanted was to spend time with him. Not even a minute. She just wanted to forget he existed, that she had a marriage to do away with, that she had made such a mess of her life over the weekend, that horrific sadness gripped her chest each time she thought of him.

She glanced at Gracie's photo, her greatest happiness in a gray world, and summoned up the courage to meet Slade's gaze.

"What's up?" she asked, pushing her glasses up the bridge of her nose.

He came into her office and shut the door behind him. "We need to talk."

"Not again."

"Did you call a lawyer today?"

"I did." She'd called during the lunch she'd practically inhaled while sitting at her desk. "I have an appointment to meet with her on Friday morning. Did you?"

His lips thinned. "Yes. Oddly enough, I have a Friday morning appointment as well."

Although she hadn't invited him to, he sat down in the seat on the other side of her desk and studied the photo she'd just been looking at. He sat in silence so long, Taylor cleared her throat to remind him she was in the room.

His skin drawn tightly over his cheekbones, he glanced up. "She's a beautiful little girl."

"Thank you."

His gaze drifted back to the photo. "She looks just like you."

"I am her mother." What was he doing?

"What about her father?"

Enough was enough. "Really? You want to discuss Kyle again? Because I don't."

"Does he see Gracie?" Slade persisted.

She eyed him with what had to be pure venom flowing through her veins. Really, that's what the caustic substance sloshing around inside her felt like. Venom. "He doesn't want anything to do with Gracie. He signed away all rights to her."

"Foolish man."

True. As far as Taylor was concerned Kyle had been an idiot to give up his rights to their precious daughter.

"Selfish as this may sound, I'm glad he doesn't want anything to do with her, because I don't believe he'd be a good influence or father. I'd worry about her if she had to spend time in his care and it just makes life simpler that she doesn't have to go back and forth between two houses. As much as I wish he could have been a good father to her, that's not who he is. Gracie has a lot more stability this way."

Slade's gaze met hers. "If Gracie were my daughter, I would spend time with her."

Despite the fact that he'd said he didn't want a wife or kids, he sounded so definite, she didn't doubt his claim. Irrational fear gurgled in her stomach. "Then it's a good thing she's not yours, because I'd worry about her if she was in your care, too."

She didn't add that she worried about Gracie no matter who was watching her. She supposed it was a mother thing, but she wanted to protect her daughter from all the bad things in the world. Leaving her with anyone was difficult. Even leaving her with Nina for the long weekend had been rough, and she trusted her best friend implicitly.

Slade leaned back in the chair and watched her a moment before asking, "Despite how we were this weekend, you don't like me much, do you?"

"Not really."

"Why not?"

"You're not the kind of man I prefer to spend time with."

"Yet you married me."

A vicious throb pounded at her temples. "Don't remind me."

"Why?"

She rubbed her temple, hoping to ease the pulsating pain that she'd begun to associate with thoughts of him. "Why what?"

"Why did you marry me, Taylor?"

She grimaced. "Haven't we already had this conversation?"

"Tell me again."

"I wasn't in my right mind," she said flippantly, wishing she hadn't stayed to do her charting, but had rushed straight out the door as soon as she'd finished with her last patient.

"I haven't been in my right mind since I kissed you in the backseat of that limousine."

His comment surprised Taylor and she met his intent blue gaze. "How so?"

"We're filing for divorce, which is the right thing. I don't want to get entangled in your life, yet I can't stay away from you. I can't go ten minutes without thinking about you." His gaze dropped to the photo of Gracie again, and he winced. "There are a million reasons why I shouldn't, why I should stay away from you and just do as we decided on the plane, but I can't get past the simple fact that I want you, Taylor."

# CHAPTER SEVEN

*I WANT YOU.* Three little words and Slade had Taylor's lungs shriveling up to oxygen-deprived uselessness.

"We don't always get what we want in life, Slade."

Not that she was complaining about her life, but she certainly hadn't.

"Besides, you just want what you can't have."

He shrugged. "We both know that if I kissed you right now, you'd kiss me back."

"I don't know that."

His brow arched. "You think I'm wrong?"

"I think you're wrong," she insisted. In theory, her claim sounded good, but she wasn't so sure he wasn't right. The man's mouth held some kind of power over her.

"Prove it."

Why was she staring at his mouth? Why were his words—"I want you"—echoing through her mind over and over and causing all sorts of jittery reactions inside her body? Want wasn't their problem. They'd wanted each other this past weekend just fine. It was everything else that had been the problem.

"W-what?" she stammered out.

"Prove that my kisses don't affect you." Was it just her or did he look inordinately confident, perhaps even a little arrogant?

"How would I prove that?" Not that she didn't immediately realize the trap he'd set. Darn him. Darn her body's reaction to him.

"Kiss me."

She crossed her arms, realized she probably looked ridiculous and dropped her hands into her lap. "I don't want to kiss you."

"Chicken."

"I'm not going to respond to such a childish taunt."

"Because you know that I'm right." His lips twitched. Oh, yeah, he'd gone from perturbed to haughty.

"You aren't right."

"Unless you prove otherwise, I am right."

Ooh, she really didn't like him.

"Fine, kiss me. But don't be offended when I go rinse my mouth out with peroxide afterwards."

He frowned but moved around the desk, took her hand and pulled her to her feet and into his arms.

The moment her body came into contact with his, she knew she was in trouble. Big trouble.

How could she have forgotten how hard his body was? How good he smelled? How could he even smell that good after working all day? But he did. His spicy male scent teased her nostrils with memories, with acknowledgment that she wanted him.

She expected him to immediately take her mouth, had braced herself for it. Instead, he slipped his fingers around her neck, slowly raking over the sensitive flesh, then pinching her hair clip and releasing her hair.

His fingers threaded into the locks, massaging the base of her scalp, every touch seducing her toward relaxation.

*Just get it over with*, she wanted to scream.

Or maybe it was just, *Kiss me!* she wanted to shout at him.

Either way, he was taking his dear sweet time and she was growing more and more impatient.

"I said you could kiss me, not maul me."

His eyes sparked with something akin to fire, but he didn't respond except to continue his caress of her and to lower his head.

His lips kissed the corner of her mouth. A soft, brief touch. Then he kissed the other corner.

She fought turning her mouth toward him and somehow managed to stand superstill, as if she was totally unaffected. As if she'd been telling the truth, that his kisses didn't affect her.

But he wasn't finished. He continued his soft rain of kisses, gliding across her temples, her forehead, even the tip of her nose.

"I don't have time for this," she warned.

He just smiled. Probably because her voice had wavered and hadn't sounded convincing at all. She'd sounded as if she *was* affected. Darn it.

He lowered his mouth back to hers, dipped to where only millimeters separated their lips. "My kisses may not affect you, Taylor. But kissing you affects me. My heart is racing and my lungs feel they can't drag in enough air. This weekend wasn't enough. Right or wrong, I need more."

*Stop it. Please, just stop talking*, her brain warned. Her mouth, unfortunately, didn't say a word. Then again, that might be a good thing because she might admit to how her own heart raced and her own lungs had deflated at his "I want you," at his tender touching of her skin with his lips.

"The anticipation of knowing I'm about to taste your sweet mouth drives me crazy, Taylor," he admitted, his voice low, husky. His gaze lifted to hers. "You drive me crazy."

He drove her crazy, too. She didn't like him and yet…

His lips touched hers. Softly at first, then not so softly, but demanding and masterful. As if he was trying to work through the craziness to some type of satisfied peace.

Only Taylor knew there was no satisfied peace with Slade.

Even after he'd taken her to the pinnacle of pleasure and

she'd thought herself completely sated, all he'd had to do was touch her and she'd been right back to craving more. Crazy. What a perfect description for the desire flooding through her.

The desire to move her lips in response to his.

The desire to wind her arms around his neck.

The desire to press her body fully to his and lean on his strength.

Yep, that was crazy.

She knew better than to lean on a man like Slade. He was a playboy. She'd seen the evidence firsthand for the past year. The fact that he kissed like a dream and his eyes promised her the world didn't mean a thing.

The fact her heart was racing didn't mean a thing.

"I don't like you," she told him the moment his mouth lifted from hers.

"I know," he conceded. "But you want me almost as much as I want you."

Probably more, but she wasn't telling him that.

But kissing him again really wouldn't hurt anything, right? After all, they'd already kissed and she'd done her best not to respond, but she'd have had an easier time stopping the earth's rotation.

Giving in to her need, she stood on tiptoe to press her lips back to his. She should have said something clever like, *Shut up and kiss me*. But talking at all just seemed unnecessary.

Feeding the hunger within her was what was necessary.

Only she knew from experience that kissing Slade wouldn't satisfy her hunger. Instead, his kisses were like an appetizer that made her crave the main course all the more.

She was starved.

Then she recalled how their kiss had started. He'd been proving a point about his kisses affecting her.

She pulled back from him. "I guess I lose."

"Seriously?" Mixed emotions twirled in his blue depths.

"I don't see how sharing that kiss could possibly qualify you as a loser. That kiss makes us both winners."

"If you say so." She took a step back, trying to put some distance between them. "You aren't my type."

"I think we just proved that I'm exactly your type. Do you need a reminder?"

Um, no. She wasn't likely to ever forget that kiss. "That's just sex."

"Sex is a very important part of a relationship."

She rolled her eyes. "Spoken like a true man."

"I am a man, Taylor, but I'll go on record as saying that if you believe sex isn't important to women in a relationship, you're wrong. Sex, whether it be a desire for more of it or less, is an important sharing between a man and a woman."

He was right. But both of her sexual relationships hadn't been about love, just appeasing physical attraction. Kyle had been good, but not like Slade. Not even in the same class.

"What do you know about relationships? You change girlfriends on a monthly basis," she accused, needing to establish some distance between them. "There was the one you went skydiving with, the one you hiked Everest with, the one you did the medical mission trip to Kenya with, the one you—"

"I don't need a recap. I have dated a lot of different women," he interrupted. "But just because my relationships with them didn't last long doesn't mean we didn't have a good relationship while it lasted."

She shook her head. "Again, spoken like a true man. I wonder what the women think."

"I'm still friends with most of them."

She twirled her finger in the air. "Yee-haw for you."

"Are you always so negative?"

"Always. You should stay far away." She waved her fingers at him. "Bye. See you in divorce court."

His expression serious, he said, "Actually, that's what

I'm here to discuss. Have you told anyone we plan to divorce immediately?"

His question had heat infusing her face. Was she supposed to have sent out an office memo? "Only Nina."

"Good," he surprised her by saying.

"Why is that good? What does it even matter? We are immediately filing for divorce."

"But I think it's better if no one know that. At least, not until after Christmas."

"What does that matter?"

"Go to dinner with me tonight so we can discuss exactly that."

"I can't. I have Gracie."

He winced, reminding her of how he'd reacted to knowledge of her daughter, to seeing Gracie, to even looking at her photo. Had he momentarily forgotten?

"If it's the only way you'll agree, then your daughter can come, too."

She shook her head. Not going to happen. "Wow, with such sweet talk, how can I resist?"

"Do you want me to sweet-talk you, Taylor? I want you, but the reason I want to take you to dinner has little to do with that want."

"Then what does it have to do with?"

"Say yes, and I'll tell you."

Did he think he could manipulate her into going? But then an idea struck. Slade had enjoyed their sexual rendezvous where there had just been the two of them and no real-world responsibilities other than their presentation. He enjoyed kissing her and seeing her as a woman. She needed to give him a dose of her real world. In the real world she was the mother of a rambunctious six-year-old. A six-year-old whom he obviously had issues with.

She smiled a Cheshire-cat smile. "Okay. We will go to dinner."

"Okay." Surprise lit his face, and also a look that was

somewhere between relieved that she'd agreed and terrified that she had. "Good. We really do have a lot to talk about. What time can I pick you up?"

"Seven." She gave him her address.

"Okay, then." He took a step back then nodded almost as much to whatever was running through his head as to their conversation. "I'll see you in a little while."

"Taylor, dear, your father's partner said he'd heard a nasty rumor this weekend."

Taylor cringed. No. No. No. She shouldn't have answered the phone. Especially since Slade would be arriving any moment.

"Craig told him that you'd gotten married over the weekend. Your father assured him that was poppycock."

Poppycock? Who said that other than Vivien Anderson?

Then again, perhaps there was no better word for the fact she and Slade had gotten married. Poppycock. Yep, that's what the whole weekend had been. What tonight was.

"Why is the idea of someone marrying me poppycock?"

"Now, Taylor, don't take this the wrong way, but you're not exactly a prize."

Trying not to be hurt, Taylor closed her eyes. Not a prize? Wasn't her mother supposed to see her as the greatest prize a man could win?

"How else is one to take her mother saying she isn't exactly a prize other than the wrong way?"

"Don't go making this about me," her mother warned. "Just tell me you didn't go off and marry someone on a wild whim in Vegas. Surely you know such a union is doomed before it's even started?"

Sure she knew that, but she wasn't admitting to a thing.

"You don't believe in love at first sight?" Why was she being so ornery? Why wasn't she just coming clean that her mother was right and that she'd made a mistake?

"Taylor! Please, tell me you didn't!"

She could lie and tell her that, but her mother's attitude rankled and for once, rather than kowtow, Taylor injected her voice with a perkiness she didn't feel. "It's hardly love at first sight, though. I've known him for a year."

"It's true," her mother gasped, her horror real and thick. "You got married. In Vegas."

Her mother made her words sound as if she had committed the most heinous crime. What else was new? Almost everything she did failed to impress her parents one way or another.

"To a doctor, Mother. He's a very successful man. You should be happy."

But rather than exclaim with joy, her mother rasped, "You're pregnant again, aren't you?"

Taylor cringed. "Do you not think a man might want to marry me just because he wants to be with me?"

Not that that was why Slade had married her, but still.

"In Vegas? Oh, Taylor, you know you wanted a church wedding!"

Had she? Taylor supposed that if she thought about it she would say she had the same wedding fantasies that a lot of women had. A day that was all about her, a gorgeous gown, flowers, a man who loved her with all his heart waiting at the end of an aisle. Not necessarily in a church, but she doubted a place named after the North Pole would have made the top one hundred.

"Vegas was much more exciting, Mom. Not everyone gets married by Santa Claus." Okay, in reality, being married by a minister in a furry red suit wasn't on her mom's top one hundred list either.

"Please, tell me you are joking."

"In a gingerbread house rather than a church. There were real elves and everything." She was bad, knew she was being bad, but she so didn't need her mother condemning her right now. She had enough of her own regrets. "It was a really unique ceremony."

"Your father is going to be so disappointed that he didn't get to walk you down the aisle."

Her mother was so disappointed she didn't get to have the huge social-club reception to show off to all her friends. Her father? She thought about the stern businessman who, although devout and good, wasn't an overly emotional man. Perhaps her mother knew a side she didn't. Perhaps her father really did want to walk his only child down the aisle. Maybe she'd stolen that experience from him, too.

Taylor felt a twinge of remorse. Her parents had been good parents, had sent her to the best schools, had made sure she'd had the best advantages in life, had always been there if she'd physically needed something. Was it their fault she'd constantly been a disappointment to them? That she'd failed them miserably when she'd gotten pregnant in medical school? That she'd accidentally gotten married in Vegas?

"I'll reserve the club for a reception." Her mother confirmed Taylor's earlier thoughts. "With the holidays, I may have to call in several favors to get the main ballroom, but I'll do my best."

"Mom, I don't need or want a wedding reception." She didn't even want the marriage.

"Nonsense. All our friends and family will be offended if they don't get to share in such an important event."

Taylor took a deep breath. Several of her coworkers had suggested throwing her a bridal shower. She'd put them off with claims of the holidays being so busy.

"Mom, it isn't fair to your club to make them shuffle around their holiday schedule to fit in a reception."

"But—"

"No buts. I have so much going on right now with Gracie, the holidays, with work."

"Fine," her mother conceded. "I'll book the first thing available for after the holidays."

Planning a reception for after the holidays was as useless as planning one for before the holidays. Unless one gave receptions to celebrate the dissolution of one's impromptu Vegas vows?

Taylor tried arguing with her mother, but to no avail as Vivien cut the conversation short. No doubt to call to book her club.

Was it wrong that she had given Gracie a glass of soda prior to Slade's arrival? That she wanted Gracie in full-chatter, full-tilt mode? That she wanted to push Slade out of his comfort zone? To play on all his worst fears about being around a kid? For him to see her as a woman who was a mother who had real-world responsibilities and not as the woman he'd slept with in Vegas?

"Mommy!" Gracie called when the doorbell rang. She jumped up and down, her blond ponytail swishing wildly. "He's here. He's here."

She'd told Gracie that a friend from work was coming to take them to Pippa's Pizza Palace. Gracie had been ecstatic because they usually only went to the designed-for-kids restaurant for birthday parties or special occasions.

Knowing she wasn't supposed to unlock the latch, Gracie bounced back and forth in front of the foyer door. Taylor had her step aside so she could let Slade in.

When she swung the door open, he gave her a wary smile that made her question how long he had been standing out there on her porch.

"Hey."

"Hey, yourself," she flung back, moving back so he could enter the foyer. "Gracie, do you remember Dr. Sain? You met him briefly at the airport."

"I remember." Gracie beamed at him, dancing around at his feet. "He took care of Vegas."

Oh, he'd taken care of Vegas all right. Her daughter meant the bear, but Taylor couldn't help but think of the real ways Slade had taken care of Vegas. She'd hoped Gracie would rename her bear, but the name had stuck so far.

Vegas had bumped Foxy as Gracie's favorite toy and she kept the bear close.

"That's right. Let's grab your coat and be off so we can get you to bed at a decent time for school tomorrow."

Gracie ran to the living room where her jacket and bear lay on the sofa.

Slade's gaze followed the bouncing little girl out of the room, then shifted to Taylor. "You look great."

Taylor laughed at Slade's compliment. She'd purposely put on an old sweatshirt and jeans, scrubbed her face clean and pulled her hair into a ponytail. Great wasn't the right adjective by any use of the word. Neither was it the adjective she'd use to describe how he looked. He looked as if he'd rather be anywhere other than here.

"Got them," Gracie announced proudly when she returned with her jacket and bear.

Her daughter handed her bear to Slade while Taylor made a great production of helping Gracie into her coat. Let him realize firsthand why she had no time for playboys.

"Be careful with her," Gracie warned him. "She is a delicate princess and has to be treated royally. She would probably like it if you pretended to be a prince come to rescue her."

What popped out of Gracie's mouth had stopped surprising Taylor long ago. Her daughter was brilliant and readily got people to do her bidding. Slade, despite whatever was bugging him, was no exception, and whatever the problem had been he seemed to have overcome it, at least for the moment.

"Who says I'm not really a prince?" he asked, bending to Gracie's level. He held the bear to where he was staring into her painted plastic eyes. "Vegas, did you forget to tell Gracie that I am Prince Charming come to sweep the two most beautiful girls in the world off their feet?"

Gracie's eyes widened. "She did forget to tell me."

"Vegas," he scolded the bear with a gentle click of his tongue. "How could you forget something so important?"

Taylor rolled her eyes, wondering if she'd made a horrible mistake in letting her daughter spend time with Slade. She'd expected him not to want to deal with a six-year-old girl, for them to have a short evening with Slade and Gracie not having time to form any attachments. What she hadn't counted on was Slade actually playing along with Gracie's imaginings. She liked that and she didn't need anything else to like about the man.

"Let's go," she growled, irritated at herself. "I'm hungry."

"Uh-oh, Vegas." Slade's voice sounded concerned. "Princess Taylor has spoken and we must do her bidding."

Gracie giggled. "She's not Princess Taylor. She's Queen Mommy."

*Good girl, Gracie. Remind him of my real role in life.* The most important role in her life. That of loving and raising her daughter to the best of her ability.

Even if she had loaded her with sugar prior to his arrival.

As if she'd read her mind, Gracie started bouncing again. "Mommy let me and Vegas have soda pop!"

Hmm, maybe she should have let Gracie in on the fact that she hadn't wanted that little tidbit shared.

Slade just looked at her, raised his brow, then grinned, his stress seeming to melt away with that revelation. "Wow. It must be a special night if she let you have soda."

Gracie nodded. "It is. We're going to Pippa's Pizza Palace."

"Pippa's Pizza Palace?" Slade's gaze went to Taylor for confirmation. She nodded.

"Well," he continued, giving Taylor a look that said he knew exactly what she was up to. "It is a palace, so of course that's where princes and princesses should go."

Ha. Wasn't he in for a surprise if he expected any kind of royal treatment at Pippa's Pizza Palace. Overpriced pizza, kiddie rides and games were hardly regal.

Totally enamored, Gracie slipped her hand into Taylor's and headed out the front door. "Vegas is really excited about going to Pippa's Pizza Palace. She wants her very own crown."

"Then her very own crown she shall have," Slade promised. "After all, she is a very special princess who traveled from far, far away."

Taylor followed Slade to his car.

"Let's load you up into your chariot," he suggested to Gracie. He looked more confident than he had when he'd first arrived. Too bad he was about to have his bubble burst.

Also having figured out there was a problem, Gracie glanced up at Taylor in question. Taylor had to fight to hide her smile.

"We should take my car instead," she suggested from behind him, watching his face closely.

"Why?"

"I think you're forgetting something. Princess Gracie is only six and has to be in a children's car seat."

His expression was priceless. "Is there a seat we can just put in mine?"

Taylor hesitated a brief moment, then shook her head. "Nina has my extra seat and the one in my van is built-in."

"Your van?"

"I drive a minivan. That's what we soccer moms do."

She was driving her point home that they were on opposite ends of the spectrum. Whatever he was thinking, he didn't say anything to her, just grinned at Gracie as if he found dealing with her easier than Taylor at the moment. "You play soccer? I love soccer!"

Gracie nodded at her new hero.

"What position do you play?"

Gracie shrugged and glanced at Taylor for an answer.

"You're a forward."

"A forward," Gracie told him, puffing out her tiny chest as she did.

"That's a great position," he praised, then turned to Taylor. "Can we take your minivan instead of my car?"

She glanced toward his car. She'd seen the sporty coupe in the parking lot at the hospital, knew that's what he drove. The expensive car fit him and was perfect no doubt for impressing the women he dated.

Seven years ago Taylor would have been impressed, too. Now flashy toys and good looks didn't impress her that much. What was on the inside of a man, his morals and his character, that's what she valued. Not that Slade would have guessed that after their wild Vegas rendezvous. He probably thought deep down she was no different from the other women who had been in and out of his life.

Only as she unlocked her garage door she couldn't quite convince herself that Slade saw her the same way as the other women he'd dated.

He hadn't married any of the other women in his life.

Sure, they'd married on a silly lust-fueled Vegas whim, but they had married.

He stood next to her, taking in each step of Gracie being safely buckled into her seat. Once Taylor was confident Gracie was properly buckled in, she handed her van keys to him.

"You're going to let me drive?" he asked, obviously surprised.

"Boys are supposed to drive," Gracie piped up from her seat.

"Don't ever let any guy tell you he's supposed to drive. If you want to drive, drive."

Gracie giggled. "I don't know how to drive."

"What?" He pretended shock. "Well, I guess princesses should be chauffeured around anyway."

Taylor watched their interaction with suspicious eyes. Of course Slade was on his best behavior. She'd thought being around Gracie would make him see her as a mom and not as the woman he'd spent the weekend with in Vegas. Perhaps she'd made a mistake.

Then again, the night was young.

# CHAPTER EIGHT

SLADE WRAPPED HIS fingers around Taylor's keys, watched the play of emotions across her face, then opened the passenger door for her.

"Your chariot awaits, Queen Taylor." He made a production of bowing, and earned claps and praise from Gracie. Not that he'd had much experience around kids, or even wanted that experience, but he admitted he enjoyed her honest reactions to the things he said and did.

"This is my chariot, too," the little girl informed him. "My royal chariot. For me and Princess Vegas."

"Absolutely."

Taylor rolled her eyes. She climbed into the front passenger seat and he shut the door, winked at Gracie, who winked back, then he slid her door closed, too.

So far, so good. Which he didn't think was supposed to be the case since even in his limited experience he knew sodas hyped most kids. He'd bet anything Taylor was one of those moms who limited her daughter's sweets. Tonight was not supposed to be a success. Too bad. He was determined it would be. He had a proposal to make. One that had been nagging at him from the moment it had occurred to him. One he hoped Taylor would agree to.

Gracie chatted nonstop, mostly about Santa and Christmas, on the drive to Pippa's Pizza Palace, which, despite the castle-shaped sign, didn't look like a place fit for a princess to eat. The building was a bit run-down and the parking lot needed repaving. Still, when they got inside, the interior was colorful and clean, if dated.

Gracie obviously didn't care. First getting a nod from her mother, she took off toward a row of machines and kiddie rides on the opposite side of the large open room.

Before they had placed their order Gracie was back, asking if she could have some coins.

"Let's get dinner ordered first."

"I'm not hungry," Gracie insisted, tugging on her mother's hand. "Can I play now?"

Taylor shook her head. "Not until you've eaten."

Gracie's lower lip drooped, and her shoulders sagged to where she looked like a deflated tire. "Do I have to?"

Taylor nodded, then, while Gracie ran back over to watch one of the video-game monitors, she turned to the cashier, placed an order for a small cheese pizza, a salad, a lemon water and a juice. The cashier glanced toward Slade, but Taylor shook her head.

"Our orders are separate."

"You'll have to excuse my wife. She doesn't understand the concept of 'date night,'" Slade explained to the cashier. "I will pay for their order and mine."

"No."

"Yes. Get us a table, please, and I'll finish here, wifey."

"I didn't say yes so you could buy dinner or call me 'wifey.'"

"Odd, because I did ask you to dinner so I could buy your dinner."

She pursed her lips, looking as if she'd like to argue, but instead she did as he'd suggested. He watched her walk over to a clean booth and put her purse on the seat. Then he turned back to the cashier and completed the order, along with purchasing some coins for Gracie.

"You didn't have to buy coins," Taylor said when he slid into the booth with his huge stash.

"Because we came to the Pippa's Pizza Palace to watch other kids play?"

"We came to eat."

"Pretty sure Gracie would be disappointed if she only gets to eat." As he said the words realization hit. "Unless that's your plan?" He studied her, noting her pink cheeks. "You'd like tonight to be a failure so you can add it to your reasons why we don't belong together?"

"We don't belong together." She made it sound like a disease. "I thought we agreed on that."

"We do."

"Then our being here makes no sense."

He glanced toward where Gracie covetously watched two kids whacking at clowns popping up from the top of a machine shaped like a cannon.

"Actually, our being together does make sense short-term." He needed to explain his proposal, but didn't get the chance as Gracie skipped back to their table.

"Mommy, after I eat, can I hit the clowns, too?" Gracie's eyes sparkled, her cheeks glowed and her voice held excitement.

"I'm not sure how I feel about a game where you beat up poor defenseless clowns," Taylor mused, smiling at her Mini-Me.

"Are you kidding me? Clowns are some scary business. We should both help just to be sure we get them all."

Giving Slade a beatific grin, Gracie nodded enthusiastically. "You should!"

"Don't tell me you are afraid of clowns?" Taylor asked, eyeing him with a slight smile.

"Terrified," he admitted, half-serious. He'd never been one of those kids who liked clowns. Maybe he'd watched one too many scary movies involving weirdos in clown suits.

"I'm not scared of clowns," Gracie announced, taking his hand. "Mommy's not either. We'll protect you."

"Phew. Thanks."

"Do you want to watch with me? We could look at the other games and pick out ones to play," she suggested, her eyes big and pleading.

Slade glanced toward Taylor to get her permission. Should he wait until after Gracie had eaten?

Taylor nodded. "I'm pretty sure that the games haven't changed since the last time we were here, but you should definitely show Dr. Sain all your favorite ones."

"You can come too, Mommy."

Taylor shook her head. "You two go ahead. Mommy will watch for our food. Plus, I have a phone call to make."

Gracie tugged on Slade's hand. "Come on. You have got to see the frog game! It's amazing."

Slade gave one last look toward Taylor, who, he knew, had purposely set him up to go off alone to supervise Gracie, then he devoted his attention to the child holding his hand. Something about her warm little hand gripping his, about the excitement with which she spoke, made him want to pick her up and hug her. Getting attached would be nothing short of stupid. Yet he'd jumped at the chance to spend time with Taylor. So he could ask her a favor. Nothing more. Not really.

If she'd agree to a no-strings affair, he'd jump at that chance, too. Too bad he knew she'd never offer that.

"Amazing?" he asked the girl, forcing his mind away from Taylor. "The frog game?"

Gracie nodded with great emphasis. "Amazing."

"Okay, let's go see this amazing frog game."

He let the little girl lead him over to a game where you had to squirt water onto a lily pad to make a frog move from the lily pad to where a fly was. Interesting.

But not interesting enough to keep his gaze from wandering back to the woman sitting in the booth, talking on her cellular phone. She laughed at something said, then glanced his way, caught him looking at her and frowned.

"Rolling the balls is my favorite game, but I'm not very good," Gracie informed him, tugging on his hands to take him away from the frog game and farther into the maze of games. "Mommy is really good."

She stopped in front of a row of Skee-Ball lanes.

Slade glanced over at the booth where Taylor sat, talking on her cellular phone, smiling and laughing. Her face was relaxed, beautiful, almost carefree. Who was she talking to? She'd told him she wasn't having sex with anyone, but had she been dating? He'd never asked if there was some-one special in her life. There couldn't have been anyone too special or she wouldn't have married him, wouldn't have had sex with him.

Gracie continued to talk about her mother's awesome-ness at Skee-Ball.

Slade smiled down at the excited little girl. "Your mommy likes to play this game?"

Gracie nodded. "It's her favorite. She's really good. She gets lots of tickets, but she always gives them to me to get the prize." The little girl gave him a pointed look, wanting to be sure he knew that giving her the tickets was the right thing to do.

Slade's gaze wandered back to Taylor. She twirled a loose strand of hair around her finger and still talked animatedly to whoever she was on the phone with. Jealousy wasn't a pretty thing and he was definitely jealous. He wanted her smiling and laughing like that with him, the way they had on the night they'd gotten married.

"That's nice of her."

Gracie nodded. "She's a nice mommy. My friend Sarah Beth, her mommy isn't nice." Gracie wrinkled her nose and looked so much like Taylor, Slade couldn't suppress the melting of his heart. There might be traits of her father present in Gracie, but when Slade looked at the little girl all he saw was a miniature version of Taylor.

"She screams and cries a lot," Gracie continued, her face and hand movements dramatic.

Slade wasn't exactly sure how he was supposed to respond, but decided a response wasn't necessary because Gracie kept right on talking and waving her hands.

"Sarah Beth says it's because she's pregnant and the baby in her belly kicks her a lot. Sarah Beth's daddy says this baby is going to be a soccer player, too. Sarah Beth is on my soccer team, but soccer season won't start back till this spring. You should come watch my games. I am very good. Mommy tells me so."

Slade took a breath for Gracie because she seemed too busy chatting to breathe. But she must have been sneaking breaths in somewhere because she kept going without being the slightest bit winded, pointing out several other games that she really hoped to play when they finished eating.

"Do you have kids?"

Gracie's random question in the middle of her rundown of her classmates caught him off guard. He shook his head.

"No, I don't have kids." For the first time in his life he almost felt as if he was lacking something by that answer. Perhaps it was the sad little look Gracie gave him, as if she was offering him comfort that he didn't.

"Are you married?"

While he racked his brain for a way to answer honestly without telling her anything her mother wasn't ready for her to know, Gracie leapt up and down.

"Yummy!" she called, grabbing his hand and not waiting for an answer when she spotted their food being delivered to the table. "Pizza. I'm a pizza-eating machine."

She made a pretense of gobbling air bites.

"Me, too," he agreed, grateful for the distraction as they headed back to the table.

"Sorry, Nina, but I've got to go. I'll talk with you tomorrow at work." She paused while the person on the other end of the phone line said something. "Okay, see you then. Have a good night."

"Nina doing okay?" he asked, to verify that she'd been talking to her best friend. He really didn't like the green flowing through his veins, the green that had flowed through his veins at the thought that there might be someone in Taylor's life. It shouldn't matter. If anything, he should want her to have someone in her life who could give her all the things she wanted for her and Gracie. All the things they deserved. It was probably some natural instinct for him to feel jealousy where Taylor was concerned. After all, she was his wife.

"She checked on Mrs. Jamison for me. They admitted her overnight for observation, but otherwise she's good."

"Mr. Slade is going to play games with me when we finish eating," Gracie announced while Taylor squirted hand sanitizer onto her tiny hands. "He's going to come to watch me and Sarah Beth play soccer this spring, too."

Slade hadn't really agreed to that, but he wasn't going to correct the child's claim. Catching Taylor's glare, he should have, though. She offered Slade the bottle and he took it, their hands brushing against each other. Zings shot up his arm. How could a single touch cause such a wave of awareness throughout his entire body?

He glanced at her to see if she'd felt the electricity that had zapped him, but she refused to look at him, her focus totally on her daughter as she put a slice of pizza onto a colorful paper plate.

"Mmm, pizza," Gracie said, continuing to talk a mile a minute.

Slade handed the sanitizer back to Taylor and found it interesting that she managed to take the bottle without a single touch of their skin this time. Had that been intentional?

"What is on your pizza, Mr. Slade, because I only like cheese pizza." Gracie took a big bite of her pizza to prove her point.

"I got a little of everything on mine," he told her, reaching for a slice of the house special. He eyed the rather bland-looking salad Taylor had ordered. "You want a slice? I'll share."

She shook her head. "I'll finish off what Gracie doesn't eat of her pizza."

"Cheese is your favorite?"

"No, but she won't be able to eat it all."

"I will be able to eat it all," Gracie corrected her. "I'm starved." She sucked in her tiny belly and lifted her shirt to show Taylor.

Taylor smiled at her daughter and a piece of Slade's heart cracked at the love that showed in her eyes, a love he hadn't seen in years. That's what he'd lost when his mother had died, why he'd dedicated his life to breast-cancer research, why he was determined to prevent other kids from losing the same.

"Guess you better get to eating, then, before you blow away, hungry girl. But not too big bites, please," Taylor added, when Gracie took a huge mouthful, oblivious to the emotional turmoil playing out in Slade's head.

Gracie ate a slice, then eyed the games. "I'm full. Can I go play now?"

"You can, but we're not finished eating so it'll be a few minutes before we join you. Stay where I can see you."

"Okay." Gracie looked at Slade. "Hurry so I can show you how good I am at the frog game. I will beat you."

Slade watched her bounce back over to the games. "She's precious."

"I think so."

"But you didn't want me to think so?"

"I didn't say that."

"You didn't have to. You gave her soda."

She sucked in her lower lip. "So?" she challenged. "Lots of kids drink soda."

"But you don't normally give Gracie soda."

"Not usually," she admitted, impressing him that she'd been honest. He got the impression Taylor was an honest person who truly tried to live her life to a high standard.

Was that something her parents had instilled in her or just who she innately was? Speaking of honesty...

"Gracie asked me if I was married."

Taylor's stomach sank. Had Slade told Gracie they'd married? "What did you tell her?"

"Not what you apparently think I did."

Which didn't really tell her a whole lot. "Then what did you say?"

He set another piece of pizza on his paper plate. "I didn't answer because we were saved by the pizza arriving."

She watched him take a bite of the loaded pizza. Her stomach growled in protest at her salad.

"I've changed my mind about telling her. I'll tell her when she's older, when she'll understand better."

He paused with his pizza midway to his mouth, an odd gleam in his eyes. "Do I embarrass you, Taylor?"

"What?"

"I'm just curious because you haven't wanted anyone to know that you married me. I was curious if you were ashamed of me."

Was that what he thought? If anything, he should be ashamed of her. She was the one who was so different from the women he'd dated. "Of course not. That's ridiculous."

As if he were no longer hungry, he set the pizza back on his plate. "Is it?"

"Of course. If I was embarrassed by you I would not have agreed to go to dinner with you tonight."

"But dinner wasn't supposed to be a success. Dinner was supposed to shove in my face that you aren't a carefree woman who can have an affair until our divorce is final."

Busted. "I didn't say that."

"You didn't have to," he pointed out, leaning slightly across the table toward her. "I have a proposal to make."

A proposal? Her stomach knotting, she eyed him suspiciously.

"Let's not tell anyone that we plan to divorce until after the holidays."

Taylor swallowed back what she was positive wasn't disappointment because she hadn't really expected him to propose they continue their weekend fling yet again.

"I can't see what the point would be," she told him, even if staring at him across the table made her want to drag him under the table and... She swallowed again.

"It would make things easier at work if we waited."

Taylor thought back on her conversation with her mother. Now there was a buzz killer. The thought of telling her that she'd been planning her divorce less than twenty-four hours after saying "I do" turned her stomach.

He picked at the edge of his paper plate then met her gaze again. "Plus, keeping the truth quiet would make things better for my family. I don't celebrate Christmas, but they do. I'd rather not ruin their holidays by having them worried that I'm facing divorce in the New Year."

He didn't celebrate Christmas? She wondered why, not liking the way her heart raced at how he was looking at her, at how her heart broke that he missed out on the joys of the holidays.

"I don't want anyone to know that our marriage isn't real," he admitted, his sincerity drawing her further into the spell he cast with such seeming effortlessness. "I know you've told Nina, but she wouldn't say anything if you asked her not to."

"You've not told anyone?"

"No. I started to tell my dad last night, but I couldn't do it. He's already worried that I've gotten married so suddenly that I just didn't have the heart to tell him."

She closed her eyes. She couldn't condemn him for not telling his father. After all, she hadn't set her mother straight. Still...

Was she strong enough to pretend they were happily married? He affected her as no other man ever had, made her heart race and her body ache, made her heart long for dreams that had been shattered long ago. He made her want and feel all kinds of scary emotions.

"I'm sorry. I just don't think I can do pretend."

"Sure you can. We did pretend in Vegas and it was amazing."

"That was different and you know it."

He considered her a moment then leaned toward her, his face only inches from hers as his gaze dropped to her lips, hesitated, then lifted back to her eyes in challenge. "Play me for it."

She couldn't breathe. Couldn't hear for the pounding of her chest. "What?" she choked out.

His grin was lethal, warning her she should just say no to whatever he was offering. "Play me to decide if we tell everyone now or wait until after the holidays."

Was it just her or had someone cranked up the heat in Pippa's Pizza Palace? Surely the thermometer was set on flaming-inferno mode. "That's ridiculous."

"Be that as it may, I'm serious." His gaze didn't waver from hers. Could he see that she was sweating? Would it be too obvious if she fanned her face?

"Why would I agree?"

"Because, if you really think about it, it's the right thing for both of us. But if you insist otherwise, if you win, I will give you what you say you want. I'll leave you alone and we'll go back to the way things were before Vegas. Plus, I will quit trying to engage you in conversation or asking you to dinner or even acknowledging that you exist."

His smile should have her running, but instead she considered what he'd said. How could she not when she could feel his breath against her lips? Or was she just imagining the soft caress that made her want to lean in and close the gap between them?

She frowned and leaned as far back in her seat as she

could without looking as if she was auditioning for a human contortionist act.

"I'll quit trying to convince you to let me strip you naked and repeat all the naughty things we did last weekend, even though I will probably still be thinking about those things and wanting them, wanting you."

Her heart squeezed and she felt a little panicky at the thought of what he'd promised, of what he'd said. Not panic. Excitement. Anticipation. Slade leaving her alone was what she wanted. What she needed. She wasn't strong, and what if she gave in to the physical sparks that burned so potently between them? Especially when he kept saying he wanted her? What if he kissed her and she forgot everything but the fact that she was a woman and he made her glad of it? What if she acknowledged that he hadn't epically failed with being around her daughter tonight?

Play a game, win and he'd back off trying to convince her to have an affair destined to lead nowhere but to heartache for her. That's what she needed. Wanted. So what was the catch? "Not that I'm agreeing to anything, but what would we play?"

"Your choice."

Her choice? "Let me get this straight. I get to pick the game and if I win, you avoid me at all costs? No changing your mind?"

"Yes," he agreed, not looking in the slightest worried. "But if I win you will give me a month of pretending to be happily married and if you happen to decide you aren't opposed to continuing our physical relationship, well, that would be an added perk."

She ignored the little voice inside her head reminding her of the last time he'd *proved* something to her, of just how tempting she found that added perk. "A month?"

"A month. That puts us at New Year."

She bit the inside of her lip. She didn't really think he could beat her at Skee-Ball, but a month…

This was crazy. He was crazy. Why was she even considering his suggestion?

"I don't want my daughter hurt."

His blue eyes twinkling, he looked more relaxed than he had all evening. "So you admit even before we start that I'd win?"

She lifted her chin a notch. "I'm not admitting anything."

His grin was wicked. "But you aren't denying that I'd win either."

She glanced over at her daughter, who was watching another child play a coin-toss game. Her gaze lit on the Skee-Ball lanes. She could do this. She could beat him, remove all temptation and just move past the events of the past weekend. It's what she needed for her sanity because being around him made her crazy.

"Any game?"

His smile broadened. "Any game."

"Skee-Ball."

He didn't hesitate, just nodded. "Best of five?"

Why had the air in the room gotten so thin?

"Best of five," she agreed, wondering what she'd just agreed to. Not that it mattered. She couldn't recall the last time she'd lost at Skee-Ball.

"We both get a warm-up game?"

She shook her head. She just wanted to get this over with. "I don't need a warm-up game."

He looked impressed. "Okay. But don't say I didn't offer."

Taylor smiled. "No changing your mind when you lose. We'll tell everyone the truth and you'll leave me alone at all times. No looks, no flirting, no daring me into kisses, no anything. You'll stay completely away from me. Tonight will be the last time I have to deal with you."

"No changing your mind when you lose," he countered. "You agree to a month of pretending to be happily married to me, spending time with me, and tolerating my looks, flirts and dares to kiss. Although, in private, win or lose, you call the shots and I'll honor your wishes. In January, we'll announce our divorce plans and go our separate ways."

There went her throat, gulping again. "If I refuse to play?"

"Then regardless of what we tell others about our marriage, I will actively pursue what I want, which is you in my bed."

Panic tightened her throat for a brief second, then she reminded herself that he was not going to win.

"Unless you're willing to admit that you want me as much as I want you, you have nothing to lose by playing me."

No way was she admitting that to him. Sure, there was no way he couldn't know how he'd made her body explode and implode and reload over and over in Vegas, but she was not admitting a thing.

"You're right. Because I won't lose."

Not looking in the slightest intimidated by her bravado, he grinned. "Such confidence. I like it."

She picked up a piece of Gracie's leftover cheese pizza and took a bite. "I'm good at Skee-Ball."

He watched her eat, and if he was attempting to hide that eyeing her mouth gave him pleasure he failed. "Gracie mentioned that."

Yet he'd agreed. That threw her. "You knew and you still let me pick which game we played? Do you want to lose? Is this some kind of sick joke?"

"In case you haven't figured this out yet, despite how many times I've told you, I want you. And for the record I don't like to lose or fail at anything. Something we have in common."

When she just stared blankly at him, he elaborated. "Our competitive spirit."

She didn't think she had a competitive spirit, but there was something about the man that made her want to get one up on him. Plus, she wasn't 100 percent sure he wasn't just toying with her. Maybe he sensed how much she struggled with her attraction to him and out of boredom he planned to prove his point on that score as well.

Either way, all she had to do was win and, whatever his motive, it would be a moot point.

# CHAPTER NINE

AT GRACIE'S ENCOURAGEMENT, Taylor and Slade played three of the frog games first. Gracie won each time. They also played several of the other electronic games, including whacking the clowns.

Hearing Gracie, seeing the joy on her daughter's face at their antics, eased Taylor's nerves.

Knowing that she would win, that Slade would quit pursuing their physical relationship, helped calm her fear of how he made her long for things she shouldn't.

He didn't seem nervous. He'd been laughing and mostly at ease with Gracie, the kiddie games and with the whole chaos of Pippa's Pizza Palace. Every once in a while she'd catch him responding a little awkwardly to Gracie's exuberance, but otherwise he'd impressed her.

"Ready to win Gracie a bunch of tickets?" His eyes sparkled with challenge.

"Oh, yeah." She was ready to get the game over so they could go home. Not that she wasn't having fun. Of course she was having fun. Slade was a fun guy. Fun wasn't the problem. But he wasn't what she wanted in a man, in a father for Gracie. He'd hurt her, hurt Gracie, if she gave him the chance. That was the problem. Why she'd needed a stronger barrier to her feelings to begin with.

That plan sure had backfired. Gracie hung on to his every word and wanted him beside her for each game they played.

She'd even caught her daughter batting her lashes at Slade. The man was a charmer. Age didn't matter. Females flocked to him and her daughter was no exception.

She ran her gaze over his handsome profile and admitted that he was definitely flock worthy. He made her want to flock, too. If only...

He turned, caught her watching him and grinned.

Taylor rolled her eyes. No need to give him a bigger ego than he already had. If he knew how much she thought about him, about their wedding night and how she wished the way he'd kissed her had been real and that he wanted a month with her to win her heart rather than to have an affair, he'd definitely tease her. Likely, he'd break her heart if given the chance. That's why she needed to accept his challenge, to beat him at his own game, so he'd back off from pursuing her and hopefully she'd walk away from their marriage without any mortal wounds.

Gracie took the center lane and they watched her play a game prior to their dropping coins into the next lane.

"You go first," she offered.

Slade shook his head. "Ladies first."

Taylor shrugged, then picked up a ball and smoothly rolled it down the lane. It dropped effortlessly into the highest point slot.

"Oh, yeah!"

Gracie high-fived her.

Slade nodded in approval. "Nice."

Unfortunately, her next two dropped into the next to highest point level slot. Frustrated that she wasn't rolling a perfect game, the remainder went into the same just-below-perfect slot until she ran out of balls.

Her score wasn't her highest, but it wasn't bad. She stepped aside. "Your turn."

"Do you want to do all five of your games first, keep a score tally and then me go?"

She shook her head. "I thought we were going to play

against each other and have winners each time. The best of five, remember?"

"Either way is fine."

He dropped more coins into the slot. A new set of balls rolled down. Slade picked one up, rolled it down the lane, and plopped it into the highest point slot.

When he repeatedly dropped the balls into the same slot, Taylor began to feel clammy.

"You're pretty good."

He rolled the remainder of his balls. "I dated a girl in high school who worked in a place like this. I killed a lot of time playing this game while waiting for her shift to finish."

His rolls didn't remain perfect, but his final score was higher than Taylor's.

Gracie jumped up and down, clapping. "You're good, Mr. Slade! You beat Mommy. Look at all those tickets."

Slade tore off the long string of tickets. "These are for you, princess. We'll have you more in just a few."

"Yay," she squealed, waving the tickets around.

"Okay, then," Taylor said, her palms sweating. Of course he'd dated someone who'd worked at a place that had Skee-Ball lanes. He'd probably dated a professional Skee-Ball player and coach, too. If there was an international Skee-Ball game, he'd probably won gold. Urgh. "I guess it's my turn."

"That it is." Slade looked as if he was having the time of his life. The fink.

Taylor started the new game and took her time to make sure she sank the balls into the highest scoring slot. She did well and upped her score by forty points, which would have beaten Slade in the previous game. She smiled as she stepped back.

Excited, Gracie gathered the tickets the machine was spitting out.

"Nice job," Slade agreed, obviously not concerned. He started his game and tied her score with almost effort-less ease.

"Hmmm," he mused. "We didn't discuss how to handle a tied score."

Annoyed at how calm he was, she stretched her arms over her shoulders. She just needed to loosen up a little to beat him. "We'll just keep playing. One tied game may not make a difference."

But Slade tied her next two scores. Gracie was ecstatic. Taylor was not. Three ties and he'd won the first game. She had to win this next one.

Putting all her focus into the game, she picked up her first ball and dropped it into the highest point slot. Yes. She repeated that time and again, the ball only dropping into a lower slot once. An almost perfect game. It was the highest score of the night.

Finally! Breathing much easier, she glanced at Slade. "Your turn."

"That's a pretty high score. What happens if I tie you or get a higher score?"

"You won't," she said dismissively, more for her benefit than his.

His lips twitched. "But if I did?"

"You would win because you won that first game."

"If I don't tie you?"

"We'd have to play a sixth game to break the tied score."

"I just wanted to be clear."

Slade rolled the ball and it dropped perfectly into the highest point slot. Each and every time. He only had one more to have a perfect game. He'd be up two wins to her none. If he tied her, he'd still win. Only if his ball dropped into a lower point slot would she win. Even then, they'd possibly have to play a tiebreaker. Knots twisted her stomach.

He surprised her by holding out the ball.

"Gracie, would you like to roll my last ball?"

The little girl, who had been enthusiastically gathering tickets, jumped up and down and nodded, her ponytail bouncing almost as excitedly as she had been. "I would."

He handed Gracie the ball and the little girl looked up at him, suddenly uncertain. "Will you help me, Mr. Slade? I want to do good and get more tickets."

Taylor wasn't sure anyone could resist such a sweet, innocent plea, and Slade was no exception. He stood behind Gracie, helped position her body just so, pulled her arm back and helped guide her through the motions. Gracie let go and the ball dropped into the second from highest slot, tying Taylor's score.

Taylor's knees almost gave way beneath her. No.

"That was good!" Eyes wide, Gracie jumped up and down, superenergized about her success.

Slade picked her up and twirled her around. "Princess, you are amazing!"

She giggled and patted his cheeks. "Did we win?"

He nodded. "We did win. We make a good team."

"Yea." Gracie high-fived him. "Princes and princesses always make good teams."

Taylor watched them, wondering at the doomed feeling in her gut, wondering at the emotional pangs at how her daughter was so quickly responding to Slade.

With a suddenly serious expression Gracie looked up at Taylor with her big green eyes. "You're not mad 'cause I helped Mr. Slade win, are you, Mommy?"

Oops. Her silence had gotten her daughter's attention. Oh, Slade was slick. He'd used her daughter against her. If she showed disappointment, Gracie would think her a poor sport.

Pasting a smile on her face, Taylor gestured to the long strand of tickets. "Nope. I think with as awesome as you just did you're going to run the machines out of tickets. Did you see all those?"

"Wow." Gracie's eyes grew large. "I'm going to get a stuffed monkey."

"A what?"

Gracie pointed to where the prize booth was. Hanging

from the ceiling was a big green stuffed monkey with a yellow banana in his hand. "I want him."

Okay. "How many tickets does he take?"

Gracie shrugged.

"Let's find out." While Gracie and Slade ran their tickets through a counter, Taylor asked the teenaged cashier at the booth how many were needed for the monkey.

"That many?"

The boy nodded.

"Mommy, we have over a thousand tickets!"

"We're going to need them."

Slade grinned. "Takes that many for a big green monkey, huh?"

Ignoring his expression, she told him.

He whistled. "Expensive monkey."

"He's worth it," Gracie assured them, eyeing the monkey with longing. "He's the king of the jungle and has been trapped up there for months and months. He needs to get back to his kingdom."

Slade looked intrigued. "He does?"

All seriousness and in full Gracie-imagination mode, she nodded. "Plus, he has to find a princess to go to the jungle with him and lead his people."

"You're a princess," Slade reminded her, getting into Gracie's active imaginings.

"I'm a princess," Gracie agreed with a *duh* expression. "But he's going to fall in love with Princess Vegas." She took on a worried expression. "Let's hope she likes big green monkeys because not all princesses do, even though they are so cute and cuddly."

Slade's gaze lifted to Taylor's and despite still reeling inside that he'd won, that he'd brought Gracie onto his side, she smiled at his rather bewildered, overwhelmed, yet totally enamored expression.

Probably a similar expression to the one she wore that for

the next month she would be pretending to be happily married to Slade and he'd be actively pursuing an affair with her.

An affair she couldn't afford emotionally.

"I want the biggest tree they have," Gracie informed Slade and Taylor as they pulled up to the Christmas-tree lot in Taylor's van the following Friday evening. "A gigantic one so I can climb high into the sky!"

"Christmas trees aren't for climbing."

Gracie scrunched her face at her mother's comment. "They should be. Christmas would be so much fun if I could climb the tree." Her face lit. "I could be an ornament."

"Or the angel at the top," Slade suggested, parking the car and not quite believing that Taylor and Gracie had convinced him to come along on this trip. The less he had to do with Christmas, the better. "You are quite the angel."

Gracie giggled, then added, "Angels fly and I can't fly. I need a Christmas tree I can climb and hang on a branch 'cause I'm a Gracie ornament."

The logic of a six-year-old had quickly come to fascinate Slade. He grinned at the miniature version of Taylor. His wife. A week ago today they'd gotten married. How crazy was that?

Was it even crazier that he'd convinced her to play along with their marriage for a month? All for the sake of not wanting news of a pending divorce to possibly reach Grandview Pharmaceuticals as it might hurt his chances of landing his dream job and because he didn't want his dad to stress over the holidays. His father had experienced enough rough Christmases over the years. Slade wouldn't be the cause of ruining this one.

Plus, he wanted Taylor so much he couldn't think of anything else but touching her again. Which was proving a little difficult since she kept Gracie between them at all times they weren't at the clinic.

Realizing her argument wasn't working, Gracie changed

tactics. "I bet you'd like to climb a Christmas tree, too, wouldn't you, Mr. Slade?"

Smart kid.

Taylor sent him a warning look.

"Not really. Christmas trees aren't for climbing. But maybe someday soon I'll take you out to my dad's farm in Franklin and we'll find climbing trees."

"Really?" Gracie rubbed her hands together, then climbed out of her car seat and jumped to the ground. "Are there chickens on your farm?"

"No chickens," Slade told her. "But there are horses and cows."

"Princess Vegas has never ridden a horse," Gracie informed him very matter-of-factly. "She thinks she would really like riding a horse. Especially a white one who looks like a unicorn."

"Hmm, I'm not sure if there are any that look like unicorns, but we'll see."

Gracie nodded, then pointed out a family who were also tree shopping. "Look!" She waved at her grinning friend whose face was barely peeking out from beneath her high-collared coat, hat and scarf. "Mommy, can I go say hi to Sarah Beth?"

Sarah Beth, as in the Sarah Beth who was on her soccer team and whose mother screamed and cried a lot?

Waving at a very pregnant woman bundled up in several layers of coats and scarves, Taylor nodded. "That's fine, but walk, don't run."

Doing what could only be called a fast walk, Gracie headed to her friend and hugged her as if it had been months since they'd last seen each other.

Her gaze still on her daughter, Taylor sighed.

Slade stared at her, but she kept her gaze trained on where Gracie and Sarah Beth chatted away, waving their gloved hands around animatedly. "You shouldn't say things to make

Gracie think you're going to be a part of our future. I don't want her hurt."

"Neither do I. But even after we sign divorce papers, there's a ninety-day wait before we go before the judge."

Taylor's attention snapped to him. "You talked to your lawyer today, too, then?"

"Yes. You knew I had a Friday morning appointment, the same as you." He nodded. "He said it'll be after the holidays before anything gets rolling."

Her eyes returned to Gracie. "Mine said the same. Guess it's just as well we didn't open ourselves up for more gossip at work."

He'd spent every evening this week with Taylor and Gracie. They'd eaten, played whatever games Gracie wanted to play, watched cartoons, read her stories and last night they'd pulled boxes out of Taylor's attic and stacked them in the corner of her living room in anticipation of Christmas decorating this weekend.

He could do without the Christmas decorating, but apparently if he wanted to spend time with Taylor, he'd have to endure Christmas festivities. He and his dad had quit celebrating Christmas the year his mom had died. His dad had since started again. His new wife had seen to that. Slade, on the other hand, although not a Scrooge, just didn't see the point.

Each night he'd helped Taylor straighten any mess they'd created, then, while she'd put Gracie to bed, he'd driven home to a house that really wasn't a home at all. Funny how he'd never noticed that before. He'd always liked his uptown condo with all its modern conveniences. Now the place just seemed empty. Good thing he hoped to be moving to New Jersey soon.

Half expecting Taylor to pull away, he grabbed her gloved hand and laced her fingers with his, clasping it tightly as they walked toward Sarah Beth's family. Beneath the fabric he could feel the outline of the wedding ring Taylor still wore. Just as he did beneath his gloves. For their pretend month.

Sarah Beth caught sight of Slade and leaned over to stage-whisper, "Who is he?"

"That's my boyfriend," Gracie informed them, not in a stage whisper. "He's my Prince Charming. When I grow up I'm going to marry him and we're going to live in a magnificent castle and throw grand balls for all our kingdom to enjoy."

Everyone's gazes went to Slade, including a wide-eyed, slightly amused Taylor. Stunned by Gracie's announcement, he cleared his throat.

Laughing, Sarah Beth's mother stuck out her hand. "Hi, I'm Janie. Gracie is my Sarah Beth's best friend. Together they are quite the pair. The entire family will expect an invitation to the wedding, of course. And frequent invitations to visit at the castle."

"I can only imagine." He instantly liked the very pregnant woman, even if she reportedly screamed and cried a lot. Seeing her so pregnant made Slade wonder what Taylor had looked like pregnant with Gracie, what she'd look like if she were pregnant with his child even now from their Vegas weekend. Lord, he hoped she wasn't. He glanced toward her, but she refused to meet his gaze. Her cheeks and nose were already pink from the cold. She was beautiful.

He smiled at Janie. "And, of course, on the castle invitations."

"Janie, this is Slade Sain. He's…" Taylor hesitated and Slade wondered how she would label him. Not husband, not boyfriend, not lover, but who?

"A friend of the family."

Friend of the family? That was accurate up to a point. He was friends with her and Gracie, even if about half the time Taylor treated him more as if he were her enemy. Still, she was cooperating on the pretend month and even smiled at him at work.

"Hoorah for handsome friends, eh, Taylor?" Janie laughed, then, placing a hand on her belly, glanced toward her husband. "We just got here and have to find a tree. My parents are visiting next week and they will be livid if we don't have a tree up for Sarah Beth."

"I hear you. I dread it when my parents visit on Christmas Day."

Real dread showed on her face. Did she not get along with her parents? He'd give anything to have the opportunity to spend time with his parents together again. Then again, maybe her dread had to do with her all-too-real pretend marriage. What had she told her parents?

"We'll let y'all get to it." Taylor glanced around the tree-filled lot. "Hopefully we can find a tree quickly and get in out of this cold."

They went their separate ways. Gracie latched on to Slade's free hand. "Can we put real candy canes on our tree?"

"Sure." After he answered, he realized he should have gotten confirmation from Taylor, but she didn't look upset that he'd answered Gracie's question.

"We could make paper chains to put on it, too."

"If that's what you'd like to do," he agreed.

"It is." Still clinging to his gloved hand, Gracie skipped beside him as if completely unfazed by the cold wind whipping at them. Taylor, on his other side, shivered. In the middle of them, Gracie was holding his one hand and Taylor his other. Warmth spread through Slade's chest. He felt... cozy. He swallowed and fought the feeling down. This was temporary and he was just making the best of a bad situation. It wasn't cozy. Just convenient.

"I think paper chains are beautiful," Gracie continued.

"I'm sure anything you made would be beautiful, princess." Convenient? Could he really lie to himself to that extreme? Spending time with Taylor and Gracie was more than a convenience.

"Mommy always thinks so." Gracie beamed up at him, causing Slade's heart to do a funny chest flop.

Taylor pointed to a blue spruce she spotted a few trees down from them. "It's gorgeous, but it may be too tall. Do you think we can get it inside the house?"

Would it fit through the back double doors of her house?

Slade inspected the tree, thinking that if he'd liked Christmas and had felt the need for a Christmas tree, then Taylor had made a good choice. Perfectly shaped with full branches.

"If not, we could trim some to make it work," he offered. "What do you think, Gracie?"

Gracie eyed the tree and gave him a puzzled look. "How are we gonna fit it inside the van?"

He laughed. Smart, smart kid. "You don't think it'll fit in your seat?"

Gracie giggled. "No way. We could put it on top of Mommy's van. I saw that on a cartoon."

Slade scratched his head. "I'm not sure that's going to work, princess."

"If you don't think we can get it on top of the van, we can pick a smaller tree," Taylor suggested, but her eyes still lingered on the blue spruce.

This was the tree she wanted. The tree he suddenly wanted her to have, even though he saw no logical reason to stuff a tree inside a house and throw glittery decorations on it.

He shook his head. "This is the perfect Christmas tree."

"This Christmas is going to be a perfect Christmas," Taylor mused, almost sounding as if she really believed so.

Not that he'd celebrated Christmas in years, but he was getting sucked into the holiday by a woman so sexy she filled his every waking thought and her six-year-old princess-wannabe daughter, because he wanted to give her that perfect Christmas, to make her holidays filled with joy.

"It is," Gracie agreed, nodding. "Princess Vegas thinks so, too."

"That settles it. Princess Vegas has the best taste." Slade winked at Gracie, got a wink right back that melted him despite the cold wind. "This is our tree. We'll pay and I'll come back later in a truck to pick it up."

"You have a truck?" Taylor looked skeptical. "I can't see you driving a truck."

"No, but my dad does and of course I can drive a truck. I grew up on a farm." Granted he'd spent as much time study-ing, volunteering and fundraising for breast-cancer aware-ness as he had hauling hay or herding cattle. But he could do any job on the farm that needed to be done. He loved the land, loved riding his horse and still got a kick out of taking off on a four-wheeler for a carefree afternoon in the country. Nothing like breathing some fresh air and getting up close with nature.

"He lives close?" Taylor still didn't look sure. "We don't want to be a bother. I could call a service and have a tree delivered."

"There's no need to pay inflated prices to a service. My dad's in Franklin. It's about a twenty-minute drive, depend-ing on traffic. I want to do this, Taylor. Let me."

"Of course." Taylor became pensive. "What will you tell him if he asks why you need to borrow a truck?"

"I'll tell him the truth. That I need a truck to pick up a Christmas tree." Or maybe not because wouldn't that cause a slew of questions? His dad knew how he felt about the holi-days, and although he and Slade's stepmom both repeatedly invited him over to celebrate the day, he always refused. "Do you want to go to?"

She immediately shook her head. "I don't think that's a good idea. He might…realize the truth."

No doubt both his dad and his stepmom would question

him like crazy regardless. It would be the first time he'd seen them since returning from Vegas. Had he wanted to take Taylor as a way of curtailing their questions?

Glancing down at where Gracie was checking out a cocoon attached to a different tree, Slade whispered back, "You might be right. He does want to meet you, though."

Taylor's brows shot up. Horror paled her face. "Definitely not a good idea."

"I agree. For now."

"This is such a mess." Taylor's lower lip disappeared inside her mouth.

"Only because of Princess here. After you've told her, I think it's a grand idea." He placed his hand on top of Gracie's head and the little girl beamed up at him from beneath the hood of her coat.

"What's a grand idea?"

"Hot chocolate and marshmallows?" he suggested. It wasn't his place to tell her more. Maybe he'd just tell his dad Gracie didn't know because they wanted her to get to know him first. Once they announced their break-up, telling Gracie wouldn't be an issue. Why did the thought of their having to do that bother him so much?

"Mmm-hmm. I'm cold." Gracie wrapped her arms around her body. "Can we go home for hot chocolate?"

"I'll pay for the tree, make sure the guy marks it as sold, then come back with the truck."

"Thank you, but I'll pay for the tree. It would be silly for you to pay for my and Gracie's tree when you'll still have to get one of your own."

"I don't put up a tree, Taylor."

"No Christmas tree?" Gracie piped up, staring at him incredulously. "Are you crazy? What if Santa thinks you don't believe and he doesn't leave you presents? You've got to have a Christmas tree, doesn't he, Mommy?"

"Absolutely. So I'll pay for this one and you help pick out another for his place. We can help decorate it."

Before Slade could argue, Gracie grabbed his hand. "Come on, Mr. Slade, you gotta have a tree for Christmas."

# CHAPTER TEN

"SORRY I TOOK so long," Slade told Taylor when she opened the front door much later when he arrived with the tree.

She'd changed from her business clothes into yoga pants and a snowman sweatshirt. Her long blond hair hung in a braid. She'd scrubbed her face clean of the light makeup she'd worn to work that day. Each night was the same. She dressed down. Purposely? To scare him away? He wanted to tell her that it didn't matter what she did. He still wanted her.

"Not a problem." She moved aside so he could enter. "I got your text letting me know you'd been delayed at your dad's."

Closing the front door behind him, Slade frowned. Despite the fact his hands were cold, he grabbed Taylor's warm ones and pulled her gently to him. "Warm me up?"

"Now?" She laughed a little nervously and glanced around her foyer as if seeking an excuse to flee a crime scene.

"Can you think of a better time?"

Her hands trembled within his. "How about never?"

He laughed. "It's hard to believe a week ago I had never met Gracie or held your hand." He squeezed her hand for emphasis. "That I had never kissed you."

"A week ago you had held my hand and kissed me," she corrected, staring at their hands. "As far as Gracie goes, she adores you."

He studied her face, her pensive expression. "Does that bother you? That she likes me?"

She shrugged, making the snowman's hat bell jingle on her shirt. "Should it?"

"No, but I can see that it does." He laced his fingers with hers. "I'm not going to hurt her, Taylor."

She wouldn't meet his eyes. "I hope not."

"Surely you believe I'd never intentionally cause her pain?"

Finally, she lifted her gaze. "I do believe that."

"It's true." He glanced around the foyer and beyond to the living area. "Where is my favorite princess?"

"Asleep. She didn't want to go to bed before you got back but she was fading fast. I promised her we'd get the tree ready to decorate tomorrow." Her expression became pensive again. "I probably shouldn't have promised her that since…"

"Since?"

"Since I shouldn't make plans that include you without your permission. Especially as you don't celebrate Christmas."

He could hear the curiosity in her voice about that, but the last thing he wanted to do was have a conversation with her about his mother's death.

"I'm here, Taylor. Right where I told you I'd be."

"I know."

She refused to look at him again and he'd had enough. He cupped her chin, forcing her gaze upward. "You think I'm going to skip out on the decorating?"

"Tomorrow is Saturday. I'm sure you have other things to do."

"I've rearranged my other obligations for the next month." Normally, he spent his Saturdays with his dad and stepmother, helping out on the farm, unwinding from the week's stressors. All other spare time was spent volunteering with various breast-cancer awareness organizations. "I want to be with you, Taylor."

He wasn't sure he'd ever said truer words. Crazy how a week could change a person's life. He'd always admired her, wanted her, from afar, but now...now she was all he could think about.

"Just because you won it doesn't mean you have to be over here all the time," she clarified. "You shouldn't put off your responsibilities because of me."

He traced his thumb over the smooth lines of her face. "You need to quit trying to back out of giving me my prize."

She met his gaze full on. "You're not getting that prize."

Awareness that they were touching and essentially alone fell over them. Awareness that had her pulling her hands away from his and walking over to where she'd cleared out a corner for the tree.

"I took a pregnancy test at work today. It was negative. I know that's no guarantee and I'll probably do tests weekly until I get my period, but I thought you'd want to know."

"That's good." Because they didn't want her to be pregnant. Emotion hit him. Whether relief or something else, he wasn't sure. Just that strong emotion weighed heavily upon him.

"Yes. The timing was all wrong anyway, but I did the test just to be sure."

He nodded, feeling as if he should say something more but not really knowing what else to say.

"What do you think?" She gestured to the cleared-out corner. "This is where we put our tree last year, but it wasn't nearly as big as the one we picked this evening." She turned questioning eyes on him. Her green gaze searched his, clear, bright, full of sincerity and a good amount of uncertainty, too. "Will it work?"

He'd make it work. He planned to make a lot of things work for the next month.

* * *

"Not there, Mr. Slade. Over here." Gracie directed Slade's top-of-the-tree decorating like a miniprofessional, even framing the tree between her tiny fingers and examining it with one eye closed.

Taylor pulled another ornament out of a box. One that had Gracie's first Christmas photo inside a golden frame. Taylor's heart squeezed. My, how time flew. Not so long ago her little girl had been a precious baby.

"Hey, that's me." Gracie caught sight of what Taylor held and came over for a closer look. "I was so cute."

"And so modest," Taylor mused. She hugged Gracie to her and they both looked at the ornament.

"Not sure modesty comes into play when she's just telling the truth," Slade said, coming down the ladder and checking out what they held. "Hey, you're right. You were cute."

"I was a little baby," Gracie pointed out needlessly. "I was inside Mommy's belly just like Sarah Beth's mommy has a baby." Then she had both adults scrambling for a response. "How did I get inside your belly, Mommy?"

Slade hid a grin and waited to see how Taylor would answer.

"Babies are a special gift and once they are inside a mommy's belly they grow until they are ready to come out into this world."

The look Gracie gave her mother made Slade wonder if the girl would accept the simplified answer. With her schooling, no doubt Gracie knew a lot more about worldly things than Taylor would like. For that matter, probably more than he would like.

He glanced down at her innocent face and felt a protectiveness that made his knees wobble. He'd thought it had been figuratively, but perhaps it had been for real because Taylor and Gracie both stared at him.

"You okay?" Taylor asked.

"Fine."

Only he wasn't. He felt claustrophobic.

He didn't want this. A family. Something he'd not had since his mother had died. Maybe he shouldn't feel that way. He had his father and stepmother, but it just wasn't the same. He was glad his father had found peace. He himself hadn't. Perhaps losing his mother had left him incapable of ever experiencing those bonds again.

He had a purpose, vows he'd made on the day his mother had died, and a wife and kid didn't figure into the equation. Good thing this was only a temporary setup or he might go into a full-blown panic.

"Maybe Mommy should hang the top ornaments." Gracie brought his attention back to the present. "You look drunk."

Determined not to think about the past, or even the future, he stepped down and tickled Gracie's ribs until she pleaded for mercy amidst giggles. "Drunk? What do you know about being drunk?"

Still giggling, she gave him a *duh* expression. "I watch cartoons."

He looked to Taylor for help, but she just gave him a blank look.

"Drunks on cartoons. Who knew?"

"Well, yeah, when the mouse falls into the barrel and comes out all hiccupy and stuff," Gracie clarified very matter-of-factly.

"You think I'm all hiccupy and stuff?" He faked a hiccup for good measure, causing Gracie's eyes to widen and then for her to burst into more giggles.

"Mommy, Mr. Slade is drunk."

He scooped Gracie into his arms and twirled her around. "If I spin enough, we'll both be drunk."

Gracie begged for more when he stopped.

"You don't know what you've started," Taylor warned, watching them with an expression he couldn't quite read. And not because his brain had yet to catch up with his spinning body.

"Gracie, with you around I wouldn't need to go to the gym." Slade collapsed onto the sofa next to Taylor.

Gracie crawled into his lap and flattened her palms against his cheeks. "More. More."

"You've tuckered him out," Taylor informed her daughter. "He's old and needs his rest. Besides, you need to finish hanging your ornaments."

"I don't want to."

"Gracie."

Gracie's chin dropped so low it almost dragged on the floor. She cut her gaze to Slade. "Maybe we could spin more after I hang the rest of my ornaments?"

"Slade may have other things he needs to do today beside help you hang ornaments."

"Do you?" Gracie pinned him on the spot.

He shook his head. "Despite being old and needing my rest—" he gave a pointed look at Taylor "—I'm yours all day, princess."

"I'm glad." Gracie wrapped her arms around him and squeezed tight.

"Me, too, princess." He soaked up the goodness of her hug and ignored the panic threatening to resurface. "Me, too."

Taylor and Gracie eyed their finished product. A fully decorated Christmas tree with twinkling colorful lights.

"It looks magical," Gracie breathed.

They'd decorated the tree before Slade had left to take his dad's truck back, but had just finished decorating the rest of the room with garlands and bows and pretty knickknacks. During that time daylight had disappeared and they'd just clicked the remote to turn on all the Christmas lights in the room.

Taylor glanced at her daughter. Gracie stared at the tree with wide eyes and awe. Through the eyes of a child. Nothing had ever seemed so magical as the wonder reflected on her baby girl's face.

"You're right," she agreed. "It does look magical."

"Just wait until Mr. Slade sees it. He's gonna love it."

Slade had said he'd come back. That had been a few hours ago. It was now early evening. On a Saturday. Despite what he'd said, no doubt he would have more exciting things to do. Why would he keep hanging around when she would barely even kiss him, much less all the other things he wanted from her?

How she was holding out she didn't know. It sure wasn't that she didn't want him. With each passing day the need within her grew more ferocious. She couldn't give in. To give in would only further complicate their situation. At least on her part. She couldn't have sex with Slade and not get emotionally attached.

But wasn't that happening with spending time with him? With watching him with her daughter? Sure, he was awkward at times, but overall the man had Gracie wrapped around his finger. Or was it the other way around?

"I think you're right," she agreed with Gracie. "How could anyone not love such a magical tree?"

The song playing on the Christmas station they were listening to changed and "Rockin' Around the Christmas Tree" came on. They looked at each other. Taylor cranked the volume up several notches. Grabbing each other's hands, they began to shimmy and shake and rock in front of their Christmas tree.

Happiness filled Taylor at her daughter's laughter. The song was their Christmas favorite and one that they always stopped what they were doing and danced to. She couldn't remember when they'd started the tradition. Probably when Gracie had been two, although perhaps it had been three.

Taylor treasured those happy, silly, giggly times.

They bounced around, twisting their tushes, laughing, slinging their arms around.

"I guess you didn't hear when I knocked," Slade said, leaning against the living room door frame. "Now I see why."

Mortified that he'd seen her shaking and shimmying, Taylor felt her giddiness evaporate and she stopped moving.

Or tried to.

Gracie grabbed her hand and waved her arms as she continued to dance with all her little heart. "Come join us, Mr. Slade. We're doing the Christmas rock, Mommy-and-Gracie style. We rule."

Unable to resist her daughter's enthusiasm, Taylor began a somewhat modified version of her earlier dancing. There was nothing stylish about the way she was twisting, but she refused to let Slade ruin their fun.

She met his blue gaze, daring him to make fun of her. She wasn't quite sure what she'd do if he did, but she'd figure that out on an as-needed basis.

His eyes twinkled with mischief, but he didn't comment on her dancing skills—or lack thereof. "I'll just watch the show."

She arched a brow. "Chicken?"

About time she turned his teasing around on him.

"Come on, Mr. Slade." Gracie bounced to the beat of the music. "It's fun."

"Yeah, Mr. Slade, come on. It's fun," Taylor taunted, crooking her finger and enjoying herself more than she'd have believed possible when she'd spotted him.

Slade pushed off the door frame and strolled toward them. Strolled because walk didn't begin to describe the swagger to his gait as he crossed over to them.

"Okay, but just remember you two asked for this and I did try to spare you." His gaze locked with Taylor's, he joined in, taking one of Gracie's hands and one of Taylor's, and began moving.

Heat spread up her arm at the feel of his skin against hers. He squeezed her hand, smiled, and Taylor couldn't keep from smiling back. Darn him. She didn't want to like him or enjoy that he was touching her or to share her Mommy-and-Gracie Christmas dance with him.

Only she was and it felt so right. All of it. Everything about him.

It had only been a week and already she was weakening in ways that went beyond the tingles attacking her senses. What was she going to feel like at the end of their month? If only she didn't know he was a player, and once a player always a player. Men might be able to change for a short while, but ultimately they always went back to playing.

It's what had happened with Kyle. It's what would happen with Slade.

He'd even said as much. He wasn't promising ever after or anything more than a monthlong affair.

The song ended, but another upbeat song about a Spanish Christmas came on. Gracie let go of their hands and began wholeheartedly singing along with the words she knew.

Taylor seized the opportunity to pull her hand free from Slade's and to step away.

"Taylor?"

Feeling choked, she shook her head and walked over to a stack of plastic bins. She fiddled with the empty boxes and bags inside, rearranging items, then closing the lid.

"Taylor?" he repeated.

"Don't you have somewhere you need to be?" she snapped, hating it that her eyes watered.

"Mr. Slade, did you see the tree?" Gracie interrupted, tugging on his hand and demanding his attention.

"Yes, when I was dancing I saw the tree. You and your mom did an amazing job."

"We did. You, too."

"I only put stuff where you told me to," he reminded her.

"That's still helping, right, Mommy?"

"Right," she agreed, grateful for Gracie's interruption so she could regain her composure.

"Are you two fabulous Christmas decorators hungry?"

Gracie nodded. "Famished." She dramatically put her hands across her belly.

"Can I take you somewhere?"

"Pippa's Pizza Palace?" Gracie piped up.

"Probably not again this soon," Taylor said, thinking she couldn't stomach greasy pizza tonight.

"She's just saying that because she knows I'll beat her at Skee-Ball again."

"Sure. That's the reason I don't want to eat overpriced mediocre pizza again this soon," she assured.

"It wasn't that bad."

"It wasn't that good either," she reminded him.

Although his gaze still searched her face, Slade laughed. "So, what's another restaurant Gracie likes?"

Gracie yelled out the name of her favorite Japanese hibachi grill.

Slade's brow rose. "You like sushi?"

"She'll eat it, but she's more into the steak and the show."

"Kid after my own heart. Hibachi it is."

Three weeks had passed since Taylor had married Slade. Three weeks in which her pregnancy tests had remained negative and she'd spent an inordinate amount of time with him. He really had set aside whatever his other obligations were because he spent every moment he wasn't at work with her and Gracie.

"It's only five more days until Christmas," Slade pointed out to the little girl in his lap.

Five days. Then her month with Slade would soon be over and then…and then what? He'd wanted the month so he could actively pursue having an affair with her. The sexual chemistry was always there, burning just below the surface, simmering and threatening to rise to a boil, but other than light touches that sent her nerves into overdrive, lingering looks that made her want to both run and hide, and strip him naked, and his lightly flirtatious comments, he hadn't pushed. Why not? She was so on edge she almost wanted him to push just so she could get angry at him.

She glanced at the other end of the sofa where Gracie was curled up in his lap. They were studying a department-store sales flyer as if it contained all the secrets to the world.

"I think Princess Vegas might like this one best." Gracie pointed to an item on a particular page.

"You think?" Slade studied the page with all seriousness. "I don't know. Princess Vegas might think getting a kitchen set to be insulting. After all, princesses don't cook."

"Princesses can cook if they want to cook," Gracie educated him. "Princesses just don't have to cook if they don't want to cook. Someone else has to do the dishes. Princesses never do the dishes."

"Unless they want to," Slade added, to which Gracie frowned and Taylor fought a smile.

"Gracie, I'm not sure that toy kitchen set will fit in Santa's sleigh."

"It will. Santa's sleigh is magic. If it can fly, it can hold all the toys for good boys and girls. Besides, some people get ponies and stuff. How do you think they all fit?" She paused for effect. "Magic."

"She makes a good argument." Slade looked as if he was fighting back a smile.

Taylor nodded. Her daughter was pretty sharp. "Well, let's hope you've been a very good girl this year, then, so Santa can bring you that."

"The kitchen is for Princess Vegas, but I have been a very good girl, Mommy."

"I think you have, but who knows what Santa's been told?" Taylor teased.

Gracie thought about that a few seconds. "Sarah Beth is getting her picture taken with Santa tomorrow at the mall. I should go and make sure Santa knows I've been a good girl."

"I think you should." Slade glanced toward Taylor.

"What do you think, Mom? You up for a trip to the mall tomorrow?"

"No parking places, crowded stores, long lines waiting to see Santa? Bring it on," she agreed. How could she not at the image of Gracie and Slade on the sofa, both looking so expectantly at her?

Slade laughed. "You've obviously done this before."

"A few times."

"You two will have to humor me. I've never done the Santa-at-the-mall thing."

Taylor frowned. So he didn't have kids and didn't want kids, but what about when he had been a kid? "Where did you grow up? Siberia?"

"Here, in Nashville."

"Then how did you avoid Santa at the mall?"

"I may have been when I was really small but, if so, I don't remember. My mom got sick when I was pretty young and we just didn't do that kind of thing."

"What kind of sickness?" Gracie rubbed his cheek in what Taylor assumed was her way of trying to comfort Slade.

"Breast cancer." His eyes were focused on the flyer he and Gracie still held.

Taylor's gaze stayed fixed on him and her hands wanted to rub his cheek, too, if it would give any comfort to the raw ache she'd heard in his two words. "Breast cancer?"

"Yes."

His mother had died of breast cancer and now he was an oncologist? Coincidence? Taylor doubted it. "How old were you?"

"When Mom was first diagnosed? Five. I was twelve when she died. She put up a great fight."

"I'm sorry."

"Me, too."

"Me, too," Gracie added, just to remind them that although she hadn't been saying much she'd been taking in their conversation.

Slade pulled her to him, kissed the top of her head, then changed the subject. "So, what do you think Santa needs to bring for your mom?"

Gracie put her finger to the side of her mouth and looked thoughtful, then scooted farther up in his lap and whispered in his ear. She glanced toward Taylor and giggled, then said something else.

Slade's eyes got big. "Seriously?"

Gracie nodded. "It's what she really wants."

"Interesting." Slade gave Taylor a look that made her feel nervous. "Does Santa do that?"

A puzzled look came over Gracie's face and then she shrugged. "He's magic, remember?"

Curious, Taylor crossed her arms. "What are you two up to?"

Gracie giggled. "Plotting your Christmas present."

"She put in a pretty tall request, but since it's what you really want..."

"I guess I'll find out in five days if I've been good or bad this year."

"Or maybe you've been really good at being bad?"

Gracie giggled. Taylor arched a brow.

"I'm pretty sure Santa is going to leave a bunch of coal in your stocking, Slade Sain." She paused. "Did you ever get your tree decorated?"

He shook his head. "It's in my living room, but that's it. I'm not much on Christmas decorations."

"Gracie and I should help you decorate." Maybe it was how his voice had cracked, how he'd tried to look so un-affected when he'd said his mother had had breast cancer, but Taylor wanted to do something for him. Goodness knew, he'd done enough for her and Gracie over the past few weeks.

"I'd like that."

"Then that's what we'll plan to do tomorrow after we go to the mall."

"That'll work because I'll have to pick up some ornaments and the like while we're there."

"You don't have ornaments?" Gracie sounded stunned. "How old are you?"

He shook his head. "We won't talk about how old I am but, no, I don't have any ornaments."

"I should make you some," Gracie offered.

"I'd like that."

Taylor would swear that his voice broke and that his eyes glistened more than a little.

Gracie climbed out of his lap and headed to her room.

"She is a wonderful kid, Taylor."

"I think so." Needing to be closer to him, to bring a smile back to his face, Taylor scooted near to where he sat. "What was Gracie's suggestion for my Christmas present?"

Looking grateful for the distraction from how emotional he'd gotten moments before, he shook his head. "Ask Gracie."

"I'm asking you."

"I'm not telling."

"Why not?"

"Because it's for me to know and for you to find out."

"That is so childish."

"Guilty as charged."

She picked up a sofa pillow and tossed it at him.

He caught it. "You wanna play?"

"Not really," she denied, but her gaze stayed locked with his mischievous one. She much preferred this look to the sad one that had taken hold in his eyes.

"Then you shouldn't have started something you didn't want to finish." He scooted closer, the pillow in his hands.

"Don't do it."

"Or what?"

"Or…or…" She couldn't think of any threat that even

halfway made sense, so she grabbed another pillow, whacked him over the head and shot off the sofa.

He caught her before she'd taken two steps, pulling her down into his lap. "Naughty, naughty, Taylor. Don't you know Santa is watching?"

"Santa isn't real," she told him, twisting halfheartedly to free herself from his hold, but his arms tightened around her.

"Don't you let my girl hear you say that."

"She's my girl, and I'd never say that in front of Gracie. I want her to believe in all things good."

Was he staring at her mouth? Because she really thought he was staring at her mouth.

She held her breath.

He was definitely staring at her mouth. "I want to kiss you, Taylor, but Gracie is just in her room."

"I know." She did know.

"Do you want me to kiss you?"

"I'm not going to answer that."

"Because you do?"

"I'm not going to answer that either."

He laughed.

Taylor didn't. Because she wanted him to kiss her. They'd been married for three weeks. Three weeks. They were getting divorced.

Yet she couldn't imagine her life without him.

Which really wasn't good because she didn't want to become dependent on him.

She started to rise from his lap, but he hugged her to him. "Don't go."

"I have things to do," she argued, needing to get away from him so she could clear her head. "I need to check on Gracie."

"We'll both go."

He made everything sound so good, as if life was full of possibilities, as if they could make this work. Then again, she'd believed Kyle when he'd convinced her of that, too.

# CHAPTER ELEVEN

KYLE WOULD HAVE been cursing before they'd even pulled into the mall parking lot. Taylor's father would have made one loop, declared the whole thing a disaster and told her there was no Santa but that he'd buy her one item off her list so to choose wisely.

However, Slade dropped Taylor and Gracie off at the front entrance so they could secure a place in line to see Santa. Then, still whistling a tune, he drove off in her minivan to search out a most likely nonexistent parking space.

Twenty minutes after letting them out at the front mall entrance, Slade joined them in the Santa line.

"You're just in time," Gracie told him excitedly. "It's almost my turn."

"Glad I didn't miss it. I wanted to see you with Santa."

"Sorry this is so much trouble," Taylor apologized.

Slade just shrugged. "This isn't that much trouble. Besides, if it makes her smile and you smile, it's worth a whole lot more than the effort to find a parking space."

"How come you're so nice?"

"Because I know what's beneath your clothes and I want another peek." He waggled his brows.

Taylor's eyes widened, surprised at his reply and a little flattered, too, even though she said, "Typical male response."

"I am a man."

"So all this is about sex?" she whispered, for his ears only. "Because you haven't even kissed me."

And maybe because she didn't quite believe that his answer hadn't been a cover because he hadn't wanted to tell her why he was really so nice to her and Gracie.

His eyes searched hers. "Have you wanted me to kiss you, Taylor? I asked you last night and you wouldn't answer. If you'll recall, our agreement was that I'd only do what you wanted me to do. I want you. I've been blunt about that. What do you want?"

She was saved from answering by Gracie excitedly tugging on her hand. "I'm next."

Fortunately, her daughter's full attention was all on the Santa and, unfortunately, Slade hadn't been distracted at all.

"Well?"

She shook her head. Discussing this in line to see Santa wasn't the right time or place. "It doesn't matter."

"It does."

"I was just making a point that if all this is about sex, then it doesn't make sense that you haven't, well, you know, pushed for sex."

Slade smiled and looked so smug that you'd think it was him next in line with Santa. "You've been thinking about Vegas."

"It's my turn!" Gracie grabbed their attention. "Mommy, take my picture."

"Actually, you can't," an elf informed them. "Picture packages with Santa are available for a small fee." He pointed his finger to a table on the other side of the line. "When she finishes with Santa, just head over there and they'll fix you up with all the pictures you want."

Taylor and Slade watched Gracie whisper a long request to Santa, for Santa to look their way, then her to nod and say more. The Santa looked an awful lot like the Santa who had married them in Vegas, but, then, they were both impersonating a jolly old man wearing red and having a snowy-white beard. For that matter, the elf kind of reminded her of the limo driver…but that was crazy.

She shook her head, thinking Slade's comment about Vegas must have put the notion in her mind.

"There's no telling what she's asking for," she mused, mostly to make sure the subject didn't go back to sex…or the lack thereof.

"You think she's changed her mind from the toy kitchen?"

Still studying the Santa and his elf helpers, wondering at the resemblance to the Vegas Santa and his helpers, Taylor shrugged. "Kids tend to change their minds a dozen times before Christmas actually arrives."

"I hope not."

Something in the way he said it made Taylor look at him more closely. "Why?"

He grinned. "Because this Santa went online and ordered a certain toy kitchen set."

"What if I've already bought that for her?"

"Then I will cancel my order," he immediately offered, not looking upset in the slightest.

Again, a very different response than her father or Kyle would have had if she'd done something that had messed with their plans. She knew she shouldn't compare Slade to them, but she couldn't seem to help herself.

"Have you?" he prompted.

"I haven't, but you didn't need to buy her such a big item."

"I'll keep that in mind when I buy your present." His eyes twinkled.

Heat warmed her insides. He planned to buy her a gift? Why did that mean so much more than it should? "I know you don't celebrate the holidays, so don't bother getting me a present."

"There's one to me under your tree. Gracie had me shake it and try to figure out what it was."

So maybe he was just getting her a gift in response to her gift. Still, it was the thought that counted and for a man who claimed not to celebrate Christmas to make the effort did funny things to her insides.

"It's just a little something."

"I'll get you a little something, too," he promised.

"Did you see me with Santa?" Happiness shone in Gracie's eyes. "He said I had been a very good girl and that I was going to get all kinds of presents this year."

"He did?" Taylor shot a concerned look toward Santa. Man, he looked a lot like Vegas Santa. But no way could it be the same guy. The dude really shouldn't build up kids' expectations so high. A lot of parents would do well to buy one or two of the items on their kids' lists.

"Yep, he said you were going to get what you wanted for Christmas this year, too. That he's sorry about last year, but you never said anything until Christmas Day and then it was too late."

"He did?" she repeated, yet again looking at the Santa. The man's attention had already turned to the next kid climbing into his lap, but he glanced up and winked at Taylor.

What? Taylor stared in slight disbelief at the resemblance, telling herself to stop being silly and to pay attention to her daughter.

Gracie showed them the little stocking filled with a few pieces of candy that Santa had given her and then they were ushered over to the photo table where a computer screen had pictures of Gracie with Santa pulled up.

They couldn't decide which of the three shots they liked best, so Taylor ended up buying two of them and Slade bought the other because he thought it might have been his favorite and he couldn't leave the print behind.

They shopped for a few gifts Taylor still hadn't picked up, Gracie helping to decide between several items for Nina, then they drove to her favorite hibachi grill.

By the time they got to Slade's house, had the small tree decorated with the ornaments Gracie had made him with construction paper, glitter and glue, and a string of colorful lights, Gracie was tired and curled up on his sofa to watch a movie on television. In less than five minutes she was asleep.

"I guess we should be going," Taylor said, feeling awkward in his condo now that Gracie was out like a light.

"We were so busy decorating my poor little tree that you never saw the rest of the condo. Let me show you."

"Okay," she agreed, not knowing what else to say.

His place was beautiful, airy, spacious and clean. No toys or little handprints anywhere. Everything modern, high-tech and looking like it should be featured in a magazine article on the perfect bachelor pad.

They came to his bedroom. She refused to look at the bed. Then they went into his bathroom and he had an amazing rain shower and tub. Flashbacks to that last morning in Vegas and the shower they'd shared had her face heating. Oh, my.

"That is seriously cool." She eyed the tub and tried to keep her mind off Vegas. "Gracie could swim in it."

They both stared at the tub. "It's a shame I don't use it more often."

"Just let me know when and I'll come make use of it for you." Ugh. Had she really just said that? She hadn't meant… Or maybe she had. What was wrong with her? Thoughts of Vegas? Part of her wished she could blink her eyes and they would be back to that weekend away from reality.

"Anytime, Taylor."

His voice changed, taking on a raspy quality, and her gaze lifted to his. He watched her with awareness, hot and heavy, as if his mind was filled with the image of her in his tub, of them in his tub. Was he thinking about Vegas?

Her heart rate kicked up. "Sorry, I didn't mean…"

"Taylor?"

"Mmm?"

"Shh." He grabbed her wrist and pulled her to him.

Her cheek pressed up against his chest. The material of

his shirt was soft, smelled of him, made her want to snuggle in closer to the sound of his heartbeat.

His fingers were in the pulled-up tangles of her hair. His lips were brushing the top of her head. His thumbs caressed her face.

"I know Gracie is asleep in the living room, but I need to touch you, Taylor. Even if just a little. Tell me that's what you want, too."

She knew what he meant. Being pressed against him felt so good. But she couldn't forget Gracie was just a few rooms away and could wake anytime.

He gently sucked against her nape.

Taylor almost moaned. Okay, so she did moan, the sound jarring her back to reality. She bit the inside of her lip.

"I know what you say you want," he continued, his eyes flickering with emotion. "When we touch, when you look at me, your body says something completely different."

She willed her body to silence. "We both know you are an attractive, skilled man. Of course I respond to you. It doesn't mean anything."

"So if we kiss and touch, it's nothing more than appeasing our sexual appetites?" he elaborated, moving even closer to her.

"Right." Had her voice cracked?

"Which means there's no reason why we shouldn't kiss, why we shouldn't give each other pleasure, because we both know the score."

"Right." That time she knew her voice had cracked.

He spun her so she was facing herself in the mirror that ran the entire length of the massive sink and countertop. He moved close so that his body pressed against hers, so that his hardness pressed into the softness of her backside. Taylor gulped.

He shifted against her. Excited shivers shot through her body. He kissed her, thoroughly, completely, making her practically gasp for air. His hands traveled over her body, leaving a wake of awareness, of need.

"None of this matters because a few months from now it will all be as if we never happened," he continued. "We'll go on with our lives just as if Vegas never happened."

Her gaze searched his in the mirror. She was reminded of the night he'd made love to her in Vegas, when he'd stripped her in front of the mirror. He'd been full of tenderness and passion. Now his eyes burned with something different, something she couldn't quite label.

Something that made her long for things she knew better than to long for. She wouldn't be able to forget him, wouldn't be able to think of Christmas without thinking of him, of their wedding ceremony performed by Santa, of his decorating with her and Gracie, of how wonderful the past few weeks had been with him at her side.

Because he made her want to believe in the magic of the holidays, that dreams could come true, even crazy ones that seemed almost impossible, such as a playboy changing into a Prince Charming. Her Prince Charming.

Only he wasn't and that was like a bucket of cold water over her head.

"You and I did happen, Slade, and that changed everything," she admitted, so softly she was surprised he could make out her words. He must have, though, because rather than resume kissing her, as she'd expected, as she'd longed for, panted for, he stepped back, turned from her, and walked out of the bathroom with a growled comment about going to check on Gracie.

"Ho-ho-ho, merry Christmas!" Slade called out as he pushed the front door to Taylor's house closed. A house that felt more and more like home to him. Which was why he needed to forget having an affair with Taylor, see her and Gracie past the holidays, then push them from his mind.

In two days he'd be flying to Newark to tour Grandview Pharmaceuticals and negotiate the offer for his dream job.

The call had come the day before and although he'd been over the moon, he'd found himself unable to tell anyone other than his father. His father, who had asked yet again when Slade was going to bring his new family to the farm for a visit and what they thought of moving to Newark. He had hummed and hawed enough to let his dad know that what Taylor and Gracie thought really wasn't a deciding factor in his decision.

They weren't.

This was the opportunity he'd dreamed of, the perfect smokescreen for Taylor and him to quietly divorce without any holiday or life drama for either of them, without Grandview bigwigs discovering that their new clinical research director had married and planned a divorce the same weekend. A win all the way around.

"Mr. Slade!" Gracie almost toppled him over as she launched herself at him, hugging him tightly.

Forgetting Taylor and Gracie wasn't going to be easy. She'd been right when she'd said they had happened and it had changed everything. Only he refused to let it change everything. He knew what he wanted, what his life goals were, and nothing was going to stand in the way of that.

Nothing and no one. He'd enjoy his time left with them, then he'd leave and not look back.

"Hey, princess." He set the packages he held on to the wooden foyer floor and hugged the little girl to him, loving the warmth and genuineness to her embrace. "You ready for Santa Claus to come tonight?"

Gracie nodded. "It's going to be amazing."

"That good this year, eh?"

Blond curls bounced up and down again. "Do you want a cookie? Mommy and I have been baking them for Santa."

Slade caught sight of Taylor standing in the doorway, watching them. As usual, she stole his breath.

His wife. But not for much longer. Soon he'd pack his belongings and move to another state, live the life he'd always wanted. A life where he focused on finding a cure for a disease that had robbed him of so much. That had robbed so many of so much. He had no regrets.

"Hey," she greeted him, a bit breathy sounding herself.

"Hey, yourself." He soaked in every bit of her. From her caught-up-in-a-ponytail hair, to the Christmas sweater and yoga pants, to her washed-clean face. He was leaving in two days. The thought made him want to grab her, throw her over his shoulder and lock them in her bedroom for the remainder of the time they had left.

"Come on, Mr. Slade. Come see the cookies we made. I put icing on them and sparkling things you can eat." Gracie tugged on his hand, reminding him of why he wouldn't be doing any of the things he longed to do with Taylor.

"Help me carry these to the tree." He motioned to the brightly wrapped cartoon-princess-covered packages. "Then lead me to the cookies."

Gracie giggled and began inspecting the presents. "Are these all for me?" she asked, big eyed.

He nodded. He'd gone overboard, but he'd never had a kid to buy for in the past, never would in the future and he wanted Gracie's Christmas to be special. It would be the only one he shared with her.

The thought of missing her future Christmases, of missing her, shot sadness through him. Which was ridiculous. He was getting what he wanted. He should be over the moon.

Gracie smiled at him. "That's a lot of presents."

Fingering a dangling blond curl because he needed to touch her, he pointed out, "You did say you'd been a really good girl this year."

She nodded, grabbed up a package and took off toward the living room where the tree was.

"You didn't have to get her so much."

"I had fun shopping for her." True. Even though it had

been years since he'd bought more than a gift card, he had enjoyed searching out gifts for Gracie.

"I can see you now in the little-girl section of the toy store," Taylor teased.

Slade took her hand, pulled her to him for a brief kiss to the cheek. "You smell good." He breathed in the scent of her hair.

"Like cookies?" She didn't pull away. Which surprised him. Thrilled him. Made him wonder what else he could do that she wouldn't pull away from.

"Like you."

"Flatterer."

"It's the truth."

"Do you always tell the truth, Slade?"

Her question seemed an odd one. Did she know about Grandview? Was she testing him to see if he'd tell her? Or was that his guilty conscience because she didn't know? He would tell her. Tonight. He studied her expression, then shrugged. "I try to be honest."

"It's a good policy. Prevents confusion down the road."

"Yeah." If she knew he was leaving, why didn't she just say so? Then again, how could she? He'd just found out the day before.

The timer on the oven dinged.

"Time to take out the last batch. You want to help decorate? The other batches should be cool by now."

He soaked in her smile, the warmth of her expression, and wondered how many nights he'd spend thinking about her in Newark. He suspected too many.

"Sure," he agreed. "But I have to warn you, I'm more of an expert cookie eater than decorator."

"Will you read me another good-night story?" Gracie yawned and stretched out in her bed. "I'm not sleepy."

"I can see that," Taylor agreed, smiling down at her

daughter. "I guess we can do one more story, since it's Christmas Eve and all."

Gracie turned big green eyes on Slade, who stood in the doorway. "Will you lie down next to me and listen, too?"

"Gracie—" Taylor began, but Slade dismissed her concerns.

"Sure."

Despite his looking a little uncomfortable, he lay next to Gracie and she snuggled into the crook of his arm, grinning up at him. "Mommy is a very good storyteller."

His expression difficult to assess, he answered, "I've heard."

"I'm not sure about that, but I can read a book." They'd just finished *The Night Before Christmas*, so Taylor reached for one of Gracie's all-time favorites about a mischievous little girl with an active imagination.

Gracie looked up at Slade. "You're going to love this. It's so good."

Taylor began to read. Occasionally, Gracie would giggle and poke Slade. "See," she'd say.

Taylor kept reading until Gracie's eyes closed, then she finished the chapter and closed the book.

She stared at the image of Gracie tucked against Slade and her heart melted. That's how it was supposed to be, she thought. How it should be.

Her gaze shifted to his and so many emotions shot through her. Mostly emotions of longing. Not just for the physical things he did to her body but for the way he'd turned her and Gracie's lives upside down over the past weeks. She had one week left with him. Then what? They told the world they'd made a mistake and were divorcing? Would he still be a part of their lives or would he go back to how things had been before Vegas?

She set the book back on Gracie's shelf and began untangling her daughter from Slade.

"I love you, Mommy," Gracie mumbled, not really awake.

"I love you, too, sweetheart."

"I love you, too, Mr. Slade."

Taylor's gaze went to Slade's. He stared at the sleeping little girl, but didn't respond other than to lose color from his face.

She might be getting all soft and mushy on the inside, but Slade wasn't. She'd do well to remember that.

Her throat constricting, Taylor moved away from the bed and left the room. She went into the kitchen and began unloading the dishwasher. He hadn't said the words back to Gracie. Because they weren't true? Because he'd told her earlier that he tried to always be honest?

Yes, she was biased, but how could he not have fallen for the little girl as much as Gracie had fallen for him? Right or wrong, she believed he had. So why hadn't he been able to admit it?

"Do you know if you're pregnant?"

Not having heard him come into the kitchen, she jumped, startled at his presence as much as at his words. Gracie's sleepy declaration had made him wonder if Taylor was pregnant. She paused midway to the cabinet, cup in hand. "I'm not."

"You're sure?" His voice was rough. Rougher than it should be, asking such a sensitive question. Or maybe she was just being too sensitive because she'd cried when she'd started her period. Tears of relief and tears of loss. How crazy was that?

"I'm sure. I told you I wasn't after the last negative pregnancy test, and I finished my period yesterday so I know I'm not. I guess I should have told you about getting my period, too."

He nodded as if that's what he'd expected her to say. "I thought you had. You drank coffee at work this week."

The man was observant. She'd give him that. "That made you think I wasn't pregnant?"

"Despite your negative pregnancy tests, you'd not had a cup since Vegas."

Yep, he was too observant for his own good.

"I started vitamins and stopped my bad habits just in case, but nothing came of Vegas."

*Nothing came of Vegas.* The words ripped at her heart. What had she wanted to come of Vegas? Nothing. Nothing at all because she'd never planned for Vegas to happen.

"I'm glad," he told her. "A pregnancy would have made everything more difficult."

Taylor gulped back the stab of pain she shouldn't be feeling. "You're right."

Because they were temporary, were getting a divorce, were only together to keep from having so much life turmoil with family and at work right before the holidays. Yet she'd not met his father or stepmother. Since Slade claimed not to celebrate the holidays, she supposed it made sense, but he'd not even mentioned her and Gracie meeting his family since the night they'd bought the Christmas trees.

Why didn't he celebrate Christmas?

She put a cup in the cabinet, shut the door and dared him to look away from her. After his not responding to Gracie, she just dared him to ignore her. "Tell me about your mother."

His face paled almost as much as it had when Gracie had told him she loved him. "My mother? Why?"

Why? Good question when they were only pretending. Only was she really? Would his comment about her being pregnant have hurt so much if she was only pretending?

"I want to understand you," she admitted. She wanted to understand why he changed relationships so often, why he felt the way he did about marriage and kids, to understand why he'd not said three simple words back to a child he obviously adored.

"There really isn't a point, is there?"

Exactly what she'd just thought, but she couldn't let it go.

"It's Christmas Eve. Humor me."

He raked his fingers through his hair. "Let's go sit in the living room. I'll tell you, but it's really not that interesting a story."

For a not so interesting story, they talked until almost midnight. Once he started talking he couldn't seem to quit. Maybe to distract himself from the panic that had gripped him when Gracie had told him she loved him. Maybe because he'd almost said the words back. But he couldn't love the little girl. Sure, he cared about her and Taylor, but he didn't love them. So instead of analyzing all the unwelcome emotions that had taken hold of him he told Taylor about when he'd first realized his mother was sick, her frequent trips in and out of the hospital, about the sticky notes she'd write him every day.

"That's why you give your patients those notes?"

He nodded. "It just feels right, like I'm keeping a part of her alive."

"You keep her alive just by being you."

Talking about his mother helped, reminded him of his life goals, grounding him to the future he'd chosen. "She was a special lady."

"I wish I could have met her."

He pulled out his wallet and withdrew a photo. It was a family shot of him, his dad, and his mother. Slade had been about five at the time.

She'd been upset when they'd started talking, but her attitude had softened long ago. "You look a lot like her."

"Thank you."

Taylor studied the picture. "How old was she when she died?"

"Thirty-three." The words tore from his heart.

Taylor grimaced. "That's so young."

He nodded. "Too young to have dealt with the things she dealt with." He stared at the photo, lots of old memories slamming him. Good, he needed those memories to keep his mind on track. He slid the picture back into his wallet, wondering why he'd let Taylor convince him to talk about his mother. Then again, maybe he'd told her because it was the perfect lead in to telling her that he was leaving, that he was taking a job to fulfill the vow he'd made in his mother's memory. Definitely he'd wanted a distraction from Gracie's sleepy words and their shattering effect.

"You were too young to have dealt with the things you dealt with, too," Taylor mused, taking his hand. "I'm sorry."

His heart squeezed and he didn't like the jitteriness shooting through his veins. Neither did he want her pity. "It's okay."

"Not really, but I understand what you mean."

They sat there, holding hands and staring at the Christmas tree for long moments, each lost in their own thoughts. He knew where his mind was, where he needed their conversation to go, but instead they sat in silence. Finally, Taylor stood.

"I guess it's time for Santa to show."

Slade arched a brow at her. "Santa?"

"You know what I mean and, no, I'm not putting a red suit and beard on."

The image of Taylor dressed as Santa had a real smile tugging at his lips. "Too bad. You'd rock a red suit and wig."

"Maybe, but Gracie will be just as happy with Santa arriving and eating his cookies sans a wig and red suit."

"I could help take care of those cookies for you," he offered, wiggling his brows and wondering why he wasn't redirecting their conversation to Grandview.

"Have at them. She also left a glass of milk, but since it's been out of the fridge a few hours I'd recommend tossing it rather than drinking it."

Taylor disappeared into her bedroom and came back carrying some plastic bags. Wondering at himself, at his reluctance to bring up a subject that he suspected would ruin their remaining time together, Slade made haste with the cookies while she pulled out stocking stuffers and gifts from the bags.

"She's going to be so excited when she wakes up."

"I wish I could see her," he murmured, not realizing he'd said the words out loud until Taylor's head spun toward him. How much he meant the words surprised him. He really would like to be there when Gracie woke, when she stumbled half-asleep into the living room and saw her gifts.

But not because he loved the little girl. Just that he'd spent so much time with Taylor and Gracie over the past few weeks that of course he wanted to be there when she experienced Christmas morning.

He watched Taylor consider offering to let him stay. His lungs didn't seem to be working correctly. He wanted to stay, to make love to Taylor, to wake up next to her, and experience Christmas morning with her and Gracie. Part of him wanted to take her into his arms and seduce her into letting him stay. Another part had his lungs constricting so tightly he had to go.

He couldn't stay, couldn't complicate the fact he was leaving the day after Christmas by having sex with Taylor when he suspected doing so would make leaving more difficult. For them both.

"What time is too early for me to arrive?"

"It's Christmas. She'll probably be up at the crack of dawn." She met his gaze. "It's already very late. You won't get but a few hours' sleep at most. Maybe you should stay?"

"I'll be fine heading home. I can sleep when I'm old." Or when he was in Newark. Alone.

*Fulfilling his lifelong dream.*

Disappointment and uncertainty flickered across her face. He was doing the right thing in going home so why didn't he feel better about doing the right thing?

"Whatever time is fine, then, but I should remind you that my parents will be here about noon."

She'd mentioned that they'd be over on Christmas Day.

"They'll bring Gracie lots of frilly clothes and maybe some mutual bonds or Fortune 500 stock."

At first he thought she was kidding, but at the serious look on her face he decided she wasn't. "Interesting Christmas choices for a six-year-old."

"Six. Two. Either way, it's never too young to start preparing for one's future."

Not liking the tension now etched onto her face, he nudged her shoulder. "They sound like party animals."

"Ha." She did smile, albeit weakly. "That they are not. More like some idealistic television couple. He's an investment broker. She's a country-club stay-home wife. They live in a plastic bubble of utopia."

"And you?"

"I'm not a chip off the old block. More like the daughter who should have been a son and has been a big disappointment at every point along the way."

"I doubt that. You're a very successful woman."

She gave a wry smile. "I guess that depends on what perspective you're looking from."

"From where I'm sitting, you're accomplished, beautiful, intelligent, compassionate and a good mother to Gracie." He didn't mention sexy since he didn't think that would be a trait her parents would appreciate, but he definitely appreciated that about her. "What more could they want from their child?"

Her cheeks turned pink and he could tell his praise pleased her. Guilt hit him that he hadn't complimented her more over the past few weeks, that he hadn't realized just how much she questioned herself. He should have told her over and over how amazing she was.

"They would have preferred for me to live a bit more within the rules."

Her comment seemed hard for him to fathom. "You a rule breaker, Taylor?"

"Apparently only on the big things."

His comment had been a tease, but her slight shrug made him wonder at her past. "Such as?"

"I didn't go into investments, but a doctor was a respectable profession, so they supported me in med school. Then I got pregnant with Gracie. That didn't win me any accolades in their eyes." She took a deep breath, then gave another shrug as if what she was saying didn't matter so much, even though it obviously did. "Now I've married a man I barely knew and am going to be the first in my family to divorce."

Good thing he knew she didn't want to be married any more than he did or he'd feel all kinds of guilty. As it was, he still felt a heel that their relationship caused her grief. "They don't know we're divorcing yet, do they?"

"No, and I'm grateful I don't have to deal with that on Christmas Day, but I dread their reaction when I do tell them. They've already told me how disappointed they are yet again in my life choices. If you decided not to show tomorrow, I wouldn't blame you."

"I'll be here." As uncomfortable as it might be, he would be there for her parents' visit and would hopefully be able to show her parents a glimpse of the woman he saw.

Before heading home, Slade brought in the large box containing Gracie's toy kitchen. "Is it okay if we set this up tomorrow, or would you rather put it together tonight?"

She shook her head. "Tomorrow is fine."

"Then I'll be going."

She nodded. "Tomorrow will be a long day, full of highs and lows."

"We'll focus on the highs."

"You're right. I have a lot of reasons to be thankful." Her eyes searched his, confused, tempting. "You're one of the things I'm thankful for, you know."

He stared at her a moment, wished things were different, acknowledged that they weren't and that he would also focus on the positives. He was getting the opportunity to make a difference in a deadly disease, to strive toward his goal of a cure. He didn't acknowledge her words, because what could he say that wouldn't reveal too much of the turmoil inside him?

He grabbed his coat. "I'll be back first thing in the morning."

# CHAPTER TWELVE

"TELL ME THEY weren't like that growing up."

Drying the plate she held, Taylor laughed at Slade's expression. "They weren't."

"They were worse?" Slade said, helping her dry the dishes and put them away.

Taylor just smiled. Her parents had descended on them, brought presents, criticized everything from Gracie still being in her pajamas at noon to Taylor looking tired to they really should have had Christmas at their place and Taylor should be more co-operative. They'd been polite, though barely, to Slade initially. Her father had quizzed him like a drill sergeant.

Which had seemed ridiculous since they were going to divorce anyway. Only she hadn't told her parents that and neither had Slade.

Slade had laid on the charm. Halfway through their visit her father had actually seemed to accept him. Her mother's only direct comment regarding Slade had been that, after seeing him, she at least understood Taylor's temptation, even if she didn't condone her choice.

Taylor had bitten her tongue and smiled at her parents, regardless of their words. Although not touchy-feely with her, they hadn't been bad parents, just ones caught up in their own lives and expectations to where they hadn't been able to understand when their daughter acted outside those standards.

Gracie loved her grandparents. For the little girl, they had genuinely smiled as Gracie had shown them the toy kitchen, which she and Slade had put together while Taylor had made breakfast, plus all her many toys and new clothes.

Gracie had also given Slade the presents she and Taylor had picked up for him. Not once while they'd been opening presents had he mentioned a present for her. Although a little disappointed that he'd changed his mind about picking up a little something for her, she supposed it didn't really matter. More than anything she'd been curious about what he'd choose for her.

"Mr. Slade, I made you some yummy bacon and eggs." Gracie carefully offered the plastic plate of toy food.

"Looks good." Slade pretended to eat the food as Gracie beamed at him. He might not have said the words back to Gracie, but his actions were those of deep affection.

Taylor's muscles seemed to freeze as she watched them, as she tried to wrap her mind around the man playing with her daughter, the same man who'd spent the past few weeks being the perfect guy, the same man who'd gone through at least a dozen girlfriends during the past year and who had the reputation of a ladykiller. Because he was.

Or was he?

Gracie giggled as Slade pretended to sip tea.

Taylor swallowed. A vision of him walking out of her Vegas hotel bathroom wearing nothing but a towel popped into her mind. As attractive as that image was, the image of him on the floor, playing with her daughter, attracted her in so many more meaningful ways.

Who was she kidding? Everything about the man attracted her. Because she was falling for him.

Had fallen head over heels.

Just as she'd fallen for Kyle. Only her feelings for Slade were so much stronger than anything she'd ever felt for Kyle.

Her heart ached at the knowledge and moisture blurred her vision. She wanted to believe Slade was different, that he'd changed over the past few weeks.

He glanced up, caught her eye and grinned.

Maybe, just maybe, he had fallen, too. If not, she suspected she was in for some major heartache.

Slade glanced up in time to see Taylor swipe at her eyes. Was she crying? Because of her parents? They'd been uptight but hadn't been that bad surely? He'd thought by the end of their visit that they'd started warming to him. He wanted to ask if she was okay, but she scurried away as if she'd forgotten something in the oven.

He immediately glanced up when she reentered the living area. Whatever he might have seen earlier, now she was all smiles and focused her attention on Gracie.

They spent the rest of the day playing games with her, checking out her new toys. Then, with Gracie half lying on Slade, half lying on Taylor, they watched a movie she'd gotten in her stocking from Santa. Halfway through the movie she was out like a light.

"I think she had a good Christmas." Slade watched Taylor twirl a curl around her finger as she played with the little girl's hair. Prior to dozing off, Gracie had done the same, playing with Taylor's hair, which, after her parents had left, she'd loosened and worn down.

"I know she did. She was so excited over the kitchen and all the dishes and toy food. Thank you, Slade."

"I've had a great time with her today." The perfect last day with Gracie and Taylor.

"She's crazy about you." She glanced down at her conked-out daughter. "With as early as she got up this morning, she's probably out for the night."

"Do you want me to carry her to bed?"

Surprise registered on her face. "Sure. I'll go turn her covers down."

Without waking her, they tucked Gracie in, then made their way back to the living room. Taylor picked up the remote and turned off the movie. Slade, however, went to the coat closet and dug in his pocket.

"I have a little something for you."

"You do?"

He grinned. "You didn't think I'd forgotten your gift, did you?"

"You didn't need to get me anything."

"I wanted to. I just hope you like it."

"I'm pretty easygoing so you shouldn't worry about me not liking my gift," she said with a smile. "I'm not that ungrateful a person."

"I know you're not." She wasn't. She was sweet, kind, thoughtful, passionate, beautiful and his, only not really and not for much longer.

He'd put a lot of thought into her gift. Thought hopefully she truly would understand. He'd wanted to give her a gift that meant something, a gift she wouldn't toss out after he was gone from her life. A gift she'd treasure and keep forever that was from him. Why that was so important he wasn't sure, but it was.

"Here." He handed her the present.

She opened the package, saw the jeweler's box inside and hesitated. "You said it was a small gift."

"It is a small gift."

"I thought you meant cost wise," she responded, looking uncertain.

"Just open the box, Taylor."

She did and glanced up at him with tears in her eyes. "Oh, Slade. It's perfect."

Pleasure rippled through him. Mission accomplished.

"I took the photo with my phone the other night when you had her in your lap and printed it for the locket."

She pulled the necklace out of the velvet box. "Help me."

He did, clasping the gold chain around her neck and

stroking his fingertips over the smoothness of her nape because he couldn't resist the feel of her skin.

She touched the locket, which fell between her breasts. "Thank you." Then she surprised him by throwing her arms around him and hugging him.

What was Taylor doing? She knew better than to touch Slade like this. Only his gift was so sweet, so thoughtful, so perfect, she couldn't not express her gratitude.

"I take it you like it?" he asked, holding her close.

"I love it." She should move away now. Hug time was past. So why wasn't she removing her arms from around him? Why was she snuggling closer, letting the feel of him wrap around her, letting his scent envelop her, letting her body melt against his?

"I'm glad."

She nuzzled his neck lightly, knowing she should move away but needing more before she could. "What made you think to get me a locket with a photo of Gracie and me?"

"My mom used to wear one with a photo of me and her. She treasured it. I thought you might, too."

Had he just kissed her hair? He shifted. He had definitely kissed her hair. Her cheek. His lips hovered over hers, so close they almost touched, so close she could feel the warmth of his breath.

His blue eyes stared into hers, so many emotions stormed there. Emotions she recognized. Desire. Longing. Need. Confusion. She closed the tiny gap between their mouths. A guttural noise sounded deep in his throat and he kissed her back. He held her close and kissed her over and over. Sweet, seductive, hungry kisses that cast her further and further under his spell.

When he pulled away he brushed a strand of hair back away from her face. "We shouldn't do this."

Disappointment hit her. Disappointment she shouldn't

feel. She didn't want him to go. Not tonight. Not last night. Not ever. Which scared her.

She started to push him away, to tell him to leave and not come back, because truly that would be best for protecting her vulnerable heart.

Instead, said vulnerable heart pounding in her chest, she whispered, "I want this, Slade. I want you."

*I want you.* Had he ever heard sweeter words? More precious words? More torturous words?

He should go. He knew that. Or should at least tell her about his flight plans for the next morning before they did what they were about to do. He couldn't walk away from her. Not when he knew tonight was the last time he'd hold her, kiss her, make love to her.

He was beyond thinking about anything other than the fact that she wanted him and was giving herself to him. He couldn't walk away, couldn't do more than cherish her gift.

Hand in hand, they walked to Taylor's bedroom, pushing the door to and locking it. Slowly, in the low lamplight, they undressed each other, kissing, touching, needing, giving.

"I want you so much, Taylor." He rained kisses over her throat, her nape. It was true. With time and distance he'd get past Taylor, would move on, have other women in his life, but at the moment he couldn't imagine ever touching anyone but her. Couldn't imagine even wanting to.

"Show me," she urged, arching into his kisses.

He intended to show her just how amazing she was, and did. By the time he had pushed her back onto her bed, had prepared her body for his, Taylor whimpered.

"Please."

Please. He should be the one begging her for the privilege. Slipping on a condom, he thrust inside her, giving her everything he had to give. More. So much more because he was positive that when he left he'd be leaving behind a part of himself.

He couldn't fool himself otherwise.

Higher and higher they climbed. Heat built a sweet pinnacle that promised to topple them over the edge. So much more than anything they'd shared in Vegas. So much more than he'd dreamed possible.

Just as he reached the point he could no longer hold back the mounting pleasure, Taylor softly cried her own release and he was a goner.

Gone. Gone. Gone.

He collapsed onto the bed next to her, gasped to catch his breath, to overcome the fireworks flashing through his mind and body. Damn.

He rolled over to tell her how amazing she was, to tell her about Grandview and that he was leaving in the morning, but that maybe she could fly to Newark from time to time to see him. Or vice versa.

He wasn't opposed to a long-distance affair with her. Actually, the idea appealed a lot. There was no reason to deny themselves the phenomenal chemistry they shared.

"I don't want a divorce, Slade," Taylor told him when their gazes met. Her heart shone in her eyes and her fingers clasped the locket he'd given her. "I want our marriage to be real. For us to be real."

*Oh, hell.* Pain spasmed in his chest while he searched for words to say he was leaving.

If Taylor had harbored any illusions that Slade felt something for her, that he wanted the same things, the look of horror on his face quickly dispelled them. What a fool she was. What had she expected? That sex with her again would magically morph him from playboy to Prince Charming like in some fairy tale?

Just because she'd fallen for him, it didn't mean he had fallen for her. Sex was just sex to Slade. Just as it had been to Kyle. She shouldn't forget that.

"I'm sorry. I shouldn't have said that," she began, scooting away so their skin wouldn't touch. She didn't want to be touching him. Couldn't be touching him.

"Don't," he told her, grabbing her arm but not hanging on when she pulled loose. "I'm the one who is sorry, Taylor."

"You have nothing to be sorry for," she assured him, picking up her clothes off the floor and scurrying to put them back on. After all, she'd known he was a playboy, had known his reputation long before Vegas. Plus, he'd told her he didn't want to be married. For that matter, she'd told him the same thing. She'd been under no illusions except her own. Because she'd gotten caught up in their pretend relationship and wanted to believe. "This is no big deal."

"You look like it's a big deal."

Yeah, she supposed she did. Sex was a big deal to her. Always had been. She couldn't turn that off. Not the way the men in her life could.

"I've known all along that our marriage was pretend, that we were divorcing, and I had sex with you anyway. That's my problem, not yours."

"Taylor…" Her name came out as a sigh.

"It doesn't matter, Slade. I'm an adult and knew what I was doing. You played by the rules we set. This is my fault, not yours."

"I'm leaving."

She hadn't really expected him to stay the night, not after her words and his reaction, but she hadn't been prepared for his abruptness. Had she secretly hoped he'd tell her she was wrong? That he was willing to try?

Oh, God. She had.

"I know." She forced her voice to remain steady despite the pain racking her insides, making her want to curl up in the fetal position and cry at her foolish heart. "You can't stay the night. Gracie."

"That's not what I mean." He sat up in the bed, raked his fingers through his dark hair and looked so guilty she could only stare at him and wonder what he'd done. "I'm leaving as in moving."

Her knees shook and she sank onto the edge of the bed. "Moving?"

"My flight is booked for the morning."

Moving. His flight was booked. In the morning. As in he'd known he was leaving before he'd arrived this morning, before they'd spent the day together, before she'd invited him into her bedroom, before she'd told him she wanted their marriage to be real. How long had he been playing her for a fool? Was he just laughing at how easily she'd caved?

Anger hit her.

"You spent the day with me and Gracie knowing you're moving in the morning and you never said anything until *now*? Did you not think that was an important piece of information for me to have before…before what we just did?"

He had the grace to look remorseful. "Technically, I won't be moving for a few weeks, but I am flying to Newark tomorrow morning. I got the job with Grandview."

Was she missing something? "What job?"

"The one I interviewed for in Vegas."

She was definitely missing something because she'd not known he'd interviewed with Grandview. Her mind? Her heart? Her sanity? All of the above? "I'm confused."

"I told you about my mom, about how I want to make a difference, a real difference in the fight against breast cancer. I interviewed for a position with Grandview and I got the job. This is my opportunity."

She took a deep breath. "So you've known all along that moving was a possibility, but never said anything to me? Your *wife*?" She put emphasis on the last word.

"You're acting as if you're really my wife. We've just been pretending the past month, Taylor, to make things easier at work and with our families. Nothing more. We both agreed to those terms."

He was right. It had all been pretend. But she'd gotten

caught up in the pretense and had lowered her defenses. She'd fallen for him and he'd kept right on being himself. Could she even fault him for that?

"I'm sorry, Taylor. I told you from the beginning I didn't want a wife or kids. Had you been pregnant, it would have complicated our situation, but you aren't. We took precautions just then, so pregnancy shouldn't be an issue from tonight, but if so we'll deal with it."

Ugh. Hearing him talk about their making love, about a possible child they'd made, so clinically, so coldly, hurt.

"All this was to make both of our lives easier rather than face grief about marrying and filing for divorce so quickly right before the holidays, to prevent our mistake from affecting my chances with Grandview, too..."

Light finally dawned.

"That's it, isn't it?" she accused, forgetting to keep her voice down. "That's what all this was really about. Not your family or office gossip or keeping things calm until after the holidays or even sex. All this was because you didn't want Grandview finding out you'd married a woman you didn't know and planned to get divorced because you were afraid that revelation would hurt your chances with your precious dream job because they might think you flighty?"

His jaw worked back and forth. "You can't deny that this way was better all the way round, including for you."

She gritted her teeth and fought the urge to hit him. "No, you jerk, it's not better all the way round because a month ago I didn't know I loved you!"

"Taylor," he began, his expression strained. He raked his fingers through his hair again. "Please, calm down and listen to reason."

"There is no reason. You used me. The least you could have done was be honest about it so I wouldn't have bought all the looks and touches, and believed you actually cared about me and Gracie. I'm such an idiot. I knew better."

\* \* \*

Slade pulled his jeans on and slipped his T-shirt over his head. This wasn't how he wanted the night to end. Maybe he'd known it was inevitable. Maybe that's why he hadn't told her the moment he'd found out he'd gotten the job. He'd known she'd be upset.

What he hadn't counted on had been Taylor saying she loved him. She didn't. She was just confusing unbelievably great sex with emotions.

Not that he didn't understand how she could make that mistake. He knew better, knew he was incapable of love, but he could almost convince himself he loved her, too. Almost.

The best thing he could do would be to leave. Her anger would help shield her from hurt and soon she'd realize she didn't love him. With a little time she'd acknowledge that his leaving had been the right thing.

It was the right thing.

So why did doing the right thing feel so very wrong?

# CHAPTER THIRTEEN

TAYLOR MADE IT through the workday without having to answer too many questions about why Slade wasn't at work. Had Nina told their colleagues there was trouble in paradise or the truth? That Slade had left her? Either way, Taylor was grateful that the office seemed to still be on a holiday high and content to ignore her misery.

She picked Gracie up from her extended school program and focused on cooking dinner while Gracie colored a homework picture.

"I miss Mr. Slade." Gracie pouted, not looking up from where she was coloring the picture at the dining room table.

Heavyhearted, Taylor stared at her daughter. Gracie had gotten used to spending time with him every day. She'd commented repeatedly each evening that she missed Slade. No doubt this evening wouldn't be very different. Her daughter loved him. Wasn't that what she'd feared, what she'd wanted to avoid all along?

Look at what she'd allowed to happen. Not only had she failed to protect her own heart, she'd failed to protect Gracie's.

"I know, baby, but Mr. Slade is a busy man. He has important things he has to do." She'd told Gracie that Slade had gone out of town on an important trip. "He helped us a lot this Christmas, but he's not always going to be around. He has his own life, his own family."

Gracie's little face squished up. "He's married?"

That hadn't been what she'd meant. She'd been talking about his father and stepmother. Her heart thudded in her chest.

"About that..." Should she tell Gracie? What would be the point, other than that she didn't keep things from her daughter? Not usually. Why had she waited so long to tell her daughter the truth? "When I went to Vegas, Mr. Slade went with me, and we made a mistake while we were there."

Gracie stopped coloring and frowned. "What kind of mistake?"

"We accidentally got married."

"Accidentally got married?" Gracie didn't understand and Taylor fully understood that. She didn't understand any of it herself.

"I know it sounds confusing and that's because it is confusing. That's why Mr. Slade has been around so much the past few weeks. But our time with him is up."

Gracie's expression remained pinched. "Because you won't be married anymore?"

What had she done? Letting Gracie be exposed to Slade, letting her fall for his charm, letting her come to depend on him as being a part of her life? Maybe her parents were right. Maybe she was destined to always let down those she loved.

"Something like that," she admitted.

"Can't you accidentally get married again?" Gracie asked with the reasoning of a child.

*Oh, Gracie!* Taylor hugged her daughter to her. "Life doesn't work that way."

Gracie didn't look convinced. "Why not?"

"Mr. Slade and I didn't really want to be married."

With a wisdom beyond her young years Gracie considered all that Taylor said. "That's why it was an accident?"

"Yes."

"But why can't you want to marry him? He's really nice."

"That he is," Taylor admitted.

"Plus, he likes us." Gracie pleaded Slade's case, breaking Taylor's heart a little at how much hope she heard in her daughter's voice. "I know he likes us."

"Of course he likes us, baby," she agreed, trying to figure out how to explain her and Slade's relationship without hurting Gracie even more. "Slade especially likes you. He thinks you're wonderful."

Gracie's face took on a serious look. "Then we should keep him because I like him, too."

Taylor closed her eyes. Keep him. Sounded simple enough. Only he hadn't wanted to be kept.

"Besides, he's your Christmas present."

"What?" Taylor blinked at her daughter.

"He is your Christmas present. I know he is," Gracie insisted. "I heard you and Aunt Nina talking last Christmas when you thought I was asleep. You told her you should have asked Santa for a man." The little girl gave her a solemn stare. "At school, when we had to write letters to Santa, I asked him for a man for you, but my teacher made me write a different letter because she said she couldn't post that one on the wall."

Mortification hit Taylor at Gracie's teacher reading the letter with Gracie asking Santa for a man for her mother. Oh, my.

"So I wrote another for the wall, but Miss Gwen promised she'd send the first one to Santa. I asked him at the mall and he told me you'd gotten your present early so I knew he was talking about Mr. Slade."

"Gracie, I…" Taylor paused, not sure what to say in response.

"We should keep him," Gracie repeated. "He's a good Christmas present."

Taylor saw the longing in her daughter's eyes, knew there was a similar longing in her heart.

But she'd told him she loved him and he'd left. There was no denying that they wanted different things. Yet how did she explain that to her child? No matter what, she didn't want Gracie hurt any more than she already was. She'd known better than to let someone into her and Gracie's world, to risk someone hurting them. Lesson learned.

She pasted on a bright smile and hugged her generous-hearted daughter. "Slade was a great Christmas present, Gracie, and we got to spend Christmas with him and that was wonderful." No matter how much she ached inside, spending the holidays with Slade had been wonderful. If only doing so hadn't come at such a high price. "But now Slade gets to enjoy his Christmas present, which is to work at his dream job. As much as you and I miss him, we do want him to be happy, right?"

Taylor did. She supposed. Mostly, she just wanted Gracie not to suffer because of her mistake in forgetting who Slade really was. A playboy who wouldn't ever truly settle down.

Gracie frowned in thought. "Yes, but wasn't he happy with us?"

"He was." She believed he had been. But Kyle had been, too, at the beginning of their relationship. Men like them enjoyed life, but quickly got bored and moved on. It's just how things were. "But his new job is what he's always wanted. Because we care about him, we are happy he got what he's always wanted."

Gracie's nose curled. "I guess so."

As angry and hurt as she was by his actions, as much as she doubted she could ever forgive herself for allowing him into their lives and hurting Gracie, as much as she would never trust him again, Taylor knew so.

Grandview Pharmaceuticals was everything and more that Slade had craved for years. The clinical research director position being dangled in front of him gave him the opportunity to work directly on developing a promising new chemotherapy drug.

He'd be heading up the team.

They'd agreed to his contract terms and were having the legal documents drawn up. In the morning he'd meet with them, sign the papers and start the rest of his life.

So why was he lying in a hotel bed, staring at the ceiling and wondering if he was making the biggest mistake of his life?

Because Taylor had said she didn't want a divorce or for their marriage to be pretend? Because she'd said she was in love with him?

They never could have been anything more than pretend. He wasn't the marrying kind. He was a career man.

He thought over the past month, of the time he'd spent with Taylor and Gracie, and his insides ached.

Ached.

Because in such a short time they'd become such an integral part of his life.

Which should make him grateful the Grandview job had come through when it had. He didn't need distractions from his true destiny. He didn't need emotions blinding him to his real purpose. He'd vowed to help others, to make a difference in the fight against breast cancer, to find a cure for a disease that had taken his mother and continued to take lives.

Despite the ache inside him, that's what he needed to stay focused on. His goals. His purpose. His dreams.

Taylor wasn't a part of that.

Couldn't be a part of that.

She was better off without him.

He didn't need distractions. Just look at how thinking of her was distracting him even now.

He closed his eyes, prayed sleep would come.

In the morning he would sign his name on the proverbial dotted line and achieve a goal he'd set for himself when he'd been twelve years old.

Nothing and no one would get in the way of that.

* * *

The following evening Nina and Taylor picked up Sarah Beth to give the new big sister some playtime away from all the baby attention, and headed to Pippa's Pizza Palace. The two little girls whacked clowns, squirted lily pads and were having a great time.

Actually, Gracie had seemed much perkier when she and Nina had swung by the office to pick Taylor up. She'd had so much paperwork to wade through that she'd worked late and taken up Nina's request that she pick up Gracie and then get them dinner.

She hadn't exactly been thinking Pippa's Pizza Palace, but to see Gracie's smile, to hear her laughter, to see the sparkle in her eyes that had been missing was worth enduring greasy pizza.

Unfortunately, she couldn't stop thinking that this was where it had sort of started. Vegas was where it had truly started, but her and Slade's first real date had been here.

"You're doing it again." Nina snapped her fingers in front of Taylor's face.

She blinked. "Doing what?"

"Thinking about him to the point you totally lose touch with reality."

"Believe me, I'm in touch with reality."

"Which is?"

She stared blankly at her friend. "What do you mean?"

"What is your reality, Taylor?"

"That I lost my mind in Vegas and married a man I knew was all wrong for me. I agreed to a month of pretending our marriage was real for Lord only knows what reason. And before long, I'll be divorced from a man I never should have trusted."

Why did her words feel like daggers in her chest?

Nina frowned. "Is that what you want?"

Taylor shrugged. "It's better this way. I told him how I

felt and he left. I'm not sure why that shocked me so much. Leaving is what men I have sex with do."

Nina shook her head. "Don't compare him to Kyle. Kyle was an idiot who couldn't keep his pants zipped when there was a willing woman around. You were an impressionable young woman who'd been kept under her parents' thumb too long. He was your teenage rebellion, not the man you are in love with, like you are with Slade."

"I was in my twenties."

"You were a late bloomer," Nina quipped without missing a beat.

"Tell me about it." Taylor sighed, knowing her friend was right. Kyle hadn't been fit to spit shine Slade's boots.

"So…" Nina prompted.

"So what?"

"You completely ignored what I said about Slade."

Taylor frowned. "I've been paying close attention to everything you've said about him."

"Yet you didn't comment on the fact I said you are in love with him."

"That's not something I didn't already know so I'm ignoring that."

"Why?"

"Because it doesn't matter. Love without trust is nothing. He left Gracie and me. Honestly, it's best that he did. Better to just get his leaving over with before Gracie and I became even more dependent on him."

"I hope you don't mean that," Nina said, so oddly that Taylor raised an eyebrow.

"Why?"

But Nina didn't answer her, just indicated toward where there was a commotion in the games section of the restaurant.

Taylor turned, but didn't initially see what had caused the commotion. Neither did she immediately recognize who was causing the commotion. When she did, she almost fell out of the booth.

Slade, followed by a posse of children, Gracie and Sarah Beth included, headed toward her.

He had lost his mind. There could be no other excuse for his current foolishness.

Well, there was one other excuse.

He'd lost his heart.

To a woman who'd fascinated him long before she'd carried on a simple conversation with him and her bubbly little girl who had, along with Nina, helped him come up with a foolproof plan to win Taylor's forgiveness.

He had to pray their plan would work.

The glare she was currently giving him wasn't an indication this was going to be easy.

Recovering from her surprise at seeing him, she murmured something to Nina about leaving and stood up.

Nina grabbed her wrist and stayed her. "At least hear him out."

"I don't want to hear anything he has to say, even if he is dressed like that."

"Sure you do, and he's gone to a lot of effort so sit down." Nina's tone brooked no argument.

Looking a bit stunned, Taylor sat back down.

A good thing because otherwise he'd feel like an even bigger idiot in the Prince Charming getup Nina and Gracie had helped him choose. They'd also ensured that Taylor would show.

He turned to the little girl who was bouncing beside him. "Princess Gracie, will you take your friends over to play so I can talk to your mom for a few minutes?"

With a really big wink at him, Gracie nodded and gathered the group of kids together, shooing them back toward the games. Several times she turned back toward them, both excitement and worry shining in her green eyes.

Maybe he shouldn't have involved Gracie.

If Taylor couldn't forgive him, would it make things more difficult that he had let the little girl in on his surprise visit? No, because he refused to fail.

"I'm going to go supervise the kids." Nina stood, paused at the end of the table and gave Taylor an encouraging look. "Remember what I said about Kyle. Don't let the past color the present."

Slade didn't fully understand her comment but supposed Taylor had lumped him into the same category as her ex. As much as he hated the thought, perhaps he deserved as much.

When they were alone, Taylor gestured to his outfit. "I take it the Grandview job didn't work out and you've hired on as a local clown?"

He glanced down at his costume. "Is that how you see me? As a clown?"

Not looking directly at him, she shrugged. "I don't want to see you at all."

"Then don't look at me, but listen to what I have to say."

"What's the point? We've already said everything we have to say to each other."

Aware that other parents in the restaurant were staring at him—and no wonder—he asked if he could sit down.

"Suit yourself, but you might have more success going in search of sleeping beauties or women with fairy god-mothers."

"I might," he agreed, wondering how he could ever have been so foolish as to leave. "But I'd rather spend the rest of my life convincing you to forgive me."

"Ha," she scoffed, still not looking at him. "You really would have more luck with a pair of glass slippers and a magic wand."

"Too bad, because there's only one woman whose Prince Charming I want to be."

She rolled her eyes. "What, did Grandview realize you hadn't brought your wife with you and you're here to convince me to play wifey again long enough to make the big-wigs happy?"

"Grandview doesn't care if I'm married or not married. Not really. Neither does what Grandview want really matter to me."

"Right, because that's so not what the past month was about."

"I don't work for Grandview, Taylor."

She met his gaze.

"I turned down their offer."

"They couldn't meet your demands?"

"They couldn't offer me the one thing in life I don't want to live without."

Her gaze narrowed. "What's that?"

"My wife."

His wife. Taylor bit the inside of her lower lip. What kind of game was he playing, showing up in a prince costume, spouting comments about not being able to live without his wife?

Her rib cage tightened around her lungs, making breathing difficult. Unable to bear to hear another word, she stood.

"I'm going outside."

She practically ran out of the restaurant, gulping in big breaths of cold air the moment she was outside the building.

"Taylor?"

No. He'd followed her. She ran to the van, opened the door.

"Please, let me finish."

She scrambled to open the driver's-side door and climbed inside. "There's no reason for you to finish. I don't want to hear anything you have to say."

She didn't. He'd left her. Left Gracie. Had broken their hearts and devastated their world.

"But I desperately want you to hear what I have to say. Please, let me tell you about this past week."

She shook her head. "No, because all I hear you saying is about you. So, you got to Newark and realized you missed Gracie and me? Is that what you're going to say? Well, too bad, because that ship has sailed."

"You don't love me anymore?"

She didn't want to admit to feeling anything for him, but she couldn't bring herself to lie. "I don't trust you anymore."

"You never did trust me."

"Sure I did. Christmas, when I wanted you to stay, it was because I trusted you, trusted what was happening between us."

"And I failed you horribly when I left?"

"Something like that."

"If I could go back, I wouldn't leave you, Taylor."

"Too bad that costume doesn't come with a magical pumpkin time machine, then, eh?"

"I never realized you had such a sharp tongue."

She leaned against the steering wheel, hid her face from him. Why wouldn't he just leave? Why was he here dressed like a prince when she knew he was a playboy?

"There are a lot of things you don't realize about me."

He walked around the van, opened the passenger's-side door and climbed in. "There are a lot of things I do realize about you. Like how much you love Gracie and how you devote your life to her. Like how loyal you are and you don't give your heart easily."

She didn't deny what he said, neither did she look up from where her forehead rested against the steering wheel. She did, however, pull the door closed to block out the chilly night air. Of course, that just closed her into her van with him.

"When you love," he continued from beside her, "that doesn't just go away because the person is a fool and lets you down."

"You did more than let me down. You let Gracie down. You left us."

"I had to go."

She lifted her head and glared at him. "Then why are you back here wearing that ridiculous costume?"

"I had to go to understand what I was leaving behind."

She swallowed the lump in her throat. "Which was?"

"My heart. I'm back because I love you, Taylor. I love you and Gracie."

His words stung her raw emotions. She closed her eyes. "You can't just pop back into our lives, say a few pretty words you think I want to hear and expect me to say everything is forgiven."

"It's what I want you to do, but it's not what I expect. Neither is it what I deserve. I know that. Which is why I'm wearing the outfit."

She shrugged. "I don't see the connection."

"I want to be your Prince Charming, but know I have to prove to you that I can be what you want, what you need, in a husband, in a father for Gracie." He reached across the console and took her hand, clasping it between his. "I want to make every day of your life living proof of happy-ever-after."

"You're crazy," she accused, but didn't pull her hand away. She should pull her hand away. Touching him had always taken away her ability to think and if ever she needed the ability to think it was now.

"I am crazy. About you. To leave you. To think I didn't need you. To not admit I loved you on Christmas night." He gently squeezed her hand. "But I am admitting that now. I need you, Taylor."

She couldn't answer him.

"You don't have to forgive me tonight or even tomorrow. You just have to give me the chance to prove to you that I am your Prince Charming."

"I don't have to do anything," she reminded him.

"Sure you do."

She arched a brow. "Or what?"

"Or else I'm driving you to my place and making love to you until you are so breathless you don't have the strength to argue with me anymore."

"That's just sex and eventually you'll tire of me."

He lifted her hand to his mouth, pressed a kiss to her fingertips. "You and I were never just sex, Taylor. Not even that first night in Vegas."

Their wedding night.

"In Newark I had a lot of time to think. I'm convinced I was half in love with you long before Vegas."

"That's crazy." Crazy seemed to be her new favorite word, but she was beginning to think it was the most appropriate word for the whole situation. Maybe they were both crazy.

He nodded. "But true. You fascinated me. I'd never met a woman who fascinated me so much, but you refused to let me get close. I'd catch myself looking for you at work, thinking about you after hours, and then in Vegas I'm not sure what happened other than I was on a high that you were kissing me back and wanted me. I think I would have done anything to have had you that night."

"You did. You married me."

"Something I'd never planned to do because I'd vowed to devote myself to fighting breast cancer."

"A noble cause."

"A lonely cause."

"Because you missed Gracie and me?"

"So much I felt like my insides had shriveled up and died. I had to come back."

"Because of me?" she asked, not really believing him.

He let go of her hand, leaving her with a sense of loss as he adjusted his fake crown. "Partially, but mostly because of me."

"But your mother... I don't understand."

He turned and faced her. "I didn't either at first. As little more than a kid, I set this goal to find a cure for breast cancer and made that my life's priority. Until you, I never let anything even get close to interfering with that."

"I never wanted Gracie and me to interfere with your goals." He'd come to resent them both for sure if they stood in his way. But more than that she wanted him to have his dreams, to fulfill them. Even when those dreams took him away from her.

"Neither did I, and you don't. You just updated them to the goals of a grown man rather than those of a heartbroken boy."

She waited for him to continue.

"As for tiring of you—" he shook his head "—I suppose that's a risk every couple takes, but I just don't foresee that happening. I love you and plan to spend the rest of my life showing you how much."

"You're planning to stay in Nashville?"

"I've already talked to Nashville Cancer Care. They welcomed me back with open arms."

"You're stepping back as if you never left."

"Have you not been listening? I left and I realized what I'd left and I want it back."

"You can't have me back."

"You're saying you don't love me, Taylor? Because I don't believe you."

"It doesn't matter if you believe me or not. I don't want you in my life anymore."

"Then you'll have to divorce me, because I plan to fight for my marriage with all my heart."

"Why?"

"Because we were never pretend, Taylor. I know you figured that out long before I did. We were always real, but I couldn't admit that. Maybe you couldn't at first either because we happened so quickly and you were scared we couldn't be real. But we were." He laced their fingers, stared at their interlocking hands. "We are real."

Tears prickling her eyes, she squeezed them shut. "How

can I believe you? How can I know this is real and that you won't leave me again?"

"You have to trust me."

"What if I can't? What if I can't let my guard down enough to trust in you, Slade?"

He took a deep breath. "Then ultimately that lack of trust will be what keeps us apart."

She nodded.

"But don't think I'll give up. Or that I won't use every resource at my disposal."

"Gracie?" she guessed.

"She is who told me I had to wear a Prince Charming costume tonight. That you had to know what she already knows."

"I can't bear my mistakes causing her pain."

"Then you have to trust me, because she loves me."

"I know she does."

"I love her, too, Taylor. More than I thought a man could love a kid. I've never known that joy before."

"If only I believed this was real."

"Believe, because this isn't a fairy tale, Taylor. It's our real-life love story."

She was crying now. A major boo-hoo fest. "I don't want to be without you."

"Then don't be." He leaned across the console, took her into his arms, hugging her close. "I love you, Taylor. Please, don't cry because of me."

She sucked back a deep breath, swiped at her eyes. "Call Grandview first thing in the morning and tell them you've changed your mind, that you'll take the position."

He shook his head. "I haven't changed my mind. My place is right here, with you and Gracie, and working at Nashville Cancer Care. It's where I want to be."

"But your dreams?"

"Are being fulfilled in a way far beyond what I could have imagined at twelve when I made my career goals. I make a difference in the lives of my patients, Taylor. Just as you do. Perhaps not on the same scale as if I helped develop a miracle chemotherapy drug, but to the patients I see each day, to the patients I hand out my sticky notes to, I make a difference."

Her heart almost burst with warmth at what he was saying, at what she was feeling. "You're right, but if research is what you want I could go with you to Newark…"

Slade's breath caught at what she'd just said, what she'd just hinted at. Not that he'd doubted that she loved him. He'd known she had. Just that he knew she was going to have a difficult time forgiving him, trusting him.

"Newark isn't what I want. I want what I thought I never wanted, what I've had the past month, only more. I want you to be my wife, Taylor. In every sense of the word. That's what I came here to show you tonight."

She met his gaze. Tears glistened in her eyes, on her cheeks. "I'm scared."

"Me, too, but what scares me most is the thought of not having you by my side every day for the rest of my life."

She nodded. "I do love you, Slade. So much."

"I know, honey. I'm so sorry it took me so long to cherish that gift the way I should have. The way I do," he corrected. "That reminds me." He paused, reached into his pocket and pulled out a jeweler's box. "I have something to ask you." He half knelt on her van floorboard. "Taylor Anderson Sain, will you do me the honor of being my wife?"

"I'm already your wife." More tears streamed down her cheeks.

"Humor me here. I'm trying to do this right this time."

She nodded, swiping at her eyes with her free hand.

"I love you, Taylor. Say you'll walk down the aisle to me, that we'll have your dad give you away to me, have Gracie as our flower girl, have my dad and stepmom there, all our friends and family to celebrate with us. Be my bride, Taylor. My wife. Forever."

"You really are my Prince Charming, you know," she whispered as he slipped the engagement ring on her finger.

"And you are my dream woman if only you'll say yes."

Amidst tears, she nodded. "Yes. Yes. Yes."

He leaned across the console, wrapped her in his arms and kissed her. "I'm never giving up on us, Taylor. You and Gracie are mine. You know that, right?"

She nodded. "You're mine, too. My Christmas present."

"Gracie mentioned that," he said, then grinned. "I'm thinking a Vegas honeymoon."

Happier than she'd have believed possible, she smiled at the man who really was her Prince Charming and all her Christmases wrapped up in one delectable package.

"Sounds perfect. Last time I was there I got luckier than I dreamed possible."

"I'm the lucky one."

# EPILOGUE

GRACIE ANDERSON SAIN walked down the aisle toward a flower-woven wrought-iron arbor. A few dozen people sat on each side of the aisle—friends, family, some of her parents' and grandparents' coworkers.

She dropped rose petals all along the way, taking care to space them so she'd have enough until she reached her destination.

"Hi, Gracie," Sarah Beth whispered as she passed her BFF and her family. Sarah Beth's brother was sleeping, thank goodness, because, although Sarah Beth's mom had quit crying all the time, her baby brother had picked up the slack. It was almost enough to make a girl think she didn't want a baby brother of her own.

Almost.

Gracie grinned at her friend, tossed a few rose petals her way, then proceeded down the aisle in her real-life pink princess dress, complete with real tiara.

She waved at her Grandma Anderson, who'd declared her to be the most beautiful girl in the whole world, winked at her new Grandpa Sain and then took her place next to her father to wait for who she knew was really the most beautiful girl in the world.

Her mother.

Appearing at the end of the aisle, Taylor appeared on the

arms of Grandpa Anderson, who bent, kissed her cheek and whispered something that had her mom smiling up at him.

Gracie glanced up at Slade to see what he thought of his bride and grinned. Oh, yeah. That was the right look. Perfect for a Prince Charming about to marry his princess.

The rest of the ceremony went by fast and then they were kissing. Gracie had to look away even though that seemed to be all they did these days. Even in front of Grandpa and Grandma Anderson, and Gracie's new grandparents.

She liked her new grandpa, even if he did pinch her cheeks. He was lots of fun and had promised her a pony for her upcoming birthday. A pony sounded great because she liked going out with Slade on his horse. However, when she blew out her birthday-cake candles she didn't plan to wish for a pony. That would have to wait until another holiday.

Her gaze sought out Sarah Beth in the congregation. She wiggled her fingers at her friend. Sarah Beth waved back, then reached to hand her mother something out of a diaper bag.

Yeah, Gracie knew exactly what she wanted for her birthday.

Even if baby brothers did cry a lot.

\* \* \* \* \*

# THIS WINTER NIGHT

**JANICE SIMS**

Thanks to my usual support team: Shannon Criss for her editorial expertise; Maria Ribas and the rest of the staff at Mills & Boon who make writing a pleasure; Sha-Shana Crichton for ensuring I have interesting work to keep me busy; and my family for their love and encouragement.

# *Chapter 1*

Colton Riley knew a fool when he saw one. At that moment, he happened to be looking at the fool in his rearview mirror. What had he been thinking? He had driven to the Great Smoky Mountains in the midst of winter without first checking a weather report.

It was snowing so aggressively visibility was practically nonexistent. If not for GPS, he would have gotten lost, even though he'd traveled this route many times before.

He put the SUV in Park as he pulled in front of the cabin with its headlights trained on the porch. He hadn't been there in a long time but he knew there was a spare set of keys somewhere in the car. After a quick search he found them in the glove compartment, zipped his jacket all the way up to his chin and got out of the vehicle.

The fierce north wind whipped snow in his face. The temperature, which had dipped drastically since he'd left Raleigh, North Carolina, for Bryson City, a little town near the Tennessee border, chilled him to the bone. His father's recent death had been such a shock to the system he wasn't his normal rational self. Otherwise, he would have worn a heavier coat—perhaps rethought this entire trip completely.

He unlocked the cabin's front door and took a couple steps inside where he automatically reached for the light switch. He pressed the flat panel but was rewarded with no illumination whatsoever. Then he remembered the alarm and rushed over to the unit but found even the green ready light was out. Power failure. He then made his way to the kitchen where he found a flashlight in the drawer next to the stove. Switching it on, he headed to check the breaker box in the laundry room at the back of the cabin. It was as he suspected—there was no electricity in the cabin. Probably downed power lines due to the blizzard, he thought grimly. He now regretted not having backup generators put in the cabin according to his parents' objections. They liked the austerity of the place. Said they came to the mountains to get away from the modern world as much as possible. Besides, they frequented the cabin more often in warmer months than in the dead of winter, so they figured they didn't need a generator.

Next he checked the cubbyhole in the mudroom where his parents kept logs for the fireplace. Empty. That did it. He would not survive the night in a cabin without electricity in the middle of a snowstorm, not when there wasn't the remotest prospect of a roaring fire.

He made his way back through the cabin and out the front door. He suddenly remembered glancing at the fuel gauge in the SUV before he had gotten out earlier and again realized that the tank was nearly empty. He laughed roughly. His dad would have probably gotten a good laugh out of this experience for years. Be prepared for anything, he'd always said. *Well, Dad,* Colton thought, *I wasn't prepared for you dying. That kind of threw me for a loop.*

He climbed back in the SUV. Luckily, he hadn't been in the cabin long enough for the snow to freeze on the windshield. The wipers cleared away the accumulation, and he spied the cabin across the pond. Lights shone in its windows. The property belonged to Adam Eckhart. His parents had been reluctant to tell him of the purchase three years ago when his biggest business rival had "coincidentally" moved next door to the Riley family cabin. Colton had simply laughed at the time because he rarely went to the mountains. His parents had frequented the cabin more than anyone else in their family.

It made him wonder, though, just what kind of psychological games Adam was playing with him. The man clearly had no sense of business fairness. At least twice Eckhart had used underhanded methods to push Colton's construction company out of the bidding for lucrative contracts.

One of the city officials whose palms Eckhart had greased had even come to Colton and boldly said things might go his way if his gift were larger than Eckhart's had been. But the Riley family didn't conduct business in that manner. So Eckhart had gotten the contract.

Looking at the Eckhart cabin now, Colton was resigned to the fact that beggars couldn't be choosers. He would have to go knocking on his enemy's door tonight, or freeze.

Lauren Gaines-Eckhart luxuriated in the warm, soapy water of the sunken tub. She had pinned up her long, wavy raven's-wing-colored hair to keep it dry, and put a Ben Harper CD in the sound system in an attempt to banish all thoughts of Adam Eckhart. She peered up at the clock on the wall. They had now been divorced exactly three days, seven hours and thirty-six minutes. She grimaced. Sometimes she was too anal for her own good.

"Ben, Ben," she moaned. "Take me away!" But the sound of Ben Harper's beautiful voice wasn't working tonight. Like bile, hatred for her ex-husband coursed through her taut body. The more she tried to relax, the more images of doing violence to Adam flashed through her mind.

She smiled at the thought and sank deeper in the tub as she laid her head on the pillow. Finally she relaxed. As Ben Harper's sweet tenor soared she closed her eyes. Tomorrow she would think about making her way back to Raleigh for work, family and responsibility, but for tonight, Christmas Eve, she was fine with being cut off from everyone and everything in her life. She'd been in the mountains for two days and had stayed in spite of severe weather warnings that mentioned the likelihood of a blizzard. She felt safe here. As an architect, she'd designed the cabin with backup generators that would provide power for several days, insulated windows and a reinforced roof built to withstand the weight of heavy snowfall. This cabin was safer than some military installations. The daughter of a retired U.S. Army general, she knew a little about the military.

As an added bonus, her nosy sisters wouldn't be able to travel up there to commiserate with her about her divorce. She adored all four of them and knew they meant well but they wouldn't let her wallow and she wanted to wallow, at least for a few days. Then, like everyone expected of her, she would pull herself together and get on with her life.

She felt her muscles loosen and sighed contentedly. A delicious feeling of peace suffused her body. Then, just as quickly, her muscles tightened once again. Was that the doorbell? She glanced at the clock—9:25 p.m.? Who in their right mind would be out and about during a snowstorm?

She sat up in the tub and listened. There it was again, this time followed by someone pounding like crazy on her front door.

Curious, and a little ticked off by the intrusion, she rose. Tall and curvy, her brown body glistened with water droplets. Carefully, she stepped onto the plush bath rug and grabbed a towel to quickly dry off.

Pulling on her robe and slippers, she hurried into the adjacent bedroom and went straight to the closet. Pushing aside some clothes she revealed a wall safe. She quickly put in the combination, opened it and removed the semi-automatic she kept for self-defense.

Her father had made sure that all his daughters knew how to safely use a handgun. She loaded it and made sure the safety was engaged. She didn't want to accidentally shoot anyone. She would fire the weapon only if it became necessary to defend herself—a woman couldn't be too careful here in the isolated mountains. The nearest police station was miles away. And no one was going to come to her rescue in a blizzard.

Colton pressed his ear to the door as he strained to hear any forthcoming footsteps from within. Could Eckhart have programmed the lights to come on at regular intervals to deter thieves? If so, the cabin could be unoccupied. He tossed that theory aside. The power was out. If the power were out in his family's cabin, the power would be out in Eckhart's, as well. Even with backup generators, someone would have to manually start them up, right? At least he hoped so.

He was about to start pounding on the door again when a feminine voice yelled, "Identify yourself, and quickly!"

"My name is Colton Riley. My family owns the cabin across the pond…"

"I know Frank and Veronica Riley," said the voice impatiently. "Stand back so I can see your face."

Colton took a step backward. He was trembling with cold, his arms wrapped around his jacket in an attempt to hold in what little body heat he had left.

Inside, Lauren squinted as she perused his face. Yes, although they'd never formally met, she recognized Colton Riley's clean-shaven chiseled features from various charitable events they'd both attended, and from family photographs his mother, Veronica, had shown her over the years. She was clearly proud of her son and had talked about him a lot. Also, it was hard not to recognize the man her ex-husband detested. He'd bought this cabin just to irk Colton Riley. Lauren had wondered about her husband's sanity then—to buy a cabin just to rub somebody else's nose in it. The fact that he was so rich that he could move right next door to a sworn enemy and they had no control over it whatsoever. On the other hand, gaining ownership of the cabin in the divorce was a breeze because Adam hadn't gotten the rise out of Colton Riley he'd expected when he'd bought the property. He'd been summarily ignored. So when Lauren had said she wanted the cabin he hadn't put up a fight.

Now his business rival was standing on her doorstep wanting to come inside out of the cold.

"Okay, you're Colton Riley. What do you want?" she yelled.

Sure she recognized him, but who knew, he might moonlight as a serial killer on weekends.

Exasperated and freezing, Colton got riled. "Look, my dad died earlier today and, not thinking clearly, I got in my car and just started driving, going nowhere in particular. Then I looked up and realized I was headed here. So…"

Lauren had the door open and was yanking him inside

before he could finish his sentence. Colton was so grateful to feel the rush of warm air on his skin he collapsed onto the floor in a snow-covered heap. Lauren shut the door but not before the blustery conditions blew snow onto the polished wood floor. She gazed down at her uninvited guest. "Frank passed away?"

Colton's eyes met hers. In hers he saw shock and sympathy.

He stood up. He was at least six inches taller than she was and she wasn't a small-statured woman—five-eight, maybe five-nine. "Yeah, of pancreatic cancer. Kept it quiet for years. He didn't want anyone feeling sorry for him."

There were tears in her eyes. She stood there with a towel wrapped around her hair and dressed in a bathrobe with pink bunny slippers on her feet. She should have looked comical, even ridiculous, but instead she looked beautiful to him. Not just beautiful—angelic.

It could have something to do with the fact that she'd just saved his life by letting him in, he thought skeptically. "Please, don't cry," he said softly as he rubbed his arms to speed up his body's recovery from the cold.

Lauren wiped the tears away with her free hand and seeing he was severely underdressed for the weather outside and must be freezing, she sprang into action.

"Come with me," she told him, and began walking toward the back of the cabin.

"Is that a gun?" he asked cautiously after catching sight of the weapon she held at her side.

"A girl has to stay safe," she said offhandedly.

"So, it's true what they say about you Gaines girls," Colton said as he followed her.

Lauren smiled over her shoulder at him. She had been under the impression he knew nothing of her background.

But apparently her reputation, or to be more accurate, her father's reputation, had preceded her.

"What do they say about us Gaines girls?"

"That you don't mess with the general's daughters."

She laughed shortly. "Damned straight, you don't."

She led him to the guest room and switched on the light. She gestured to the closet. "I'm sure some of the clothes in there should fit you. There are towels and toiletries in the bathroom. By the time you're finished taking a hot shower I'll have something warm for you to eat and drink."

Although grateful, Colton hesitated to accept her generous offer. He stood peering down into her upturned face, an expression of surprise on his own. "Are you sure this is okay with your husband?"

He wanted to avoid being caught naked in the shower by an irascible husband who'd stalked in from somewhere else in the house.

"Ex-husband," Lauren informed him tightly.

He looked confused. "I'm sorry. I didn't know."

"Nondisclosure clause in the prenuptial," Lauren said briskly. "I can't speak to the media about our divorce or about anything that happened in our marriage. He thinks it might reflect negatively on him, from a business standpoint. Now, I'll leave you alone."

She left before he could say anything else, closing the door firmly behind her.

Colton looked around the spacious room with its pine floor, vaulted ceiling with exposed beams, and a natural stone fireplace. He'd heard she was an architect. As a builder he could see the thought and skill that had gone into its design.

Right now, though, a nice warm shower was what he needed. He wasted no more time peeling off his clothes and stepping into a steamy bath.

\* \* \*

Having taken the time to put on jeans and a long-sleeved cotton shirt, Lauren stood in the kitchen, heating up some of her hearty beef vegetable soup she'd made earlier that day. As she stirred it with a wooden spoon, she wondered how Veronica was doing. Veronica and Frank had to have been married nearly forty years. What did you do when you lost someone you'd been with for that long? Someone you adored? Frank had a reputation for being a hardnosed businessman but with Veronica he'd been nothing but loving. The time Lauren had spent with them up in the mountains, sharing meals and playing chess with Frank who once told her that she and Veronica were the only women who'd ever bested him at the game, would now be dearly cherished memories.

Their son, though, was a mystery. She knew only what others had told her about him. He'd taken over the company when his father had retired. The Rileys had been in the construction business for more than half a century in the Raleigh area. They were known for being trustworthy and for producing quality private homes and commercial buildings. On the other side, Lauren had spent the entire length of her marriage listening to Adam complain about "those damned Rileys" who "have had a monopoly in this city for too long." Adam was the upstart, and in order for the newcomer to triumph over the standard-bearer, deals were made that might be conceived as manipulative, perhaps even downright illegal. In return, Lauren had started to dislike her ex-husband long before she discovered he was having an affair.

Back in the guest room, Colton had showered and brushed his teeth, and then found a pair of jeans that would fit him and a soft denim shirt in the closet. No underwear, which was fine with him. Unless he found a pair of briefs fresh out of the package, he wouldn't be wearing anything that had once been *that* close to Adam Eckhart's body.

He did find a package of thick, white athletic socks, which he opened, selected a pair and pulled onto his feet. Appropriately dressed now, he went in search of his hostess. He let his nose lead him to the kitchen. Whatever she was cooking smelled wonderful. He hadn't realized how hungry he was. He'd left Raleigh hours ago, his trip a meandering blackout until he recognized some familiar landmarks and realized he was headed to the family cabin, a place where he'd spent many an idyllic summer fishing, swimming, hiking and kayaking and generally making his older sister, Jade's, life miserable. She'd been such a neat freak that he'd gotten a kick out of throwing her in the pond, or putting frogs, snakes and insects in her bed. He'd been a total jerk to her back then. It was a wonder they had such a close, loving relationship today. He'd left Jade in Raleigh with their mother. Which reminded him, by now they must be worried sick about him. He needed to call and tell them that he was fine. He felt bad for making them worry on top of the grief they were feeling due to his father's recent death.

Where was his cell phone? He found his jacket by the front door where Lauren had hung it on the coat tree to allow it to dry. He rummaged through the damp pockets until he found it. No lit-up display indicated it was in need of a recharge.

A few seconds later, he was walking through the kitchen doorway. Spotting Lauren ladling soup into a bowl, he said, "Thanks. I think my body temp's back to normal again."

She looked up and smiled, "Good. You're not a vegetarian, are you? I've got some beef vegetable soup. Would you like coffee? Or maybe hot chocolate?"

Colton sat down at the place setting she'd provided for him at the high-counter kitchen island. "No, I'm definitely not a vegetarian. That soup sounds good. And a hot chocolate, please," he said. "Thank you…"

"Call me Lauren."

She smiled again, and his heart skipped a beat. He hoped he wasn't becoming infatuated with Adam Eckhart's ex. It didn't help that the woman was kind and generous to a fault. She was also drop-dead gorgeous with her fresh face, skin so clear and golden-brown with a hint of red as if she was blushing underneath. She'd taken the towel off her head and her blue-black hair fell in waves about her heart-shaped face. She was adorable without makeup. He'd seen her all dressed up at the Black and White Ball last year. She'd been on Eckhart's arm with him beaming like an idiot, and no wonder—she'd been the belle of the ball. She'd been breathtaking then but not as appealing as she looked now, so vulnerable, as if her emotions were barely being contained. He supposed she was hurting from the divorce. Could that be why she was up here alone—contemplating her lost marriage? He would not broach the subject. Even if he'd known her for more than an hour, which he hadn't, he would never bring it up.

"This looks good," he said just before sampling the soup. It was savory with a tomato base, tender chunks of beef, and just the right amount of red pepper for spice. He looked up at her with appreciation. "You made this?"

"Homemade," she confirmed with a smile.

"Delicious," he said.

"I'm glad you like it," Lauren said softly as she busied herself making hot chocolate.

Momentarily, Colton put down his spoon and regarded her. "I'm sorry for intruding on your downtime. But when I got to the cabin I found out there was no electricity, and no wood for a fire, so I had no other choice but to come knocking on your door."

She was smiling as she poured hot milk into two mugs. "You don't have to explain. I know Veronica and Frank never had backup generators put in. I tried to convince them to but they insisted their place was more rustic and somehow more romantic without the generators."

She stirred cocoa, sugar and a touch of vanilla into each mug. "They were the perfect couple."

Colton cleared his throat when he felt a lump forming in it, and tears at the backs of his eyes. He couldn't start bawling in front of a stranger, even if she was a sympathetic stranger.

He took a deep breath. "Yeah, they were pretty devoted to each other."

Lauren placed a mug of hot chocolate in front of him and sat down across from him at the kitchen's island. "You don't have to talk if you don't want to. I understand. I got out of Raleigh shortly after I got word my divorce was final. I wanted time to myself before my family began to smother me, wanting to know if I was all right."

He noticed she spoke with a smile that didn't reach her eyes, which by contrast were sad. Because he didn't like her ex-husband he couldn't imagine a woman not being overcome with joy after being declared free and clear of the buffoon.

He ate his soup in silence as she sipped her hot chocolate.

Although neither of them actually looked at the other, there were a lot of quick secret glances. Lauren had noticed his short, naturally dark brown hair was still damp from the shower and he had strong hands. He ate slowly, savoring each bite, which made her wonder if he did other things in that manner, as well. No rush, just lingering and appreciating, enjoying the moment. His skin was the color of cinnamon, and his eyes were dark gray, like his father's. His photographs didn't do him much justice, and the few times she'd seen him at public functions she had not given him much thought because after all she had been a married woman.

Colton could not help inhaling the clean feminine scent of her. Fresh out of a bath, he figured since she had opened the door in her bathrobe. Even half-frozen, he hadn't missed that. Her silhouette was classically beautiful, the slender neck, that square chin with the dimple in its center, angling up to a full mouth with lips that looked soft and inviting. Damned if a near-death experience didn't make you more observant, and appreciative, of things you might never have noticed before. When she breathed in and out, he imagined her full breasts heaving with desire, for him.

Once or twice while he was finishing his meal they smiled at one another, but uttered not a word. When he was done with the soup, he looked up at her. "That was wonderful. You saved me."

Lauren laughed nervously as her eyes met his. "What was I supposed to do, let you freeze to death?"

His gaze went to her mouth. Her tongue flicked out and moistened her lower lip. She rose and reached for his bowl. "Can I get you some more?"

Suddenly, his heart was thudding in his chest, and his manhood, already going commando in his borrowed jeans, began to stir. He knew he had to get out of her presence before he said or did something that would embarrass them both.

"Um, no, thank you. I think I'll just go to bed. I'm more tired than I thought."

If he wasn't mistaken, she looked relieved at his announcement. Was she feeling the same attraction he was feeling?

"Of course," she said, hurriedly crossing the room to put the bowl in the sink. "You know the way. If you need an extra blanket, they're on the top shelf in the closet."

"Good night, then, and thank you," Colton said hoarsely.

"Good night," she said softly, chancing a shy glance in his direction. "Hopefully, we'll have better weather tomorrow."

# Chapter 2

Colton got all the way to the door of the guest room before he realized he hadn't asked Lauren if the phones were working. He could not with good conscience go to bed without attempting to let his family know he was safe.

Lauren was washing dishes at the sink when he returned to the kitchen. She heard him enter and placed a dish on the draining board before turning to face him. "Is there a problem?"

"My cell phone's out of juice and I have no way of recharging it. Do you have a working phone I can use?"

She was drying her hands on a dish towel as she walked toward him. "The landline's down due to the storm, but I have a satellite phone you can use."

"A satellite phone?" Colton mused. "You have to be outside when you use that, right, underneath open sky?"

"Mmm-hmm," Lauren confirmed with a smile. "I take it with me when I hike in the woods or the mountains."

She hung the dish towel on a rack attached to the oven door and walked over to the large window in the kitchen and drew aside the curtains. The wind had died down and it wasn't snowing any longer. Colton joined her at the window.

"It's not as bad as it was out there earlier," he said contemplatively.

"There's a hooded, insulated jacket in the front hall closet that should fit you. You won't even feel the cold in that baby," Lauren told him.

"All right," Colton agreed, "I'll go put on my shoes and try on that jacket."

"And I'll go get the phone," Lauren said. He watched her walk away, the gentle sway of her hips a thing of beauty.

They met up again at the front hall closet where she helped him into the jacket, reminding him of his mother bundling him up for the cold when he was a child. Then she explained how to use the phone. "It's simple, and it works anywhere in the world, so there shouldn't be a problem reaching your mother."

"How'd you know I wanted to phone my mother?"

"Your father just passed away and you're missing, whom else would you want to phone? You're not married, are you?"

"No, I've never been that lucky," he said, marveling at how easy it was to talk to her.

She smiled sweetly as she handed him the phone and said, "Tell her my thoughts and prayers are with her."

Lauren had been right, the phone was a cinch to use. He got his mother on the first try. She was sick with worry. "Colton, oh, my God, where are you?"

"I'm in Bryson City, Mom, at the cabin, or rather I'm

at your neighbor's cabin. Our cabin didn't have power, so Lauren offered me her guest room."

"That's hours from here," Veronica Riley cried. "And I heard there was a snowstorm expected in that area tonight."

"Blizzard is more like it," Colton said. He looked up at the sky. Stars were starting to peek through the cloud cover. "But things are clearing up. With luck, I'll be home tomorrow."

"Lauren is a sweetheart," Veronica said. "Have you told her about your father?"

"Yes, and she cried," he said, his throat getting full again. "She says her thoughts and prayers are with you."

"Of course they are," said Veronica fondly. "It's not that I'm not glad she was there when you needed her, but why in the world is she up there alone in that godforsaken weather?"

"She told me she wanted to get away from well-meaning people sympathizing with her over her divorce."

"She's divorced?" Veronica sounded startled. "I didn't hear anything about it."

Colton didn't want to go into the nondisclosure clause that Lauren had earlier told him about over the phone. "It was kept quiet," was all he said. A moment of silence passed. "Mom, I'm using a satellite phone under the stars. I'd better go. I'll call you again tomorrow."

"Okay, baby, I'm glad you were able to let us know where you are and that you are safe. You're in good hands," Veronica said confidently.

"Good night, Mom," said Colton with warmth.

"Good night," said Veronica softly.

He'd gone a few yards from the cabin to make his call and now he turned and carefully walked back. The snow came halfway up his legs with each step. He took it slowly, not wanting to fall down in the powder. He'd had enough of the cold for one night.

He guessed Lauren had been watching him from a window because as soon as he reached the cabin, she was there in the doorway, wearing a hooded jacket as if she was ready to come to his rescue should he need her. "Hey, did everything go okay?"

"Yeah, no problem," he assured her.

"Good," said Lauren, "Then get in here. It's freezing!"

Colton was more than glad to oblige. Feeling sure of his footing, he jauntily put one foot on the bottom step, slipped, lost his balance, and went flailing backward, arms windmilling in an attempt to regain his equilibrium. He wound up on his back in the snow. He was thankful the snow was all he'd landed on.

He found the whole situation ridiculous and started laughing uproariously.

Lauren, in her rubber-soled boots, was off the porch and by his side in a matter of seconds. Laughing, she helped him to his feet and brushed snow off his coat. "Are you all right?"

As they held each other upright, Colton peered into her beautiful face. "No, I haven't been all right all day. My father's gone and I seem to have lost my senses. I drove up here on a whim and ended up unknowingly intruding on your solitude. But now that I've met you and put a personality to the image of you I've seen over the years, I find that I'm strongly attracted to you. I'm definitely not all right."

Lauren's heartbeat accelerated at his admission. "Well, that's normal," she said, her voice warm and gentle. "We're both hurting, needing comfort. And we're here alone. The situation is rife with potential for sexual attraction. I've been checking you out, too."

They took the steps together and made it to the door

without another mishap. Inside, Lauren shut the door and they quickly removed their jackets. She then busied herself hanging the damp jackets on the coat tree, appearing to Colton that she wanted to drop the subject.

But he wasn't ready to do that just yet. "And what do you think?"

She looked up at him with big brown eyes and said as innocently as she could muster, "About what?"

Colton smiled. "You know what."

She turned away and began walking toward the back of the cabin. "I think you know you're hot, Colton Riley. How could anyone not? You look in a mirror every day."

"Are you saying I'm conceited?"

"No, I'm saying I'm hot, you're hot, but we should just leave it at that. Any further discussion could lead nowhere good."

"Oh, I think it might lead to somewhere good and something memorable," he contradicted her. "And you think you're hot, too?"

This made her turn to stare at him. "Are you saying I'm not?"

"Hell, no. I think you're smokin' hot. I like the fact that you don't deny it and try, like a lot of women I've met, to fish for compliments. You're confident in your sexuality. I like that."

"Honey, there is nothing wrong with my sexuality. Just because my ex was a cheating bastard doesn't mean I wasn't holding up my end!"

"Touchy subject, huh?" asked Colton. "You don't have to convince me that your ex is a bastard. I don't like him, never have."

"He doesn't like you, either."

There was a calculating light in her eyes that made him

wonder something. "Did he tell you how he cheated me out of several contracts?"

She harrumphed. "I didn't know and didn't want to know anything about his business dealings. And if you think you can get back at him for some dirty deal by sleeping with me, think again. He doesn't care about me. I'm a starter wife, his first wife, but apparently not his last. He's already engaged to number two."

"I don't even think like that," Colton vehemently denied. "My wanting to sleep with you has nothing to do with Adam Eckhart. Does your wanting to sleep with me have anything to do with the fact that he hates me and if it got back to him it might piss him off?"

"No!" Lauren cried.

"Then you do want to sleep with me?"

"Yes, but…"

He moved in. Lauren looked him in the eyes. Her stare was penetrating, as though she could see right through him. He found her scrutiny thrilling and invited it. He had nothing to hide. He wanted her to plumb deep and discover that for herself. He didn't wonder why he was unafraid of being so vulnerable. He just knew she made him grateful to be alive at this moment.

At last, she spoke. "There have to be some ground rules. You don't have a girlfriend, do you?"

"There is no one special in my life," he assured her.

She was looking at him suspiciously. "I won't have a part in another woman getting hurt over infidelity."

"Scout's honor," he said with a straight face.

She seemed to be satisfied with his answer. "Okay, then. What happens here stays here."

"Done," he promised.

"You can't tell anyone."

"Understood," he agreed. "That goes for you, too. Not even your girlfriends."

"Not even your boys," she countered.

"Not even your priest," he said.

"Not even God," she said with a smile.

"I think He already knows," said Colton as he backed her against the wall and planted a sensual, bone-melting kiss on her sweet mouth.

Bodies pressed closer and warmth ensued shortly afterward. By some silent consensus they agreed that this seduction would be slow and deliberate. When they came up for air from that first kiss, their eyes met and they smiled. It was confirmed. They were a good fit. She unbuttoned his shirt, curious to know whether his chest was hairy or smooth. She was rewarded with a hairy, muscular chest and a washboard stomach.

He was patient as she ran her hands over his pectorals and admired his biceps after she had finished removing the shirt. "I like your guns," she said.

"Speaking of guns, you don't keep yours under your pillow, do you? I don't like those kinds of surprises in bed."

She laughed sexily. "No, it's back in the safe. The only thing exploding in my bed tonight will be you."

After that there wasn't very much talk. She took him to her bedroom, which was two doors down from his. When he walked in the room, he saw that her bed had been turned down already, and there was a book on it. She had obviously planned to read until she fell asleep.

He watched as she began removing her clothing piece by piece.

First, her jeans, revealing long, shapely legs and a see-through pair of panties. Then her blouse, under which she wore a lacy cream-colored bra that matched her bikini panties. Her body was lush and feminine yet athletic and she had an ass that a man like him would love to hold in a fit of passion.

After she'd gotten down to her underwear, her gaze fell to his lower half. He unbuttoned the jeans he wore but did not pull them past his hips. "I'm not wearing anything underneath," he warned.

"I'm a grown woman," she told him. "You haven't got anything I haven't seen before."

She removed her bra to make him feel more comfortable. Her breasts were full and everything he desired, not too big, nor too small, just right for palming in his big hands, and the erect nipples were ripe for licking. His mouth watered.

He pulled the waistband of the jeans down past his hips and heard the audible intake of breath from her. He was well-endowed, but not monstrously so. It was nice to know she liked what she saw.

Lauren, suddenly faced with the manifestation of her wanton desire, was having second thoughts. She was pretending to be someone she was not. Adam was the only man she'd ever made love to. She had made it seem to Colton as if she had more experience with men than she actually had. Adam was not nearly as blessed as Colton was when it came to sexual "equipment." She wasn't sure if she could accommodate him.

Too much time had passed with Lauren staring at him for Colton's comfort. "Lauren, is something wrong?"

"No," she denied.

He walked toward her, totally naked, his muscles flexing enticingly, his manhood semi-erect. She couldn't help it. Her body reacted to the sensual image he made. The man was sex personified, and she'd been too long without a lover, a good lover. She was beginning to wonder if

Adam had ever been a good lover. After all, she had nothing to compare him to.

There was only one way to find out.

She removed her panties, tremblingly. Colton stopped in his tracks and took all of her in. He sighed with satisfaction. She was not one to mow the lawn, so to speak. She was beautifully natural, which was refreshing as far as he was concerned.

There seemed to be nothing separating them now as he pulled her into his arms, and they fell onto the bed. She molded her body against his. He was fully erect now, and their bodies, his skin a darker cinnamon than hers, wrapped themselves around each other. Their kisses were deep. The taste was like a drug, and her body writhing beneath his worked him into a sexual frenzy.

The smell of her, the silkiness of her skin fed his need. When she opened her legs to him, somewhere in the back of his mind, he remembered condoms. He didn't know if she had any. He hadn't even thought about them until now. But it wouldn't do. No matter how much he wanted her he wouldn't risk getting her pregnant just to satisfy his needs. "Do you have any condoms?" he asked huskily.

"They're in the nightstand drawer," she said with a gesture of her head. He got up and looked in the drawer she'd indicated. Once he had the condom in his hands he tore it open and put it on. He looked back at her to see that she was watching him. He supposed he should feel self-conscious. They were strangers in every sense of the word, especially in a physical sense, but this felt natural.

But he was a man who'd been brought up right. He was a gentleman. So when he pulled her into his arms once more, he looked into her eyes and asked, "Are you sure about this?"

"Yes," she breathed. The expression in her eyes left him no further doubt.

Her willingness pleased him, and his penis grew harder at the thought of penetrating her. But first, her pleasure. He got on his knees and pulled her toward him to the edge of the bed. Her legs were splayed wide, and it was apparent that she was ready for him from the wetness of her sex. He'd been wondering what she tasted like and now he bent his head and devoured her. His tongue moved slowly around her clitoris, inciting a current of electrically charged sensual pleasure throughout her body. She felt it down to her toes. Her moans were low at first and grew louder as her impending orgasm drew nearer.

He left her clitoris and licked the sides of her labia. This made her thighs tremble. She whispered, "Yes, yes, yes…"

Though he was happy she was enjoying his efforts, he wasn't satisfied with that reaction alone. He wouldn't be content until she started calling on a deity. He redoubled his efforts. She rose up on her elbows, "Oh, my God, what are you doing to me?"

He merely smiled.

When she climaxed, she not only released pent-up sexual energy, but she also came to the realization that there was a lot she didn't know about sex, and here was the man who could teach her.

Colton got up and while she was in that malleable state just after an orgasm, when your mind was blown and sensual pleasures were magnified, he entered her. She was just as he imagined she would be—hot, tight and more than capable of handling him.

Never had Lauren had such an enthusiastic, energetic lover, one who seemed to give even more than he got. Her body reveled in it. Felt as if it had been waiting for him all her life. She knew that this feeling was what people were trying to describe when they said that sex was the closest thing to heaven on earth. She'd never felt so alive.

Colton couldn't believe his luck. This woman was his equal in every way. Not content to lie there and accept his thrusts, she was giving it back to him with as much fervor as he was giving it to her.

When he came it was a monumental moment for him. He didn't know if it was because his emotions were so intense tonight after the day he'd had, or there was something unique about Lauren. She was smiling up at him. She looked exhausted but supremely happy. He was glad he'd had something to do with that.

# Chapter 3

"I've done it now," Lauren said jokingly as they lay in bed wrapped in each other's arms. They'd gotten up and showered together and climbed back in bed.

Colton smiled. "What have you done?"

"I've become the Gaines girl who's not only divorced but who, after the divorce, jumped right in bed with the first available man. I left Raleigh to get away from it all and a hunk shows up on my doorstep."

"Life isn't fair," Colton said sympathetically.

Lauren laughed softly. "Darn right, it's not. I was determined to give up men."

He reached out and brushed a tendril of hair behind her left ear. "How long would that have lasted? You're a vital, passionate woman, Lauren. I can tell that much from the little time we've spent together. Don't let Eckhart turn you off men."

"Please don't say that name," said Lauren.

"All right, I'll just say 'the asshole' from now on," Colton said.

"Don't even refer to him at all. I came here to forget he exists."

"Then why'd you come to a place you shared?"

"He was rarely here," Lauren explained. "He bought the place and came a couple of times, met your parents who, as you can imagine, gave him a cool reception. Then after a while, he stopped coming at all. I didn't care. What he didn't know was that I had an ulterior motive when he announced he was buying the property."

"Which was?"

"My granddaddy Beck, my mother's dad, lives up here near the Cherokee reservation. He owns a lodge. I go to see him whenever I come up here. Grandma died about five years ago and he doesn't have any family in the area. My sisters and I make sure one of us goes to see him at least once a month. I was delighted when my ex bought this place. And, thanks to you, I got it in the divorce settlement."

"Thanks to me, how?" Colton wondered.

"Because he got no reaction out of you when we moved across the pond from your place, he lost interest and gave it to me without a fight."

Colton understood. "So when you come up here, it's like going home."

"Exactly," she answered with a contented sigh.

"The only place I'm able to feel that way is my parents' home," Colton told her. "I own a home but it's just a house. A very nice house, mind you, but it has no sentimental value."

"Maybe you haven't been in it long enough," she suggested.

"I bought it six years ago," he replied. He smiled at her.

"You're an architect. Maybe you can come take a look at it and tell me what's missing about its design that's preventing me from caring about it."

"That implies that we're going to take this further than this nonreality bubble we're presently in," Lauren warned him.

"Is that what you think is happening here?" Colton asked, the humor gone out of his tone and his eyes. Up until now they had been talking good-naturedly. True, her insistence about keeping this a secret had indicated that she believed this was to be a one-night stand, but after making love he no longer wanted it to be just that. He envisioned seeing her again, slowly getting to know her. He had assumed she felt the same way.

"Wasn't that what we agreed on earlier? That *this* remains our little secret?"

"Yes, Lauren, but I thought you were thinking of your reputation. I didn't believe that you were really going to kick me to the curb afterward. Not if we both enjoyed ourselves. And I know you enjoyed yourself."

"I did *enjoy myself*," she confirmed as she freed her arms from his and sat up in bed. "I simply didn't want to set myself up for disappointment. I wanted you to know that there were no strings."

"Just pleasure," he said as he sat up while maintaining eye contact with her. "I understand not wanting to be hurt, Lauren. Believe it or not, I've been hurt before, too. On the other hand, I don't want you to sell yourself short. Of course I want more than a tryst in the mountains."

"You say that now after sex, but you may feel differently when we get back to Raleigh and to our everyday lives. Plus there's the trauma you are under due to your father's death. People do strange things when they're grieving."

"And you're worried that you might have slept with

me just to get your ex out of your system, is that it?" he wanted to know.

Lauren shook her head, but her eyes told a different story. She was undecided. "I'm an emotional wreck right now," she admitted. "I don't know up from down. I only know that I enjoyed being with you tonight."

"That's an honest answer," he said softly as he pulled her back into his arms.

Lauren smiled again as she got comfortable in his embrace. "Let's talk about anything except what might happen after we get back to Raleigh. For instance, how old are you?"

"I'll be thirty-five in October," he easily replied. "And you?"

"I'll be thirty next month."

"How do you feel about that?"

"Same as I felt about twenty-nine—indifferent. I'm not afraid of getting old, I'm just afraid of not accomplishing what I want to in life."

"Which is?"

"To be happy," she simply said.

"What would make you happy?"

"To be successful at what I do," she began. "To have a marriage that is as loving and lasting as my parents' marriage or your parents' marriage, for that matter."

"They did it," Colton reasoned. "I don't see why you can't."

"The world has changed," Lauren said. "What was important to our parents' generation isn't important to ours. Couples get married today knowing there's an easy out. Couples from our parents' generation actually did it believing they were in it for a lifetime."

"I don't agree with that," Colton countered. "I think

young people want the same things. We just go about it differently."

"The odds are stacked against us," Lauren said. "Fifty percent of marriages end in divorce."

"Is it that high?" Colton asked incredulously.

"I'm probably quoting old statistics and it's even higher by now," Lauren said.

"You're seeing the world through newly divorced eyes," Colton told her. "Give yourself a few months and you'll see things differently. Now, let's talk Christmas. You know in a matter of minutes, it's going to be Christmas Day. What do you want for Christmas this year?"

"I didn't even bother to get the decorations out of the attic," Lauren said. "I'm not in the Christmas mood this year."

"Humor me," Colton insisted with a coaxing smile.

"Peace on Earth, good will toward men?" Lauren ventured.

"Okay, besides that."

"A warm, sexy man in my bed," Lauren said, grinning at him.

"I think Santa already gave you that, young lady," Colton said and kissed her soundly.

When they broke off their kiss, she asked him what he wanted for Christmas, "For a moment like this to last," was his only reply.

The next morning Colton awakened before Lauren and took the opportunity to observe her while she slept. He could barely hear her breathing, she slept so deeply. She had braided her hair after they'd made love last night for the final time and now it fell in a single tress down her back. She slept on her side and was literally hugging her pillow. He smiled. She looked so young in repose, nowhere near thirty.

He was still watching her when she opened her eyes and smiled at him. "Is it morning already?"

The sun filtered through the sheers at the window. She squeezed her eyes shut against the glare. "Why didn't I put up blackout curtains?"

"You obviously like sunshine in the morning," said Colton as he swung his legs off the bed and stood up. "I have electric shutters in my bedroom that block out everything."

"What are you, a vampire?" she teased.

"If I were, you would be one by now, as well," he told her.

He got down on the floor and began doing push-ups without a stitch of clothing on. Lauren sat up in bed to watch. This was the strangest man she'd ever met. She stopped counting at a hundred.

Climbing out of bed, she said, "I'm exhausted just looking at you. The general would love you. I bet he's out jogging right now."

"I'd love to meet him," Colton said.

But she was gone. He heard the bathroom door close as he switched and began the sit-up portion of his morning regimen.

Momentarily, he heard the sound of Lauren brushing her teeth. After a hundred and twenty sit-ups he got to his feet, gathered his clothing that he'd discarded in the heat of passion last night and went to the guest room to shower and dress.

When he emerged a few minutes later, dressed and ready for his day, whatever it might bring, he heard music and followed the sound to the kitchen where Lauren was cracking eggs into a bowl. She looked up. "There you are.

The electricity's back on and the phone's working again but according to Grandpa who knows the guy who drives the snowplow, the roads won't be cleared up here until tomorrow morning. I'm sorry."

Before he said anything, he kissed her good-morning. "Why are you apologizing? You didn't cause the storm."

"I thought you might be worried about your mom being alone at a time like this," she said, concerned.

For a few hours Colton had been able to allow his mind to rest from the constant assault of grief over his dad's death. Lauren had given him that, and he was grateful to her. But now it all came rushing back. "My sister, Jade, and her family are home from Miami. They're with her," he said.

"Oh, that's good," said Lauren. She turned back around and resumed cracking eggs. "Scrambled eggs and toast all right with you? I don't have any breakfast meats. I'm not a big eater of bacon or sausage and I wasn't expecting guests."

He smiled gently. "Why don't you let me cook for you? You cooked for me last night."

She readily agreed and moved aside to let him take over. He did appear as if he knew his way around the kitchen. He effortlessly whisked the eggs in the bowl and then placed butter in the skillet. At just the right temperature, he added the eggs. He didn't cook them too long, turning off the stove before they congealed, and when he put them on two separate plates they were of a fluffy consistency.

"Where'd you learn that?" Lauren asked.

"The Riley men are all competent in the kitchen," he said. "Grandpa Riley was a chef at a restaurant in New Orleans before he got in his head to come to Raleigh and start a construction business."

"Cooking and building don't seem to go together," Lauren said as she put two slices of bread into the toaster.

"They don't," Colton agreed. "That's only a bit of Riley family trivia."

When the toast was ready, they sat down at the island where Lauren had already put two place settings. She poured orange juice in their glasses. "Coffee?" she asked with the carafe poised over his cup.

"Yes, please," Colton said, smiling at the domesticity of the scene. It was as if they did this all the time. He was very comfortable in her presence.

A local radio station was on in the background. The announcer reported, "That was the worst snowstorm we've had in these parts in years. As our listeners know, we're used to milder winters."

Another voice broke in with "Yeah, Bob, let's hope the temperature doesn't rise too swiftly because if it does we're going to have a muddy mess out there."

"How'd your granddad fare?" Colton asked once music resumed on the radio program.

"He says the lodge is none the worse for wear. That place is built like a fortress," Lauren said fondly.

"He lives alone?"

"Yes, but his business keeps him so busy he isn't lonely. Hunters and fishermen stay there year-round. He has a great staff but I'm afraid at eighty, he's getting a bit old to run the place. I'd never say that to his face because he'd probably bite my head off. He's never going to willingly retire."

"He sounds great," Colton said.

"He is," Lauren was quick to say. "Our mom, Virginia, is his only child. She's been trying to get him to move in with her and the general for years but he says if he and the general lived under the same roof, one of them would wind up shot." She laughed. "He was only slightly exaggerating. He and Daddy don't get along. He never forgave Daddy for marrying his daughter and taking her all over the world. Daddy's been stationed quite a few places and Momma followed him. But then she decided she wanted us to have a more permanent home and that's when they settled on Raleigh. It was a fairly large city and not too far from her father. She got a degree in English and took a job as a teacher and worked her way up to principal. Daddy's retired now, but she's still working and like her own father, shows no signs of retiring anytime soon."

"She sounds like my mom," Colton said. "Only dad's illness got her to slow down. She wanted to spend as much time with him as possible toward the end."

Lauren squeezed his hand in sympathy, but didn't say anything. She always felt that if you didn't know what to say to comfort someone it was best to say nothing at all. Just be there for them.

Colton took a deep, trembling breath. "I feel so helpless. I mean, I'm usually the guy people go to when there's a problem that needs solving. But with this one, I feel totally out of control, unable to cope. It took everything out of me to watch him die in the hospital. Then to see my mother appear to age twenty years right before my eyes after he was gone hit me even harder. Her pain was palpable. I had to get out of there, and I'm sorry to say, I took off. I'll always regret leaving her alone with my sister."

"I'm sure they understand."

"They love me—" he paused "—so they'll say they understand, but deep down I believe they'll think I abandoned them."

"No, no, please believe me, Colton. Everyone responds differently to the death of a loved one. You had to distance yourself for a while. Your family won't hold that against you."

"Even now," he admitted, "I don't want to go back. I was grateful when you said the roads wouldn't be clear until tomorrow. There's the funeral to plan, the casket to pick out, a suit for dad to wear. I should be doing that. I'm his son."

Since Lauren had known Frank for several years, she felt she could now share with Colton an observation she'd made about his father.

"You're worrying about insignificant things," she said. "The Frank Riley I knew and was very fond of didn't leave matters like his final requests up to chance. He probably left minute details as to exactly how he wanted his memorial service to progress. And even if he didn't, Veronica certainly has in mind how she wants him to be honored. Couples who've been together that long usually have things worked out in advance."

"You think?" Colton was hopeful that she was right because he was at a loss. A big, strong man like him was completely stumped.

"The phones are working," Lauren reminded him. "Phone Veronica after breakfast and ask her."

Colton breathed easier as he finished his breakfast. Lauren had a calming effect on him.

Twenty minutes later he had his mother on the phone.

"Everything's been arranged for some time now," Veronica told him. "Your dad left specific instructions. The only thing I haven't been able to arrange is the New Orleans–style jazz band that'll play him all the way to the cemetery. His words, not mine. Jade's on it. You say you're going to be stuck there another day? Today's Wednesday. The funeral is on Saturday. That's plenty of time for you to get back home."

"I'm so sorry I'm not there with you," Colton told her sincerely.

"I know you are, baby," Veronica said with warmth. "Don't be so hard on yourself. You've always been too hard on yourself. Your father used to wonder if maybe when he was teaching you to run the business he forgot to teach you when to let go. Life isn't all about making money and living up to everyone else's expectations. It's about knowing yourself and knowing when to relax and enjoy the fruits of your labor. You're thirty-four and you haven't fallen in love yet. What's stopping you? Your father and I used to play this game whenever we met a nice young lady. 'She would be perfect for Colton,' I would say, and your father would laugh at me and say, 'Let Colton decide who is perfect for him. Just like I decided you were perfect for me.' That shut me up for a while, but I still wonder whenever I meet a nice woman whether or not she's the one for you," Veronica said with a sigh. Before she said goodbye she reminded him to give her best to Lauren.

Lauren was having her own conversation on the satellite phone as she walked outside on hard-packed snow. Her sister, Amina, a captain in the army who had recently finished a hitch in Afghanistan and was trying to get used to civilian life, was threatening to steal the general's Hummer and come up there and collect her. "It's Christmas," she whined, making Lauren remember when they were kids and Amina, two years younger than herself, began to moan and groan until she wore her down. "No one should be alone on Christmas."

Lauren told her about Colton's unexpected arrival last night.

"It was the damnedest thing. I was in the tub at the time."

Amina screeched with delight on the other end after listening to Lauren's account. "Desiree says he's man-candy. And you know she doesn't say that about just anybody. Is he still there? We're getting in the car now if he is."

"No, you're not," Lauren said with some satisfaction. "The roads aren't fit for driving and won't be until tomorrow."

"Damn!" Amina said disappointedly.

Apparently, Desiree took the phone from Amina because it was her voice that Lauren heard next. "Colton Riley, huh? Women in Raleigh have been trying to trap him for years. He's either very wily or a confirmed bachelor. Be careful. You're very vulnerable right now."

Desiree was a psychotherapist who specialized in relationships. She had a diagnosis ready for any male her sisters came in contact with. She was so busy solving everyone else's relationship problems she had no time for a relationship of her own.

"You don't have to worry. I just offered him a warm place to stay last night," Lauren said, mindful of the agreement she'd made with Colton. "There's no relationship here for you to analyze, Desi."

The next voice to speak belonged to her sister Meghan. "Hey, sis, don't listen to these two. I hope you're taking advantage of the isolation and getting to know Mr. Riley better."

Lauren smiled at the naughty suggestion coming from Meghan. If any of her sisters could be stereotyped as bookish and a bit of a nerd it would be Meghan who was a history professor.

"It's nothing like that, Meg," she assured her. "He's just the son of my neighbors."

"All right, okay," said Meghan hastily. "I'm just saying that if you let loose and went for it, you're way overdue."

*Isn't that the truth,* Lauren thought. Her behavior had

been exemplary up until now. She could be forgiven for one indiscretion, couldn't she?

Amina was in possession of the phone again. "All right, we won't come up there. But stay in touch and let us know when the roads are clear. We've got to go check on Grandpa. He says he's fine, but he always says that."

"Will do," Lauren promised, "Bye, girls."

She heard them call "Bye!" in unison.

She disconnected and put the phone in the deep pocket of her jacket. Around her the world was snow-covered and looked like a winter scene in a Currier and Ives painting. The pond was frozen over, the tiny dock layered with frost. The oak and pine trees that surrounded the property were snow-laden. They were definitely having a white Christmas.

"Everything okay?" she heard behind her.

Colton had walked out to meet her. She wondered how much of her side of the conversation he'd heard. "Yeah, my sisters threatened to come up here but I told them the roads weren't clear yet."

"You have four sisters, right?"

"Yes, but only three, Desiree, Amina and Meghan, are in the area. Petra's a zoologist studying the Great Apes in Africa."

"No kidding, like Jane Goodall?"

She smiled. There were many facets to him. "Yes, she's been there for over two years now."

"What does she do when she's not studying apes?"

"Actually, she studied to be a veterinarian and worked at a big city zoo before deciding to specialize and become a zoologist. Now she lectures and has written a couple of successful books on the subject."

"She sounds very accomplished."

"Growing up in our household we were all told to aim

high. And even if we didn't hit the mark, we would be giving it our best shot."

"That's a good way of looking at things," Colton said, smiling down at her.

They began walking back to the cabin. "What did Veronica say?" Lauren asked.

"Pretty much what you guessed she'd say," he answered. "They've got it under control. The funeral's on Saturday."

"I'll be there," she said easily. "Unless you don't want me…" She hated that now that they'd been intimate she was wondering if her presence at his father's funeral would make him uncomfortable and perhaps make him relive their time together when he should be focusing on his father. But such were the repercussions of spontaneous sexual relationships. She figured she should expect some awkward moments.

"Please come," he said. His tone was gentle and sure. "I'd like for you to be there and so would Mom."

# Chapter 4

"What would you like to do today?" Lauren asked once they were back in the warmth of the cabin.

Colton turned to her with a humorous glint in his eye. "I want to take you on a date."

She laughed shortly as she shrugged off her coat and hung it on the hall tree. "A date, huh? Where are you planning on taking me?"

"A movie, dinner and then, dancing," he said with confidence.

She looked at him as if he'd taken leave of his senses but she was excited by the idea, so she accepted. "What time will you pick me up?" she asked.

"Let's make it six," he said. "I'm eager to get to know more about you."

"What am I supposed to do in the meantime?" she asked. She had thought they would spend their last day together in bed, like any normal snowbound couple.

"Do whatever you would do if I weren't here," he suggested.

So for the remainder of the day she worked in her office. She devoted a considerable amount of time to making a three-dimensional model of the building she was designing in Raleigh using a program on her computer. It allowed her to see the building from all angles and to visualize it more accurately. At around one o'clock her stomach growled, and she went in search of lunch to find Colton in the kitchen already fixing them sandwiches.

"Hello, Miss Gaines," he said. "You don't mind if I call you, Miss Gaines?"

"Not at all," she said, going to him and planting a kiss on his cheek. She hadn't kissed him since this morning. Colton put down the knife he'd been using to cut the sandwiches in two and pulled her into his arms for a proper kiss.

When he let her go, Lauren was breathless. "Are you sure tonight's our first date? That kiss was kind of fresh if it is. Actually, we should only be shaking hands at this point. And don't even think about getting lucky tonight. Sometimes I don't even kiss a guy good-night on the first date."

When Colton grinned, she noticed he had a dimple in his left cheek but not his right. How could she have missed that up until now? She peered closer. "What happened to your other dimple?"

"A genetic anomaly," he said with a short laugh. "I'm the third Riley who has only one dimple. What can I say? I'm a freak of nature."

"Another bit of Riley family trivia?"

"I've got a long list." He handed her a smoked turkey sandwich on a plate. "Will you be having your lunch in here with me, or will you be taking it back to work with you?"

"Oh, I'll have it in here with you if I'm not disturbing your date planning," she said with a bit of skepticism.

He let it slide. She may not have confidence in his ability to pull this date off but he was having fun. They sat down at the island and ate their sandwiches. "What kind of movie are we going to see?" Lauren asked after swallowing her first bite.

"Unfortunately, this theater has a shortage of romantic films starring African Americans," he told her regrettably. "However I trust the owner's taste and I'm sure whatever's shown will be worth watching."

Lauren smiled. It was true. She hadn't brought many DVDs with her on her visits to the cabin over the years. Her real collection was at home in Raleigh. "Well, how're you doing on dinner and dancing?"

"The restaurant I'm taking you to has a wonderful menu. You're going to dine on roast chicken, twice-baked potatoes and broccoli in a butter sauce."

"Wow, the chef must be a genius," she quipped. "The last time I visited that restaurant they didn't have roast chicken on the menu."

"Roast chicken, canned chicken, why quibble?" he asked good-naturedly. "It's going to be a culinary masterpiece."

"If you say so," Lauren said. "And dancing?"

"Ben Harper, Ray Charles and Otis Redding are all appearing at this little club tonight," he told her proudly. "I was able to get reservations."

"How nice of Ray Charles and Otis Redding to make the journey back from the Other Side to entertain us," Lauren said with laughter in her voice.

"I thought so, too," Colton agreed.

Lauren smiled at him. "It sounds wonderful."

* * *

Promptly at six that evening, Colton knocked on Lauren's bedroom door. She opened it to find him standing there looking handsome in the clothes he'd first arrived in except he'd freshly laundered them, taken a bath and shaved. He smelled heavenly.

She, too, had paid close attention to her appearance tonight.

She was wearing one of the few dresses she had in her closet: a short sarong-style silk dress in a rich shade of red. It was a summer dress but she figured that didn't matter since they weren't leaving the cabin.

She'd put her hair up and she wore a pair of black sandals with three-inch heels. She'd even applied a bit of makeup for the first time since Colton's arrival. Mascara made her lashes appear longer and the red lipstick gave her mouth a pouty look.

"You're a vision," Colton said appreciatively.

"And you look very handsome tonight."

He offered her his arm. "Shall we?"

She put her arm through his. "Yes, please."

The first thing Lauren noticed as they walked into the living room was that Colton had raided the attic and put up the artificial Christmas tree and decorated it with all her special ornaments. She stood stock-still for a moment, touched by his efforts. She turned to him, her eyes dancing, "It's beautiful."

Colton smiled, warmed by her reaction to the tree. "Merry Christmas, Lauren."

"Merry Christmas," Lauren murmured back, her heart filled with the warmth of the season despite her attempts to block it out.

Colton led her over to the couch and they sat down in front of the TV. He had already put the movie in the

DVD player. Now he picked up the remote, and he said, "I hope you haven't seen the new Larenz Tate/Nia Long movie yet."

Lauren laughed at his description. He'd found a copy of one of her favorite romantic movies. She'd forgotten she owned it.

"No," she said, going along with him. "What's it called?"

*"Love Jones,"* he replied.

Lauren, who'd seen the film at least a dozen times before, thoroughly enjoyed it with Colton. Turned out he had never seen it and initially tagged it a "chick flick." But he admitted, at the end, that it was well executed and dealt with real issues couples faced.

They kissed as the credits rolled. Lauren's lipstick was nearly gone as they'd kissed so much during the movie. She loved the taste of him. Clean, fresh and inviting. Kissing had not been a big part of her life lately. She realized now that she and Adam hadn't shared a memorable kiss for a couple of years before their divorce. She should have known the love had gone out of their marriage when he'd stopped kissing her the way he used to.

Colton looked deeply in her eyes after the kiss ended. He seemed to have sensed a change in her. "What is it? Am I too rough?"

"No," she was quick to reassure him. "I'm enjoying myself. I'm just trying to shake some memories."

He hugged her close. "It's going to take time," he said gently. He frowned. "Was he abusive?"

Lauren didn't answer immediately. Instead, she gave the question some thought. Adam never hit her but he was sometimes verbally abusive. He wanted her to stop working and support him in everything. He said his wife didn't need to work. He was her job. She should be like the wives of other rich men they associated with, women who were content to decorate their houses, attend social functions and look beautiful on their arms. These wives were happy to be at their husbands' beck and call. In return they wore designer clothes, lived in lavish mansions and spent money like it was going out of style. Marriage was a compromise, Adam used to say. And Lauren wasn't willing to compromise. She told him she hadn't spent years in college to simply let her degree gather dust.

She'd been raised to be an independent woman, not to depend on a man for everything. What kind of role model would she be for their future daughters if she were a sycophant with no backbone whatsoever? The subject of children was another bone of contention between them. Lauren wanted them. Adam didn't. He had been raised by a single mother who struggled every day to put food on the table. His no-good father hadn't contributed a cent to him and his two sisters' upkeep. If Lauren had known Adam didn't want children, she wouldn't have married him. There were quite a few revelations he laid on her *after* their wedding. Another was his obsession with youth. He was ten years her senior. She assumed their age difference was enough for him. But he insisted that she dress like someone barely out of their teens. She refused to do that, as well. He wanted her to get breast implants. She believed her breasts were fine just as they were. Nothing she did seemed to please him. Then she found out that at forty he'd found a twenty-two-year-old mistress. That was the last straw. Lauren filed for divorce.

"No," she finally answered Colton. "He wasn't physically abusive, but it became impossible to live with him after a while."

"I know you don't feel comfortable talking about what went on in your marriage, and I'm not going to press you," said Colton. "But I want you to know that if you do feel

like you want to talk to me at some later date, I'll be there
for you."

He got up and reached for her hand. She smiled at him
as he pulled her to her feet and said, "Dinner time, Miss
Gaines."

Because they were unable to go out for groceries Colton
had improvised with what was in the refrigerator and the
pantry. He made a chicken and broccoli stir-fry with
canned chicken breast and frozen broccoli seasoned with
onions and peppers over a bed of rice. Lauren couldn't figure out how he'd done it, but it was delicious. He'd found
half a bottle of white wine in the refrigerator and served
the two of them with a flourish.

He sat down across from her. His gray eyes danced with
good humor. "My dad used to say it's better to eat a bowl
of vegetables with someone you care about than a sump-
tuous feast with someone you hate."

Lauren squeezed his hand across the table. "You Riley
men really do know your way around a kitchen."

"Eat up," Colton coaxed her. "We need to be at the club
by nine."

She insisted on washing the dishes while he went into
the living room to set up "the club" by moving aside the
couch and rolling up the rug that covered most of the hardwood floor.

When she heard Ray Charles's distinctive voice singing, "Night time is the right time…" she went into the living room to find Colton waiting for her with open arms.

Because they didn't want to leave each other's arms
they slow-danced their way through Ray Charles's greatest
hits, even when the tempo picked up. Her head was on his
shoulder, his strong hands on her back, his touch sending
delicious sensual currents throughout her body.

She tilted her head up and looked him in the eyes.

Should she tell him that he was her first affair? She wanted him to know that this time had been special in case they came to their senses and decided not to see each other again once they returned to Raleigh. No, she told herself. It would make him feel self-conscious. So she didn't say anything. She would let him think she was as sophisticated as he was. This kind of situation was obviously not new to him. He was one of Raleigh's most eligible bachelors, after all.

An upbeat Ben Harper song filled the air and Colton said, "I see you like alternative rock."

"He's not an alternative rocker," Lauren defended her favorite musician.

"Sounds like alternative rock to me," Colton said.

"I'll have you know that Ben Harper is a Renaissance man. He's adept at many styles of music. He's rock, yes, but he's also rhythm and blues. I would follow him anywhere."

"Do I detect a slight crush on Mr. Harper?" Colton asked playfully.

"Maybe," Lauren admitted, equally as playful.

"You're a groupie?"

"I am not," she denied, appalled. "I just buy all of his CDs and go to any of his concerts that are within a hundred miles of Raleigh. But I wouldn't call myself a groupie."

"No, baby, you're definitely a groupie," Colton teased. Then he bent and kissed her forehead. "That's okay, though, I'm not jealous, much. There's one thing I've got going for me that Ben Harper doesn't."

She looked up at him with a challenge in her eyes. "What's that?"

"I'm here," he said simply.

She laughed. "That's a good point."

He placed her hand on his chest. She could feel the

steady thud of his heart against his rib cage. "When you touch me my heart sings."

She looked deeply in his eyes. She knew this was only a fantasy. Their emotions were heightened for different reasons but it all added up to the same thing. They were comforting each other in their time of need. That's all it was. Yet, in this moment, it felt so real. In her present emotional state she could see herself loving him forever. That was why complete strangers got married in wedding chapels in Vegas and regretted doing it the next morning, she thought wryly.

She'd abandoned her shoes during the movie and now she had to rise to her tiptoes to kiss him. Colton breathed a satisfied sigh and let her in. He couldn't remember kissing a sweeter mouth. And the things she did with her tongue made him harden in a matter of seconds. He didn't even believe she was aware of her effect on him.

Her eyes were drunk with passion when they surfaced for air. "I want you now," she said. She'd turned into a tigress. Her golden-hued eyes told him in no uncertain terms that he was hers tonight. She would not be denied.

He followed her to the bedroom with his eyes on the sexy sway of her hips in the little red dress she wore. The hem was hitched up high and revealed her long, shapely legs. In the bedroom, she turned to him and unbuttoned his shirt. He let it drift to the floor after it was past his shoulders. Her sultry gaze met his. "Admit it, you knew I was a sure thing tonight," she teased.

"A boy can only hope," Colton breathed. His erection was straining against the confines of his jeans. Lauren noticed the bulge.

She touched him and smiled. "You were a master of self-control today," she complimented him. "As I tried to concentrate on work, all I could think about was making love to you."

"Ditto," Colton assured her.

That was all the small talk they could manage. Colton quickly removed his jeans, briefs and socks. Lauren loosened the folds of her sarong and Colton peeled the dress off her body. She wasn't wearing a bra and had on flesh-colored panties beneath. At first glance she appeared as though she were naked.

Colton kissed her shoulders as he pulled her closer to him. He cupped her breasts, after which he began rubbing her nipples between a thumb and forefinger of each of his hands. Lauren sighed with pleasure and languidly arched her back.

Colton took turns licking each nipple until she felt weak in the knees. She stood in front of him only in her panties. He raised his head, his lips wet from licking her nipples. Sitting on the edge of the bed, he pulled her to him. He kissed her belly, ran his tongue around her belly button and then stuck the tip of his tongue inside, which caused an interesting sensation within Lauren.

When he began pulling down her panties, Lauren stayed his hand. "Last night, you pleasured me. Tonight, I treat you."

"I'm grateful for the offer," he said with a smile, "but the feel of your mouth on me would be more than I could bear right now. Even the thought of that…" He gestured downward with his gaze.

She followed his line of sight. His penis was even harder than it had been earlier.

She took his advice and she let him remove her panties and coax her onto her back on the bed. Colton ran his hands along the insides of her thighs, enjoying the view.

Her curly black thatch hid a pink jewel of a clitoris. He bent and sought out the pearl.

Lauren startled at the initial touch of his tongue on her but soon relaxed. A delightful sense of letting go washed over her and then pure sexual pleasure. Honestly, she didn't know whether she was coming or going. It felt so good. Could something that felt this good be wrong?

As his tongue worked its magic, his hands gently massaged her hips, which heightened her experience that much more. His large hands squeezed and squeezed. A sexual explosion spread out from her feminine center to the rest of her. Her thighs trembled with the release, and a satisfied sigh escaped her lips. She was his.

Colton got up and put on a condom. Returning to her, he got on his knees on the bed and straddled her. "Open up for me, baby, and wrap those beautiful legs around me as tightly as you can."

She was a quick study and performed splendidly. With each thrust his pleasure increased. He felt as though he were climbing higher and higher to heaven. Lauren met each thrust with a push of her own. Her insides quivered. The power within Colton was transferred to her and for one incredible moment they were in sync. She once again scaled the peak and met him up there. They collided and sparks flew. As they came down together, their pelvises pressed so close together they could have melded in the heat of the moment, all she could think was, if this wasn't love, she didn't know what was. And that was the crux of the problem. The reason she was up here in the first place was because she hadn't known what love was and had married the wrong man.

She could not make the same mistake twice. That was why she knew that once she and Colton were back in

Raleigh, she would not seek him out. She had to get her head straight first.

Colton, on the other hand, knew that he wanted to see her again, and as often as possible. He had never met a woman quite like her. He would pursue her with every ounce of his being.

# Chapter 5

The next morning they didn't make a big production out of saying goodbye. They made love upon awakening, showered separately, dressed and had a quick breakfast. Then Colton walked across to his family's cabin to make sure the storm hadn't caused any damage. Satisfied, he returned to Lauren's place. They did think to exchange business cards, and each of them quickly scribbled their personal cell phone numbers on the backs of them.

He got into his SUV and Lauren leaned in and briefly kissed his lips. "Safe trip," she said warmly. "I'll see you on Saturday." She had made a promise and she intended to keep it.

"I'll look forward to it," he replied lightly.

He put the car in gear and drove off. Earlier that morning the snowplow owner had been true to his word and now the roads were navigable.

Lauren stood and watched the SUV all the way to the

county road turnoff. Then she went inside. She would be leaving shortly herself. Before returning to Raleigh, though, she would check up on Grandpa Beck.

"What were you thinking heading to the mountains when you knew they were expecting a snowstorm?" Virginia Beck-Gaines cried when she saw her daughter later that evening. "I was worried sick about you!"

"I found out about the storm after I got there and I only came by here to give you an update on Grandpa," Lauren said irritably. She and her mother were known to butt heads, but she was in no mood to get into it right now. She was tired from her trip. They were in the big kitchen of her parents' five-bedroom house on the outskirts of Raleigh. The house sat on ten acres of land. Their closest neighbor was half a mile away. They liked their privacy.

Virginia, called Ginny by her husband, was short and slender. Anyone who knew her joked that she stayed too busy to gain weight.

She wore her long black hair with silver streaks in a twist at the back of her neck. Her caramel-colored skin was wrinkle-free except for the beginnings of crow's feet. Half African American and half Cherokee, she had the high-cheekbones of her ancestors. Her daughters had inherited her bountiful hair and their various shades of brown skin were crosses between their mother's golden brown skin and father's darker brown shade.

Her size belied her strength and her influence on her family. There was no doubt that she ruled the roost, even though the rooster was six-four and over two hundred pounds.

"Ginny, would you let the girl get a word in edgewise?" Lauren's father asked in her defense. "She's safe and sound and that's all that counts." He regarded Lauren. "How is the old reprobate?"

Retired general Alfonse "Fonzi" Gaines had been trying to ignore them by concentrating on his crossword puzzle, but no such luck. Fonzi was completely bald. He'd been shaving his head since his mid-forties when his hairline started receding. A disciplined ex-soldier, he jogged each morning. He had a weakness for his wife's cooking so he had to stay active in order to maintain his trim physique.

"He's fine," Lauren answered gratefully. "He's got a family of twelve up there celebrating Christmas at the lodge. They're from Florida. He says they were thrilled with all the snow. He had to nearly tie them down to keep them from going skiing the next day, but he explained that if anyone got lost out there they would freeze to death before rescue workers could get to them due to the road closures. That took the wind out of their sails."

"What is this I hear about your having a guest for the past two days?" Ginny wanted to know.

Lauren had expected an interrogation. She wished she had sworn her sisters to secrecy. She calmly gave her parents the tame version of Colton's visit. And the reason he'd dropped in.

Ginny had a concerned expression on her face after Lauren had finished relating the tale. "I did read in the paper that Frank Riley had passed away. He was well respected in this town. I'm sure there'll be a huge turnout for his funeral."

On Saturday, Lauren arrived early for the memorial service with her sister Desiree, who had insisted on accompanying her. The two of them found a parking space as close to the church as they could get, which happened to be on the street because the church's parking lot was already packed. On West Edenton Street, St. Paul AME Church was the oldest African American church in Raleigh. Inside, the pews were as packed as the parking lot. Lauren and Desiree, both wearing dark, tailored skirt suits, were able to squeeze into a pew in the middle of the church. Shortly after they were seated the choir began to sing a mournful spiritual.

Lauren strained to see if she could catch a glimpse of the family on the front pew, but she couldn't see much. Women's stylish hats blocked her view. She noticed the casket was closed and there was a poster-size photograph of Frank on an easel to the side of it. It was not a recent photo and she could easily see Colton's resemblance to his father. They had the same color eyes and the same square shape to their jaw.

An usher had given her a program when she'd walked through the door and she read it now. She saw that Frank had been the eldest son in a family of four children. He was survived by a sister and two brothers. He and Veronica had had two children, Franklyn Colton Riley, Jr., and Jade Veronique Everett. Jade had given them two grandchildren.

Looking around the ornately decorative church that had been built in the Late Gothic Revival architectural style, Lauren noted several town officials, including the mayor in attendance.

The stained-glass windows caught her attention momentarily. Bright sunshine streaming through gave the colors in them a kaleidoscopic effect. After the choir finished its selection, a minister took the pulpit and offered a prayer. Lauren's heartbeat quickened when the minister sat down, and Colton walked onto the stage and began the eulogy. He had not mentioned he would be doing the eulogy. But then perhaps he'd been encouraged to do it after he'd gotten back home.

He was a natural. At first his voice trembled slightly with emotion, but he soon got hold of himself and he went on to speak reverentially about his father. "Like most sons," he said, "I resented my father giving me advice on how to live my life. I thought his suggestions were old-fashioned and were designed to ensure I would follow in his footsteps. Thinking I knew better than he did, I didn't listen to his advice. I made my own decisions.

"Those of you who know me are aware that I went through a period of time when I wanted to party 24/7. I worked in the family business, yes, but my heart wasn't in it. I worked from Monday to Friday but at quitting time I was ready to have a good time. And Saturday and Sunday, I didn't go to church—those were my days to really cut loose. I drank too much and I lost count of the number of women I went through. Seeing I was wasting my life, my dad pulled me aside and said, 'Son, what do you value most?'

"I gave him some insincere answer about valuing family. He laughed at me and told me that if I truly valued family I would be doing everything in my power to make sure that when the time came I would be ready to take the reins of Riley Construction instead of slowly killing my body with alcohol and my soul with womanizing. Of course, I didn't listen. I didn't get it until he told me he was dying. Then, I was slapped in the face with reality and I knew he'd been right. If I cared about my family I would be preparing myself to pick up where he left off. I still drink but I don't do it excessively. I've learned what moderation means. And I respect women. I've become the man my family needs, but it was at a terrible expense. My father's gone. I miss you, Dad."

She'd been wrong. It wasn't a eulogy Colton had given.

It had been a personal goodbye to his father. Not the story of his father's life, but the story of a son's redemption.

There were tears in her eyes when he finished.

It was Frank's eldest brother, Tad, who gave the eulogy after Colton sat down. By the end of the service Lauren and several people around her had shed plenty of tears.

When they stood to watch the casket being carried out by the pallbearers, she whispered to Desiree, "I know I told you I wouldn't be going to the cemetery but I changed my mind. Will you be okay getting a taxi home?"

Desiree, who had said earlier she didn't want to go to the cemetery because those places gave her the creeps, now relented. "I'm not going to desert you. I can see how emotional you got after Colton's speech. It's almost as if you care about him."

"I'm not the only person here who found what he said touching," Lauren pointed out. She realized Desiree was not being mean-spirited but she wished just once her brainy sister would not be compelled to voice her opinions.

They fell silent until the procession with Frank's body had passed. Then they filed out of the church with the more than five hundred other people who had come to pay their respects.

Outside, Lauren took a deep, cleansing breath and carefully made her way through the throng of people who were milling about chatting instead of making their way to their cars to follow the hearse to the cemetery.

She looked around to see if she'd lost Desiree in the crowd. But she soon saw that her sister had been waylaid by a tall, broad-shouldered man in an expensively cut black suit.

As she stood there debating whether or not to go back for Desiree, a voice from behind said, "I thought I spotted you."

She turned at the sound of Colton's voice and her stomach muscles constricted painfully at the sight of him. He was dressed impeccably in a black suit, crisp white shirt and burgundy silk tie with highly polished wingtips on his feet. But his face was tired and drawn. Her heart went out to him.

She wrapped her arms around him when he came in for a hug. He squeezed her tightly and spoke hurriedly. "We're heading to the cemetery now, but I'd love it if you'd come to the house." He slipped a card in the palm of her hand. "Here's the address." He looked in Desiree's direction. "Is that one of your sisters?"

"Yes. Desiree," she said.

"Don't worry about her. That's my cousin Decker with her." He pecked her on the cheek. "I've got to go. They're waiting on me in the limousine. You will come?"

"Yes," she found herself saying even though she didn't think it would be a wise thing to do. Already her emotions were betraying her. Instead of reacting mildly to his presence after not seeing him for twenty-four hours, she had been ridiculously glad to see him.

He jogged away as soon she acquiesced. As he climbed in the back of the limousine he smiled at her and gave her a little wave. Desiree caught up with her a few minutes later after having finally shaken Colton's cousin.

"Oh, my God," she complained, her voice low, "I can't believe I've just been hit on at a funeral. He's a prime cut of man-beef. But really, this isn't a typical pickup venue."

Lauren laughed softly. "That was Colton's cousin Decker."

Desiree flashed a business card. "Mr. Decker Riley, Esq.," she read. "Shakespeare had it right when he wrote, first kill all the lawyers. Mr. Riley's really full of himself."

"I'm sorry you feel that way because my plans have

changed," Lauren told her regrettably. "We're not going to the cemetery after all. We're going to the Rileys' home."

They began walking toward the street where Lauren had parked the car. The crowd had thinned somewhat so the path was clear. Desiree, a bit shorter than her long-legged older sister, had to nearly run to keep pace. "I kind of feel like the best friend in a romantic comedy," she said a bit breathlessly. "First you told me you were going to the funeral because you were friends with Frank and Veronica Riley and it was only right to show up to pay your respects. Then you tell me you're extending your respects by going to the cemetery. Now you tell me you're getting in even deeper by going to the Rileys' home."

When they were nearly there Lauren remotely unlocked the doors. "I'll explain on the drive over," she promised.

The black late-model Range Rover wound its way through traffic as they traversed downtown Raleigh and turned and headed out of town to the suburbs.

"What's going on, Lauren?" Desiree asked. "While I was talking to God's gift to women, I looked back and saw you hugging Colton as though you two hadn't seen each other in years. That's not how people act who have just met and are casual acquaintances."

"I'm emotionally raw," Lauren admitted. "Maybe I'm experiencing what people say happens when you save somebody's life. I feel responsible for him now."

"You're getting way too attached," Desiree said, stating her opinion once more. "You did what any decent human being would have done. You let him in out of the cold, nothing more." Her eyes narrowed, her expression grew contemplative. "Or, is there something you're not telling me?"

"If I were keeping a secret, do you think that question would get it out of me?"

"Then something did happen between you two when you were snowed in!" Desiree exclaimed triumphantly.

"Really, Desi, you should learn to curb your imagination. I simply like the Rileys, both Veronica and Colton. I've known Veronica for more than three years. I've just met Colton, but he seems like a decent man. A man who reminds me of his father, whom I enjoyed knowing."

"Oh, please," said Desiree sarcastically. "You're backpedaling so fast smoke is coming out of your ears. You like Colton Riley like I like chocolate and you know I love the stuff. I would marry it if it were possible."

Smiling, Lauren said, "You and most of the women in the world. Seriously, I'm not in love with Colton Riley."

"Then you're in lust with him," said her very wise sister.

Lauren didn't deny it. "Should I make an appointment with you to talk about it?"

"That depends," said Desiree. "Is he in lust with you, too?"

"I would say yes," Lauren said confidently.

Desiree sighed deeply. "I can see now that all my earlier warnings came too late. But you know what? Your falling off your pedestal has been a long time coming. You were a virgin when you married Eckhart and I'm sure you never cheated on him, even though you probably had plenty of provocation."

"Could you speak plain English on occasion?" Lauren asked. "I know you're the brain in the family, but give us poor average people a break."

"You're not that average," said her sister sweetly. "Anyway, what I'm saying is, so what? You had a fling with Colton. It's nothing to get all guilty and repentant over. You're both free agents. Wait, he isn't involved with anyone, right?"

"He told me he isn't," Lauren confirmed.

"Okay, then," Desiree continued, "my only concern is that you're newly divorced and have probably not gotten over the hurt yet. Although, I don't see why you don't recognize the fact you're well rid of that snake."

"I'm realizing it more every day."

"Good. So, I'm just worried that you got it on with Colton because you wanted to test whether or not you were still desirable and Colton got it on with you because he was distraught over his father's death and found comfort in your bed. Other than that, I say go for it."

Lauren laughed shortly. "You hit the nail on the head. Should I keep seeing him for the hot sex, or cut my losses because a relationship based on a fling has no future?"

"It was hot, huh?" Desiree asked, observing her sister's face. Lauren couldn't hide the longing expression that fleetingly crossed her face.

"Honestly, the best I ever had," Lauren said.

"Well, come on now," said her sister, throwing cold water on that statement. "You've only had two men so far. I've had more lovers."

"Interesting," said Lauren. "Care to tell me how many more lovers you've had?"

"Four more," Desiree answered nonchalantly. "A couple of them weren't worth the effort. Bad is an understatement to describe their performances in bed. I'm not saying you can't have great sex without being in love, but my best experiences were with Noel, and I loved that man more than chocolate."

Lauren sighed sadly in sympathy for her sister's loss. Noel Alexander had died tragically in a boating accident during Desiree's senior year of college. They had been engaged.

"So from personal experience, I think what you're feeling for Colton might be more than mere lust. Perhaps you made a personal connection. The only way to find out is to let this play out. To do that you'll have to risk getting hurt again. Are you willing to risk it?" Desiree asked.

Lauren didn't answer immediately. She knew Desiree expected her to give it some thought. Her first instinct was to guard her heart and oftentimes her first instinct had turned out to be the wisest choice. But Desiree had been right when she said it was about time Lauren fell from her self-imposed pedestal. It was time she took some risks.

No one accomplished great things without some risk. "I think it's worth it," she finally said. "What if he's the one for me in spite of the unusual way we met?"

Desiree seemed pleased with her decision. "I can't wait to tell Mina and Meg," she said with a big smile.

"You can't tell anyone else," Lauren said hurriedly. "Colton and I promised each other that our affair would be just that, our affair. Aren't therapists supposed to keep what patients tell them confidential?"

"You're not my patient. You're my sister," Desiree pointed out. It was apparent she was eager to share what she'd learned with Amina and Meghan. "I won't breathe a word of it to Mom and Dad, but you've got to let me tell the girls."

"No, Desi." Lauren wouldn't budge.

"Then you'd better give me a dollar," Desiree caved in.

"Why should I give you a dollar?" Lauren asked.

"Payment for my services," Desiree said. "I consider what I do to be as important as what lawyers do. Legally, you're not my patient until there has been an exchange of legal tender for my expertise."

Busy driving, Lauren briefly glanced at her sister to see if her expression was serious. It was. "Oh, okay, look in my purse and get a dollar. But I want a receipt!"

# Chapter 6

The Rileys' sprawling three-story antebellum-inspired house sat on a hundred acres of verdant land near a lake. Ancient oak trees with branches covered in moss dotted the property. It was the picture of genteel Southern living.

Lauren guessed this was a gathering exclusively for family and close friends because when she and Desiree arrived there were only about thirty cars parked in the circular driveway.

The housekeeper greeted them at the door and directed them to the solarium where waitstaff carrying trays of canapés circulated among the guests. A bar was set up in the corner of the room.

"They certainly have class," Desiree whispered.

"Lauren!"

Lauren heard her name being called from across the room and looked up to find Veronica heading their way. In her late fifties, Veronica was tastefully dressed in a black sleeveless A-line sheath with a matching jacket and black pumps. Her shoulder-length dark-brown hair had gold highlights that brought out the gold in her eyes. Lauren was enveloped in her arms. She fondly pressed her cheek to hers and then released her to get a good look at her. "I was glad when Colton told me he'd invited you. It gives me the chance to thank you for what you did for him. Thank you, dear."

Lauren smiled shyly. "There's no need for thanks, Veronica. He was the perfect houseguest. He cooked and did his own laundry." Lauren thought it best to keep things light. The day had probably been unbearably sad for Veronica.

Veronica laughed softly as she took notice of Desiree for the first time. "This must be Desiree. It's a pleasure to meet you."

"The pleasure's all mine," Desiree said sincerely.

She and Desiree clasped hands briefly, and Veronica looked at the sisters side by side. "There's a strong resemblance," she said. "There are five of you altogether, right?"

"Yes," Lauren answered, "Although only four of us live in the area."

"Ah, yes, one of your sisters is studying the Great Apes in Africa."

"I'm afraid I tell my mom everything," Colton said as he joined them. "But I didn't know she actually listened to me."

He offered Desiree his hand. "It's wonderful to meet you, Desiree."

Desiree firmly shook his hand and smiled up at him. "Likewise, Colton," she said. "I'm so sorry for your loss."

"Thank you," he said simply. Then he turned to Lauren, and said, "I have something to show you." He looked apologetically at Desiree. "You don't mind if I steal her for a few minutes, do you?"

Desiree was magnanimous. "Of course not. Keep her as long as you like. I was getting tired of her anyway."

Lauren quickly cut her eyes at Desiree before turning to follow Colton.

In Colton and Lauren's absence, Veronica moved closer to Desiree. "I don't know about you but I'm famished. Would you join me for something to eat?"

"Sure," said Desiree and she followed Veronica out of the solarium to the kitchen.

"The staff is circulating with finger foods," Veronica explained, "but who can satisfy their hunger on that stuff?"

Desiree found Veronica Riley was a woman after her own heart.

She'd missed breakfast that morning and the array of Southern dishes displayed on the huge island in the center of the kitchen made her mouth water. She was putting a slice of juicy ham on her plate right next to a serving of potato salad when Decker Riley strode into the room. "Auntie, I've been looking everywhere for you. The pastor has to leave and he wanted to speak with you about something before he left." He stopped in his tracks when he spotted Desiree and smiled broadly. "We meet again," he said, the delight evident in his deep baritone.

Veronica was chewing a mouthful of collard greens and cornbread. She swallowed. "Child, tell the pastor to come back here. I'm not leaving this kitchen until I'm full as a tick. Desiree will be here when you get back. Won't you, Desiree?"

Desiree smiled politely. "I'm not going anywhere."

Decker reluctantly spun on his heels and went to give the pastor his aunt's message.

Veronica smiled at Desiree. "He comes off a bit too strong but he's really a decent young man."

Desiree had good instincts about people and she believed Veronica Riley was the type of woman who saw things clearly and consequently spoke her mind. "We met earlier at the church and 'player' was the first impression I got."

Veronica sighed. "I don't know why young men these days think that image appeals to women. I think it turns off more women than it attracts. I feel that some so-called players are really insecure. It seems to be all a facade they hide behind in order to protect themselves from getting hurt."

"You're very perceptive," Desiree told her. "That's my theory, as well."

Veronica smiled. "I knew when I met you that we were two of a kind."

When Colton had said he had something to show Lauren, he hadn't been using that as an excuse to get her alone. He really did have something to show her. However, they had to run an obstacle course to get where he was taking her. His dad's study.

They were stopped by his sister, Jade, as he and Lauren began climbing the stairs to the second floor. Lauren found Jade to be as charming as her mother and brother. She was tall and full-figured. Her skin was dark chocolate like her father's and she had jewel-like golden-brown eyes that sparkled with happiness. Her husband, Manu Everett, who was half Samoan and half African American, was a couple inches taller than Colton's six-two frame, but he was about the size of a refrigerator.

"Colton, is this Lauren?" Jade asked excitedly.

Colton introduced them. Lauren couldn't help smiling. Jade's face was so animated. *How does she manage to look this happy,* Lauren wondered, *when they just buried their father today?*

That was when Manu walked up, grinning, and greeted them. He had the same light of natural happiness in his eyes. He playfully picked up his wife from behind and set her back down on the floor. "Hey, everybody," he said warmly.

"Manu," Jade said, "This is Lauren, the woman who saved my crazy brother's life."

Manu's face broke into an even wider grin. "We're indebted to you, Lauren. I don't know what we'd do if something happened to this dude." He playfully punched his brother-in-law on the arm. Lauren knew from Colton's wince that it had hurt.

"He was actually company for me," Lauren graciously said. "Without him I would've been trapped in a blizzard all by myself."

"I hope he was a good houseguest and didn't leave his wet towels on the bathroom floor," Jade joked.

Lauren looked up at Colton in mock horror. "You don't really do that, do you?"

"I have no idea what Jade is talking about," Colton denied. "Now, if you two will excuse us, Lauren and I have something to discuss in private."

Manu hugged his wife. "Well, go on, my brother. No one's stopping you."

"Mommy, Daddy!" Two adorable children, a boy of about six and a girl of about three came running up to them.

Manu grabbed both of them to either side of him with powerful arms. "Didn't I tell you to stop running?"

In that instant, Lauren had her answer to how Jade managed to look so happy on such a sad day. She had love in abundance.

Lauren was delighted to be introduced to Colton's niece

and nephew, and then Colton took her firmly by the hand and led her upstairs.

Colton stuck his head in the room to make sure that no one else had sought a bit of peace and quiet in his dad's study before ushering Lauren inside the bookshelf-lined room.

Elegant, yet homey, the room reflected its late owner's tastes. A huge cherrywood desk sat atop a Persian rug in front of a bay window. There was the faint scent of a sweet variety of tobacco in the air. Leather sofas faced each other with a large square coffee table between them. Frank's antique chess set was the only thing on the tabletop.

Lauren remembered it fondly. She used to joke with him that she hoped the elephants whose ivory the chess pieces had been carved out of had died of natural causes. Frank had found that hilarious. "And I suppose that chicken you're eating committed suicide?"

A dark brown leather Queen Anne chair sat near the fireplace, a reading lamp next to it. A red wool throw was on back of the chair. It looked so inviting that Lauren couldn't help but sit in it, her mind on its previous owner. She looked around admiringly. Frank had left an indelible imprint on this room.

Colton locked the door behind them so they wouldn't be disturbed without advance warning.

Lauren noticed his actions and smiled, but she didn't move from her seat. She hadn't come here today to find an empty room and make out with Colton. She'd come to show support. As always, though, her body betrayed her loftier intentions. She wanted to kiss him, and deeply.

To mask her desires, she started talking. "What you said today was very touching."

"It was the truth," Colton said as he slowly walked toward her. "I've worked hard to change. But I'm far from perfect. I'm always discovering something I need to work on. What I've discovered lately is that I have the capacity for becoming one of those annoying people who is completely obsessed with someone else. So obsessed that they think about them all the time, crave their touch and even dream about them."

As he said this and walked toward her, he held her captive with his mesmerizing gaze. His gray eyes were dark and stormy and so damned sexy. Her body, it seemed, rose from the chair of its own accord. She fairly floated into his arms. And the kissing began.

They moaned with the sheer pleasure of their mouths finally being able to come together in this common but astonishing manner. Colton had read somewhere that kissing raised levels of neurotransmitters like dopamine and serotonin. They made you feel happy and horny and that was what made kissing such an enjoyable act. He was a man of nearly thirty-five years old and he didn't remember ever getting such a thrill from kissing as he did when he engaged in it with Lauren. She was beautiful, yes. But he'd dated many beautiful women. So what *was* it about her?

"We're back in Raleigh," he said softly, "And I, for one, don't want to forget what happened between us. I want to date you, in public. That's my decision."

Lauren went with her heart. "I'm in total agreement."

Colton grinned. "Great, because I need a date for the Black and White Ball."

"That's on New Year's Eve," said Lauren in a near panic. Last year, she'd gone with Adam and it had been one of the worst experiences of her life. The ball was attended by premier businesspeople in Raleigh. The attendance fee was a grand and most of the proceeds went to local charities. To Lauren, that was the only reason to participate. However, Adam attended to network and to be seen. Last year's event had certainly been memorable, to say the least.

"My marriage crashed and burned at the ball last year," Lauren told Colton.

His brows arched questioningly. "I remember seeing you there. You looked exquisite. You were smiling as if there was nowhere you'd rather be."

"I became very good at pretending the last year of our marriage," Lauren said sadly. "Do you want to hear what happened or not?"

Colton had been holding her by her arms. He let go of her and gestured to one of the couches.

"No, thanks," Lauren said. "I'd rather stand for this."

She could still see the scene that had unfolded in the ladies' room the night of the ball. She had used the facilities and emerged from the stall to wash her hands and check the state of her makeup only to be accosted by a young woman in a white gown. The women in attendance wore either a black gown or a white gown. She'd worn white that night, as well. Her gown had been a Grecian-inspired one-shoulder creation. The other woman wore one with a plunging neckline and a side-slit almost up to her waist. She had curves in all the right places and meant for them to be seen.

A redhead, her skin was the color of toasted almonds and her eyes were blue. Lauren remembered thinking she must not be a real redhead because redheads generally had paler skin, not brown skin. At any rate, she could have given a supermodel a run for her money. "You're Mrs. Adam Eckhart, aren't you?" she asked Lauren. Her tone had been friendly and admiring. Lauren's guard was down because this wasn't the first time a young woman had approached her to try and get in her good graces. Adam Eckhart was a rich, powerful man and it could be to a young woman's advantage to get in good with his wife. It got you closer to the great man himself. And if you failed to get to him, at least you would be in his orbit and there were other successful men who ran in his circles who were worth latching on to.

Lauren wrongly assumed the redhead was one of these women.

"Yes," she'd replied, equally friendly. "I am, and you are?"

They were standing in the middle of the ladies' room, other women moving around them. The redhead looked Lauren straight in the eye, her stare unflinching. "My name is Joy Summers and I'm his mistress."

She hadn't even lowered her voice, just said it out loud for everyone to hear. Several women gasped and immediately turned to stare at this vulgar young woman who'd chosen to confront her lover's wife at the social event of the season.

Lauren felt sick to her stomach. She'd suspected Adam was cheating but suspecting it and having proof of it were two entirely different things.

She recovered fairly quickly, though. Years of inculcation by her mother and father to always be poised and behave intelligently in public came to her rescue. She met the redhead's challenging gaze, and said, "And what does that have to do with me?"

The redhead's eyes bugged out. She had not expected such a response. "I thought you'd want to know."

The other five women in the room showed no signs of leaving. They stood rapt, hanging on every word. Lauren calmly said, "I already knew, thank you. Is there anything else you'd like to say? For instance, you're sorry for not telling a married man to go to hell when he first hit on you? Because you must have known Adam Eckhart was married. Or do you specialize in married men?"

"Don't kill the messenger," said the woman, smiling as though she'd exacted a coup with that comeback.

One of the onlookers sniffed derisively. "If it was me I'd do more than kill you."

Lauren looked sharply at the woman. "I've got this."

"Handle it, sister," encouraged the woman.

"Obviously you feel confident in your status as his mistress," Lauren said, "Or you wouldn't risk his wrath. Married men like keeping their affairs quiet. That's the point of an affair. It's a naughty delight. It loses its appeal after it's been revealed." She circled the woman much like a lioness checking out her prey before pouncing. "Maybe you think I'll divorce him and then he'll come running to you. I've never heard of that happening but you might get lucky. Who knows?"

"I'm pregnant with his child," the redhead tossed out as her trump card.

"Then that's why you've come here with this desperate attempt to win a permanent place in his life," Lauren surmised. With that, she turned to leave.

"I'm sorry for everything," the redhead shouted at her retreating back. "I had no alternative but to show up here and embarrass him into taking responsibility."

"Good luck with that," Lauren had called back.

"She really was his mistress," Lauren said to Colton now. "But that stunt she pulled was the end of her. Adam dropped her soon after. He's engaged to someone else now. I have no idea if there was ever really a baby involved."

Colton hugged her close. "Forget the Black and White Ball then. We'll ring in the new year together anywhere you want."

Concerned by his state of mind so soon after his father's death, Lauren asked while looking him in the eyes, "Are you sure you're up for a celebration?"

"Dad wouldn't have had it any other way," Colton assured her. "For years the Black and White Ball has been the big blowout of the year for the company. We make generous donations to local charities. It made Dad feel like Santa Claus at the end of the year."

"All right," she relented, noticing the look of pride on Colton's face. "I'll go with you."

"But what about your bad memories from last year's ball?"

"I'm no longer married to that cheater," she reasoned. "I doubt I'll be cornered in the ladies' room by one of his mistresses again."

Colton hugged her tightly. "I'm going to make sure you have a good time. Now, for what I wanted to show you."

Lauren's brows arched in surprise. "You mean you really did have something you wanted to show me? I thought that was a ploy to get me alone."

"Only partly," Colton said, releasing her and walking over to his father's desk. He opened a drawer and withdrew an envelope and walked back over to Lauren and handed it to her.

Puzzled, Lauren looked down at the envelope, which was made out of expensive vellum paper in a rich cream shade. Her name was scrawled on it in cursive.

"It's from Dad," Colton said.

Tears sprang to Lauren's eyes at the thought of Frank thinking enough of her to leave her a personal message. She eagerly opened the envelope and read the enclosed note aloud, "Lauren, I want you to have my chess set because you and I spent wonderful evenings both challenging and getting to know one another. If I'd had a second daughter I would want her to be just like you. By the way, I inquired and the pieces were made from the ivory of an elephant by the name of Hannibal. He spent his last days at a retirement home for elephants in Botswana where he died in his sleep. Being an environmentalist himself, I'm sure Hannibal wouldn't mind your having a part of him. Frank."

Lauren cried even harder after reading his message. Colton pulled her into his arms.

He bent and kissed her, tasting her tears. "Stop crying now. Dad didn't want anyone crying over him. You know what he wrote in his letter to me? He said, 'Colton, I can't tell you how to remember me. You'll have formed your own opinion of me over the years. But I hope you'll remember that I liked to laugh and I worked hard. I loved your mother and you and your sister and when I made friends I kept them for life. I don't want you to waste a minute of your life. Don't cry for me. Be happy that I knew how to have a good time while the getting was good. I wish you happiness, son.'"

"That's so sweet," Lauren said.

Colton laughed. "Only you and my mother would describe Dad as being sweet. He was a tough SOB, but he was fair and honest and he loved his family. He was a good man. The kind of man I aspire to be one day."

"You're already a good man, Colton Riley."

Someone knocked on the door. Colton shot an irritated look in its direction and reluctantly released Lauren to open the door.

Veronica stood on the other side. "Um, hi. Wouldn't you and Lauren like to come downstairs and join us? There's food in the kitchen. You two must be ravenous by now."

Colton immediately knew he'd been tattled on by his sister or perhaps his brother-in-law. Both were equally immature and loved playing practical jokes on him. They'd probably told his mother he'd taken Lauren upstairs with seduction in mind. True, he'd wanted to steal a kiss, but he'd never make love to Lauren and risk embarrassing her in a house full of people on the day of his father's funeral.

He looked back at Lauren and laughed. "Shall we go down before all the potato salad's gone?"

Lauren wiped her tears away and smiled. "I am a little hungry."

She noticed Veronica was observing her closely as they started downstairs. "Have you been crying, dear?"

"I gave her the letter Dad left for her," Colton explained.

"I see," said Veronica sympathetically. She pulled Lauren into the crook of her arm and held her close to her side all the way downstairs. "I helped him write the letters. He was in good spirits the day he wrote yours. He smiled the whole time and when he finished, he said he knew you'd get a kick out of that."

"He was right," Lauren assured her. Taking Colton's advice that Frank didn't want anyone crying over him, she took a deep breath and smiled.

# Chapter 7

Lauren was pleased to return to work on Monday. Work centered her. Her current commission was to design the new children's hospital. She'd been with the architectural firm of Lawrence, Mayer and McGill since she was twenty-two. She had interned there and the senior partner, Albert Lawrence, had liked her so much he'd offered her a permanent position after she'd graduated from Duke University. For some time family and friends had encouraged Lauren to start her own firm. But she enjoyed being part of a design team. She also liked being able to concentrate fully on her work and not have to worry about renting an office space, hiring reliable staff and all the other hassles of running your own firm. Maybe one day, she had thought.

When Lauren stepped off the elevator, she greeted the firm's receptionist, Meredith, a stout middle-aged black woman who wore her long gray hair in a large bun. Meredith genuinely loved people and made everyone feel at ease.

"Good morning, Meredith," Lauren said cheerfully.

Meredith put down the coffee mug she'd just taken a sip from. Her brown eyes twinkled. "Hello there! How was your Christmas?"

Lauren smiled. She was searching for a suitable response because she hadn't discussed her divorce with Meredith. So saying she'd holed up in a cabin while she wallowed in self-pity then had rescued a gorgeous hunk whom she had spent two days making love to, wouldn't do at all. She kept it simple and told a little white lie. "Wonderful. We went to the mountains. There was snow."

"I heard," said Meredith, "A blizzard. But I'm sure your mister kept you warm."

Lauren had found over the years that Meredith believed a little romance could cure anything that ailed you. Reading romance novels, which she could be found doing each day at lunchtime, was her favorite pastime.

"Oh, yes, I had a big strong man to keep me warm," Lauren confirmed. She smiled. It was the truth and it ought to satisfy Meredith's romantic imagination.

"And how was your Christmas?" she inquired.

"Too much family," Meredith complained. "The house was so full you were stepping over warm bodies to get to the bathroom. But we had a real good time."

"I'm glad to hear it." Lauren continued walking toward her office. "Have a great day!"

"You, too," Meredith said and resumed drinking her coffee.

At around ten that morning, Albert Lawrence tapped on her office door. Lauren could see his portly outline through the opaque glass in the top of the door.

"Come in, Albert," she called, her tone welcoming.

In his sixties, Albert had a head full of curly white hair, which he kept shorn close to his head. In spite of his excess weight, he was invariably impeccably dressed. Today he wore a dark blue pinstriped suit with a white dress shirt and a red silk tie. His dress shoes were always shined to a high gloss.

He closed the door behind him and approached Lauren's desk at a turtle's pace. "Hello, Lauren. I thought I'd drop by and see how you were doing. Holding up? I went through a stressful divorce myself some years ago. Initially, I didn't think I'd survive without her. She left me for a younger man, you know, and back then, the courts were always on the side of the mother when it came to custody rights. I not only stood to lose a wife, but my children. So, I understand what you're going through."

Lauren smiled. "Albert, I believe those are the most words you've ever strung together in a conversation with me."

She gestured to the chair in front of her desk. "Please, sit."

Albert looked at the chair as though he were debating whether to sit or not. Then, he sat down. "Only for a few minutes," he said, "I don't want to disturb your work flow."

"You're not," she assured him. Albert was a worrier. He was a talented architect who was not stingy with his knowledge. She'd learned so much from him over the years. "And I'm doing fine, really. I haven't given Adam much thought at all during my break."

"Good, good." Albert hedged.

But instantly Lauren knew something was wrong and it concerned her ex-husband. "You sound like you have something to tell me," Lauren said suspiciously.

Albert didn't like giving people bad news, and usually left that task, particularly when the need arose to fire someone, to one of the other senior partners. Albert simply didn't have it in him.

He looked at her, his dark brown eyes full of sympathy. "I wouldn't even mention this but you are the principal architect on the project. The client says your ex's company has put in a bid to build the hospital."

Lauren's expression didn't change. She had known that she would one day have to work with Adam's company. He owned one of the largest construction companies in the state. Architects had to go on sites and check to make sure the building was being constructed according to specifications. That didn't mean she would encounter Adam on her frequent visits to the site. In fact, as head of the company he probably delegated much of the onsite work to someone below him on the totem pole.

"Don't worry," she said to Albert. "Even if his company wins the bidding war, more than likely I'll never run into him."

Albert looked appeased as he rose. "I hope not," he said. "The way he treated you was atrocious. I don't want him to upset you further. Well, I should let you get back to work."

Lauren rose and walked him to the door. "Thanks for your concern, Albert. You're very nice to think of me."

Albert blushed and hurried out. Lauren closed the door and returned to her desk. *Somewhere in the city,* she thought, *that bastard is probably having a good laugh thinking that I'm trembling in my boots, dreading the possibility of having to interact with him. We'll see who gets the last laugh.*

She returned to her computer and the 3-D image she was working on. Architects used to spend hours building models of the structures they designed. The models were then presented to the client so that they could visualize how the finished project would look. More and more these days, models were built using computer programs and her presentation to the client was usually in the form of a PowerPoint slide show.

Her cell phone rang, and she picked it up and checked the display. It was her sister, Meghan. "What's up, Meg?"

"Are you free for lunch?"

"I was planning to work through lunch," she said regrettably. "Why?"

"You have an event to go to in less than forty-eight hours," Meghan reminded her. "Don't you think you should devote some time to shopping for it? Mina, Desi and I aren't going to let you wear something you've already worn before. Our reputations are at stake."

"What do you mean your reputations?" Lauren asked, amused.

"How you look reflects on us," Meghan said reasonably. "After all, you're the oldest and you're supposed to set the example. Although, God knows, you've never taken that seriously. But things have changed. You're divorced. Undoubtedly your ex is going to be at the ball with his barely legal fiancée and we're not going to let you go unless you're put together."

Lauren laughed. "Oh, I don't think he wants to go to jail. She's probably over eighteen."

Meghan snorted. "Yeah, he's such a prince."

Getting them back on subject, Lauren asked, "What are you going to do if I refuse to go shopping with you? Kidnap me?"

"If we have to," Mina cut in. "I can bench press two hundred pounds. I should be able to hogtie you."

"Fine," said Lauren, still laughing. "Pick me up out front at noon. Don't be late because I can only spare an hour for this shopping expedition of yours."

* * *

The girls were in Meghan's baby-blue Mustang when they pulled up to the curb. Desiree was riding shotgun so Lauren climbed in back with Amina. All of them were dressed differently. Meghan, with her long black wavy hair in a smooth chignon, was in a business suit like Lauren because she was taking off from work, too. Amina, who wore her black hair in a huge Afro, was the most casual of them all and was wearing jeans, athletic shoes and a leather jacket over a pullover shirt. She was not employed yet following her last hitch in the army. Desiree, who'd recently had her long hair shortened to chin length, was wearing a designer dress and shoes. She was the fashionista in the family and one who knew where to find designer clothes at bargain prices.

The air in the car was redolent with fast-food smells. "Where's my lunch?" Lauren asked, inhaling the enticing odor.

Desiree turned around and handed her a Wendy's bag and a large drink. "A single and a Diet Coke," she said.

"You remembered. Thank you," Lauren said, accepting the bag and paper cup. She sat back and ate in silence while her sisters debated where to go.

After deliberating, they headed to a consignment boutique downtown where Desiree knew the owner and he promised they would get their money's worth.

"You mean my money," Lauren said. "Remember, I don't have Adam's credit cards anymore. I'm on a single girl's budget."

"Don't worry," said Desiree. "We've decided to treat you."

"Yeah," put in Mina. "I've got a chunk of money in my account and no one to spend it on."

"Spend it on you," Lauren suggested. "You deserve to be spoiled with all you've been through."

Lauren immediately felt the mood change after she spoke and quickly regretted her words. Amina was a helicopter pilot and her last assignment had been in Afghanistan. She had been credited with saving hundreds of soldiers by air-lifting them to safety. Like many soldiers, she lived with the knowledge that each day she woke up in the morning could be her last day on earth. She was ready to lay down her life for her country. But when the man she loved was killed in action, she'd lost it. Six years in service seemed long enough. When Keith was alive she had thought she would make the military her life's calling. After all, he had been in it for life. But when he died, her heart was no longer in it. She didn't reenlist when her time ran its course.

Amina laughed shortly. "Stop tiptoeing around me, you guys! I'm handling it. And don't think I don't know what you've been thinking but have been afraid to say out loud. It's the Gaines girls' curse. First Desiree lost the man she loved and now I've lost the man I love." She met Lauren's gaze. "I'm sure you and Meg are wondering if the same thing's going to happen to you."

"Never," Lauren vehemently denied. "I don't think that way. My heart just goes out to you and Desi. I wish I could take the pain away."

"Well, I have," Meghan admitted softly. "I tried not to think that way but it makes you wonder. I mean, what are the odds that two sisters would lose the men they love, and both before marriage?"

"If you're going to think superstitiously," Lauren reasoned, "then Adam should have died before I married him. Instead, we were married for nearly six years, and he's still very much alive. There is no curse, just life, and life can be hard enough without adding a curse to the equation."

"Amen," agreed Desiree. "Let's leave the curse alone, shall we? There is nothing preventing us from being happy in a relationship except finding the right man and having moderate good fortune. After all, Momma and Daddy have been together for thirty-two years."

A few minutes later they were pulling up to the consignment shop. Once inside Lauren immediately began to model dresses while her sisters commented on her choices. Since women who attended the ball were asked to wear either a black dress or a white dress, Lauren selected dresses with only those colors. But after half an hour and no sure winner, Desiree handed her a vintage halter gown by Halston that was vertically half black and half white. Lauren tried it on and stood in front of the full-length mirror. It fit perfectly. The sisters gathered around her, approval written all over their faces.

The dress had an invisible zipper up the back and the material was thick and soft. It felt like silk against her skin. "I look like one of those 1930s pinup girls," she said wistfully.

"Wear your hair up," Desiree advised. "We want Colton to be able to see your bare back."

"And wear red lipstick to complete the 1930s pinup girl look," Amina chimed in.

"Of course, you might not even make it to the ball once Colton sees you in it," Meghan joked.

They all laughed.

Lauren smiled at her reflection. She couldn't wait.

The night of the ball, Colton got home late from work. Earlier that day he'd filled in for a welder on the downtown skyscraper site because the hired one hadn't shown up for work. Further investigation revealed he'd been in an accident. With no time to get anyone else, and with work in need of completion in a timely manner, Colton had gone on-site. Though, it wasn't unusual for him to get his hands dirty on the job. He'd started at the bottom. His dad had him working as a carpenter's helper when he was sixteen. By the time he was eighteen he was proficient at any number of skills from bricklaying to welding, plumbing and electrical wiring. His father told him he wanted to be able to say his son knew the business inside and out, and in the future when he became the head of the company it could be said that he'd earned the position.

As he entered his house, he was beginning to feel the effects of a long, physically taxing day. Then, he thought of Lauren and how she would look in her ball gown and he got a boost of energy. He hadn't seen her since the day of his dad's funeral. They had spoken several times, but both of them had been busy with work. He could see now that he was involved with a woman who enjoyed her work as much as he enjoyed his. He liked that about Lauren because he wanted her to be fulfilled. He was smart enough to know if a woman was happy with herself, she was more prone to be happy with her man.

He smiled as he showered. Was it too soon to think of himself as her man? Maybe, but he didn't care. He was going with the flow, eager to see where this would lead.

Thinking ahead, he'd laid out his clothing for the ball before he'd left for work that morning. The tuxedo was his. He'd stopped renting tuxes after thirty, believing a grown man, especially one who had occasion to wear a tux several times a year, should own at least one. It had been tailor-made to fit his wide shoulders, muscular chest, trim waist and long legs.

He switched out the cummerbund from time to time. He owned three different colors. Tonight he was simply wearing classic black. Lauren had told him her dress was black-and-white. He thought the traditional tux would complement her dress nicely.

He drove his Lexus to her house. The SUV was too sporty for tonight. When he rang the bell he felt a nervous tremor in his stomach. He tugged at his bow tie. He couldn't believe that after making love to her in every conceivable position up at the cabin he was anxious about taking her to a dance.

Lauren opened the door and flashed him a smile. "Wow, you really clean up well, Mr. Riley."

Colton was speechless. Her skin, her hair, the way her dress hugged her curves and, God help him, her juicy lips, all worked together. Her sexuality was personified even though the dress was not in the least immodest. No cleavage was spilling out of it. Her legs were entirely covered. Just her shoulders and back were bare and that was enough. Her golden-brown skin with its red undertones glowed with health. Her hair shone. Her eyes were clear and beautiful.

"If you don't say something soon I'm going to think you don't like my dress," Lauren teased.

Colton snapped out of his reverie and pulled her in his arms and kissed her. Lauren smiled at him when they parted. "That's more like it."

"You're exquisite," he said huskily. He held her face in his hands. "Maybe we can skip the ball."

Lauren laughed. "No, we're not skipping the ball. I'd have to tell Meghan she was right."

"What?" Colton asked.

"I'll explain on the way," she promised and grabbed her clutch and wrap from the foyer table.

* * *

The grand ballroom at the Marriott was more than five thousand square feet and elegantly furnished. Large round tables were placed around the periphery on the room. The chairs around the tables were upholstered with gold brocade fabric. Navy blue tablecloths topped the tables and elaborately folded gold cloth napkins adorned the white china. Centerpieces consisting of deep red long-stemmed roses in clear glass vases claimed pride of place at each table.

Two-hundred and fifty couples were in attendance. Colton and Lauren immediately spotted the Riley table and made their way across the ballroom past the highly polished wood dance floor and the podium.

"You made it just in time," Veronica greeted them. "They're getting ready to start serving."

She rose and accepted Colton's peck on the cheek. Then she and Lauren exchanged a greeting. Also at the table were Jade and Manu, Veronica's escort and nephew, Decker, and three other couples associated with Riley Construction.

"Lauren, you look lovely this evening," Veronica said with warmth.

"And you, Veronica," Lauren returned. "Your dress is stunning."

Veronica wore a simple sleeveless V-neck black gown. With her gold highlights and gold jewelry, she was the epitome of style and sophistication.

"Thank you," Veronica said. "Jade picked it out."

"Good call, Jade," Lauren complimented her. "You look fabulous tonight also. That gold brings out your eyes."

Jade had on a white gown with gold accents including a thick gold belt at her waist.

"You can't go wrong with classic lines," Jade said, smiling gratefully.

"What about us? Aren't we pretty?" Manu said, gesturing to himself and then Decker.

Manu and Decker were attired in black tuxedos similar to Colton's.

Jade laughed. "*Pretty* is not a word I would use to describe you, Manu. *Imposing* would be a better description. Shoulders like yours do not belong in a tuxedo. But Decker's kind of pretty tonight."

Decker frowned at his cousin. "Don't start with me, cuz. People are already going to wonder if I can get a date on my own since I'm here with Auntie."

Veronica looked affronted. "Nobody twisted your arm. You wanted to come. I'm sorry Desiree wouldn't come with you but you don't have to take your disappointment out on us."

Decker appealed to Lauren. "What's wrong with your sister? Why won't she go out with me?"

"There's the problem right there," Veronica pointed out. "You asked what's wrong with Desiree. You should have asked what's wrong with you."

"There's nothing wrong with me," Decker proclaimed. "I'm one of the most eligible bachelors in Raleigh. I have a great job, I'm good-looking, healthy and I've got money in the bank. What else does she want in a man?"

"I can't speak for Desi," Lauren said. "I don't know why she won't go out with you. You'll have to ask her."

"Yes," said Veronica. "Go to the source."

Decker rose. "I will." He took his cell phone from the inside pocket of his jacket. "Excuse me."

In his absence, Veronica said, "That boy has it bad." She whispered to Lauren, "You can tell me, I won't say a word. Why won't she go out with him?"

Before Lauren could answer, Colton interjected hoping to change the subject. "Don't worry about Decker. He always lands on his feet."

The event's host, a distinguished-looking silver-haired man in a black tuxedo, walked onto the stage and spoke into the microphone at the podium. "Good evening, ladies and gentlemen, and welcome to the fiftieth annual Black and White Ball."

Shortly after the host finished speaking, a small army of waitstaff began serving dinner, which was a choice between prime rib, lobster or vegetarian lasagna with various side dishes. Decker returned after everyone had been served. He sat down and began to eat.

Veronica looked at him and asked, "Well, what did she say?"

"She said she won't go out with me because I'm not ready for her yet. She says I may never be ready for her." He sighed. "I have no idea what that means."

Veronica shook her head sadly. "No, I don't believe you do."

While they ate their meals, Lauren looked around the room. She recognized several couples at nearby tables, including a woman who had been in the ladies' room last year when Adam's mistress had confronted her. The woman was African American and looked to be in her forties. She was tall and shapely and wore her natural hair in a very short Afro. She caught Lauren watching her and smiled.

Lauren smiled back. She hoped seeing the woman would be the only thing to happen tonight to remind her of last year's embarrassment. But walking toward their table was Adam Eckhart, with a voluptuous woman in white on his arm.

Lauren hadn't seen him in months. She couldn't discern anything different about his six-foot frame. He was still fit. His goatee was expertly trimmed. Grooming and presentation meant a great deal to him. He looked perfect in his black tux.

He stopped beside her chair. Lauren steeled herself for an insult of some kind.

"Good evening, Lauren," he said pleasantly. She hadn't realized it until now that when she'd spotted him she'd put her hand on Colton's thigh to steady herself. Now she felt his thigh muscles tighten reflexively. He clearly was not glad to see Adam, either.

She squeezed his thigh underneath the table, communicating to him to calm down. She could handle this. "Good evening, Adam," she said as she looked up at him.

"Riley," Adam directed at Colton with a slight smirk across his face.

"Eckhart," Colton replied. The two men's eyes met. Neither of their expressions was friendly.

"This is my fiancée, Nichole Kelly," Adam said, smiling at her.

Nichole was in her early twenties. Tall and buxom, her gown displayed her full breasts for all to see and admire. Lauren thought spillage was imminent. Knowing Adam, however, Lauren could not be certain that she'd chosen her own gown. Adam was very controlling. He'd probably told her what to wear, what to say and how to say it.

"Miss Kelly," Lauren said politely.

"I love your gown," Nichole Kelly replied a bit breathlessly.

"Thank you," Lauren said, a bit stunned. She seemed sweet.

Adam, looking irritated by Nichole's behavior, went on, "Did you hear I won the bid on the children's hospital?"

"No, I left work early today and haven't listened to my

messages," Lauren said stiffly. She was not going to congratulate him. His coming over here was a ploy to unnerve her and possibly get a dig in at Colton.

Colton congratulated him, though. "Good for you, Eckhart."

Adam smiled. "Thank you. I noticed your company didn't have a bid in."

"No, we already have enough to keep us busy for a while," Colton was pleased to note.

"Excellent," said Adam. His gaze rested on Lauren. "This will give me the opportunity work with Lauren. When we were married we never got to work together. It'll be a new experience for me, and I like challenges. Good evening, all." With that he turned and led his fiancée away.

"What a pompous ass," Veronica said after he was out of earshot. "Lauren, are you okay?"

"I'm fine," Lauren assured her, but she was fuming inside.

# Chapter 8

"That man is so irritating," Lauren said for Colton's ears only. "He only came over here to plant seeds of discontent in us. He can't stand to see me happy. And what's up with Nichole Kelly? She seems almost sweet. As if she's unaware of what kind of man she's with."

Colton's gaze locked with hers. "Mission accomplished, then, huh? Here you are carrying on about him. Are you going to let him spoil our evening?"

Lauren rolled her eyes. "As if you didn't want to punch his lights out," she accused. "I could feel how tense you were."

He didn't try to deny it. "I've made no secret of the fact I can't stand him. But I wouldn't have hit him."

In the background the band started to play and the host again took the stage. "I hope everyone's enjoying their meals. Now it's time to get up and dance the night away. Let's bring in 2014 on a high note!"

"Good idea," said Colton, reaching for Lauren's hand. "Let's dance."

Lauren was glad to get up and stretch her legs. They were among the first couples to walk onto the dance floor. Above them a crystal chandelier sparkled with golden light. The band's chanteuse, a lovely young African American woman in a black gown, began singing Alicia Keys's latest hit.

She sang it with soulful intensity. The speed with which she sang was just right for slow-dancing. Lauren relaxed in Colton's arms and gazed up at him. He smiled tenderly. She regretted bringing Adam up. She had vowed she wouldn't allow his little games to get to her. Now here she was, tense, because of something he'd said. He couldn't have been serious about looking forward to working with her on the children's hospital.

"I'm sorry," she said sincerely.

"Baby, I'm holding you in my arms," Colton said softly. "No apology needed."

She sighed and laid her head on his chest. The thump of his steady heartbeat steadied her. Closing her eyes she let him lead her, her trust in him implicit. She could feel the powerful muscles in his thigh where his leg touched hers. As she relaxed she was becoming aroused. The song was so sexy. Images of them making love came unbidden to her mind's eye.

Colton tried to control his emotions. He wanted to be aware of everything about Lauren in this moment. But when he did that he was also aware of the warmth of her body, the soft seductiveness of her skin, her scent and the rhythm of her heart. Because he was unable to separate his desire for her from her physical being he was soon turned on by her closeness. Plus there was the fact that he'd been dreaming of making love to her ever since he'd left her on Christmas Day a week ago. It had been a whole week since they'd been intimate, which was too long.

Lauren looked into his eyes. He knew she could feel his erection.

"Do you want to get out of here?" she asked playfully. "Find an empty closet somewhere?"

He chuckled at her suggestion. "I'm shocked you would say such a thing, Miss Gaines. Give me a minute. I'll calm down."

"You've got that kind of control?" she asked innocently. "Maybe you can teach me how to do that."

"You, too?" he asked, his eyes smoldering.

She loved those smoky-gray eyes of his. She'd heard of women being seduced by a pair of sexy eyes but it had never happened to her until she'd met him.

"Yes," she happily confessed. "I've been unable to stop imagining you naked and on top of me for any length of time since we parted." She peered deeply into his eyes. "And in my nighttime dreams I'm insatiable. The problem is I know the reality is as good, or better, than my dreams. So you see I'm a lost cause. Because of you I'm completely obsessed with sex. I was a normal person until you showed up."

"I'm sorry?" Colton said with a beguiling smile.

"You should be," she teased.

"I'm sure you'll think of ways to punish me later," Colton said, not looking apologetic in the least. And his erection was not going away as he'd promised.

"Why wait for later?" Lauren asked. "I'm going to punish you now." She wrapped her arms around his neck and drew him down for a long, sensual kiss. Her tongue sweetly caressed his and the sensation was orgasmic.

When they came up for air, he grinned at her. "You're a bad girl."

She smiled. "So, punish me!"

But Colton was aware that they had become the center of attention and refrained from meeting her challenge there on the dance floor. He pulled her back in position and they resumed dancing. "Behave yourself. We're becoming a spectacle."

At his company's table, Adam watched them with fascination. He had come here tonight relatively certain that Lauren would be in attendance. However, he was shocked to see her on Colton Riley's arm. He knew he was being unreasonable but the fact that she was involved with his biggest business rival felt like a personal affront. Of all the men in Raleigh, or the world for that matter, she was with him?

"Sweetie, let's dance," Nichole pleaded.

He smiled indulgently at her and rose, offering her his hand.

She giggled. He hated it when she giggled. She sounded even younger than her twenty-two years. Intellectually, she was nowhere near being his match. But she was stunning and very susceptible to suggestion. Already she was willing to do anything to please him. Of course, her malleability got tiresome after a while. Once you had someone under your thumb it was inevitable that you would lose respect for that person.

As he held Nichole in his arms his attention was riveted on Lauren and Riley as they danced a few feet away. There hadn't been another kiss after that outrageous public display they'd put on. Lauren was becoming a cliché, a divorced woman who played fast and loose with her reputation, he thought.

\* \* \*

Colton and Lauren returned to their table and Colton asked his mother to dance.

"No, I'm fine," Veronica graciously declined. "I'm fine just watching you all."

"Mom, when you and Dad attended this affair you were always on the dance floor. Let's go." Colton would not take no for an answer.

Veronica took her son's arm. "Very well," she said resignedly. "If only to prevent your father from visiting me in my dreams and accusing me of moping without him."

After they'd gone, Jade said to Lauren, "She's not joking. Since Dad's death she's dreamed about him every night. I'm beginning to think she lives for her dreams about him. I'm trying not to worry."

Lauren had some experience in this area. "There's nothing wrong with Veronica. People who're widowed often dream about their spouses. It helps with the grieving process. My Grandpa Beck dreamed about my grandmother a lot after she died but the dreams have tapered off. Now he only dreams about her every once in a while. That doesn't mean he loves her less. It's just that he's accepted she's gone and his mind's at peace. At least that's how he explained it."

Jade smiled at her. "Thanks for that, Lauren. You put my mind at ease."

"She's a worrywart," Manu said. "Always has been."

"Come on and dance with me," Jade told him, pulling him up by the hand. "Work off some of that prime rib."

Lauren sat watching them once they were on the dance floor. Manu moved surprisingly well for a big man. Jade's dance skills were obviously more advanced than his but from the brilliant smile on her face, Lauren could tell she was having a wonderful time in her husband's arms.

After a couple of songs, a male singer replaced the chanteuse. His song was one designed for lovers. Lauren spotted Colton and Veronica leaving the dance floor.

When they got back to the table, Veronica was laughing. "I don't think I'll ever get used to songs that openly talk about sex," she said. "In my day it was inferred but not explicitly so." She smiled at Lauren. "He's all yours, dear."

Colton laughed as he held out his hand to Lauren, "Sweetheart?"

Lauren smiled when he referred to her as *sweetheart*. Up until now, only *baby* had been his term of endearment for her.

Colton planted a kiss on the side of her neck as she settled in his arms. "Mom was right. This is not the type of song you dance with your mother to. This is baby-making music."

"Then I'd better sit this one out, too."

Colton laughed again. "Do you know how much fun you are to be with? Your beauty and accomplishments aside, you're still one of the most fascinating women I've ever known. But I had a clue you would be when you opened the door with a gun in your hand."

"We were in the middle of nowhere," she reminded him. "You could have been the Abominable Snowman for all I knew."

"I never asked, but do you have a permit to carry a gun?"

"Yes, Officer," she quipped. "Plus, I've put in many hours at the shooting gallery. The general made sure of that. We practiced shooting like other kids practiced their basketball game. It was just another pastime that we enjoyed and were proficient at."

"What else did the general make sure you girls were trained to do?"

"Hand-to-hand combat was taught and we were put in a martial arts class when we turned seven," Lauren said. "For physical conditioning, not to learn to kick someone's butt. Our sensei stressed respect and control of anger. We were taught that martial arts were only to be used in self-defense or to protect someone else."

"Which discipline?" Colton asked.

"A lot of kids were in tae kwon do," Lauren said, "But the general signed us up for karate. He said it was more suited to a woman's body."

"Why is that?"

"Karate is the Japanese art of self-defense in which blows and kicks are targeted to sensitive parts of the opponent's body. Women have more strength in their lower bodies, so the general believed women would be very adept at kicking the crap out of anyone who attacked them."

"And were you good at it?" asked Colton, his eyes alight with humor.

"I earned a black belt by the time I was seventeen," Lauren said without a trace of bragging.

Colton laughed softly. "I'm impressed." He hugged her tightly and wistfully said, "Why didn't mom and dad invite you to the house years ago when you were neighbors in the mountains? We've got a lot of time to make up."

Lauren was touched. "Your parents did invite me to their home here in Raleigh, but I politely declined. Adam tolerated my associating with them in the mountains because the cabin's isolated. But here in Raleigh it would have gotten out that I was a friend of the Rileys. In his mind you all are the enemy."

Colton sighed. "You're right. It's all in his mind because I rarely give him a thought let alone think of him as my rival. He's the one who started this by bribing people to beat us out of at least two contracts that I know of. Personally, I wish he'd realize that there's enough work to go around without resorting to such tactics."

"There's a possibility he has a screw loose," Lauren offered with a laugh. "And I'm not saying that because I'm bitter. Okay, maybe I'm a little bitter. There's nothing wrong with a woman being a little bitter. It's my prerogative to be bitter. Long live the bitter!"

Colton laughed. "You crack me up."

She laughed, too. "Okay, I'm not leaving the house without my meds anymore."

Colton kissed her forehead. "You're even more beautiful when you let go and laugh like that."

Following their dance Colton escorted her back to their table, after which he went to the men's room. When he was returning from the facilities he encountered Adam coming in the opposite direction in the corridor.

He had planned to simply ignore him, but Adam was having none of that. "You know, Riley," he said, "I thought taking my sloppy seconds when it comes to business would be enough for you. But no, you had to try out my ex-wife, as well. That's poor sportsmanship."

Instantly angered by his vulgar suggestion, Colton stopped short and stared at Adam. His big hands balled into fists of rage. His gray eyes became even more stormy than usual as they narrowed and focused on Adam. "You are one small-minded prick, Eckhart, if you think that Lauren is a possession that you once owned. What happened? You realized you've made a mistake by letting her go? Sloppy seconds, you say? Lauren is nobody's sloppy seconds. She's wonderful and you know it. That's why it rankles that she's finding happiness after being shackled to you for years." He circled Adam and their actions were beginning to draw the attention of passersby who stopped observe them.

"Happiness," Adam scoffed. He chuckled. "You believe you can make her happy? Did you even go to college? You're a roughneck. You still do menial jobs. Oh, yes, I heard about that. You probably think it makes you a part of the team. But real powerbrokers know that you have to separate yourself from the team. You have to stand above them. Your father's death was the worst thing that could have happened to Riley Construction. Your leadership will bankrupt it within the year. You're a boy trying to fill your old man's shoes."

"I'm not going to stand here and defend myself against accusations that are unfounded," Colton said. "Time will tell whether or not I'm fit to run my family's company. Time will also tell whether or not I can make Lauren happy. But there's one thing we both already know. She's not with you, she's with me. And that's where she wants to be."

"I could get her back if I wanted to," Adam calmly claimed with a smirk. "She was in love with me once. I can get her to fall in love with me again. Care to make a wager?"

"There's nothing you won't stoop to, is there?" Colton wondered aloud, genuinely taken aback by his crassness.

"Are you afraid you're going to lose?" Adam sneered. "Because, my friend, you don't stand a chance since for the next year or so I'm going to be spending a lot of time with Lauren on the children's hospital project. I'll probably see her more than you. Lauren and I have a past. I assure you she still has feelings for me. You don't just stop loving someone because you're no longer together."

"What about your fiancée?" Colton asked.

"She's a dalliance, a pretty distraction," Adam said nonchalantly.

"You really do have a screw loose," Colton told him, shaking his head in wonder.

Adam was outraged. Colton's words suggested that he'd been discussing his sanity with someone, and that someone could only have been Lauren. "Is that what she said about me?" he yelled. "That I have a screw loose?"

Colton was silent on the matter. He gestured to the audience they'd attracted. "You're making a case for that right now."

Several of the men and women who'd gathered around them nodded in agreement.

"Can we have some privacy?" Adam yelled at them.

"This is a public hallway, bruh," said one of the men. He was also dressed in a tuxedo. "I've got your back, Colton, if something jumps off."

Colton acknowledged the guy's offer with a nod in his direction. "Thanks, Joe, but nothing's going to jump off. The theatrics are over." He glanced at his watch as he turned to leave. "It's nearly midnight. I'm going to usher in the New Year with my lady."

"Remember what I said," Adam called after him. "She'll be mine again within the year."

"Keep dreaming," Colton said in parting.

Adam stood alone, fuming. A screw loose, indeed. He would show them exactly how it felt to go up against someone who was as determined to succeed at whatever they set their mind on as he was. Lauren had been the one to begin divorce proceedings. He had asked her, begged her—and he was not the sort of man to beg—to forgive his infidelity and continue their marriage. But she said that she had lived for a long time with the suspicion that he was cheating on her and now that she had proof she could not go on fooling herself. It was over. From that point on, what could he do but put on an act and tell her that she'd never supported him anyway? If she had been the wife he needed her to be he wouldn't have sought solace elsewhere. That had torn her up. He still remembered the hurtful expression in her eyes. He couldn't back down then though. He told her a man of his standing deserved a trophy wife. She was getting a little long in the tooth.

He'd in essence bitten off his nose to spite his face. He'd made a mistake. Now that he was engaged to the trophy-wife-to-be, he'd tried to be satisfied. But Riley was right. He did want Lauren back. That old saying, you don't miss the water until the well runs dry, was true.

The baiting of Riley was simply a way to strengthen his resolve to win Lauren back. He was fired up now. He'd prove to Riley that he wasn't a man to be counted out.

# Chapter 9

Colton tried to shake off the madness that had ensued in the hallway as he strode back into the ballroom. His eyes went directly to his table where his mother and Lauren seemed to be deep in conversation. They were leaning toward one another, their heads nearly touching. The warm feeling he got from knowing how much his mother and Lauren enjoyed each other's company almost dispelled the seed of doubt his confrontation with Adam Eckhart had planted in him.

Could Lauren still have feelings for Eckhart? He was at war with his conscience. On one hand he wanted to be completely honest with Lauren and tell her exactly what had transpired a few minutes ago. On the other, he didn't want to ruin her evening by telling her about Eckhart's lunacy. So he decided he'd tell her later.

His mother smiled up at him when he joined them. "Colton, did you know that both Lauren's mother and I attended Shaw University? Now, I've got to go look in my old yearbooks and see if I can find a Virginia Beck. Beck's her maiden name."

Sitting down on Lauren's left Colton said, "No, I didn't. You two might have known one another."

Veronica frowned. "Seems like I would remember a Virginia, but I don't."

Lauren smiled at Colton. She looked into his eyes and seemed, to him, to detect that something was amiss. Or maybe it was his guilt at deciding not to tell her about his encounter with Eckhart until later that was niggling at him.

A look of askance crossed her face. "Is something wrong?" she said, her tone soft but urgent.

Ever since Lauren had seen Adam again she'd had this sense of foreboding lying just below the surface, trying its best to rear its ugly head.

"No, no," Colton assured her and rubbed her arm comfortingly. He leaned toward her, kissed her cheek and whispered, "It's almost midnight."

Around them, couples were returning to their tables from the dance floor. Tradition at the Black and White Ball dictated that at the stroke of midnight, champagne would flow like water and everyone would toast the New Year in.

Waitstaff entered the ballroom pushing trolleys laden with bottles of the bubbly spirits. On stage the host was counting down the seconds. "Ten, nine, eight, seven," he intoned.

Promptly at the midnight hour the sound of corks popping filled the ballroom. "Happy New Year!" everyone exclaimed with joy. Those who had them blew paper horns. Silver and gold confetti rained on them.

At Colton and Lauren's table, champagne glasses were filled and everyone offered toasts to one another. Colton looked into Lauren's eyes and said, his voice husky, "I hope this year will be the best you've ever had."

"It will be with you in it," Lauren said, smiling happily.

They gently touched their glasses together, took sips of champagne and put their glasses on the table.

Colton leaned in, his gaze on her mouth. "Our first kiss of the year," he said, his voice rife with longing.

"Make it a good one," she whispered back as she wrapped her arms around his neck and pulled him down to meet her mouth.

They got lost in one another. The rest of the world receded as if there was only the two of them, high on the euphoria that new love causes. When they parted and peered into each other's eyes both of them knew something vital had changed between them.

"Colton," Veronica said.

To Colton her voice sounded far away. Then, he came back to the present and realized that hadn't been the first time she'd tried to get his attention.

He smiled at his mother. "I'm sorry. What did you say?"

"I was saying," Veronica said with a laugh, "that I'm going home." She rose and the rest of the family got to their feet also. Everyone had varying amounts of confetti in their hair and on their clothing and was picking it off themselves. "I hate this stuff," Veronica complained.

She looked around for her nephew, but Decker was nowhere in sight. She sighed. "When Decker gets back," she said to Colton and Lauren, "tell him as an escort, he sucks."

Then she hugged Lauren and Colton. "Enjoy the rest of your evening."

She left with Jade and Manu, with Manu giving Colton a thumbs-up on the way out.

Colton and Lauren were left at the table alone. The other

Riley Construction staff and their dates were on the dance floor. For many, the party really got started after midnight.

Lauren smiled at Colton. "Going home sounds good to me."

Colton was about to say something when her cell phone started making its distinct text message buzzing sound that reminded her of a tiny chainsaw. She laughed thinking it was probably one of her sisters texting to say Happy New Year.

"Excuse me," she said to Colton as she slipped her hand into her clutch and got her cell phone. Quickly pressing a couple buttons she frowned and murmured, "Oh, no, no, it can't be."

When tears sprang to her eyes and she thrust the cell phone at Colton as if she wanted it far away from her, Colton's first impulse was to comfort her. He pulled her into his arms and held her against his chest as he read what was on the cell phone's screen. The message consisted of only four words. *I still love you.* And it was from Adam Eckhart.

"Please erase it," Lauren said as she clung to him.

Colton did as she asked. Then pressed the phone back into her hand. "It's gone, sweetheart." He pulled her to her feet. "Come on. Let's go home."

Lauren wiped the tears away with the pad of her thumb as they made their way across the ballroom to the exit. "Why doesn't he just leave me alone?" she wondered aloud as Colton made sure her wrap was securely around her before they ventured out into the chilly night.

"Sweetheart, we need to talk," he said, "but not here. Let's wait until we're in the car on the way to your place."

She nodded numbly, sniffing. "I hate him so much," she said, her voice barely a whisper.

Colton was in a pensive mood for the first few minutes

as they drove along the streets of downtown Raleigh. Traffic was light at the moment since most revelers were already where they wanted to be.

Why had Lauren reacted with tears when she'd gotten Eckhart's text message? Why not with derision, or laughter, calling him a nut or a sap to send such an idiotic admission of love to his ex-wife? There were many ways she could have reacted, but tears? Tears were connected to emotions. She apparently still felt something for him.

"Lauren, on my way back from the restroom I ran into Eckhart and against my better judgment I let him draw me into an argument."

Lauren turned in her seat so that she could see his face while he spoke. "What did you argue about?"

"You," Colton said, his voice cracking. He cleared his throat. "I don't want to go into detail because some things were said that were inflammatory, things I don't want to have to repeat. But the gist of it was he's angry with me for dating you and he threatened to do everything in his power to get you back."

Lauren gave a great sigh of relief. "So he threw down the gauntlet," she said with a short laugh, "challenged you to a duel at dawn and attempted to make a gentleman's bet on who would come out on top?"

Colton looked at her, amazed by her change of attitude. "What brought back the Lauren with backbone? A minute ago you were crying."

"That was before I knew that this was just another one of his games," she explained. "I got emotional when I got the text because I thought he was genuinely still in love with me and he was going to make an effort to get back in my life. That part terrified me, but it's not unheard of for a divorced couple to reconcile. Not that I had any intention of doing so. But I remember the love I used to have for him, too, and occasionally it tries to break through to the surface. Those are the times I suffer and wonder what I did wrong to make him cheat on me."

"A cheater is a cheater no matter the provocation," Colton said. "I sincerely believe that. You didn't do anything for him to cheat on you."

She smiled at him. "I know that now but for months after I had filed for divorce I wavered between righteous indignation and feeling that maybe I should take some blame for his actions, too. Anyway, I no longer believe I did anything for him to go looking for a mistress."

"So, why do you think he's playing games with you and he's not sincere about still being in love with you?"

"It's that old rivalry thing again," Lauren said calmly. "You have something he believes is rightfully his. *Me.* If he hadn't approached you tonight and said all those things you're avoiding telling me because you think my feelings will be hurt, I would have taken that text message seriously." She sighed again and ran her hand over his muscular thigh. "Let him try his best. There's only one man I'm interested in and I'm touching him right now. And as soon as I get him home I'm going to be touching him all over."

Colton let out a soft sigh of his own. The sound of her sexy voice and the feel of her hand on his thigh aroused him. He was glad he'd come straight to her and told her about his conversation with Eckhart. Now that their cards were on the table there was nothing left that could come between them. In a few minutes not even their clothes would be separating them. He would see to that as soon as they walked through the door of her apartment. He pressed down a little harder on the accelerator of the Lexus.

She had him flat on his back on the thick rug atop the hardwood floor of the living room. They hadn't made it to the bedroom before they'd begun ripping their clothes off. The lamps on the end tables were dimmed and the room was quiet except for their heavy breaths.

Their naked bodies in two shades of brown, his dark cinnamon, hers more caramel, were joined in a timeless dance. Lauren's head was thrown back in ecstasy, her full breasts shaking with each thrust. Colton gave her every inch of him. She reveled in it and her body asked for more.

Unable to keep her orgasm at bay any longer, Lauren's thrusts increased in frequency and the climax claimed her at the same moment as Colton came with a ferocity that made him want to howl. He controlled it and groaned loudly instead.

Lauren moaned languidly and lay on his chest, her vaginal walls quivering around his shaft with her release. She peered into his eyes, her own dreamy. A smile turned up the corners of her generous mouth. "Now, that's how Cinderella should end her night at the ball."

Colton smiled and hugged her tightly. "I'm glad you enjoyed yourself."

Two weeks later, Lauren attended the groundbreaking ceremony for the new children's hospital. It was a Monday morning and the January air was cold, the wind brisk and the sunshine bright.

Lauren sat on the platform that had been erected for the occasion, waiting to get up and say a few words after the director of the hospital introduced her as the architect. Local news stations were covering the event and there were perhaps two hundred people sitting on folding chairs in the cleared field that was the site for the hospital.

Adam sat on the opposite side of the podium at which the hospital's director was delivering his welcome speech. Lauren had made the mistake of making eye contact with

Adam on one occasion but he'd looked so hopeful she had refused to look at him again. Since the night of the ball he had sent multiple text messages. None of which she'd responded to.

After the groundbreaking ceremony, the media briefly interviewed both Lauren and Adam. She finished first and beat a hasty retreat. He caught up with her on the street where she'd parked the Range Rover.

"Lauren, Lauren," he cried, running across the street, car horns blaring at him.

He was wearing a dark blue suit with a black overcoat. His goatee looked freshly trimmed. Lauren stood with her back to the driver's side door of the Range Rover, her eyes narrowed.

"I have nothing to say to you," she warned as he stopped in front of her and opened his mouth to speak.

Adam clamped his mouth shut and took a deep breath. Then he gave a hopeless shrug and started talking. "Well, I've got something to say to you. I'm forty years old and I'm still immature. Instead of appreciating you when we were together I did nothing but find fault with you, which is something I now realize I did because I was so in awe of you. There was nothing wrong with you. Instead, there was something wrong with my values. Money and position were the only things I cared about and I thought that you didn't fit into my plans. I accused you of not supporting me. It was I who didn't support you. I can see that now."

"Hold on a minute," Lauren told him as she opened her car door, leaned inside and ejected a CD from the CD player. She put the CD back in its case and handed it to Adam. "Listen to track four," she told him.

A few minutes later after he'd watched her drive away and walked back to his SUV Adam put the CD in his CD player and jumped to track four. "I don't believe a word you say..." Ben Harper sang.

Smiling, Adam relaxed on the car seat. He had to give it to her. She had style.

Lauren looked at Adam in her rearview mirror. She remembered when his charm didn't seem in the least bit smarmy to her. She'd eaten it up. She'd been thrilled that he was interested in her at all. When they'd met he was already a successful builder and because of his success and his attractiveness to women, he was considered one of the best catches in Raleigh. In spite of objections from her parents who after meeting him later told her in private that he was not to be trusted, she had given him her heart. Thinking of her parents reminded her that she was taking Colton to Sunday dinner at her parents' house this weekend. She wondered what they would say about him in private after meeting him.

"I'm nervous about meeting your dad," Colton admitted on the drive to Lauren's parents' home on the outskirts of Raleigh.

Lauren tried to laugh it off. "You're not the first guy who's been nervous about meeting the general. But I'm going to let you in on a secret—he's not the one to look out for. That would be Momma. Daddy's easygoing. All he cares about on a Sunday afternoon is the amount of time he gets in front of the TV watching football. He's devoted to North Carolina State and you follow that team, too, so you already have one thing in common. With Momma, no man is good enough for her daughters, period. Even if she likes you you're still not good enough. So, I suggest you relax and be yourself."

"And your sisters?" he asked.

"Don't worry about my sisters. They think you're perfect for me. They're very smart girls, my sisters."

When they pulled into the driveway, Virginia was standing in the doorway, a warm smile on her face. "Colton, it's a pleasure to meet you finally." She shook his hand and led him into the family room with Lauren bringing up the rear.

The large family room was furnished in comfortable leather seating. The décor was more suited to a man's tastes with dark brown being the dominant color. Colton was introduced to Lauren's father who got up and shook his hand. Fonzi was a couple inches taller than he was, but Colton had broader shoulders and he was more muscular. "Good to meet you, Colton," said Fonzi. "Let me introduce you to my father-in-law, Benjamin Beck."

Benjamin Beck was small and wiry with solid white wavy hair that he wore long and tied back with a strip of leather. His dark brown skin was weathered from the outdoors and his jeans and plaid shirt were a bit frayed but clean. He was a man without pretension, and Colton liked him instantly.

Benjamin firmly shook his hand. "I knew your father. He was a good man."

Colton smiled. "Thank you, sir. It's good to meet you. Lauren tells me you own a hunting lodge. I'd love to see it someday."

Benjamin laughed shortly. "Oh, there's not much to it. Just plain old logs, the bare bones, I'm afraid. The people who stay at the lodge are looking to get back to nature."

"Well, I like the outdoors," said Colton. "I'm not a hunter but I fish and enjoy outdoor sports."

"Then we ought to go fishing sometime," Benjamin said. He smiled at Lauren as if to say, "I like this one."

"Daddy, before you all start planning a fishing trip let

me introduce Colton to the rest of the family," Lauren cut in sweetly.

Colton had already met Desiree since she had accompanied Lauren to his father's funeral and come with her to the house afterward. But he had yet to meet Meghan and Amina. He saw a resemblance to Lauren in each of them. Their eyes were almond-shaped like hers. They also had Lauren's honey-brown skin tone. They were all attractive women and apparently enjoyed exercising because they were physically fit and healthy-looking. Knowing what Lauren had told him about their father teaching them to shoot and signing them up for karate classes at the age of seven, he could see his influence on them.

"Hi again," Desiree said and came forward to offer a hug.

Colton hugged her back. "Desiree," he said warmly. "My cousin sends his best."

Desiree laughed. "You tell him I send mine right back."

Amina was next. She had her natural hair braided and it fell to the middle of her back. She shook his hand. "Amina," she said.

"Like the African warrior princess?" Colton said.

Amina was impressed. "You know about Aminatu, the Nigerian princess who built a fortress around the city of Zaria to protect her people in times of war?"

"I'm an African history buff," Colton admitted.

This earned him points from Virginia, who was an educator.

She continued with the introductions. "And this is the baby of the family, Meghan."

Meghan smiled up at him. "It's a pleasure, Colton. I happen to be a history professor."

Colton peered at her with a puzzled expression. "You can't be more than twenty."

"I'm twenty-four, the youngest professor at North Carolina State," she told him matter-of-factly. She laughed, "I don't really look twenty, do I?"

"I'm sorry, but you do," said Colton.

Everyone laughed.

"All right, since the introductions have been made," Virginia announced, "Colton, have a seat and enjoy the game. Girls, I know this is sexist, but let's get the food on the table."

Her daughters let out playful groans of protest as they followed her out of the room.

In the women's absence, Fonzi turned to Colton, who had sat down beside him on the big brown leather couch in front of the widescreen TV. "That's just an excuse to go talk about you behind your back."

"Oh, I know," said Colton. "That's how they do it in my family, too."

Fonzi chuckled and reached for the bowl of mixed nuts, but his father-in-law already had it in his hands and was picking out the pecans and putting them in his mouth.

"May I have the nuts, Ben?" asked Fonzi.

"You could stand to drop a few pounds," Ben teased him. "I'm doing you a favor."

"You'd be doing me a favor by passing me the nuts," Fonzi insisted.

"Wait, there's another pecan at the bottom," Benjamin said.

"Ginny!" Fonzi yelled. "Would you tell your father to behave?"

"Behave, Daddy," Virginia yelled back.

Benjamin handed over the bowl of nuts. "Big baby," he muttered about his son-in-law.

Fonzi peered into the bowl, which had been totally depleted of his favorite nut, the pecan. "You don't even like pecans," he accused Benjamin.

"I suddenly get a taste for them when I'm around you," Ben said with a smile.

Fonzi sighed and shook his head. "One of these days, old man, one of these days."

"Let's go," said Benjamin as if he were ready to step outside. He said to Colton conspiratorially, "His bark is worse than his bite."

Fonzi set the bowl of nuts on the coffee table. "Let me explain, Colton. Benjamin has never forgiven me for marrying his daughter and making her happy. He thought she should have stayed in the mountains with him and married some mountain man and stayed barefoot and pregnant instead of getting an education and traveling the world with me. And that, in a nutshell, is the reason for the antagonism between me and my father-in-law, the most stubborn man in creation."

"That's not all," Benjamin said. "I also don't like you because you didn't give me a grandson. Every time my little Virginia got pregnant I would wish for a boy so that maybe then she could stop bringing your children into the world. But the more she tried for a boy the more girls kept coming. I love my granddaughters. But couldn't you manage to shoot out one boy? It's not up to the woman, you know. It's all on the man."

"Damn it, Ben, we get the children God sends us," cried Fonzi. "Get off my back!"

Colton liked both of them. They reminded him of his dad and his uncle Tad who never got along. But after his father's death his uncle Tad had been the one to give the eulogy and there hadn't been a dry eye in the church when he was done.

During dinner, Colton sat between Lauren and Virginia.

The dining room table was laden with Southern cuisine that Virginia had modified to make healthier for her family. She never fried anything, or used fatty pork to season her greens. She used smoked turkey instead. Her menu today included baked chicken, mustard greens, sweet potato soufflé, macaroni and cheese, acre peas with whole okra and corn muffins. For dessert she'd made a golden cake with chocolate icing, Fonzi's favorite.

Everyone ate to their heart's content. Benjamin, though a small man, put away a prodigious amount of food. After he'd finished eating, he burped loudly. "Excuse me," he said sheepishly. "You know, in some cultures that's a sign you enjoyed the meal, and I did, baby girl. Everything was delicious, but now I should be getting on the road. It's a long drive back home."

"Won't you stay another night, Dad?" Virginia said in cajoling tones.

"I'm sorry, I can't," Ben said regrettably.

His son-in-law was smiling happily. "Now, Ginny, he says he's got to be back by tomorrow morning to welcome some new guests. Let him go."

Ben ignored him. Instead, he turned his attention to Amina. "Mina, I know you're feeling at loose ends after coming back home. I'd like you to consider coming to work with me. I don't have anyone to leave the business to. Your mother, as you know, is my only child and you girls my only grandchildren. Your sisters have careers. Maybe owning a lodge would suit you. You never know. Want to give it a try?"

Mina was stunned because, number one, her grandfather hardly ever made grand gestures. He was too taciturn for long speeches. And number two, because he was always lamenting the fact that he didn't have a grandson, someone he could leave the lodge to when he died.

She got up and went to hug him. "Grandpa, I'd love to give it a try. In fact, I'll go throw a few things in my duffel bag and I'll leave with you right now. I'll do the driving."

"You can drive a stick shift?"

"Grandpa, I can drive anything with wheels," said Mina with a broad grin.

Her sisters, as excited as she was by their grandfather's offer, got up and followed her out of the dining room to help her pack.

Lauren kissed Colton's cheek before she joined her sisters, "Be back soon, sweetie."

Colton was left at the table with her parents and grandfather. Virginia smiled at him. "Things happen quickly around here."

## Chapter 10

Lauren rarely phoned to make an appointment to inspect the building site of the children's hospital. She liked to drop by unexpectedly, which served two purposes. It lessened the chance that she would run into Adam, and it also kept the construction crew on their toes.

It was a Friday in mid-February. The sun was shining brightly when Lauren arrived at the site at half past eleven. She was dressed in a dark gray pantsuit and comfortable heels. Because this was routine for her, she had brought her own hard hat that she had put on as soon as she got out of the car across the street from the site. The building's substructure or foundation had been completed and the crew had begun on the ground level.

She was spotted by one of the construction workers as soon as she walked onto the site and heard him yell, "Hey, boss, the architect's here."

She smiled. They had a warning system. The foreman,

whom she knew from her previous visits, was a short, burly red-faced man in his forties with huge biceps and a broad chest. He hurried toward her, smiling. "Miss Gaines. How are you today?"

"Hello, Mr. McPherson. Fine, thank you, and you?"

"Right as rain!" he said with a smile.

"I'm just going to do a quick walk-through if it's all right with you," Lauren said casually. Specifically, she was there to make certain the materials they were using were of the highest quality and the skill with which they applied them was up to par. "If you like, you're free to join me," she told him. She didn't want to put anyone's teeth on edge. She tried to make these inspections as painless for the crew as possible. If she saw shoddy materials being used, for example, she wouldn't put the blame on them but on their employer.

Bobby McPherson nodded his agreement. "I'd be happy to."

"This is on a spread foundation, am I right?" she asked Bobby.

"Yes, ma'am," he said. "Reinforced concrete isn't as solid a foundation as a solid rock foundation but this baby will stand the test of time."

She asked him for dimensions and he supplied them. She walked the length of the foundation while around her workers were bolting together steel beams, girders and columns which would form the superstructure. The bolting was temporary. Workers would weld the steel together permanently later on.

After half an hour Lauren was satisfied with her walk-through and shook Bobby's hand as she prepared to leave.

"Looks good," she said. "Thank you, Mr. McPherson."

"Anytime, Miss Gaines," Bobby said as he walked

alongside her. He scrunched up his face. "Um, ma'am, do you mind if I ask you a personal question?"

Lauren's brows rose in surprise. Bobby McPherson had never tried to delay her leaving. On the contrary, he always seemed relieved when she exited the site. She couldn't see any harm in him asking her a question, though, so she signaled for him to continue. "No, go ahead."

"Is it true you used to be married to the boss?"

"Yes, it's true," Lauren said easily.

His face reddened further. "Sorry, I don't mean to be nosy. It's just that you go by the name Gaines."

"I went back to using my maiden name after the divorce," she said feeling a bit uncomfortable explaining this to Adam's foreman. It was apparent, though, that Adam had told Bobby McPherson about their past relationship. The question was why had he taken the time to do that?

She got her answer when she started walking back across the street to her car. Adam was waiting next to it, smiling. Bobby McPherson must have phoned him or sent a text message before coming to meet her.

"Surprise inspection?" he asked, his light brown eyes alight with humor.

Lauren removed her hard hat and held it in front of her. "You know how it is. It's my job to make sure the customer gets the building he's paying for."

"Is everything to your satisfaction?"

"So far, so good," she said lightly.

"What are you doing for lunch?" he asked. "It's practically noon. Want to go to that café we used to like near here?"

"No, Adam, I don't want to share a meal with you," she said bluntly. Her eyes met his. "Look into my eyes. Do I show any indication that I'm the least bit interested in having a personal relationship with you?"

"It's a woman's right to change her mind," Adam said hopeful. "I can't imagine that Riley's giving you something I couldn't give you if you let me."

"I'm not going to discuss my relationship with Colton with you."

Adam frowned. "Relationship," he said dismissively. "You've only known him for six weeks."

"How do you know how long I've known him?" she asked suspiciously.

"I've asked around," he said hesitantly. "Okay, I hired a private detective to find out how you met. It was in the mountains during a snowstorm. I should never have given you that cabin."

Lauren laughed. "You didn't want it."

"If I'd known you would turn it into a love nest for you and Riley, I never would have given it to you."

Lauren wanted to go but he was standing right in front of the driver's side door, blocking her from reaching for the door's handle. "I'm really tired of your games," she said with a long-suffering sigh. "You don't want me. You just don't want Colton to have me. Your possessions were always more important to you than I ever was."

"I already admitted that," Adam reminded her. "Okay, so you don't want me back. I get it. My question is, did you ever love me? If you did, you would have loved me unconditionally. You would have had it in your heart to forgive my transgressions."

"I'm not a saint," Lauren said. "I don't have it in me to keep forgiving someone for their transgressions, especially if those transgressions involve having sex with other women. Sex is supposed to be sacred. It doesn't mean the same when you're sharing your man."

"Is the sex that good with Riley?" He sounded as though any minute now he was going to start yelling.

"Did you not hear me when I said I wasn't going to discuss my relationship with Colton with you?" she asked incredulously.

"Of course I heard you, Lauren. I hear everything you say. I simply refuse to accept it. When we met you were totally innocent. I was your first."

"What has that got to do with anything?"

"You saved yourself for your husband," he said reasonably. "You believed that we would be together forever. I disappointed you and broke our bond. In some ways it broke you, too. Admit that, at least."

"I admit it," she readily said. "You broke my heart. That's why I'm not letting you near it again."

"I'm trying to restore your perfect dream," he said, his voice soft and sincere. "Your mother and father have had a long marriage. Your grandfather had been married to your grandmother for over fifty years when he lost her. So what if we had a hiccup in our marriage? We could remarry and continue the family tradition. Riley can't offer you that, he's no better than I *was*. He's a playboy. Eventually he'll grow tired of you and move on to the next beautiful woman. Could his feelings for you be anything other than lust? Maybe he's a little grateful to you for saving his life. The detective said he would have probably frozen to death if you hadn't let him in. Lust and gratefulness are all your relationship is based on. Do you know what an orgasm is? It's a chemical reaction in the body. Oxytocin, called the love hormone, is released when you climax. People mistake it for love and before you know it you're in a relationship. Think about that. You and I have a history. He's only a hormone releaser in a good-looking package," he concluded.

"Wow," said Lauren, shaking her head in awe. "You are such a silver-tongued devil I'm almost convinced you're right, that Colton is just a handsome plaything. Fortunately, I'm immune to your lies and manipulation. Now get out of my way."

She went to reach around him for the door's handle and he pulled her into his arms and tried to kiss her. She dropped the hard hat and struggled against him. She hesitated using karate on him because at her present level of anger she might seriously injure him. So she gritted her teeth and pushed him hard in the chest, putting her weight into it, until he fell backward onto the pavement.

Adam laughed as he looked up at her from the ground. "I suppose I should be happy you didn't kick me in the crotch." He got to his feet and dusted himself off. "Sorry, darling. I was desperate to show you how I feel."

Lauren stood with her hands on her hips, her legs spread in a defiant stance. "Stop calling me *darling,* and I don't care if you're sincere about wanting me back. I don't want you. So I'm telling you, once and for all, leave me alone."

Adam's demeanor instantly changed. He'd been smiling ruefully. Now his eyes narrowed and his expression became mean and calculating. "You know I hate ultimatums. If you don't want me then let's see how long your lover boy will want you after he sees you in action."

"What do you mean by that?" Seeing her in action? Then it occurred to her. He was referring to compromising photos. She laughed because she had never in her life posed for any. He'd tried to cajole her into making a sex tape of the two of them just for their private viewing but she'd balked at it. And there had been no snapping of nude photos, either. She wasn't going to be caught all over the internet in her birthday suit.

"You can't be implying that you have compromising photos of me," she said indignantly. "I never agreed to do that with you."

"That doesn't mean I didn't film us together," he said with a smirk. "Remember the night we christened our new house? We made love in front of the fire. Your body looks so good in firelight. That film makes very fine viewing."

That was when she slugged him. It wasn't a karate move, it was an old-fashioned right cross to the jaw and it took him by surprise. His head snapped to the side and there was a sharp cracking sound. Lauren thought she'd broken his jaw and for one fleeting moment, wished she had. But when he looked at her again, his eyes watering, his hand gingerly touching his face, she saw that his jaw was intact.

He blinked at her as though his vision might not be clear. "Damn, you put some power behind that punch. I used to think you were exaggerating when you said you took martial arts from a young age, but that really hurt."

"Boss, boss, are you okay!" Bobby McPherson shouted as he came running across the street with two other men in tow.

"I'm fine, Bobby," Adam said. "No need for your concern. Please go back to work."

Bobby looked from him to Lauren. "Are you sure? She still looks mad to me."

"Yes, I'm sure," Adam said decisively.

Bobby reluctantly backed away and gestured to the two men who'd arrived with him to head back across the street to the site.

Alone with Lauren again, Adam said, "That's going to cost you. I have witnesses who'll testify that you assaulted me.

"Now, I'm going to tell you what you're going to do. You're going to stop seeing Riley. After which you're going to come back to me."

"You're delusional," Lauren said, her voice harsh. She

was shaking the kinks out of the hand she'd hit him with. The pain was subsiding. "I'm not doing anything without proof that you really do have a sex tape."

He calmly reached into his inside coat pocket and retrieved a small videotape.

She couldn't believe he was producing the tape at this very moment. "You meant to provoke me from the beginning," she accused, livid. "You were prepared for this outcome."

He smiled cockily. "I'm a son of a bitch. That has been well established over the years. Too bad you didn't remember that when you started giving me ultimatums." He pressed the tape into her hand. "Enjoy the show."

He turned to leave.

"What if I call your bluff and tell Colton you're trying to blackmail me?"

He looked her in the eye. "You wouldn't do that. You'd be afraid he'd try to kill me and you wouldn't want his spending the rest of his life in prison on your conscience."

"Don't be too confident that you have me where you want me," Lauren warned.

Adam grinned. "I'll take my chances."

He left then, not glancing back. She stood there frozen, watching his retreating back and wondering what she'd ever done to deserve this.

Lauren drove around for a while, not wanting to go back to the office because she knew she wouldn't be able to concentrate on work while she had the tape in her possession. So she phoned the office, and when Meredith answered she told her she wasn't feeling well and wouldn't be in for the rest of the afternoon. She didn't have any appointments today, but asked that Meredith please inform the partners of her plans if they inquired about her in her absence.

At home, she put the tape in and pressed Play. Seeing her and Adam making love should have been old hat, but it made her sick to her stomach that she'd ever given herself to him. There was nothing particularly kinky about their lovemaking session on the night they'd christened their new home. If Colton actually looked at it, how would he react? No one wanted to see the person they were involved with making love to someone else. She knew she would be mortified if she saw a sex tape with Colton and another woman. Would it force him to quit seeing her?

Lauren sat on the couch thinking, torturing herself, working out several scenarios in her head. She couldn't allow Adam to manipulate her. That was a given. The question was, how was she going to beat him at his own game?

Maybe she could break into his house and steal the tape. But the problem with that was he might have copies hidden elsewhere. Perhaps in a safety deposit box or in a wall safe in his house. He could have even given a copy to a friend to hold on to for him.

Then something occurred to her. It was illegal to tape someone without their knowledge, wasn't it? She picked up her cell phone and quickly dialed her lawyer's number.

"Arielle Maxey's office," the secretary said brightly. "How can I help you?"

"Is Arielle in?" Lauren asked.

"I'm sorry, Miss Maxey's in a meeting. May I give her a message for you?"

"This is Lauren Gaines. Please tell Arielle to phone me as soon as possible. My ex-husband is trying to black-mail me."

There was a sharp intake of breath and an exhale on the other end of the line followed by a quick "I'll give her the message right away, Miss Gaines."

"Thank you," Lauren said and then hung up.

Lauren pointed the remote at the video tape player and switched it off. She was breathing a bit easier now. Having taken some kind of action instead of simply panicking had made her feel better.

Fifteen minutes later, Arielle phoned.

"What's this I hear about Adam trying to blackmail you?" she asked belligerently. Arielle, in her mid-thirties, was a sister who seemed to be always itching for a fight. Lauren thought she was well-suited for her profession.

Lauren explained what was going on and waited patiently while Arielle sat silent on the other end of the line for a couple of minutes. Arielle didn't like to blurt out responses. She was a thinker, a ruminator. Consequently, her responses were sometimes long and drawn out, although very thorough and logical.

"You say you had no knowledge whatsoever that you were being recorded?"

"That's something I would never agree to," Lauren assured her. "Not in this day and age."

"Oh, yes, I have several clients who have regretted letting their lovers or spouses tape them in compromising positions. Blackmail is often a part of it. They threaten to put it on the internet or send it to someone unless you do what they say. There are some sick puppies out there.

"In the state of North Carolina taping someone without their knowledge isn't illegal if the taping is being done in a public place where there is no prior expectation of privacy. But in your home where you didn't give your permission, and you can expect to have your privacy respected, it is most definitely illegal. Maybe Adam should have consulted his lawyer before trying to strong-arm you into doing his bidding. Do you want me to call him and threaten him with prosecution? It would be my pleasure to do so."

"No, wait, I have more questions," Lauren told her. "Can I sue him for all the copies of the tape?"

"We can try," Arielle told her. "But it's highly unlikely that we would find all the copies. He would probably lie about it. I think you should tell Colton what's going on and warn him that Adam has threatened to send the tape to him. He can then choose to destroy the tape before watching it."

"Do you really think it'll be that easy?" Lauren asked skeptically. "I like him a lot, Arielle. I don't want to lose him over this."

"He's a mature adult," Arielle said. "He knows that you and Adam had a sex life."

"Yes, but what if he doesn't destroy the tape and watches it? Once you see something like that it's etched in your memory. I'm in it and it disgusts me."

Arielle laughed shortly. "Because Adam disgusts you," she pointed out.

"Yes, that's true. But if the shoe were on the other foot, I wouldn't want to see Colton with another woman."

"My advice is still to tell him what's going on so he'll be prepared in case Adam sends it to him out of spite after you tell him to go to hell. You're going to tell him to go to hell, aren't you?"

"Yes, and threaten him with jail if he ever shows that tape to anyone!" Lauren exclaimed, getting to her feet. She had decided that there was no time like the present. "In fact, I'm going over there right now and tell him to his face."

"No more hitting," Arielle warned. "He could still press charges against you for assault."

"No more hitting," Lauren promised. "Thanks, Arielle."

"My pleasure," said Arielle.

## Chapter 11

It only took fifteen minutes for Lauren to reach the Eckhart Construction building on Atlantic Avenue. When she walked into the office the receptionist, a gorgeous young African American woman with silky straight hair falling nearly to her waist, inquired why she was there. Lauren wondered where Edie was. Edie had been the receptionist for years and Lauren had liked her.

Forcing a smile, Lauren said, "Tell Mr. Eckhart his ex-wife is here."

As if she suspected Lauren was there to cause a scene, a panicked expression crossed the woman's face but soon vanished and was replaced by a polite smile. "I'm sorry, but Mr. Eckhart isn't here."

Lauren hadn't expected this. Adam was a workaholic. He was always at the office unless he was onsite somewhere.

"Then he's visiting one of his sites?" she asked, her tone friendly but insistent.

"I'm not at liberty to give out that information," the receptionist replied stiffly.

Irritated now, Lauren narrowed her eyes. "Look, I just want to talk to him."

"I'm sorry," the receptionist said again, her voice rising. "Please leave before I have someone escort you off the premises."

Suddenly, Edie came walking swiftly into the outer office, a look of concern on her mocha-colored face. Heading straight for Lauren, she cried, "Mrs. Eckhart, what a lovely surprise."

Smiling, she reached for Lauren's hand and they shook. Lauren breathed a sigh of relief. "Finally, a friendly face," she said.

Edie didn't immediately let go of her hand but led her back to her office. Lauren saw from the sign on the door that she'd been promoted to office manager.

Edie closed the door behind them and then hugged Lauren. They were old friends, after all, and she'd missed her. "It's wonderful to see you. How've you been?"

"I'm doing well," Lauren said with a warm smile. "How are you and yours?"

"Oh, the family's healthy and that's what counts," Edie said. In her early forties, Edie was of average weight and height, had light brown skin and dark brown eyes and wore her shoulder-length brown hair in a straight style with bangs. "As for me, I'm overworked and underpaid, as usual."

They laughed. Once their laughter subsided, Edie met Lauren's eyes and said, "I assume you're looking for Adam?"

"Yes, do you know where he is?"

"He came in here a few minutes ago and went to his office but then he came back out and said he was going home. He was in some pain and thought taking something for it and lying down would help."

Lauren panicked. Did she hit him harder than she thought she had? Maybe he had a concussion. If so, he shouldn't take any medication or go to sleep. That could be asking for trouble. "Okay," she said to Edie, trying her best to appear as though she was in no real rush to leave but desperately wanting to run out. "I guess I'll try him at the house, then. Thanks, Edie." She gave Edie another quick hug. "Take care of yourself, and congrats on the promotion."

"Thanks," Edie said, smiling but looking at her strangely. She walked with her to the exit. "You're feeling okay, aren't you?"

"Oh, yes, yes, I'm fine," Lauren said.

Once on the other side of the door she sprinted to her car. She had to remind herself not to speed as she drove across town to the exclusive neighborhood where her former home was located. It would be foolish to speed and risk being pulled over by a police officer. A delay might be the difference between life and death.

As she drove she remembered when she got up this morning and looked out her window and thought that this was such a beautiful day. She'd been eager to get it started. Now she wished it was over. Why had she hit him? He'd provoked her, true. But all her life she'd been trained not to hit anyone unless in self-defense or in the defense of someone incapable of defending themselves. Yet she'd violently attacked Adam because he'd said something that angered her. So many times people did things in anger that they were unable to take back. If he died because she lacked anger management skills she would have to live with the consequences for the rest of her life.

She made record time getting to the house on Cone Manor Lane.

The stone Tudor Revival home had been built five years ago. Adam had had it built as a surprise for their first wedding anniversary so she had not had any say in its design. Although a beautiful home, she found it too big and ostentatious. She would have preferred a less cavernous house with personal details that made you feel at home when you stepped into its foyer. This house was two stories tall with a sweeping staircase. It had five bedrooms, five full baths and two half baths. It boasted almost eight thousand square feet of usable space and sat on two acres. There was a pool out back, and a gym and a home theater in the basement. It was an estate, not a house. Adam liked living large.

She got out of the Range Rover and ran to the front door. She was about to ring the bell when she noticed the door was ajar. She paused. Adam would not leave the door unlocked. He was usually careful about security.

Her mind racing, she tried to think what she should do, quietly enter the house and check things out firsthand? Or go ahead and phone the police? If she phoned the police and nothing was amiss she'd look like a fool. But looking like a fool was preferable to walking in and finding Adam dead on the floor from the knock on the head she'd given him. She didn't think she could handle discovering a dead body, even if that dead body belonged to her horrible ex-husband.

Unfortunately, while she was mentally debating what her next move should be, a dark figure approached the door holding a gun in her hand and demanded she enter the house.

Lauren grimaced when she saw the business end of the

.38 pointing at her and then slowly raised her gaze to look into the face of her assailant, Nichole Kelly.

"I thought I heard a car pull up. You're just the woman I want to see," said Nichole as she backed into the house, gun trained on Lauren. "Come with me, and don't make any sudden moves. You and I need to talk."

After they were inside, Nichole said, "Lock the door."

Lauren did as she was told.

Nichole went to her and shoved her farther into the house. "We're going to his office," she said, her voice calm but decisive. In the office, a large luxuriously furnished room replete with a custom-built stone fireplace, Lauren saw that Adam had been duct-taped to a chair and his mouth was sealed shut.

She wondered how Nichole had managed that. Adam must have weighed a hundred pounds more than she did. Then when she got closer to him she saw that he had a bloody gash on the back of his head. She certainly hadn't done that. She'd struck him on the jaw. Nichole must have snuck up behind him and hit him with a blunt object.

Adam had apparently been sitting in his office chair when she'd hit him from behind and while he was unconscious she'd gone to work on him with a roll of duct tape.

Lauren turned and faced Nichole. "What's going on here? Why is he trussed up like that?"

"Because I decided not to kill him right away," Nichole said. Her eyes were bright and there was a crazed expression in them.

Lauren was pretty sure her own eyes were bright, too, with desperation. She didn't want to get shot.

"All right," Lauren said slowly. "What did you want to talk with me about?"

"First," said Nichole, "what are you doing here? And

don't lie to me because I'm upset and I don't want to have to shoot you."

"I don't want you to shoot me," Lauren said with a nervous smile. "I'm here because he and I argued and I hauled off and hit Adam earlier today and when I went to his office to talk with him I was told that he'd gone home in pain. I was worried that if he had a concussion from the punch I threw, he could possibly die."

"So you came to see if he was okay," Nichole concluded for her.

Lauren nodded. "Yes."

"Why did you hit him?"

"Because he threatened to show a sex tape he'd made of us while we were married to the guy I'm seeing now unless I agreed to come back to him."

Nichole said, "Huh?"

"Do I have to repeat that? He was trying to blackmail me."

"He told me you two were still in love," Nichole said, "And because of that he had to dump me." She lowered the gun as she talked and paced the floor.

Lauren glanced at Adam who was conscious and trying his best to follow Nichole with his eyes. He reminded her of a horse with a bit in its mouth, eyes rolling from side to side. She wondered if he really did have a concussion. He'd been hit on the head by angry women twice today.

"I guess he'd forgotten he gave me the alarm code and a key to the house after we got engaged. I had planned on coming in while he was away and getting my few personal belongings as I did one day last week. But when I was here I discovered his little hobby. He has about fifty videotapes of himself and several women having sex. He labels them with the first letter of the name of his conquests. He had ten in there with the letter *N*. He had around twenty with the letter *L*."

"You bastard," Lauren cried angrily, glaring at Adam. "You only showed me one."

"I was so upset I left that day without remembering to get the belongings I'd come for," Nichole continued. "So I came back today for them and he picked today of all days to come home early from work. He never does that. I hid while he came in here and sat down at his desk. I was so angry with him for taping me without my permission that I hit him over the head with his own gun. You probably know the one he keeps in his desk drawer?"

Lauren shook her head nervously.

Nichole smiled. "You're okay."

"Thank you," Lauren said with a smile. "I thought you were very nice the first time we met. I wondered why you were with him."

"I'm sure many people thought the same thing when you were with him," Nichole returned the compliment.

Adam mumbled loudly as if he were reminding them to get back on topic. They both glared at him.

"Now I'm contemplating whether I should just off him or humiliate him."

"I vote for humiliation," Lauren said. "Death is final and mercifully quick. Humiliation on the other hand lasts a lifetime."

Nichole cocked her brow, her interest piqued. "What do you suggest we do?"

Adam protested even louder.

"Shut up, we're trying to think," said Lauren. "Mmm, what would be a fitting punishment for a pig like him?"

"We should definitely destroy his videotape collection," she told Nichole.

"Of course," Nichole agreed. She went over to an antique armoire inside which sat a flat-screen TV and bent down to open the bottom drawer. "They're all in here."

"We can burn them in the fireplace," Lauren said. "And make him watch."

In a matter of minutes they had a fire going in the fireplace and were tossing the videotapes into it. They talked while they tossed.

"You know," said Nichole. "When we met I was prepared not to like you. He talked about you like you were Satan's daughter. How you never supported him. You wouldn't quit your job to entertain his clients. To think I was preparing to quit my job."

"Oh, no," Lauren said. "You should never give up your career for a man. If he's a real man he wouldn't want you to give up something that means so much to you."

Nichole tossed a videotape with the letter *N* on it into the fire. "I'm glad I didn't quit. Where would I be now? I'd be out of a job with no way to pay my bills."

"What do you do?" Lauren asked.

"I'm a massage therapist," Nichole said. "That's how we met. I gave him a massage. I should have known he was no good when he asked me if I could please him with my hands. But I thought he was just flirting. I'm a certified massage therapist. These fingers are for healing, not for giving happy endings."

After they'd put all of the tapes into the fire, they turned their attention to Adam once more.

"I think we should videotape him in his present state and keep copies for ourselves as a guarantee that he won't try to seek revenge for what we're doing to him," Lauren suggested.

Nichole wrinkled her nose, thinking about it. "Okay, let's do that. But I also have an idea."

"I'm all ears," said Lauren.

"We can't unbind him," Nichole said. "He's strong. He may be able to overpower us. Maybe we could cut the clothes off him and film him using that expensive camcorder of his. And after we're finished we could roll him outside and leave him naked and taped to his chair on the front lawn."

Adam really started yelling then. However, with the tape over his mouth the sound was muffled and didn't carry very far.

Lauren laughed. "I wish we could do that, but there's no way to cut his clothes off him while he's duct-taped to that chair. We're going to have to leave him where he is and call 911 on the way out. He's been hit on the head twice. He might need medical attention."

Nichole looked in the middle distance for a few seconds then said, "Yeah, you're right." She glared at Adam. "You're not having a fun day are you, sweetheart?"

Shortly after that, the partners in crime got busy. Lauren filmed Adam as he thrashed around in the wheeled office chair, trying his best to hide his face from the camera. Once she had a few minutes of footage she removed the tape and put another in so that they would each have a copy. Nichole wiped down all surfaces that might have their fingerprints on them. Lastly, she wiped the gun down and returned it to the desk drawer.

Finished, the two women stood facing one another. Lauren offered Nichole her hand to shake. "I'm sorry things didn't work out well for you. You seem like a nice person."

"Ditto," Nichole said, smiling. "Do you want to call 911, or should I?"

"I'll do it," Lauren said. She picked up the phone on Adam's desk and dialed. When the dispatcher asked what the nature of her emergency was, she said, "This guy brought me home with him and he started getting rough with me.

I hit him and tied him up. I think I might have hit him too hard. I'm outta here!" She then hung up the phone. "Since this is his house phone. They'll know exactly where to come," she explained to Nichole.

Lauren reached into her coat pocket and removed a business card. She gave it to Nichole. "We're connected now. Here's my contact information."

Nichole's face lit up. "I don't have a card," she said regrettably. She walked over to Adam's desk and borrowed a pad and pen to write down her address and phone number. Walking back over to Lauren, she gave her a slip of paper and said, "Who knows, one day we might get together over drinks and reminisce."

Lauren smiled at that. "Stranger things have happened."

Then they left Adam where he sat and vacated the premises. Outside, Lauren waved to Nichole as they both hurried to their vehicles.

Too keyed-up to go home, Lauren drove around awhile, relishing the fact that she was finally rid of Adam. He no longer had the means with which to blackmail her, unless Nichole was wrong and she had not discovered his entire stash of videotapes. However, she had a good feeling they'd destroyed all of them. And there was nothing left to come back to haunt her.

While driving she put in a follow-up call to Arielle. Arielle answered her personal number. "Hey, Lauren," she said, "I don't have to come get you out of jail, do I?"

Lauren laughed and told her what had happened.

When she was finished relating the tale, Arielle said, "You must really care about Colton Riley to do all this to prevent him from seeing those tapes."

Lauren did care about Colton very much. What she felt for him was hard to put into words. "I don't know if it was out of the humiliation I felt for being secretly recorded or my fear that if I let Adam get away with what he planned that I would always be subject to his whims. I got away from him once. I wasn't going back there again."

"I'm just glad the police didn't get involved," Arielle told her. "If Adam knows what's good for him he'll keep quiet about it. But if he does decide to raise a big stink and report you and Nichole, you don't have any evidence that you were provoked to do what you did. You burned all the tapes."

Lauren patted her coat pocket. She felt the two small rectangular objects she'd secured earlier. "No," she told her lawyer. "I didn't destroy them all. I kept one with an *N* and one with an *L*. I'll send Nichole hers tomorrow and explain why I kept it."

"I knew some of my smarts would rub off on you eventually." Arielle laughed a good ten seconds, then said, "So, none of your actions had anything to do with Mr. Riley?"

"I already told you I didn't want to lose him because of Adam's treachery," Lauren said.

"Are you going to tell him what you did?"

"Yes, I can't take the chance that Adam will be vindictive in spite of everything and tell him about the tapes just to hurt him."

"He doesn't play well with others, our Adam," Arielle said wisely.

"I'm going to try Colton now and see if he's available to talk," Lauren said. "Thanks again, Arielle."

"You take care," Arielle said and disconnected the call.

# Chapter 12

Colton had just come out of a meeting with the company's accountants when he received Lauren's call. He was happy to hear from her and told her so. "You've been on my mind all day," he said, his voice husky with longing.

"You've been on my mind, too," she said, "Something's happened and I need to talk to you. Can you spare a few minutes?"

"Sure," he answered without hesitation. "Where are you? I can either come to you or you could come here."

"I'm not too far from you," Lauren said. "I'll be there in ten minutes."

"This must be important." A hint of worry was apparent in his voice. "You're not in any trouble?"

"I was," she said softly, "I think the problem's solved but you should still know about it."

"All right," said Colton. "I'm here for you."

The Riley Construction Company offices were downtown. Lauren had a hard time finding a parking space and wound up taking longer than ten minutes to get there. When she walked into Colton's office, he breathed a sigh of relief and pulled her into his arms, kicking the door closed. They hadn't seen each other since Wednesday when Colton had cooked for her at his place. The workweek kept them busy and the time between their next meeting felt agonizingly long.

He gazed down into her upturned face. He was wearing dark gray dress slacks and a long-sleeved light blue dress shirt, its sleeves rolled up, and black wing tips. His suit jacket hung from a coat tree in the corner. He'd removed the tie earlier in the day. As he peered into her eyes, he drank her in. Her widely spaced eyes were smoky with desire and he was happy he was the one who put that expression in them.

"God, I've missed you," he said breathlessly and lowered his head to kiss her sweet mouth.

Lauren had missed him, too, and returned his kiss with fervor. She moaned softly, relishing the delicious taste and feel of his mouth on hers, the slow, deliberate, extremely sexy havoc his tongue wreaked on hers. She felt the kiss down to her toes. She looked into his eyes when they parted and reached up to caress his strong jaw. *I did do it for him,* she thought, astonished. Arielle was right. In that instant, she knew that she would have done anything not to lose him. Adam's threat had thrown her into protective mode. She had thought she was protecting herself and doing what she'd always done, which was solve her own problems.

She realized now that she always wanted Colton to look at her in the manner he was looking at her right now: with admiration, longing and sensual intensity. She believed that if he had seen those tapes, he would never have looked at her in the same way again. Therefore, she'd gone with her gut and tried her best to put Adam in his place.

Her hand still on his jaw, she said softly, her gaze locked with his, "It's been quite a day."

She told him everything from the beginning. Her fight with Adam on the street, what had happened when she'd gotten to his house, and the burning of the tapes except for the couple she'd saved for insurance.

His gray eyes were riveted on her face. A frown creased his brow. His inner turmoil was evident from the pained expression in his gray depths. "Why didn't you call me?" he asked, his jaw muscles clenching in obvious irritation. "You could have been hurt going to his house like that. What if Nichole had been convinced that you were the reason he'd dumped her? What if she had shot you in a jealous rage?"

Lauren reached out and touched his cheek to soothe him, but he drew away from her. "Lauren, I think you take your independence too far," he said, his eyes narrowed in anger. "It never occurred to you to call somebody? Myself, your father or your sisters? Your first reaction was to phone your lawyer."

"For legal advice," she said in her defense. "You or my father or my sisters couldn't give me that."

"No, but one of us would have talked you out of going over to Eckhart's house after you'd hit him."

"I was afraid he'd suffered a concussion," she cried. "I had to make sure I hadn't injured him too badly. Believe me when I tell you I took no pleasure in setting foot on Cone Manor Lane again."

He sighed heavily. "You're so stubborn. You should have called me. You think that because you've got a black belt in karate and know how to use a handgun, you're invulnerable, some kind of superwoman. You're not. You foolishly risked your life today."

"I had no way of knowing what I was going to walk into when I went to his house."

"That's my point," Colton ground out. He took a deep breath in an attempt to calm down. "Why did you do it? I know you have better sense than to trust Eckhart. Why didn't you call his bluff? I wouldn't have watched that tape for anything in the world. The last thing I want to see is Eckhart making love to you."

"I know that," Lauren said as if that proved her point. "That's why I had to make sure you never got the chance to."

"You still should have called," he repeated.

"What would you have done if I had?" she asked.

"I probably would have strangled him," Colton admitted, teeth bared in a snarl.

"That's why I didn't call you."

"I don't need your protection," he practically shouted but reeled it in because his secretary was in the outer office and he didn't want his and Lauren's business all over the office.

"And I don't need yours," Lauren countered fiercely. "It's true, I'm independent. It's the only way I know how to be. Adam threatened to send you the tape he showed me unless I broke things off with you. I did what I thought was the right thing. I fought back."

"You would have done better by dumping me," Colton told her angrily.

Lauren saw red. "Okay, consider yourself dumped!" Arms crossed over her chest, she stubbornly turned her back to him.

Colton laughed. "There's that stubborn streak again."

"I'm serious," Lauren insisted, turning back around to face him. "I'm here to tell you we can't see each other anymore. I'm obviously too far gone on you for my own good if I would do anything in my power not to lose you.

So, let's call it quits, shall we? It's probably the best thing for both of us."

"You can't quit me," Colton told her angrily. They were standing facing one another in front of his desk. She was so upset her chest was heaving.

"I most certainly can," Lauren begged to differ. Her eyes bored into his. "Apparently, what we have between us is a chemical reaction."

"If that's how you look when you're getting ready to dump me, with your breasts about to burst out of your blouse, you're not very convincing," Colton said, "because you know that chemical combustion you mentioned only happens between you and me. It's unique. Stop making it sound trivial. I got angry because I was scared that I might have lost you due to the fact that you're so stubbornly independent you couldn't call me when you got into trouble. That pisses me off. I'm a man and a man has to feel needed. We are cavemen in that respect. Got that? It's our duty to protect our women. Superwomen like you don't understand that, or don't want to understand it. Your father loved you but he did you a disservice when he taught you to be so remarkably self-sufficient. If you ever do anything as foolish as you did today, you won't have to quit me. I'll be forced to let you go." Then he roughly pulled her into his embrace and kissed her hard. He kept the kiss intact until she fell limply into his arms.

After they came up for air she looked up dreamily at him. "You win this round. I'd better go."

She reluctantly left his warm embrace and turned to leave.

"Are you capable of driving?" he teased with a broad grin.

"Shut up," she said as she walked to the door on wobbly legs.

\* \* \*

Colton had every intention of letting it go. The remainder of his workday he tried to put Adam Eckhart and what he'd done to Lauren out of his mind, but he hadn't been able to shake it, so he decided to have a man to man talk with him. It wasn't hard to track him down. He went to the closest hospital to Eckhart's home address. When he got there he tried the emergency room and, masquerading as Eckhart's brother, he learned that they were keeping him overnight for observation. Apparently, he'd taken a good beating. He found him asleep in a semiprivate room, the other bed occupied by an elderly man channel-surfing and mumbling about nothing being on TV.

When the guy looked up and saw Colton, he said, "Who're you looking for?"

"Adam Eckhart," said Colton.

"That's sleepyhead," Adam's roommate said. He laughed. "But if I'd been hit over the head like that I'd probably want to sleep, too."

Colton strode over to Adam's bed and loudly cleared his throat.

Adam startled awake. When he saw who was standing beside his bed, his eyes narrowed with hatred. "What the hell do you want?"

"Just checking to see if you were still alive," Colton said with a smile. "How does it feel to get your ass kicked by two women?"

Adam winced as he sat up in bed. The back of his head had a huge bandage on it and he was wearing a hospital gown. "Go ahead and issue your threat, Riley. I know that's why you're here. Lauren came running to you and now you're here to demonstrate what a big hero you are."

"No," Colton denied calmly. "I'm not going to threaten you. I'm going to make a promise to you. I vow that should you ever even look at Lauren funny I will put you in the ground, not the hospital." He smiled. "Are we clear?"

Adam didn't say anything. The color had drained from his face, and he felt dizzy. "I suppose it makes you feel better coming here and threatening me in my weakened state. I can't defend myself. But, yes, we are clear."

"Listen, if you'd like to revisit this when you're healthy again, you know where to find me," Colton offered. "I just wanted to state my case and be done with it. Trying to blackmail Lauren was despicable. But I'm sure you already know that. Plus, the fact that you taped unsuspecting women for your viewing pleasure is plain sleazy. It amazes me that a man as successful as you are can't find something better to do with his time. Seek help, Eckhart."

"I'm not a head case," Adam said, holding his head with both hands. "Get out!"

"I'd be happy to," Colton told him. "Just repeat what I said to make certain you understood me."

"Yeah, yeah, I'm not to ever go near Lauren again. I got it. Good riddance to her. She never appreciated the finer things in life. She wants to roll around in the gutter with the likes of you."

Colton laughed softly. "You're a piece of work, Eckhart."

"What, are you surprised I'm unrepentant? Was I supposed to cower and say I'm sorry for what I did? I'm just sorry it didn't succeed. I was looking forward to her starring in more of my home movies," Adam said with a smirk.

Colton almost hit him when he said that. Restraint was aided by the sudden appearance of a nurse who had come to take Adam's vitals.

Colton turned on his heels and left. He didn't know if his talk with Eckhart had gotten through to him. He simply had wanted to make sure Eckhart knew that in the future he would be prepared to deal with him in a deadly and final manner should he resume his harassment of Lauren.

As the weeks passed, to Lauren's relief, she never ran into Adam when she visited the children's hospital site. He did phone her one day when she was on the way home from work. She'd looked at her cell phone's screen and seriously thought of not answering but she did because she wanted to know if he'd fully recovered from his head wounds.

"Yes, Adam, what do you want?"

"I'm surprised you answered," he said.

"Don't waste time making small talk."

"This is hard for me to say," he began almost timidly.

"Well, I have no trouble telling you to go to hell if you've called to make further threats. The fact is I saved your life. Nichole had snapped. She was going to shoot you. If I hadn't been there I don't know what would have happened."

"That's why I'm calling," Adam said, "To thank you for saving my life. I do believe Nichole hated me in that moment. She might have done something crazy."

"Yeah, yeah," Lauren said skeptically, "What's the catch?"

"No catch," Adam disavowed. "I'm not incapable of learning from my mistakes, you know. You don't have to worry about me anymore. No seeking revenge or any of that. I, um, I wish you the best."

At that point she was really suspicious. "What brought this on?"

"Almost dying can have a spiritual effect on a man," was all he said. "Goodbye, Lauren."

After hanging up Lauren had wondered if indeed Adam had changed. Only time would tell.

Nichole had phoned Lauren after she received the tape

Lauren had sent to her. She'd had misgivings about destroying all of the evidence and was glad that Lauren had had the foresight not to. They had agreed to keep in touch.

Spring was soon upon them and Lauren and Colton planned a long weekend at her cabin to enjoy the season in the mountains. They set off early one Saturday morning in April in Colton's SUV.

"Grandpa Beck wants us to come to the lodge tonight for dinner," she told Colton as he drove. "Since Mina has been there he's becoming a lot more social. And she's transformed the lodge by adding a few decorative touches and bringing the place into the twenty-first century with internet connections. Could you believe he didn't offer Wi-Fi? She sent photos. His rustic lodge now appeals to a whole new clientele. Bookings have doubled. Grandpa Beck complains that they'll never have any downtime if things keep up like they have been lately."

"Good for him," Colton said.

Lauren laughed. "Mina says he complains all the time, but she can tell he's secretly pleased."

"What about Mina?" Colton asked. "Does she like living up there?"

"She loves it. It keeps her mind occupied, and Mina likes to stay extremely busy so she doesn't have to think too hard. When she thinks she invariably comes back to the fact that she lost the man she loved."

"That must be hard to forget no matter how much she works," said Colton.

"It is," said Lauren sadly. "But what else can she do but take one day at a time and continue living? She knows Keith would want her to find love again."

The day was bright and sunny. As they drew closer to

the mountains the air got crisper. The leaves on the trees had turned from orange and yellow to green.

Colton had been looking forward to this weekend. Although he and Lauren tried to see each other at least once or twice each week, it was never enough time. Many of their weekends were spent with each other's families. There had been birthday parties, Sunday dinners and a big get-together to celebrate Lauren's parents' anniversary. He enjoyed getting to know her family. But what he really wanted was more alone time with her.

He glanced over at her. She was thumbing a text message to someone, her face scrunched up in concentration. Her long wavy hair was in a ponytail, and she was wearing well-worn jeans and a short-sleeved Duke University T-shirt. She'd kicked off her sandals miles back. She knew how to relax.

In fact, she was good at many things, including making him fall in love with her. It had been four months since they'd met on that fateful winter night.

He smiled as he returned his attention solely to his driving. He was remembering a conversation he'd had with his mother a couple days ago. She'd come by the office because she wanted to tell him that she was going back to work. For years she had been an interior decorator. His father would build the houses and she would design the interior of the model homes. His father often said that the houses he built were structurally sound and built to last, but if not for his mother's contribution no one touring them would see them as homes.

That day in his office, Colton had said, "Why would you want to go back to work? Dad left you financially secure. You don't ever have to work again. Why not enjoy life? Go to Paris. Run with the bulls in Pamplona. You can do anything you want to."

"Running with the bulls is a man thing," Veronica had said with a smile. "Besides, working is what I want to do, not be on a perennial vacation. I need purpose in my life. I need to contribute something to society."

"You're contributing something to society by being my mother," Colton said in response to her plea for purpose. "I still need you. Jade needs you. You've got two grandchildren to spoil. A lot of mothers would be trying to marry me off, and you're looking to go back to work."

"Honey, you're a hairbreadth away from fulfilling your father's and my wishes for marrying you off," Veronica told him smugly.

That had gotten Colton's attention. He'd stood up behind his desk, rested his hands atop it and glared down at his mother who had the grace to squirm a little in her comfy leather chair across from him. "I know that tone," he began, his voice firm. "What do you know that I don't?"

"Darling, do you remember my telling you about that game your dad and I used to play? Whenever we'd meet a young lady we thought would suit you we'd say, could she be the girl for Colton? Well, Lauren was at the top of our list. Of course back then she was married to that horrible Eckhart man but we always held out hope. After your father died and you went to our cabin and had to spend time with Lauren I figured it was fate. I'm delighted that you and Lauren finally got together. I'm sure your father is somewhere laughing."

Colton had sat back down behind his desk, his eyes on his mother. Shaking his head in wonder, he said, "When were you planning on telling me this?"

"On your wedding day," said Veronica, smiling. "But since the wedding's on lock I'm telling you now."

"The wedding isn't on lock," Colton told her. "I haven't even told Lauren that I'm in love with her yet."

This put a look of concern on Veronica's face. "You don't love her?"

"Yes, I love her," Colton said out loud for the first time. "I love her but I'm trying to pick the right time to tell her. Lauren's experience with Eckhart left her heart bruised and battered. I don't think she's going to want to be in love anytime soon, even if she does love me."

"Huh?" said Veronica. "Speak English, please."

"Eckhart swept her off her feet," Colton explained. "Our relationship has been a whirlwind, too. How we met, the quick attraction—everything points to it being too soon to declare my love. She'll never take me seriously."

"You can't be sure of that unless you tell her," said his mother.

Now, as he drove toward Bryson City, Colton wondered exactly how he was going to convince Lauren that the love he felt for her was real and not infatuation or lust. At some point in a relationship built on lust a transition to love has to be made for the couple to stay together, right?

This weekend he resolved to let her know how much he loved her.

# Chapter 13

"Oh, my God, girl, you look good!" Lauren exclaimed upon seeing Amina later that evening. She and Colton had driven over to Grandpa Beck's lodge after resting awhile then showering and dressing for dinner upon their arrival at her cabin.

Lauren had barely set foot out of the SUV before Amina hugged her tightly. "So do you," Amina said in her ear. "Being in love suits you."

The sisters both had on jeans and dressy blouses, but Lauren had on heels and Amina wore her trusty athletic shoes.

Lauren looked at her sister whose skin was glowing with good health. "I can't hide anything from you."

The lodge, a ten-thousand-square-foot three-story building made of hand-hewn pine logs stood in the midst of a pine forest. The lodge itself had eight guest rooms but there were also six small cabins dotting the property.

Spring was Benjamin's busiest season even before Amina had become his partner. They were fully booked.

Her grandfather came out of the lodge and hugged her after Amina let her go. She stood eye to eye with him. "Grandpa, you remember Colton," Lauren said, gesturing to Colton who was coming around the SUV to shake Benjamin Beck's hand.

Ben looked up at Colton with a smile on his weathered face. "Sure, I do. How are you, Colton?"

"Just great, sir," said Colton. His gaze took in the charm of the lodge and the splendor of the surrounding woods. "This is quite a place you have here."

"Wait until you see the inside," said Benjamin proudly. All four of them began walking toward the two-story entrance of the lodge. Huge tree trunk columns stood sentinel on either side of the intricately carved door that reminded Colton of a totem pole. In the wood of the door there were images of forest animals and eagles soaring in the sky.

Inside the foyer the ceiling rose two stories, and a curved staircase led to the guest rooms. Pine floors polished to a high gleam stretched as far as the eye could see. A fireplace large enough to roast a pig in was the main focus of the lobby.

Heavy pine furnishings with beige cushions composed the seating groups near the fireplace and African and American Indian art in the form of wood sculptures and woven throws on the couches and chairs lent a Western charm to the décor.

"I like it," Lauren said appreciatively to her sister and grandfather after observing the touches Amina had added to the lodge since her arrival. "It's not as masculine as it used to be."

"I could see the wisdom in Mina's ideas," Benjamin said. "Women enjoy getting away to the mountains, too, and now they'll feel more comfortable here. When I first opened this place I catered to hunters and fishermen. They usually left their wives at home. These days the wives come along. I'm not a stick in the mud, you know. I can change with the times."

"Lauren," Amina said, "let me show you the new kitchen."

Benjamin laughed shortly. "We'll skip that, if you don't mind. Come with me, Colton."

While Lauren and Amina went off to explore the kitchen, Benjamin led Colton to the lounge. Unlike the lobby, the lounge was more laid-back and was the designated place for guests to have a cocktail or catch a game on TV. It looked like a large den except there was a fully stocked bar in the back and a burly bartender ready to mix your favorite libation.

"What's your poison?" Benjamin asked as he and Colton took seats at the bar.

"I'm not much of a drinker," Colton said. "How about the house beer?"

"Two drafts, George," said Benjamin.

George, a tall black guy in his late forties, must have weighed three hundred pounds, but it was distributed in such a way that he just looked stocky rather than overweight. "Anything you say, Ben," he said with a smile.

"George, this is Colton Riley," Benjamin introduced them. He glanced at Colton. "George has been with me for ten years. He's my right-hand man."

"Which is Ben's way of saying I do a little bit of everything around here," George joked as he drew two beers from a steel keg under the counter.

He set the mugs of beer before them. Foam spilled over the tops, and he wiped it away with a white dish towel.

"Thank you," said Colton.

"My pleasure," said George good-naturedly and turned away to fill another guest's order.

Colton and Benjamin drank their cold beers companionably before Ben broke the silence. "So, Colton, you and Laurie seem to be going strong."

"That's the first time I've ever heard anyone call Lauren Laurie," Colton commented.

"I'm the only one who calls her that," said Benjamin. "All the other girls have their names shortened, but no one ever called Lauren by a nickname. I don't know why. Maybe because she was the oldest. She was a serious child. Her grandmother used to say Laurie was so serious-minded. And that she did everything fast, from taking her first steps as a toddler to saying her first words. I don't know much about the hierarchy of siblings, but maybe my wife had a point. Laurie didn't spend much time doing childish things. That's why I'm glad to see her looking so relaxed and happy. You've no doubt had something to do with that, so I thank you."

Colton was looking into Ben's dark brown eyes and wondering what had brought this on. "If anyone's benefited from our relationship it's me. She makes me happy."

Ben smiled and changed the subject. "So, when was the last time you saw my big-headed son-in-law?"

Colton chuckled. "A couple of Sundays ago," he said. "He and Mrs. Gaines are doing well."

"Has he found a hobby since he retired?"

"He watches a lot of sports."

"He needs to get a job. My Virginia still works."

"Lauren says the general retired after more than thirty years of emeritus service, that's what's on the award he received when he retired."

"A man has the right to retire," Ben told him, explaining himself. "But Fonzi is not the type who can sit at home. He needs to be doing something productive. He hasn't been retired long enough to realize that. He will one day and if he hasn't already gone stir crazy, he'll find something to do."

"I get the feeling," Colton said, looking at Benjamin suspiciously, "that you don't dislike Mr. Gaines as much as you pretend to."

Benjamin laughed shortly. "I don't dislike him at all. He's been a good husband and father. That's all you can ask of a man. We've been sparring together for so long it's become a habit. He'd probably think I was sick or something if I didn't give him a hard time."

"And you're not mad at him for not giving you a grandson?"

"I would be one sorry son of a bitch not to be grateful for my wonderful granddaughters. They're all exceptional women. But I would be lying if I said I wasn't looking forward to having grandsons one day." He winked at Colton.

Colton laughed. "You're winking at the wrong man. Lauren and I are a long way from having kids."

"But you are heading in that direction, aren't you?" Ben asked hopefully.

"I am," Colton assured him. "I don't know if Lauren is."

"Are you going to do a little sightseeing on this visit?" Amina asked over dinner. "Or are you just going to spend all your time holed up in the cabin?" She wiggled her brows at Lauren in a leering manner.

Lauren laughed at her sister's antics then promptly ignored the innuendos. "I thought I'd take Colton to see Mingo Falls tomorrow."

"It ought to be pretty up there this time of year," Ben said. "Remember, though, the hike leading to the falls can be treacherous for those who're not used to the terrain. So be careful."

"Isn't that on the Cherokee Indian Reservation?" Colton asked.

"Yeah, *mingo* means *big bear* in Cherokee. Mingo Falls is one of the highest falls in the area," Ben answered before putting a large piece of steak he'd speared with his fork into his mouth.

"We don't need special permission to go on the reservation?"

"No, you don't need a permit," Ben said.

"Then let's do it," Colton said to Lauren.

Mingo Falls was located on the Qualla Boundary on the Cherokee Indian Reservation and just outside of the Great Smoky Mountains National Park which was the most visited National Park in the United States. Lauren and Colton were able to drive the SUV to Mingo Falls Campground but from there they had to walk.

The midmorning air was chilly, and fog could be seen in low-lying areas. The mist rose in the mountain air but it began to dissipate by late morning. The sky looked gray and the clouds portended rain.

Lauren and Colton wore sturdy walking shoes, jeans and T-shirts and jackets. In their backpacks they carried bottled water and a light lunch in the form of ham sandwiches and fresh peaches.

The climb to the falls was steep and the terrain was rocky and covered with tree roots that made it tricky to walk. It was necessary to be as careful as Ben had warned. As they strolled along the trail they encountered other hikers coming down, and when they looked back they saw others ascending. They heard the falls before they saw them. There was something spiritual about the sound of water falling over rocks.

When they finally reached the falls, they stood rapt with wonder at the one-hundred-and-twenty-foot example of nature's power and majesty.

Lauren stood in front of Colton, who had his arms wrapped around her. "No wonder people risk broken bones to get up here," Colton said softly. "This is breathtaking."

The crashing of the waterfall nearly drowned out his voice, but Lauren heard him and wholeheartedly agreed. "It seems like the most beautiful places on earth require effort to get to." She sighed wistfully. "Wouldn't it be great waking up in the morning and seeing that sight first thing?"

"If you designed the house," Colton told her, his cheek pressed to hers. "I'd gladly build it."

Lauren laughed. "It would take an architectural genius to design a house that would not only be able to be built on rocky terrain but have form and function."

"Then why don't we simply build a house together in Raleigh?" Colton suggested.

Lauren craned her neck to look back at him. "Are we building castles or are we being serious here?"

"We're doing both," he said. He carefully turned her around to face him, his hands on her upper arms so that they both kept their balance.

"I love you, Lauren," he said, looking deeply into her eyes.

Lauren was elated. She loved him, too, and she had hoped that he shared the same feelings but she'd been afraid to tell him how she felt. "I'm so relieved I'm not in this alone," she whispered. "I love you so much."

As they looked intensely into each other's eyes, Colton

wanted to freeze the moment and keep it this way forever. She loved him. He could die happy.

But then loose rocks above began rolling toward them and suddenly their footing was not so sure after all. They fell and began sliding down the rocky incline they'd been standing on. Because he was heavier, Colton was rolling downward faster than Lauren. He tried to hold on to her as they fell, but the momentum made it impossible to do so. Lauren felt their fingers disconnect. She was trying not to panic. Luckily, they weren't near a cliff. Eventually, their descent would stop and they would be able to get back up and walk out of here.

She was right. Colton ended up bumping into a huge outgrowth of a pine tree's roots and as she was rolling past him he reached out and grabbed her, thereby stopping her descent.

For a few minutes all they could do was hold each other and catch their breaths. She looked him over. He had scratches on his face but he looked none the worse for wear. As he looked back at her, the expression in his gray eyes went from concerned to relieved.

"You've got a scratch across your left eyebrow," he said, "otherwise you look okay. How do you feel?"

She managed a weak smile. "I don't think anything's broken. How about you?"

Colton's one dimple winked at her. "Never better," he said. "Do you see what falling for you gets me?"

They rose carefully to their feet. "You're so corny," Lauren said of his "falling for you" comment.

"If we make it back to the cabin I'm going to show you corny," he promised.

"You mean *when* we make it back to the cabin," she corrected him.

"Yes, ma'am," Colton said with a smile.

Hand in hand, they slowly made their way back up to the path where they encountered a couple about to embark on the same trail. The couple eyed them with curiosity. Lauren imagined they had dirt and leaves stuck on their clothes to say nothing of the scratches marring exposed skin.

"Are you okay?" the woman asked.

"The rocks are a bit loose back there," Colton told them. "So watch your step."

They continued walking. They heard the woman say to her partner, "Maybe we ought to turn back."

But her partner pooh-poohed her misgivings.

Lauren squeezed Colton's hand. "Hear that? I brought you here and almost got you killed but it was worth it."

Colton glanced down at her, his eyes alight with humor. "You told me you loved me. That was worth it."

Lauren grinned. "You say the sweetest things."

An hour or so later they were soaking in the sunken tub of Lauren's cabin playing footsies. "I'm worried about what could happen to you...now that I love you and you know it," Lauren said as her right foot found a sensitive area of his body and gently caressed it with her toes.

Colton was finding it difficult to think with her foot where it was. "What do you mean?"

"I told you about the curse, didn't I?"

He'd had his eyes closed enjoying the moment. But now he opened them and looked at her. "I thought you didn't believe in it."

"I don't," she said, "But I also didn't believe I'd ever meet a decent man and fall in love. And here we are."

"You have a way of making your life harder than it needs to be," Colton said as he sat up on his end of the tub and removed her foot from his crotch. "I command you to think only positive thoughts for the rest of the weekend." He pulled her toward him and she climbed on top of him, water splashing over the sides of the tub to the floor. He squeezed her bottom with both hands as their groins rubbed together in the warm soapy water. Lauren cooed with delight. This was infinitely better than tumbling down a hill in a national forest, she thought.

Colton had been semierect throughout their playful foreplay. Now he was fully erect and ready for her to impale herself on him. But Lauren had other ideas. She reached behind him and pulled the tub's plug. Then she kissed him briefly and got up. Thanks to the nonslip ridges in the tub's bottom she didn't fear falling when she grabbed his hand and coaxed him to his feet. "Let's move this to the bedroom, okay? I'm cold."

He was happy to oblige her. In fact, he took great pleasure in taking the removable showerhead and rinsing the suds off her beautiful brown body, then patting her down with a fluffy white towel. He liked pampering her. If she'd let him, he'd wash her hair, but Lauren had a thing about her hair. She was tender-headed and didn't trust he'd be gentle—something about his big man hands. He smiled as he held her bathrobe for her and she slipped inside it. She rose up on her tiptoes and kissed his chin. "Your turn," she murmured, her voice sexy. She dried him off and held his robe open for him in return. After he was ensconced in its warmth he bent and swept her into his arms and carried her to the adjoining bedroom.

Lauren giggled. "Don't drop me. I've been beat up enough for one day."

"I'm not going to drop you, woman, but I do believe you've put on a few pounds lately."

"I weigh the same as I did the day we met," Lauren

claimed. "But if I have gained a few you can blame yourself, Mr. Gourmet Chef."

Colton dropped her onto the bed and turned to remove his robe and deposit it on the floor. Turning back he watched her as she followed his every movement. He liked it when she couldn't draw her eyes away from him.

Lauren removed her robe and tossed it onto a nearby chair. She moved backward on the bed, her eyes riveted on Colton's cinnamon-brown body, the muscles rippling enticingly as he walked toward her. "Like what you see?" he asked as he straddled her and forced her legs apart.

Lauren arched her back, her pelvis thrust upward. "You're so damned vain. Maybe I simply admire the human body in all its aesthetic beauty, much like, as an architect, I admire a beautiful building."

Colton chuckled. "Or maybe looking at me makes you wet and horny as hell."

"Must you be so crude?" she asked, pretending to be aghast at his choice of words.

"Too titillating for you?" he asked as he bent and licked the nipple of her right breast. His hot tongue laved the hardened nipple until Lauren writhed with pent-up sexual desire. He paid equal attention to the left nipple. Then he kissed his way down past her rib cage to her belly and farther still until he was feasting on her feminine center with abandon.

Lauren moaned loudly. Her inhibitions were long gone and her will abolished under the assault of his mouth. She came with a shout and even then Colton didn't let up, but only slowed down to coincide with her trembling release.

"I love you, I love you, I love you," she cried repeatedly.

That only increased his ardor. His penis was hard and throbbing, and by the time he got a condom on he could barely contain the need to enter her. She was more than ready for him and he slipped inside, her folds welcoming him with hot intensity. Lauren clung to him, her legs wrapped tightly around him. His thrusts were so deep she felt he might tear her asunder but at that moment all she cared about was the pleasure of loving him and being loved by him. She grabbed his ass with both hands and held on. She could feel his muscles flexing as he moved. The hot steel of his shaft filled her up.

The walls of her vagina quivered with the lovely friction. She felt another orgasm coming on and at the same time that Colton growled his release, she exploded again. Together, they fell onto the bed and faced one another, smiling gently, breathing hard.

"I like this much better than hiking," she told him sincerely.

Colton laughed. "I'll keep that in mind."

# Chapter 14

Their weekend in the mountains would be the last vacation they would be able to take for months to come. Work kept them extremely busy. The building business was booming due to the improved economy and both Lauren and Colton benefited from it. In October, Lawrence, Mayer and McGill, pleased with Lauren's work on the children's hospital, offered her a partnership, which she accepted. She also hired an intern, a twenty-year-old African American woman named Deanna Lane, who was currently attending Duke University.

Colton, who usually thrived on getting out in the field, found himself more and more in the office with clients. He missed the physical labor but knew as head of the company he had to show leadership and keep them fiscally strong. That meant he had to court clients and once he landed them, keep them happy and eager to do business with them over and over again. Now he knew what his father meant when he'd said that you always had to have your business cap on.

As for his love life, it remained hot and heavy. They'd exchanged keys and it wasn't unusual for Lauren to come home from work and find him in her kitchen preparing a meal for them.

On the night before Thanksgiving, Colton came home and found Lauren not in his tub but asleep in his bed. He stood there smiling at the image she made, like a black Goldilocks snoozing away while the big bad bear arrived home and discovered her in his bed. He got undressed and climbed in with her. She awakened as soon as he knelt on the bed, and blinked at him. Smiling, she murmured, "You're home."

He kissed her and pulled her close, pulling the covers over both of them. "It's cold outside."

She snuggled into him, her warm, naked body molding itself to him. "But it's warm in here."

"Not that I'm not happy to see you," he said, looking into her eyes, "but you said you and your sisters were spending the night at your parents' house to help your mother prepare Thanksgiving dinner."

"I know I did," she said softly, "and I meant to, but Momma nixed that. She said it's time we started cooking dinner ourselves and inviting her and Daddy to our houses. So Desiree volunteered for duty. We're all going to her house tomorrow for dinner."

"Isn't that a lot of cooking on Desiree?"

"Desi's not cooking. Don't tell Momma but she got on the phone with a caterer the minute after she told us she'd handle it. She's organized like that."

"Yay, Desiree," Colton said. "Now, come here."

Benjamin closed the lodge for Thanksgiving, so he and Amina drove to Raleigh to spend time with the family. His old blue Ford pickup was parked in Desiree's driveway when Lauren and Colton arrived the next day at noon. It looked out of place next to the other late-model cars and SUVs.

Desiree met them at the door looking cool and collected and chic in a royal-blue dress and black patent leather pumps. Lauren kissed her proffered cheek. "You didn't say anything about dressing up."

She and Colton wore casual clothes. He was in navy blue Dockers and a white short-sleeved shirt, a black hoodie and athletic shoes. She wore black slacks and a lavender pullover top, a black hoodie and athletic shoes.

Desiree looked her over. "You look great. I'm a nervous wreck and I need my armor to get me through today. I've already been busted. Momma inspected the kitchen and found the containers the catered food came in. I'll never live it down."

Lauren laughed. "You're a psychotherapist. Don't you have some kind of psychological trick that'll get you through today?"

"Yes," Desiree said, "and it involves mimosas. I've got a pitcher mixed in the kitchen. Help yourself."

Lauren looked closely at her sister's eyes. They were a little glazed. "Desi, are you drunk?"

Desiree smiled. "That's a possibility."

Desiree closed the front door after Lauren and Colton were inside then gestured to the great room to the left of the foyer, which served as the entertainment room. "Everybody's in there. Make yourselves comfortable while I go check on the rolls I put in the oven a few minutes ago."

Desiree's home was immaculate like its owner. The air was redolent with enticing aromas of food cooking. Two-stories, it had high ceilings, hardwood floors throughout except for tile in the kitchen and baths. She liked open spaces so the rooms were tastefully decorated with minimalist furnishings in modern styles. Knickknacks were few and far between but she had a penchant for African American artists like Romare Bearden. Prints of his watercolors could be found above the fireplace in the spacious living room and on her bedroom wall.

Lauren and Colton were greeted as soon as they entered the great room. Virginia and Fonzi were sitting on the couch with Amina between them. Benjamin sat in a chair across from them and Meghan sat on the arm of her grandfather's chair. There was a football game on TV.

Amina got up to hug Lauren. "I haven't seen you since April," Lauren cried. She took in Amina's huge Afro. "You look like that jazz artist, what's her name?"

"Esperanza Spalding," Meghan spoke up from her perch on the arm of Benjamin's chair. "I love her."

Lauren touched her sister's hair. "You look fierce!"

"Thanks," Amina said. "I'm having fun being natural these days. My hair feels so much stronger in its natural state."

"How is life in the mountains? Have you met any nice guys?"

Amina laughed. "If I were looking for a guy I'd be out of luck up there. They're either married or Grandpa's age."

Benjamin heard that and had to add, "She's not lying. I told her a guy's going to have to drop out of the sky for her."

"Mina's not looking for a man. She's there to learn the business. How is that part going?" Virginia interjected.

"She's smart as all get-out," Benjamin said proudly. "She already knows more than I know about customer relations. The guests love her. She's going to be just fine, Virginia."

Virginia sat back on the couch beside Fonzi, satisfied with her father's assessment of his granddaughter.

"Enough about me," said Amina, her teasing gaze encompassing Lauren and Colton. "How are you two doing? You haven't taken anymore spills since Mingo Falls, have you?"

"No, thank goodness," Lauren answered for both of them. "We've stayed out of the woods."

"This is the first I've heard of an incident involving you and Colton at Mingo Falls," Virginia said, her eyes on Lauren. "When were you there?"

"In April," Lauren answered easily. "We went to Bryson City for the weekend."

"You'd only known one another four months at that time," Virginia commented.

Lauren's face went hot with embarrassment. Surely her mother wasn't going to discuss her sex life in front of everyone.

"Ginny," Fonzi said in warning tones.

But Virginia would not be muzzled. "Am I the only one in this family who thinks their relationship is going too fast?"

She turned to Fonzi. "You don't think that Lauren needs to get her head together before getting too emotionally attached to Colton? She just got out of a marriage."

"Mother, I'm standing right here. If you have a problem with me, please direct your comments to me."

"I don't like your tone of voice, young lady," Virginia told her, standing up to face her. Lauren was nearly a foot taller than her mother.

"And I don't like yours," Lauren said respectfully. "How can you possibly have a problem with my relationship with Colton? He's been nothing but a gentleman."

Virginia turned to look at Colton who had taken a seat on the chair beside Benjamin's. "You're a good man. I know that. I have no problem with you. I have a problem with my daughter getting out of one marriage and immediately getting involved with another man. A decent man whose heart she might break when she discovers that she's not ready to be everything he needs her to be. Mainly because she hasn't yet resolved issues relating to her recent marriage." Her gaze back on Lauren now, she continued, "You haven't been divorced a year. Are you over Adam?"

Lauren's eyes bugged out. Her mother obviously didn't care that she was embarrassing her in front of Colton.

"I could tell you things about Adam that would curl your hair and you would never again doubt that I'm completely over him," Lauren said, her voice strangled. "But I won't do that here and now. That's private and actually, it's none of your business. I love you, Momma, but you're too hard on the people you care about. Is it any wonder none of your daughters have been able to find happiness with a man?"

She hadn't meant to say that, but there it was. She couldn't take it back. Her expression remorseful, she said, "That didn't come out right. I didn't mean to suggest it's your fault, but we are always aiming for perfection because of your influence and because we don't want to disappoint you. My God, I stayed with Adam longer than I should have because I didn't want to admit defeat. You and Daddy told me before I married him that he couldn't be trusted and I married him anyway. Do you know how badly I felt when the marriage failed? It meant I would have to hear 'I told you so' from you, Momma!"

Desiree had entered the room in the middle of Lauren's speech and Meghan, who hated to see anyone upset in the family, was wildly gesturing to her to step in with professional advice. When Desiree remained silent, Meghan cried, "Desi, do something. Tell Lauren she's wrong about Momma."

Desiree went to put her arm about Lauren's shoulders.

She looked at Amina, who had gotten to her feet, as well. "Mina, is Lauren wrong?"

Amina went to stand on the other side of Lauren in a show of support. "No, she's not wrong." She directed her next comment to her youngest sister, Meghan. "Maybe by the time you came along Momma had run out of steam. But she was hard on us, always pitting us against each other to compete for her affections. To prove that we were good girls, smart girls, put on this earth to achieve the highest possible goals in life. Me? I was going to be a general like my father." She looked her mother in the eyes. "Sorry to disappoint you, Momma."

Desiree and Lauren hugged her tightly. Meghan got up and joined her sisters. She had tears in her eyes. "I'm sorry," she whispered over and over again.

"What is this, Beat Up On Your Mother Day?" asked Virginia incredulously. Her petite body practically trembled with indignation. "If I was hard on you girls it was because I wanted you to believe in yourselves, to know that you could accomplish anything. That's what a parent's supposed to do, inspire and cheer her children on. Apparently it worked. I got an architect, a psychotherapist, a zoologist, an accountant and a college professor out of it."

Benjamin suddenly stood up and grabbed Virginia by the shoulders and shook her. "Are you not hearing what they're saying, Virginia? You've alienated your children by being a hard-ass. Is that plain enough English for you?"

Virginia looked crestfallen. "Daddy, please don't say that. I love my children!"

"I know you love them, but you're driving them away with your attitude." He sighed heavily. "Baby girl, if I did anything to you when you were growing up to make you behave this way, I'm sorry." He let go of her and went on to explain as everyone gathered around him and Virginia,

"I wasn't always as successful as I am now. When Virginia was a child her mother and I struggled. She even went hungry sometimes. I don't know, maybe the memory of hard times made her believe she had to push her daughters to succeed so they'd never have to go through what she did. I don't know for sure." He turned to Virginia once more and smiled. "But deep down she's got a good heart. She really does believe she does what she does for the betterment of her family."

Fonzi, who was nearby, spoke up on his wife's behalf. "If you girls want to blame anyone, blame me. I was often away from home and Ginny had to do everything by herself. I'm the one who turned her into an iron soldier."

Virginia was crying silently. Fonzi hugged her close. "It's always best to get things out in the open, sweetheart. The girls aren't saying they don't love you."

Lauren, Amina, Meghan and Desiree wrapped their arms around their parents in a group hug.

Colton, standing beside Benjamin, joked, "Are all Thanksgivings with the Gaineses like this?"

Ben looked up at him and laughed, "No, this is a first. But I have a good feeling about it."

Later that night in bed at Colton's house, he held Lauren close after making love. Colton peered lovingly into her eyes. Her hair was a tangled mess. He liked it that way. Today had been enlightening. It wasn't because of the argument he'd witnessed between Lauren and her mother. He knew that no family was perfect. Every family was dysfunctional in one way or another.

What he had found interesting was the ease with which they had forgiven each other and gone on to have a wonderful time together. Some families let grudges grow and they feuded for years.

Lauren smiled at him. "What're you thinking?"

"That your family and my family are a lot alike," he said softly.

"Oh, your family's nuts, too?" she joked.

"You have an idealized view of my mom and dad because you saw them in a relaxed environment in the mountains. I saw them every day growing up. They argued as much as any other couple. But after they argued, they made up and there was never any fear of them breaking up. They were in it together, forever. That's what I want for you and me."

"I want that, too," she told him, "more than anything."

"Then let's do it," Colton said, his eyes sweeping over her face. "I think it would be romantic to get married a year from the day we met."

Lauren gasped. "Are you asking me to marry you?"

Colton laughed shortly. "Don't look so shocked. Yes, I am. I'm sorry for the circumstances, being naked in bed and all that. But this wasn't planned, it just came out. I've never asked anyone to marry me before." He reached over and opened the top drawer in the nightstand on his side of the bed and withdrew a small brown velvet jewelry box. "I do have the ring, though. I bought it weeks ago and have been trying to think of a romantic way to propose but I kept drawing a blank."

While he was rambling on, Lauren sat up in bed, snatched the jewelry box from his clutches and tore it open. She stared down at a five-carat solitaire in a platinum setting. Looking at him with an astonished expression, she cried, "You're serious!"

"As serious as a naked man can be," he said, sitting up, as well. He took the jewelry box back, plucked the ring from it and placed it on her finger. It was a perfect fit.

"You are a six. That was the jeweler's guess after I described you."

Lauren continued to regard him with a shocked expression. He cleared his throat. "I never thought you'd be at a loss for words. Say something, anything. Okay, not anything. I'm hoping for a positive response."

Tears pooled in her eyes and left wet trails down her cheeks. "Yes, I'll marry you."

She threw her arms around his neck. "You know we can never tell anyone how you proposed. We're going to have to make something up."

Colton grinned and kissed her. "It'll be our secret."

Lauren stood in the atrium of the new children's hospital. Sunlight spilled in from the glass dome above. She couldn't believe the project was so close to completion. It had been nearly a year since they'd broken ground.

It was a Sunday and the construction crew was not there. She walked the building alone, marveling at the realization of what had once only been in her mind.

"Hey, Lauren, I see great minds think alike."

She turned around to find Adam walking toward her. She immediately grew tense.

He must have seen it in her face because he quickly said, "Don't worry. I'm not here to make a scene. I saw your car and debated whether I should come in or not. I saw your wedding announcement in the paper and I wanted to wish you well."

Lauren didn't know what to make of him. She decided to take the high road and be civil. "Thank you, Adam."

He took a deep breath and visibly relaxed. Looking up at the glass dome above their heads, he said, "Great project, huh? It turned out better than I imagined."

Lauren smiled. "I have to agree. Your company did a good job."

He smiled his thanks. Then he turned to leave. "I've got to go. Nichole is cooking dinner."

Lauren couldn't let that comment go unnoticed. "Nichole?"

He smiled. "Yes, I apologized and asked her to take me back and she forgave me. We're engaged."

Lauren was genuinely surprised. "Good for you," she said, and meant it.

He smiled and gave her a salute as he continued on his way.

Lauren finished her tour of the building alone.

# Chapter 15

The club was on the seedy side of town and was not the type of establishment Colton would typically be willing to go to. But then he hadn't chosen it. His best man, Decker, had. Decker and several of the other men who'd been invited to his bachelor party were onstage gyrating with scantily clad strippers. Decker had rented the place out, as well as the services of the strippers, for the night.

The music was so loud Colton couldn't hear himself think.

A bra landed on his head, and he brushed it off onto the floor. Decker came down off the stage and plopped down across from him. "Look, cuz, this party is supposed to be for you and you're sitting there nursing a beer. Get up and dance."

"I'm danced out," Colton told him. He glanced at his watch. "It's three in the morning. Don't you think it's time to wrap up the party and head home? My wedding is in eleven hours."

Decker, who was about three sheets to the wind, sighed loudly. "You're not even married yet and she's got you on a leash."

"Nobody's got me on a leash," Colton denied. "I simply know who I am and it's not this. When you asked me what I wanted to do for my bachelor party I told you I wanted to go to a sports bar and watch a couple games with the guys. Why you kids think naked women doing degrading things is the ultimate bachelor party, I'll never know."

"Because for those of us who aren't already hog-tied, naked women doing degrading things *is* the ultimate in a bachelor party," Decker said.

"That's just why Desiree won't go out with you."

"Don't mention that devil's spawn. I ran into her at a Starbucks the other day and she was so friendly, smiling and asking me how life had been treating me but when I asked her to sit down and have a coffee with me she said she had an appointment."

"Don't call her devil's spawn just because she won't go out with you. She has her reasons."

"Such as?" asked Decker sarcastically.

"It's not for me to say," Colton told him. "You'll have to ask her yourself."

"I don't care what her reasons are," Decker declared and went back onstage where a buxom blonde threw a feather boa around his neck and pulled him against her chest. He turned his head, grinned at Colton and gave him a thumbs-up. "A girl's got to make a living!" he yelled.

Colton laughed.

"Having fun?" asked a sultry feminine voice at Colton's side.

He looked up at the curvaceous brunette and smiled. "Just great, thanks." He returned his attention to the stage, hoping she'd get the hint and leave him alone.

Instead, she sat down in the chair Decker had vacated earlier. "My name's Viveca," she told him. "If this scene isn't your cup of tea, we can go somewhere private."

"Thanks, but I'm engaged," Colton said firmly.

"I know," she said. "You're the guest of honor." Her gaze went to Decker.

"Oh, he told you to take care of me, huh?" Colton guessed.

She smiled seductively. "He was very generous."

That did it. Colton got up and walked onto the stage and dragged Decker off of it. He pulled him back to the table where the brunette was still sitting.

"Did you tell her to entertain me?" he asked Decker through clenched teeth.

Decker shook his hands off him. "Can't you take a joke, cuz? I knew you'd never cheat on Lauren. But it's traditional for the groom to be offered the opportunity to have another woman before he gets tied down to one woman for the rest of his life."

"Desiree was right," Colton told him. "You're not ready for her. I'm out of here."

"But you're my ride home," Decker protested.

Colton headed for the exit. "If I'm giving you a lift you'd better come on."

Decker started yelling to the other guys who'd been invited to the bachelor party, "Hey, fellas, we're taking off."

"Yeah," Colton yelled, too, wondering why he was even bothering to thank them for coming when all of them were so drunk they wouldn't remember his words tomorrow. "Thanks for coming!"

As he walked out the door of the establishment, he didn't bother to look back to see if his cousin was following him. In the parking lot, which was poorly lit, he went to his car and unlocked the door.

He heard a noise behind him and thinking it was Decker he whirled around to tell him to get in the car. But it wasn't Decker. It was a stranger and he was wielding a crowbar like a weapon. Colton was able to block the blow and grab the crowbar. He wrenched it out of the guy's grasp and swung it, hitting the guy on the forearm as he held up his arm to protect his head.

"Ah!" the guy yelled. "Don't hurt me. I'm sorry, I'm sorry. Please don't hurt me."

Colton finally got a good look at the man. He was thin and bedraggled. His hair was matted and he looked and smelled like he hadn't bathed in a long time.

"Cuz, what the hell's going on?" Decker cried as he ran toward Colton.

"I was attacked," Colton said, pointing the crowbar at the man who'd jumped him. "Call the police."

"Please mister, I was hungry," the man said.

Decker was already punching in the numbers on his cell phone.

Suddenly, a car came careening straight at them. The assailant ran, screaming his head off. Colton wound up tackling Decker, who had frozen in the headlights, and shoving him out of the way just in time. They ended up sprawled on their sides in the alley next to a Dumpster.

Decker got to his feet but Colton didn't get up. Decker knelt over his cousin. "Colton?" Colton didn't answer. Decker gently rolled him onto his back. Colton was unconscious and there was a gash on the side of his head. It appeared he'd hit his head on the Dumpster when he'd propelled both of them out of the path of the car that had tried to run them down.

Decker had dropped his cell phone when Colton had shoved him out of harm's way. He doubled back and found it lying on the pavement in pieces. He had no alternative but to run back into the club and make a call from there.

He looked back at Colton lying in that dirty alleyway one more time before sprinting toward the club's entrance.


Decker had phoned Lauren from the hospital as he sat in the emergency room waiting area. Half an hour later she arrived and was told the same thing Decker had been told earlier. Colton was still unconscious and they were doing everything in their power to bring him around.

Lauren paced the floor, unable to sit for any length of time. Decker sat feeling guilty for having taken his cousin to a strip club in a bad neighborhood.

A few minutes after Lauren had gotten to the hospital Desiree and Meghan showed up. Embarrassed about his part in the drama and knowing he must smell like a distillery, Decker was not overly enthusiastic about seeing them, especially Desiree. He had to repeat the story of how they'd come to be at the hospital. He imagined Desiree would dislike him even more than she already did after tonight.

About two hours after Colton had been brought in, a doctor in scrubs strode into the emergency room waiting area and asked for the family of Colton Riley. They all approached her with hopeful looks on their faces.

"He's awake," she reported. "There doesn't seem to be any permanent damage but head wounds can be tricky. We're keeping him overnight for observation."

"Thank you, Doctor," Lauren said gratefully. "Can we see him?"

The doctor smiled. "Only one of you, I'm afraid."

Lauren followed the doctor back to an examining room. She found Colton lying on his back in a narrow hospital bed. He smiled when he spotted her. "Hey, baby."

The doctor left them alone and Lauren hurried to his side.

She grasped his hand in hers and kissed his cheek. "You gave me quite the scare."

He smiled weakly. "You thought it was the curse all over again for a minute there, huh?"

"Don't even joke about that."

His gray eyes were alight with humor. "I would have to be dead to miss our wedding tomorrow."

"Stop talking," Lauren ordered him with tears in her eyes. "Do you realize what our lives were like a year ago? Frank had recently died and I was a basket case over a failed marriage. Never joke about dying. I don't know what I'd do if I lost you."

He squeezed her hand. "I'm not going anywhere."

Meanwhile in the waiting room, Desiree had sat down beside Decker. Meghan had gone in search of coffee.

"It's a good thing you were with Colton when he got hurt," she said, drawing him into a conversation. She had good instincts and knew he was blaming himself for Colton's injuries.

She wondered if she wanted to ease his pain because that was her profession, or if she was actually starting to like him.

At any rate he seemed vulnerable and she'd never been able to resist helping anyone in a weakened state.

He looked at her. "You don't have to be nice to me. I know you can't stand me."

"That isn't true, Decker," she denied. The truth was she didn't think of him at all. She couldn't say that though. It would be cruel. She didn't waste time thinking about the handsome attorney because she'd pegged him as a player from their first meeting and she had no patience with men who didn't respect women. It wasn't personal.

"I'm going to tell you something, and I hope you'll try to understand. I've been avoiding you because I have a low tolerance for men who see women as playthings. I have nothing against you. You seem like a decent guy except for the player vibe you give off. But, you see, I've had a great guy in my life and I know what I want in a man. He died a few years ago and, I'm sorry, but I've been comparing every guy I meet to him and they never stack up."

Decker just smiled at her. He knew now that he'd never win her heart. What live man could compete with the memory of a lost love?

Colton's doctor signed his release papers at ten the next morning. He was told to take it easy for a couple of days but there should be no permanent damage from his head injury.

Lauren told him they could postpone the wedding until he was fully recovered but he insisted he was fine. He could rest after the wedding.

She'd stared into his eyes as if she could discern his sincerity. He'd grinned at her. "You're just going to have to take my word for it."

She relented but promised to watch him like a hawk.

They reluctantly separated after she saw him home from the hospital. She would be at her parents' house where her mother and her sisters, including Petra, who was flying in from West Africa, would help her get ready for the wedding. The next time they would see each other would be at St. Paul AME Church, the same church where they'd had Frank's memorial service. Colton's mother had been pleased with their decision to be married there. She said it would almost feel as if Frank would be there.

Back at the Gaineses' house, Lauren sat at her mother's vanity table while Virginia put the finishing touches on her upswept hairstyle. Since their blowout on Thanksgiving Day the two of them had been less reticent with one another. Clearing the air had been a cathartic experience.

Virginia smiled at her daughter's reflection in the mirror. For her afternoon wedding Lauren had chosen not a gown but a cocktail-length dress in cream. It was sleeveless and the hem fell just above her knees. V-necked, it revealed only a glimpse of cleavage, and the waist was fitted. The soft folds of the skirt swirled about her hips and thighs. It was like wearing a confection.

"You make a beautiful bride, sweetheart," Virginia said, a lump forming in her throat. "I'm so pleased for you. I know you and Colton will be happy together."

Lauren rose and hugged her mother. "Thanks, Momma. That means a lot to me." Tears fell. Virginia took her handkerchief that she kept in her cleavage and patted them away. "None of that now," she admonished. "Today is for smiling and laughing, not crying."

"Yeah," Petra cried, coming to hug her mother and sister. "The second time is the charm!"

Lauren laughed at her petite sister. Of the five of them she was the shortest at only five-three. But Petra was still three inches taller than their mother. She had their mother's natural hair color, too, a deep brown that almost looked black.

It was wavy and long like Lauren's but unlike Lauren she'd never cut hers and it fell to her waist.

Desiree entered the room issuing orders. "Five minutes before we get into the cars and head to the church, so make sure you have everything ready to go."

"I'd better go check on your father," Virginia announced. "That man can't tie his tie without me."

All five sisters were dressed in cocktail-length dresses. Lauren had not chosen the styles and colors for her sisters, just the length. She'd left the styles and colors up to them because they knew best what they looked good in and she wanted them to feel beautiful on her special day, too.

They huddled together in their parents' bedroom. "Shall we pray that the honeymoon will be productive and make us aunts?" Petra asked jokingly.

"Yes," Meghan said, "because our older sister isn't getting any younger and Momma and Daddy want grandkids soon. Plus Grandpa Beck's been waiting for a male child to be born into this family for years and he's nearly eighty."

"Will you selfish creatures leave my uterus alone?" Lauren chimed in. "If you must pray for something, pray for good weather today. God will send me a child when He sees fit."

The weather was gorgeous. The December air was crisp and cool. The sun shone brightly and there was a light breeze that ruffled the skirts of the ladies' dresses and caused the gentlemen who wore hats to hang on to them.

Three hundred guests filled the pews of St. Paul AME church. Organ music resounded off the walls of the magnificent edifice.

The general wore his dress uniform as he escorted Lauren down the aisle. He looked very handsome.

Lauren's maid of honor was Desiree. Colton's best man, Decker, could not keep his eyes off her.

Colton, looking resplendent in his tuxedo, felt lightheaded with love when he saw his bride walking down the aisle on her father's arm. She looked innocent, sexy and sophisticated all at once. When she saw him looking at her, she smiled and mouthed, "I love you." That made him inordinately happy.

After the minister pronounced them husband and wife, the kiss lasted nearly a full minute. Then Colton bent and picked up his bride and carried her back down the aisle to an enthusiastic applause. Laughing, Lauren gazed into her new husband's eyes and said, "Don't hurt yourself. You just got out of the hospital, remember?"

Colton grinned, "Be quiet, Mrs. Riley, and enjoy the ride. It's our wedding day!"

He carried her all the way down the church's front steps and to the waiting limousine, with friends and family cheering him on.

Just as he was about to deposit her onto the back seat of the limo, Lauren cried, "Wait, wait, the bouquet!"

Colton set her down on the sidewalk and she turned her back to the crowd and tossed the bouquet over her head.

Her sisters were standing directly behind her but they all stepped aside, purposefully ducking out of the way of the flying bouquet, and Veronica wound up catching it. She laughed and held it up triumphantly, crowing, "There's some life left in the old girl yet!" which elicited laughter as they stood on the sidewalk waving goodbye to Lauren and Colton.

In the car, Colton pulled Lauren into his arms and kissed her soundly. When they parted he murmured against her cheek, "Dad must be laughing in heaven right about now."

"Why?" Lauren asked softly, her eyes sparkling with happiness.

"Because he and Mom were right. You and I were meant for each other."

* * * * *

# LET'S TALK

## Romance

For exclusive extracts, competitions
and special offers, find us online:

- facebook.com/millsandboon
- @MillsandBoon
- @MillsandBoonUK

**Get in touch on 01413 063232**

For all the latest titles coming soon, visit
**millsandboon.co.uk/nextmonth**

# MILLS & BOON
## A ROMANCE FOR EVERY READER

**FREE** delivery direct to your door

**EXCLUSIVE** offers every month

**SAVE** up to 25% on pre-paid subscriptions

## SUBSCRIBE AND SAVE

**millsandboon.co.uk/Subscribe**